Praise for Phoebe Conn's
Where Dreams Begin

"In this emotionally gripping and gritty novel, Ms. Conn creates a tale that keeps the pages turning... If you enjoy a contemporary suspense novel, then *Where Dreams Begin* is a book you should look into. It's emotional, thrilling, and has characters that the reader will enjoy."
~ *Long and Short Reviews*

"There are moments in *Where Dreams Begin* that had me right on the edge of my seat."
~ *Coffee Time Romance*

Look for these titles by
Phoebe Conn

Now Available:

Defy the World Tomatoes
Where Dreams Begin
Fierce Love

To Roxanne with Best Wishes! Phoebe Conn

Where Dreams Begin

Phoebe Conn

SAMHAIN
PUBLISHING

Samhain Publishing, Ltd.
11821 Mason Montgomery Road, 4B
Cincinnati, OH 45249
www.samhainpublishing.com

Where Dreams Begin
Copyright © 2012 by Phoebe Conn
Print ISBN: 978-1-60928-604-0
Digital ISBN: 978-1-60928-475-6

Editing by Linda Ingmanson
Cover by Kanaxa

First Samhain Publishing, Ltd. electronic publication: June 2011
First Samhain Publishing, Ltd. print publication: May 2012

Dedication

Where Dreams Begin is dedicated to everyone who works so hard to give all our children warm loving homes and the best life has to offer.

Prologue

A biting chill fogged the air, but Felix "The Cat" Mendoza was still on the prowl. He knew Hollywood's alleys better than the geeks at MapQuest and, after midnight, conducted a hasty sweep of his favorites. He wore khakis and a navy blue windbreaker. His thick, black hair was cropped short, and he moved with a brisk stride, as though he was eager to get home after work.

As he passed by, hungry kids huddled in doorways and hunched down beside Dumpsters called out to him, but his generosity was limited to the youngest girls. Whenever he noticed a fresh face with real possibilities, he'd be quick to approach her.

He would break into a shy smile as he handed her a couple dollars that first night. It might be a five the next. By the third evening, she would be waiting for him. He would buy her a meal, and before she'd finished her french fries, he would offer a warm, clean place to spend the night.

This week he'd lucked out and won the confidence of a frightened pair who were clearly underage, although should anyone be foolish enough to ask, they would swear they were eighteen. As he helped them into the backseat of his Camaro, he thought, as he often did, that "The Cat" had a real nose for pussy. He would never attract former madam Heidi Fleiss's prestigious clientele, but he more than satisfied his patrons' prurient desires with a steady stream of nubile talent.

After a quick stop at a drive-through for the hamburgers he'd promised, he planned to take the girls to one of his small, rented apartments. He would make them laugh as he fixed them hot chocolate topped with marshmallows, but like all the others, they would awaken in the morning minus any memory of the night.

To mark them as his, the rosy tips of their small, soft breasts would be newly pierced with tiny gold rings, and the ache between their legs would last for days. Drugs liberally laced with shame would keep them loyal, and as Felix closed the passenger door, he turned away to hide an all too predatory grin.

That was when he spotted the blonde. Her long, shimmering hair brushed the shoulders of her slinky red dress, and as she moved toward him on red satin heels, he paused to admire her slow, seductive sway. Unfortunately for her, he never paid for sex.

"I've already got a date," Felix bragged. "Two of them, in fact." He started around the front of his car, but the blonde veered toward him to block his way. In too great a hurry to play her games, he dropped his voice to a menacing hiss.

"*Vayase, puta.*"

Felix's insult dissolved in an anguished gasp as, after one brutal lunge, the blonde shoved against his belt buckle to withdraw her razor-sharp switchblade. Her flying curls slapped his cheek as she turned away, and he grabbed for his torn belly, but a torrent of warm blood spurted through his fingers. His eyes closed on a last glimpse of red satin, and he was already dead when his skull cracked on impact with the curb.

The two girls in the backseat of the Camaro weren't certain what they had seen, but they knew it was bad. They scrambled between the front seats, bolted out the driver's door, and didn't dare look back as they fled the scene in a frantic sprint that would have set a new high school track record back home.

Chapter One

Luke Starns badly needed a vacation. What he had instead was more work than he could accomplish in two lifetimes. That Lost Angel was such a worthwhile enterprise only added to the suffocating pressure. Worn out, he shoved his chair away from his desk and propped his heels on the only uncluttered corner. He leaned back and laced his fingers behind his head.

Now superbly comfortable, he gave in to the noisy yawn he'd suppressed all afternoon and closed his eyes to imagine a sunlit tropical lagoon where jasmine scented the gentle breeze and raven-haired beauties swam in the nude. Longing to lick off the crystal water dripping from their rose-tipped breasts, he was startled when his secretary rapped lightly at his door.

He sat up so quickly he scattered the pages of the grant application he'd been struggling to complete. "Come on in, Pam," he called.

Pamela Strobble opened the door and peeked in. An attractive African American woman with short, glossy curls, she was dressed in colorful ethnic prints. "I wouldn't have disturbed you," she whispered softly, "but there's a young woman here looking to volunteer that you simply must meet. Do you have a minute to do an interview?"

Luke reluctantly hauled his thoughts back to the present and shuffled the grant papers into the proper order before checking his watch. With his concentration shot, interviewing a prospective volunteer made a lot more sense than losing himself in erotic daydreams.

"Sure, send her on in," he replied.

"Thanks. Her name's Catherine Brooks."

Luke stood as Catherine came through the door. Her gently draped slack suit was the color of ground cinnamon and the perfect complement to her deep auburn hair and brown eyes. Fashion meant nothing to Luke, however, and the expensive tailoring of her clothes and the casual elegance of her shoulder-length hair only served to convince him that she was yet another woman with more money than sense. Unfortunately, their kind showed up whenever Lost Angel got a mention on the local news.

At first, he'd actually believed the sophisticated women could contribute more than money, but when none had lasted more than a week or two, if that long, he'd lowered his expectations accordingly. Because Lost Angel extracted the same dreadful toll on volunteers that it took on its directors, they were always in short supply, and he was forced to welcome each and every one.

He doubted his faded Madras sport shirt and comfortably worn jeans would impress her, but when the kids coming there had only a few changes of clothes, he didn't need suits. He noted the simple gold wedding band on Catherine's left hand and assumed she'd taken the precaution of leaving her diamonds at home. She'd shown considerable courage by not simply circling the graffiti-scarred block where their converted church stood and driven home.

He still had to dig deep for a smile. "Good afternoon, Mrs. Brooks. We've had nearly fifty calls today and half a dozen others stopped by to inquire about volunteering. Were you also inspired by Channel 4's piece about us on last night's eleven o'clock news?"

Catherine took the straight-backed chair he indicated and then replied in a voice that was soft and pitched low. "I'm sorry. I seldom watch the late news. It was a feature in the *Los Angeles Times* that piqued my interest."

Luke dropped back into his chair. He picked up his pencil and tapped the eraser against the desktop in a muted tattoo. "That was months ago, Mrs. Brooks, so it couldn't have prompted much in the way of interest."

Catherine cocked her head slightly and tucked her hair behind her ear. "Do you usually make fun of volunteers?" she asked.

Luke threw down the pencil and added high-strung to the list of faults he'd assigned her the instant she'd slipped through his door. She had a death grip on a slim black leather handbag that didn't appear to contain anything more substantial than her car keys, cell phone and Visa card. He doubted she would even make it through the interview, let alone return to do any useful work.

"Please forgive me. It's been a long day," he stressed. "Whatever inspired your visit, it's appreciated. If you read the *Times'* article, then you know how desperate our situation truly is."

He ticked off the statistics on his fingers. "One out of every four runaways in America comes to Los Angeles. A large percentage have been abused and actually believe if they escape a miserable situation at home and make it to Hollywood, they'll quickly become the next Brad Pitt or Keira Knightley. There's also a large number of kids leaving foster homes with nowhere to go. Both groups are preyed upon by the unscrupulous scumbags who either want to sell drugs or use the kids for sex or, in most cases, both.

"This old church was on the verge of being condemned when we took it over, but with our limited funding, it's all we can afford to rent. I'd like to believe we've actually done some good, if not nearly enough. Now all I can promise is a lot of tedious paperwork, absolutely no benefits and nothing in the way of pay. If that sort of drudgery actually appeals to you, Pam will give you an application on your way out."

Catherine scanned the office that was little more than a whitewashed cell. It was furnished with a battered desk, computer and mismatched file cabinets, but no attractive artwork, live plants nor personal items. The single window provided an unappealing view of the building's weed-strewn parking lot.

"I was hoping for something more directly related to serving the teenagers," she argued persuasively. "I know Lost Angel provides clean clothing as well as hot meals."

With long, dark lashes, she had a fawn's touchingly innocent gaze, but Luke doubted she was stupid, and he'd already brought the interview to an end. Without shame, he chose the quickest way to be rid of her. "Do you have children, Mrs. Brooks?"

For a brief instant, Catherine's gaze strayed toward the cracked linoleum. "No, but I am a former teacher."

"Really? Where did you teach?"

"I was in the English department at La Cañada High School before I married, and I loved the lively interaction with the students. It was the best part of the job."

Luke nodded thoughtfully. "I'm sure it was, but our teens bear absolutely no resemblance to the pampered college prep crowd living in La Cañada. Once you've spent a few minutes with some of our kids with purple Mohawks, nose rings and hideous homemade tattoos, you'll quickly get over any need to spread your frustrated maternal warmth here."

Catherine reached out to pluck his nameplate from his desk, then replaced it with a loud thud. "With such an impressive string of degrees, I'd expect you to come up with something less obvious. Have you simply had a bad day, Dr. Starns, or are you deliberately being nasty?"

That show of spirit took Luke by surprise, but it also provided ample evidence that she was used to getting her own way. In his book, it was another strike against her.

"Bad days are the only kind we have here at Lost Angel," he swore darkly.

"Then why do you stay?" Catherine countered. "Were you homeless yourself at one time, or do you simply enjoy playing the martyr?"

Luke recoiled slightly, then decided Catherine wasn't nearly as fragile as she looked. He left his chair and circled the desk, prompting Catherine to rise and face him. She stood five feet ten inches tall in her flats, but even barefoot, Luke grazed six feet, and his scuffed loafers added another inch. As he moved near, he surveyed the difference in their heights, but he had no intention of defending his views more forcefully than she would care to see.

Luke watched her raise her chin to maintain a challenging stare and added obstinate to his growing list of complaints. "Mrs. Brooks," he began, fully intending not to merely throw her out of his office but to forbid her return. Then it occurred to him that he ought not to let her off so easily. Encouraging a woman with her delicate sensibilities to volunteer was almost diabolical, but he just couldn't resist, and a quick grin erased all trace of hostility from his expression.

"Forgive me if I've misjudged your commitment to Lost Angel," he said. He crossed the room to the door and swung it open wide. "I'll have Pam add your name to the list for Monday's training session. Unless, of course, you've something else planned for the day?"

"Nothing I can't postpone," Catherine assured him on her way out.

When Catherine crossed the parking lot a few minutes later, she was proud of herself for standing up to Luke Starns but badly disappointed her first interview since college had gone so poorly. She'd been completely baffled to find such a caustic individual running Lost Angel and sincerely hoped that after she'd completed whatever training he might provide, they could simply avoid each other.

As she walked toward her Volvo, a plump girl with a long, thick mop of corkscrew curls came toward her. She was dressed in a chartreuse T-shirt and bib overalls. A scruffy marmalade cat with tattered ears peered out of the canvas bag slung over her shoulder. She appeared to be a regular at Lost Angel, and while Catherine unlocked her station wagon, she remained by the door.

"Hi. You got some spare change? My cat's hungry," the girl greeted her.

Catherine doubted Lost Angel encouraged panhandling on the premises, but the scrawny cat did look as though he could use a meal. She opened her purse and pulled out a dollar bill. "Von's has their house brand on special at four cans for a dollar."

"Great. I'll stock up," the girl replied. She tucked the money into her bib pocket and quickly jogged away, forcing her bedraggled pet to endure a wild, bumpy ride.

Catherine slid behind the wheel, and as she turned the key in the ignition, she caught a glimpse of Luke Starns at his window. He shut the blinds before she could wave, but she felt as though he'd caught her cheating on an exam. She could readily imagine the harsh lecture he would deliver on Monday, but she wouldn't have to listen.

Lost Angel had not turned out to be what she'd expected at all, but her first visit had been oddly exhilarating, and she felt she owed it to herself to give it a second try. After all, a

15

volunteer position wasn't like a real job, and if she didn't feel as though she were making a valuable contribution, she could always quit. There was only one problem with that strategy, however: she'd never quit on anything.

Luke Starns took several deep breaths before reviewing Catherine Brooks' application, but when he discovered that the word widow appeared under marital status, he cursed and laid the form aside. He preferred face-to-face meetings with prospective volunteers to assessing people's abilities from the dry facts they supplied on the Lost Angel application, but he certainly wished he'd seen Mrs. Brooks' form before they had met. Until the last moments of their interview, she'd projected such a touching vulnerability that he'd seen no reason to encourage her interest, and when he had, it had merely been for spite.

Now that he knew she'd lost her husband, he wished he'd engaged her in a real conversation and then gently nudged her toward another worthwhile charity. He had seen her fall for Tina Stassy's plea for money for cat food, and the other kids frequenting Lost Angel would also recognize her as a soft touch. Regardless of how generous her nature might be, however, she couldn't support them all.

"Nor should she," he murmured aloud.

Disgusted with himself for not behaving more professionally, he left his office to conduct the afternoon session where he could offer little more than a sympathetic ear and a sandwich to kids who needed far more in the way of structure and assistance than Lost Angel could provide.

As he arranged chairs in the cavernous room that had been the church's sanctuary, he took little note of the once-sacred surroundings. For him, it was merely a room where the good they did, like the ruby light streaming through the stained glass windows, would vanish with the coming night.

Dave Curtis, the center's maintenance man, joined Luke in time to set up the last of the chairs. "Sorry, boss. I should have had everything ready, but it took longer to clean out the trap under the kitchen sink than I'd expected and I'd wanted to change my shirt." He pulled his light brown hair into place with a quick yank on the elastic band holding his ponytail.

"Don't apologize. There's more work than any of us can do."
Luke stepped back and shoved his hands into his hip pockets.
"From now on, I'll let the kids arrange the chairs. It'll give them
more of a sense that this is their group rather than mine."

"Sounds good to me. You want to get a pizza later?"

Luke hesitated a long moment, then shook his head. "No, I
need to get out of here. Maybe tomorrow night."

"Sure, whenever. I'm going to give the sprinklers another
try. I need to clean out all the heads before I can judge whether
or not the pipes are still good, but I'd sure like to be able to
water what's left of the grass."

"Yeah, give it a try," Luke encouraged. He admired Dave's
initiative, and summoning what was left of his own, he
welcomed the first of the kids to arrive. It was Tina Stassy, and
while it was likely he was having more success reaching her cat,
as long as she kept coming back, all three of them had a chance
to survive.

Chapter Two

Catherine flung the red dress toward the bed where the soft, sand-washed silk fell in a bright burst of color, then pooled out over the plush ivory comforter in a spreading stain. Next, she peeled a pale, peach chiffon gown from its padded hanger and sent it flying toward the high brass bed.

"Give me a hand here, Joyce," she called to her friend. "All these party clothes have to go."

Joyce pushed her frizzled blonde curls out of her eyes and took a tentative step toward the roomy walk-in closet. "You'll regret this for sure," she warned. "You've such pretty clothes, and they'll cost a fortune to replace."

"I've not worn a one of these dresses since Sam's death, and even if I did receive an invitation to a formal affair, I wouldn't accept. Seeing them hanging in the closet just makes me incredibly sad."

Reluctantly turning toward the bed, Joyce reached for the red silk dress and folded it over her arm. "I wish we wore the same size," she remarked wistfully. "I've always envied you your height and willowy figure."

After a moment of silent debate, Catherine threw a cranberry knit coatdress on the bed. The crystal buttons caught the morning light pouring in the windows and sent a riot of shimmering rainbows dancing across the ceiling. "I thought you enjoyed being petite."

Joyce laid the red dress aside and folded the cranberry. "It's definitely an advantage where men are concerned, and there are always plenty of clothes on the sale racks in small sizes." Her carefully penciled brows formed a mere hint of a frown. "But how long can a woman rely on merely being cute?"

Joyce was thirty-seven and had gone through a bitter divorce three years prior. Catherine understood how serious her question truly was and gave it the consideration it deserved. "Cute lasts forever," she assured her confidently. "I've met women in their eighties who were as cute as they could be."

"I hope you're right, but I'm afraid a woman is really much better off being tall. Christie Brinkley was on *Entertainment Tonight* last week. She still looks so damn good, but like you, she has the height to be elegant."

Catherine glanced down at her oversized purple T-shirt and worn jeans. "Somehow I've never thought of myself as being particularly elegant."

Joyce followed the direction of Catherine's gaze and laughed with her. "Not today, perhaps, but in any of these fabulous dresses, you most certainly are. I remember the last time you wore the chiffon." Joyce's words caught in her throat. "You and Sam were such a handsome couple."

The compliment caught Catherine off guard, and a painful rush of sorrow flooded her eyes and brought a dizzying weakness to her knees. Betrayed by the force of her seemingly inexhaustible grief, she sank down on the side of the bed and recalled that last party at the club in such shimmering detail, she could almost taste the frosty key lime pie served for dessert.

"I'm sorry." Joyce gave Catherine's shoulders a quick hug. "I didn't mean to make you cry."

Catherine responded with a poignant sigh. "Please don't be afraid to mention Sam. I may cry each time you do, but I don't want him to be forgotten."

"Oh, Cathy, no one will ever forget Sam. All his friends loved him. Come on, let's take a break and have some iced tea, or something stronger, if you'd like."

Catherine brushed away her tears with trembling fingertips and laid aside a black velvet skirt as she rose. "I think it's a damn good thing I don't drink, or I wouldn't have been sober a single day this past year."

Still struggling to regain her composure, Catherine led the way through her charming Cape Cod-style home. It was too large for her now, but it contained far too many precious memories to sell.

The kitchen faced the east and opened out onto a redwood deck. On long summer nights, she and Sam had enjoyed the concerts staged at the nearby Rose Bowl from the lazy comfort of their own backyard. He had loved the Rolling Stones and been elated to hear Mick Jagger whip the paying crowd into a frenzy with "Satisfaction".

The bittersweet memory brought a shaky smile, and, cheered, Catherine poured two glasses of iced tea and added sprigs of fresh mint from her garden. She and Joyce carried them out to the glass-topped table on the deck and settled into the thickly cushioned chairs. She took a long sip of tea, then held the cool glass to her cheek.

"We can finish packing up the clothes later, but for now, there's something I'd like to run by you."

Joyce immediately sat forward. She smoothed her white slacks and tapped her pink-tipped nails against the side of her glass. "I'm no expert on anything except decorating, but I'll do my very best to help."

Catherine gazed out over the lush green lawn. Every spring, the flower beds needed attention, and she was embarrassed to have overlooked them until now. She made a mental note to buy pansies and snapdragons for some much-needed color. Unfortunately, her life was equally pale, and brightening it would not be nearly as easy as replanting the flowers.

"I'm not ready to look for a full-time job," she finally confided, "but I do want to get out more and try some volunteer work."

"Well, *alleluia*! It's about time." Joyce paused to again fluff her curls from her eyes. "The Huntington Library has a terrific program for docents. It's close, and so is the Norton Simon Museum. Or what about the Los Angeles Zoo? Wouldn't that be fun? I bet they let their volunteers hold the baby gorillas."

Catherine nodded to acknowledge the wealth of attractive possibilities nearby, but she'd already made her choice. She watched Smoky, her pampered gray tomcat, leave the shady spot beneath the camellias and welcomed him into her lap. He responded with a noisy purr, curled up and, utterly content, closed his bottle-green eyes for a nap. Catherine stroked his fur lightly as she described her plans.

"There was an article in the *Times* a few months ago about Lost Angel, an organization in Hollywood that serves runaway and homeless teens. It was such a moving story, and—"

Joyce rattled the table with her fist. "Oh no. You can't be serious. It's located in a terrible neighborhood, and you might get mugged, or worse."

Catherine wasn't altogether surprised by the hostility of Joyce's reaction, but she had a ready defense. "Just bear with me a moment. Before Sam and I were married, I taught high school English. The pressures of his law practice made our lives so hectic that there just never seemed to be a good time to get back into education, but schools have changed in the last ten years. What I need is some practical experience with today's teens. If it's good, then I'll apply for a teaching position for the fall."

Joyce shook her head in disbelief. "Sam left you well-provided for, so why you'd want to work is beyond me, but even with metal detectors at the entrances, teachers are still dodging bullets nowadays. Why take that kind of risk?"

"You're citing the extreme. Most schools have secure campuses, but it's not security that concerns me. Kids have become so sophisticated, and I don't want to walk into a classroom in September and not be able to connect with them."

Joyce responded with a derisive snort. "Oh, you'll connect, all right. You're a gorgeous woman. The boys will be hot for you, and the girls will envy your sense of style."

Catherine quickly discounted Joyce's cynical opinion. "Perhaps, but it's not the same as having a real impact on their lives. By volunteering at Lost Angel, I hope to gain some worthwhile insights, while at the same time, I might actually be doing some good."

Joyce slumped back in her chair. "God help us, but you're actually going ahead with this, aren't you?"

Catherine turned that question aside with an easy shrug. "It's time. I'll always miss Sam, but I need to build a life on my own now."

"What would Sam say about Lost Angel?"

My darling Sam, Catherine mused silently. At night, she lay awake sharing her day with him and still felt his loving presence. "Sam was quite liberal in his politics, and he always encouraged me to do whatever I wished. He'd not oppose me on this."

"Won't you at least consider other options?" Joyce pressed. "Your tennis is even better than mine, and with a little practice, we could win the ladies' doubles title at the club this summer."

When Catherine brushed aside that suggestion, Joyce quickly posed another. "What about volunteering in the literacy program at the public library? Or donating time at the charity thrift shop where you plan to drop off your clothes? You once mentioned how you hoped to someday have a daughter. How about becoming involved with the Girl Scouts? Don't they run camps in the summer?"

Catherine projected the same relaxed tranquility as the tomcat in her lap. "Girl Scouts have families who love them. What about the kids who have no one? Who's going to care about them?"

"I don't see why it has to be you," Joyce countered. "Don't get me wrong, Lost Angel does a tremendous amount of good. I just don't see why you have to become involved with it. Maybe what you really need isn't kids to teach, but a new man to love."

Stung by that unwanted advice, Catherine stubbornly refused to give in to tears and instead tickled Smoky's ears. "I'm going to pretend you didn't say that."

"All right, I apologize if it was thoughtless, or a bit premature, but one of the benefits of decorating office buildings is that I meet plenty of attractive men. Professional men," she emphasized. "You're only thirty-two, Cathy. You can't want to spend the rest of your life alone."

Catherine took a long drink of tea before offering a hushed reply. "I'd expected to spend the rest of my life with Sam. There are days when just accepting the terrible fact that he's gone is almost more than I can bear. The prospect of falling in love again is beyond imagining. Now let's finish boxing up my clothes, and don't let me forget to include the shoes I'll never wear again, either." She set Smoky aside, rose and shoved her chair into the table.

"I'm sorry if I didn't say what you'd hoped to hear," Joyce offered, "but I trust you to do what's best."

Catherine nodded, but she didn't really trust herself to do anything right without Sam.

Monday morning, Catherine sorted through her newly reorganized wardrobe, but nothing she owned seemed appropriate for Lost Angel. She'd thought her cinnamon suit would be perfect for an initial interview but now feared she'd been overdressed.

She reached for a chambray shirtwaist with a colorful beaded belt, but it was an outfit Sam had urged her to buy, and she pulled back. He'd loved to take her shopping, and at moments like this when she couldn't make up her mind, he'd always teased her about having more outfits than Malibu Barbie, then reached into her closet and yanked out the perfect choice. Whenever she went out, she still took the time to look her best, but oh, how she missed his pretty compliments.

An all too familiar ache touched her heart, but becoming a volunteer was an important first step away from that lingering anguish. She grabbed the chambray as Sam's choice and scolded herself as she dressed, because the day had never been about clothes. The chance to help out at Lost Angel was what counted, and she was ashamed of herself for losing sight of her goal.

The training session was set for ten o'clock, and after the heavy morning commuter traffic had thinned, Catherine made good time. She pulled into the center's parking lot, and after Luke's mention of a surge in volunteers, she was surprised not to find more cars. She started toward the office, but then a couple in an RV drove into the lot, and she waited for them on the walk.

The gray-haired pair were dressed in matching khaki slacks and bright blue shirts, but only the woman's breast pocket was embroidered with brilliantly hued tropical birds. Her hair was gathered atop her head in a gently poofed knot, while a mere hint of downy fringe ringed the man's ears. Both wore broad smiles and greeted Catherine warmly.

"Hello, dear. I'm Rita Tubergen, and this is my husband, Joe. I was certain I understood the directions when I telephoned last week, but we got lost as soon as we left the freeway. I sure hope we're not late for the training. Although if we are, you'll be late too, won't you?" she added with a girlish giggle. "Unless, of course, you're the instructor."

23

"No, I'm another new volunteer."

Catherine thought the couple charming, but as soon as she'd introduced herself, Rita slowed their progress toward the office with an involved description of how they'd recently sold their dry cleaning business. After a leisurely trip through the southwest, they were eager to donate their time to Lost Angel.

"And what about you, dear?" Rita asked.

Catherine had always made friends easily, but the Tubergens were the first couple she'd met since being widowed, and she couldn't bring herself to blurt out such tragic news. She wished she'd anticipated the need to supply more than her name, but for the moment, her mind was a frustrating blank. Unwilling to burden strangers with her sorrow, she simply hurried them on down the walk and was relieved when Pam Strobble met them at the office door.

The secretary's flared black dress was splashed with bold white graphics, and her black espadrilles tied at the ankle with huge bows. As she led Catherine and the Tubergens through the office and out across the courtyard to the annex, her silver bracelets chimed in time with her bouncy steps.

"This building was constructed to house the Sunday school," Pam explained as they entered. "So it's divided into a lot of little rooms. We've kept the largest for staff meetings and treat the rest as storage lockers for donations.

"Sorting those can be more trouble than they're worth, but I'll let Luke tell you what needs to be done. He'll be with you in a minute. Help yourself to the coffee. This is the only day it'll be free," she added in a teasing aside and then left them at the entrance of a long, narrow room.

Windows facing the courtyard let in the bright spring sunshine, but the room was as starkly furnished as Luke's office. There was a small table near the door with a freshly brewed pot of coffee, and Rita and Joe stopped to help themselves. A large, rolling chalkboard sat at the far end of the room, and folding chairs were arranged around a conference table where a red-haired young man and three middle-aged women were already seated.

"Come sit with us, dear," Rita urged. She and Joe edged by the young man and took the seats nearest the chalkboard.

Catherine assumed Luke Starns would stand at the front of the room and cautiously slipped into the chair at the opposite end of the table. "There's no need to be crowded," she explained. "I'll be fine here."

As friendly as she'd been earlier, Rita introduced herself and Joe to the others and again recounted the sale of their business and recent travels. Spurred by her example, the young man gave his name as Ron Flanders. Almost painfully thin, his loose-fitting green polo shirt and Dockers would have looked equally handsome left on their hangers.

"I'm working part-time in the math department at Cal State LA. How about you?" he asked the woman seated opposite him.

Her hair was dyed to the blue-black sheen of patent leather and gathered at her nape in a bright red bow that matched her long, acrylic nails. Her red dress was trimmed with black piping, and before she replied, she rose up to straighten the skirt with a nervous tug.

"I'm Beverly Snodgrass, and I was a receptionist until our firm was bought out, and the new owner laid off everyone over forty. I've been looking for a job, but they're impossible to find if you don't even know how to turn on a computer; and I can't just sit home and cry."

"My thoughts exactly," the woman beside her agreed. Her wavy brown hair was cut short, and her ample figure was disguised by a loose-fitting tunic and slacks. "I'm Alice Waggoner. My husband just retired, and he's driving me nuts.

"I need an excuse to get out of the house and Lost Angel is a damn good one. This is my friend, Betty Murray. I talked her into coming here with me." Betty looked enough like Alice for them to have been sisters, and she merely smiled and shrugged.

It was now Catherine's turn, but Luke Starns entered as soon as she'd given her name. She hadn't expected to be happy to see him, but his arrival excused her from having to provide any personal information, and for that unexpected favor, she was deeply grateful.

On his way toward the front of the room, Luke glanced at Catherine a moment longer than the others, and she wondered whether he was merely surprised to find her there or, perhaps, badly disappointed. Whatever his reaction, she was intent upon being cooperative and greeted him warmly.

"Good morning, Dr. Starns," she said.

"Please, just make it Luke. Good morning, everyone." He referred to a roll sheet on a clipboard as he greeted them by name. Then he tossed the LATEXTRA section of the *Times* on the table.

"I'm sorry to have kept you waiting, but we expected several others, and I didn't want to begin without them. Apparently they've had second thoughts, and this story might be the reason. If any of you missed it, here's a quick recap.

"A man named Felix Mendoza was murdered near here the other night, and it appears to have been a particularly vicious crime. He'd served time, most recently for pandering, and was carrying a bottle of Rohypnol." When the name brought mystified stares from several in his audience, Luke offered more detail.

"It's known as the date-rape drug, or 'roofies'. It's not available in the United States as a sleeping pill, but it's sold in a great many other countries, including Mexico. The drug not only renders a person unconscious, but also causes short-term memory loss, so when they awaken, they aren't certain what's happened to them, unless, of course, it's painfully obvious that they've been raped.

"Felix was last seen with two pretty girls, and it doesn't take much in the way of imagination to guess he planned to take them home, slip the Rohypnol into their Cokes, and then slip them something else entirely."

He paused to allow everyone to paint an appropriately disgusting scene in their minds. "A few days with Felix would convince any girl she'd been born to be a whore."

That ugly prediction brought a gasp and deep blush from Alice, Betty and Rita Tubergen, while Joe gave more of a strangled gulp, but Luke had meant to shock them. "The teens who come to Lost Angel haven't had pretty lives, folks, and the men they meet aren't passing out milk and cookies. The *Times* article makes no mention of witnesses or suspects, but rather than raise the crime rate, I'd say Felix's death has actually improved the quality of our neighborhood."

Rita raised her hand. "But, Dr. Starns, Luke, surely you don't condone murder."

"You might be surprised by what I've learned to condone since taking over Lost Angel," Luke replied drily, "but it's nothing compared to what some of the kids have done to survive. Los Angeles has approximately 5,000 homeless teens, and only 200 beds available in shelters. You do the math. It wouldn't hurt any of you to spend a few nights out on the street to gain a real appreciation of why our needs are so great."

Joe Tubergen shifted uneasily in his chair. "I think maybe we've made a mistake in coming here."

"Did you expect volunteering to be as enjoyable as coaching Little League?" Luke responded.

"Well, yeah, maybe a little bit," Joe admitted sheepishly. "At any rate, I didn't think we'd have to step over dead pimps to reach the door."

"Felix died several blocks from here," Luke corrected. "But that doesn't mean you won't trip over a corpse tomorrow, and it could be one of the kids. Every year we've lost a few to one type of violence or another."

He gave them a moment to consider that fact, then cleared his throat and continued in a more matter-of-fact manner. "Lost Angel is supported by private grants as well as public donations, and we track every penny. It's time-consuming but well worth the effort to maintain our donors' trust.

"We furnish hot showers, clean clothes and nutritious meals. We also offer group and individual counseling, and provide referrals for medical and dental care. We do our damnedest to help kids find jobs and safe places to live. Until they have both, they can pick up their mail here, and that service means a lot to them. Runaways quickly discover that being on their own is no adventure, but if they're too ashamed to call their parents and beg for money to return home, we'll take the first step and contact their family.

"I want to make it clear right now that we never make promises we can't keep, nor do we allow volunteers to take any of the kids home, because none of us can care for them all, and it wouldn't be fair to the ones left behind. Most of them support themselves panhandling, but if you come here with your pockets or purse bulging with dollar bills, you'll probably be robbed before you can pass out more than one or two."

Catherine thought the others looked a mite green, but she was curious about a point Luke had not mentioned and raised her hand.

Luke responded with an impatient nod. "Do you have a question, Mrs. Brooks?"

"What about condoms, do you supply those?" she asked.

"Oh, my goodness," Rita cried. "We're on church property, so surely that isn't allowed."

Luke reached into his pants pocket for a handful of condoms and, with an easy toss, splattered them down the table. "We have no religious affiliation, Mrs. Tubergen, and not only do we allow it, it's imperative. We're fighting to keep these kids alive and well, and we can't ignore the spread of HIV."

Joe and Rita exchanged a frantic glance and, after an uncomfortably long pause, Joe rose to help his wife from her seat. "Maybe it was the angel name that confused us, but we just don't belong here. Will you excuse us, please?"

"Of course." Luke waited until the Tubergens had passed through the door, then pulled Rita's chair around to the front of the table and sat. "If anyone else is squeamish about remaining, please speak up now so we don't waste any more of my valuable time or yours."

Ron just shrugged, and the women across from him shook their heads. Catherine nodded to encourage him to continue. He leaned back in his chair, but despite his relaxed pose, he punched out every word.

"Our goal isn't to become a homeless shelter, but to provide a safe environment as a drop-in center, as much comfort as possible, and the constant reassurance that somebody cares. For some kids, that's more than they've ever had."

As Luke continued to define Lost Angel's mission, Catherine refrained from asking how he kept from being overwhelmed by the enormity of the problems the center addressed, but clearly something drove him, and she doubted it was mere altruism. There was a real pride in his voice as he described several kids who had succeeded in getting off the streets, but his sorrow was just as keen when he cited more than one tragic failure.

Catherine swiftly realized she'd made a tactical error in taking the chair at the far end of the table, for it placed her directly opposite Luke. Seated along the side, she could have more easily avoided his often piercing gaze. She'd never met anyone with such a challenging nature and wondered what had possessed him to go into psychology, where he must surely be misplaced.

His dark brown hair was laced with gray, and he'd obviously been too busy the past weekend to get a haircut, but now that she'd seen him a second time, she had to admit his hair was no longer than many men wore theirs. Had she not had a stinging sample of his prickly personality, she would have considered him attractive, but she found it difficult to imagine him showing a woman any tenderness or relaxing long enough to make love.

"Mrs. Brooks?" Luke called.

Catherine feared her expression must have betrayed the wildly inappropriate directions of her thoughts. She promptly forced a pleasant smile. "Yes?"

"You were frowning slightly, and I wondered if perhaps you had an objection to our strict drug-free policy?"

"Why, no, absolutely none," Catherine assured him.

"Good, because I won't compromise on it."

"Nor should you," Ron Flanders concurred.

Catherine didn't draw a deep breath until Luke resumed his lecture on the center, but it took awhile longer for her incriminating blush to subside. When they finally left the room to tour the rest of the facility, she moved to the back of the small group to again stay as far away from Luke as possible. He actually laughed a time or two as he showed them the rooms heaped with donated clothing, but there was no real mirth in the sound.

When they reached the kitchen, Luke introduced Mabel Shultz, the full-time cook, and stepped back to allow her to describe the type of volunteers she required. Alice Waggoner and Betty Murray immediately asked if they could stay to help with the lunch preparations.

"Of course, you may," Luke assured them. "Just come by the office before you go home and set up your schedule with Pam."

He led the way out of the kitchen and through the church hall. Long tables filled the room, and perhaps two dozen teens were clustered about in small groups playing board games while several others sat by themselves reading dog-eared paperbacks.

Beverly Snodgrass wore a cloying perfume that made Catherine sneeze, and as they entered the sanctuary, she moved to avoid the annoying scent. Purposely lagging behind, she paused to study a remarkably beautiful stained glass window.

The pews had been removed from the large rectangular room, and Luke walked to the center before turning to face the new volunteers. "I hate to disappoint you, Mrs. Brooks, but the windows aren't on today's agenda. Before you leave, ask Pam for a pamphlet detailing their history and subject matter. You're sure to find it fascinating."

Embarrassed by his continual scolding, Catherine hurriedly caught up with the others. Then she had to stifle another sneeze. "I'm sorry. Did I miss something important?"

"Not yet. As I explained earlier, Lost Angel has no religious affiliation, but we've found the kids are far more comfortable using the hall where we serve meals for filling out job applications, playing cards and board games. So we've reserved this space for counseling. Perhaps it's merely the high ceiling and stained glass windows, but I've found even the most defensive kids are remarkably candid when we meet in here."

Beverly glanced toward the high exposed beams. "Yeah, it is kinda creepy."

Ron nudged Catherine with his elbow, but she couldn't believe Beverly had misunderstood Luke's meaning. "I imagine the stillness and subdued light naturally inspire trust," she offered for Beverly's benefit.

"Precisely," Luke agreed. "Now let's go out front, and we'll return to the office that way."

As they moved through the heavy double doors and stepped out into the sun, the kids lounging on the steps turned to look up at them. Catherine instantly recognized the girl with the cat and decided the poor animal looked no better fed than when she'd last seen him. There were several boys in the baggy shorts, over-sized hockey shirts and baseball caps worn backward that were popular everywhere. One such kid was out on the walk practicing stunts on a skateboard. That someone so young would even try to live on his own broke her heart.

"I like your boots," a girl called out. Her long blonde hair was covered by a denim hat with a rolled brim. She was wearing purple high-topped basketball shoes with her faded print dress and hugged a backpack stuffed with her belongings.

"I like your shoes too," Catherine replied.

"Want to trade?" the girl asked.

Catherine laughed and shook her head. "Sorry, this is my favorite pair."

Catherine threaded her way between the kids seated on the steps with the same graceful ease she strolled through her garden, while Beverly Snodgrass and Ron Flanders moved to the far right to walk where the way was clear.

"Hey, Luke." The boy with the skateboard came walking toward them. "You think we'd get a reward if we found out who killed Felix Mendoza?"

"I doubt anyone has offered one, Nick. It's only when someone the community admires is killed that the family, or his friends, put up a reward."

"Damn," Nick swore, and he dropped his skateboard, hopped on and spun around in an agile turn.

"Do you know something?" Luke pressed. "If you do, come inside with me now, and we'll call the police."

The teenagers gathered on the steps responded with a chorus of howls. "He won't have to give his name," Luke admonished the noisy crowd, "but it's important to provide clues."

"Why?" Tina Stassy asked. "We all know what Felix was after, and it's about time he got what was coming to him."

"I won't argue with you," Luke admitted, "but if any of you saw or heard anything significant, please let me know. I'll pass it along to the police."

Luke gestured for his volunteers to follow him, and they made their way around the hall and past what had once been a wide, green lawn. Dave Curtis was out working on the sprinklers, and he waved to them before turning them on to produce a varied mixture of sputtering sprays and one immense geyser.

"Do you think we could call this mess dancing waters and sell tickets?" Dave called to them.

"No way. Shut it off," Luke ordered.

"He just needs a couple of new sprinkler heads," Ron offered. "Do you mind if I give him a hand?"

"Not at all. The yard's too small for a real soccer game, but it would be great if the kids had a lawn were they could kick a ball around."

"I'll see what I can do," Ron replied, and he broke into a slow, loping jog to join Dave.

Now accompanied by only Beverly and Catherine, Luke returned to the office. "Whether you can volunteer a couple of hours a month or a couple of days a week, you need to set up a schedule and let us know whenever you're unable to come in on your regular day. Pam will help you with that. Thanks for coming in today, and I hope to see you both often."

Luke's handshake was firm but brief. When he quickly broke eye contact, Catherine felt certain he'd made the same parting comment to all the volunteers, but Beverly positively beamed as though his words had been meant for her alone.

When Luke entered his office and closed the door, Beverly hurriedly checked her watch. "I've got a nail appointment, so I can't stay today, but what about Friday afternoon? Would that be a good time to come in?" she asked.

Pam checked the master schedule posted on the wall by the door. "Friday is actually pretty light, so the afternoon would be fine."

"Good. I'll see you then. Catherine, was it? Maybe I'll see you then too."

"Possibly," Catherine replied.

Pam waited until Beverly had closed the door on her way out, and then whispered, "What happened to the others? Luke always manages to discourage a couple, but this is the first time he's begun a training session with seven volunteers and ended with only two."

Catherine quickly reassured Pam that only the Tubergens had dropped out, and that the others were still at work on the premises. "I'd like to stay a while longer today if I may. There's a mountain of clothes to sort. Could I ask some of the kids to help me?"

Pam shook her head. "We've tried that, but they tend to work just long enough to find whatever it is they need and then leave, so not much progress is made." She pursed her lips thoughtfully, then broke into a delighted smile. "I'm way behind on the mail." She reached behind her desk to pick up a cardboard banker's box and carried it over to the second desk.

"When the mail arrives, I sort it into bills we have to pay and stuff addressed to kids, because we want them to be able to follow up quickly on job applications, but the other letters just land in here until someone has time to sort them and post the flyers in the hall. Use this desk and see what you find. Some parents send out dozens of flyers, and we try and post the new ones every week.

"Stop whenever you get tired, or take a break for lunch and come back if you like. We're real flexible here." Pam lowered her voice to a conspiratorial whisper. "At least I am, but don't you dare tell Luke I said that."

Catherine doubted she and Luke would ever exchange any such teasing confidences. "Don't worry, I won't," she promised.

She slid into the chair at the desk, reached for the first letter and used a pair of scissors from the desk drawer to slit it open. Just as Pam had predicted, it contained a flyer of a teenage boy described as a runaway, and she set it aside to post. She'd noticed the bank of colorful flyers in the hall where the meals were served but hadn't been close enough to recognize what they were.

"Do many kids find themselves on a flyer and call home?" she asked.

"I haven't kept track, but every once in a while someone does. It's not nearly often enough, though."

"How long have you worked here?"

"Not quite two years. I was Luke's secretary at UCLA, and when he left the Psychology Department to come here, I came with him."

Catherine slit open another flyer and found a smiling girl with braces on her teeth. "He left UCLA for Lost Angel? Wasn't that an unlikely career move?"

"I'll say." Pam checked Luke's door and again lowered her voice. "It was more of a mission. Luke's sixteen-year-old daughter committed suicide. The day after Marcy was buried, he walked off the UCLA campus and never went back."

That awful news hit Catherine with the force of a tightly clenched fist, and the envelope she'd been about to open fluttered to the floor. She'd found Luke short-tempered and rude, but now she understood why his anger ran so deep. Ashamed for having misjudged him, she brushed away a tear and bent to retrieve the letter.

"I can't think of anything worse than losing a child," she murmured.

"It was a terrible shame. Marcy was such a terrific kid, but her boyfriend broke up with her just before the prom, and she took a handful of her mother's sleeping pills. Maybe she just meant to scare her boyfriend, but she didn't wake up. That was the end of Luke's marriage too."

Pam turned back to the figures she'd been entering into her computer. "How did we ever get on such a distressing subject?"

Catherine felt sick. She'd had no idea that Luke had suffered such a tragic loss, and she now felt a kinship she hadn't even dreamed they might share. Her curiosity numbed, she kept opening letters and stacking up flyers until Pam left for lunch. Then she went to Luke's door and knocked lightly. Once he'd invited her inside, she rushed through a clumsy apology.

"The other day, I made some stupid remark about your playing martyr, and I'm sincerely sorry."

Luke gestured toward the chair opposite his desk and waited for her to sit. "That wasn't one of my best days, either, so let's just say we've exchanged apologies and forget it. Now, tell me the truth. Was I too rough on the Tubergens?"

His charming grin caught Catherine completely off guard, and she could scarcely believe she was talking with the same man. The silver tint to his hair made him appear older, but now that he wore a relaxed smile, she doubted he was forty. Thoroughly distracted, she tried to recall what he'd asked, then wasn't certain how to reply.

"Perhaps rough is too strong a word."

"Pick another, then. You've taught English, so your vocabulary has to be extensive. How would you describe me?"

Arrogant, opinionated and *dictatorial* swiftly came to mind, but Catherine had come to apologize rather than insult him anew. "I'm not sure where to begin," she hedged.

Luke left his chair and came around to lean against the front of his desk. "Look, I know I was less than cordial when you came in to interview, but I've spoken with too many other lovely, well-educated women who hope to volunteer between tennis games and luncheon dates. They usually bail on us before the month is out. I was thinking of them, and that was totally unfair to you."

His obvious sincerity only served to increase Catherine's discomfort, and unable to remain seated, she left her chair and circled it to create a safe barrier between them. "I'll agree your tone was a bit sarcastic, but I misjudged you too. My only excuse is that I was unaware of your situation."

Luke's dark brows dipped slightly. "And just what situation is that, Mrs. Brooks?"

Now that Catherine had had the opportunity to see him with more than a thoughtful or threatening frown, she could appreciate how remarkably expressive his face truly was. At present, he looked puzzled, but she feared she was treading upon dangerous ground and licked her lips nervously.

"I was referring to the loss of your daughter."

Luke crossed his arms over his chest and again allowed a caustic edge to sear his words. "You must have found Pam in a talkative mood this morning."

"Oh, please, you mustn't be angry with her. Clearly she's devoted to you, or she wouldn't have followed you here from UCLA."

"Oh, Christ." Luke jabbed his fingers through his hair and, for a moment, looked as though he might yank out a handful. "She gave you the whole pathetic story, didn't she? I'll bet she even threw in the bitter divorce."

Catherine hadn't meant to upset him again, but she felt as though the floor had opened beneath her, and she scrambled to break her fall. "You're a psychologist, so you must know it's never wise to harbor such sad secrets."

Luke straightened up. "Don't lecture me on the finer points of psychology, Mrs. Brooks. There's a tremendous difference between a man willingly confiding the details of his private life and someone else blabbing them all over town without his consent."

"I can't dispute that," Catherine agreed calmly. After all, she'd had ample opportunity that morning to describe herself as a widow and not taken it. She wouldn't have been pleased if Luke had waved her application and announced it to the group, either. In boots, she was his equal in height, but she still felt at a terrible disadvantage and inched toward the door.

"I'm sorry, but I meant only to offer an apology and say that I know how lost and alone you must feel."

"The hell you do!" Luke followed her across the room, and as she reached for the doorknob, he slammed his palm against

35

the door to keep her trapped in his office until he was good and ready to let her go.

"You will never understand how wretched I feel, Mrs. Brooks, so drop the pretty pretense that you do. I want my private life kept private, and I expect you to respect that wish even if Pam Strobble doesn't. Is that understood?"

What Catherine understood was that he had no intention of opening his door until she agreed and being trapped there frightened her as badly as his fiery temper. He was standing so close she could see the golden flecks in his hazel eyes burn with a dangerous gleam, and it was all she could do to nod.

"Good." Luke swung open the door and stepped out of the way. "Now go on home, and if you pass Pam on the way out, tell her she's fired."

Chapter Three

Luke slammed the door in Catherine's face and then threw the bolt, or she would have marched right back into his office and argued that when he was furious with her, he had absolutely no right to take it out on Pam Strobble. She raised her fist to pound out her disapproval; then, refusing to sink to his level, she let her hand fall. She couldn't leave and allow Pam to face his wrath alone, but she was far too upset to continue opening the mail and simply paced the office until the personable secretary returned.

Pam came breezing in carrying a McDonald's bag and milkshake, but Catherine's anxious frown erased her smile. "What's happened?"

Catherine gestured toward Luke's door as she rushed through a highly censored version of what had actually transpired. "You needn't worry, though, because I won't allow him to vent his foul temper on you."

Pam raised a hand in a gentle, soothing gesture. "Thanks, but I've lost track of how many times Luke's fired me, and I've yet to clean out my desk. Trust me, he'll calm down once he's had lunch. Left on his own, he often forgets to eat, and then he's as cranky as a toddler without a nap."

Catherine winced at Pam's lack of understanding. "Believe me, his temper soared far above the cranky range. In fact, I'd say he was close to a murderous rage."

"Then it's a good thing I bought him a strawberry shake, because he'll agree to anything for one of these. In fact, I always wave a strawberry shake in front of him whenever I ask for a raise."

Pam appeared more amused than disturbed, but Catherine remained frantic. "Just remember that this is all my fault, and don't let him bully you."

"Girl, my husband stands six feet six inches tall and weighs 240 pounds, but he can't bully me. Luke Starns doesn't stand a chance."

Catherine braced herself, but as Pam approached Luke's door, Nick entered the office from the courtyard. He gripped his skateboard with one hand and with the other held the door open for two fair-haired girls.

They were an appealing pair with slender figures and creamy complexions, but there were dark circles beneath their wide, blue eyes. Their jeans had once been tight, but now bagged at the knees, and their cropped sweaters drooped off their sagging shoulders. One was dragging a backpack which had become too heavy to carry.

"Come on in," Nick coaxed. "Luke's a cool dude, and he'll see you're treated right. Is Luke here? I want him to hear what these girls have to say about Felix Mendoza."

Pam sent Catherine a startled glance, then shrugged and left the McDonald's bag and shake atop the file cabinet near Luke's door. "Let me tell him what's up," she said, but she took the precaution of using the telephone intercom on her desk to summon him. She mentioned Felix Mendoza the instant he answered.

"They look scared to death," Pam turned away to whisper. "You better get out here real quick."

Luke appeared mere seconds after Pam had hung up. He sent Catherine an incredulous glance but quickly swung his attention toward the girls. Then, with no trace of his earlier irascible mood, he introduced himself as the center's director.

"Would you care to come into my office, or would you be more comfortable talking out here?" he asked.

The pair had barely inched their way inside the office and quickly scanned the room with darting glances. "Out here," they responded in unison. There were comfortable chairs for visitors, but they chose to stand.

"We heard you served lunch," the taller of the two said. Her hair was pulled back in a ponytail, while her companion's fell past her shoulders in loose waves.

Pam sat at her desk, and Catherine moved around beside her while Nick took one of the visitor chairs. Appearing completely relaxed, Luke leaned back against the second desk and braced himself with his arms. "We'll be happy to give you something to eat, but first, why don't you tell me what you know about Felix?"

The girls exchanged a fearful glance, then again spoke at once. "He was just a friend."

"I'll just bet he was," Luke replied smoothly. "Tell me something more about him."

Catherine glanced down at Pam, who was taking notes in a steno pad rather than handling the center's other business as it had first appeared. The disheveled girls looked to be fifteen or sixteen, and that they might have awakened in a pimp's filthy bed turned Catherine's stomach. It was difficult to believe their lives could have been so awful at home that they would have willingly taken such a revolting risk.

"They barely knew him," Nick interjected. "But they were there when he died. Go on. If you can tell me, you can tell Luke."

When the huddled pair remained reticent, Luke prompted softly, "How long have you been in LA?"

"We got here last week," the ponytailed girl replied. "We thought Hollywood would be, well, more sparkly."

Luke nodded. "Everyone does, but the only sparkle Hollywood has comes from pretty girls like you."

Catherine marveled at how easily Luke's compliment penetrated the girls' defenses. They blushed, then interrupted each other in a rush to describe what they had seen. As Pam struggled to keep up, her once-neat writing blurred into a hurried scrawl.

"We weren't really sure what had happened that night," the girl with the flowing hair explained. "The next morning, we went back to where Felix had parked his car. We were kind of mixed-up about where it was, and by the time we found it, the police were about to tow it away. We just hung with the neighbors, who had come out to watch, until we overheard someone say Felix had been stabbed. Then we just walked away, real cool, like."

"You had a good reason to be frightened," Luke said. "But didn't it occur to you that you might be able to help the police catch the killer?"

"We didn't see much," the shorter girl insisted. "We'd just gotten into Felix's car when this woman came up to him, and we didn't hear what she said."

"Not a word," swore the girl with the ponytail.

Luke accepted that with a slight shrug. "All right. Did you see the knife?"

The girls shook their heads vigorously. "We just saw Felix double over, and we didn't stick around after that."

"Can you describe the woman?" Luke asked. "Did you notice if she were tall or short, heavy or thin?"

The girls shuffled their feet and moved even closer together. "It was dark," one complained. "I couldn't tell if she were a Latina or Chinese."

"She had white hair," the other said.

"No, it was just bleached blonde. I saw a streak of red. I guess it was her dress."

"Maybe you noticed more than you realized," Luke coached. "Could you pick her out of a line-up?"

"No way. We were just thinking about how great it was to have a place to spend the night," the pony-tailed girl blurted out. "Then wham, things got weird. Now what about lunch?"

Apparently satisfied with what they'd told him, Luke straightened up. "Sure. Let's go over to the dining hall." He nodded toward the door to the courtyard, and the girls scooted right out. Smiling wide, Nick jumped out of his chair to exchange a high five with Luke.

Before Luke followed him out the door, he turned back to offer Catherine a word of advice. "Those girls were smart enough to know when to run, Mrs. Brooks. You'd be wise to follow their example."

His voice was honey-smooth rather than threatening, but Catherine caught his meaning. She was too shaken to leave immediately, however, and instead sank into the chair Nick had used.

"Those girls witnessed a stabbing and all they can think about is having lunch? Just listening to them made me sick. If I'd witnessed a killing, I'd still be screaming."

"So would I," Pam agreed, "but most of the kids we see here have become inured to violence. It's a defense mechanism they've adopted to protect themselves from the frequent horror of their reality."

Catherine understood the concept, but it still took a large gulp to swallow her disgust. "That's such a sad way to live, especially for kids. I was hoping to straighten things out for you before I left, but now I doubt there's any point in my staying. I just don't feel up to going another couple of rounds with Luke."

Pam had been reviewing her notes but looked up to offer an encouraging smile. "Luke and I will be fine, but maybe you ought to drink his strawberry shake."

It was plain Pam was no more upset by Felix's murder than the pretty pair of witnesses, and Catherine wondered if the secretary's senses were not equally numb. She rested her head against the back of the chair and closed her eyes.

"No, thanks. Just give me a few minutes to collect my thoughts, and I'll be on my way."

Pam gave her thirty seconds. "You know why Ms. Snodgrass wants to come back on Friday afternoon, don't you?"

Catherine hated to think how long she would need to find the courage, or perhaps the stupidity, to return. She opened her eyes and sat up slowly. "I've no idea. Why?"

"You must have noticed the way she was eyeing Luke. If she's here at closing time on Friday, I'll bet you anything you name that she'll invite him out for a drink."

"Would he go?" Catherine asked, then, astonished by that spontaneous burst of curiosity, she pretended a rapt interest in her nails.

"Why don't you make it a point to be here Friday afternoon so you can see for yourself?" Pam offered coyly.

Catherine responded with a rueful laugh. "I doubt I'll have recovered sufficiently from today by then."

Pam giggled at what she mistook for a joke, but when Dave Curtis and Ron Flanders entered the office, she quickly abandoned her teasing tone. "It looks as though a couple of witnesses to Felix Mendoza's murder have stopped by for lunch."

"Anyone we know?" Dave inquired.

"No. The girls haven't been here before," Pam replied. "Luke is careful not to spook kids by asking for their names too soon, but I'll probably be able to tell you who they are later this afternoon."

"I was referring to the murderer," Dave stressed. He caught Catherine's eye and winked. "Hi, there."

Catherine could barely manage a smile for the maintenance man, but she was enormously appreciative. Everyone at Lost Angel was friendly except Luke, and she was desperately sorry not to have left well enough alone where he was concerned.

Pamela introduced Dave to Catherine, then reached out to give his arm a playful shove. "No, silly, it was just some blonde in a red dress."

Ron Flanders took a quick step toward Pam's desk. "A woman killed the guy?"

"He was a pimp," Pam enunciated clearly. "One of his girls must have been dissatisfied with his service."

"Whoever she is, the city ought to award her a plaque for sending that slimy rat to the eternal sewer," Dave proposed.

Catherine directed her question to Pam. "Even if Felix wouldn't have been nominated for Hollywood's man of the year, aren't you going to contact the police so they can question the girls?"

"Once they've eaten, Luke will convince them it's their civic duty and then let them use our telephone," Pam assured her. "He encourages all the kids to be responsible citizens. When they fail, usually with disastrous results, he helps them analyze what happened so they can show better judgment in the future. Didn't he explain that this morning?"

"He sure did," Ron Flanders replied.

Catherine feared Luke must have covered that point while she was wondering about the man himself and was embarrassed by that lapse a second time. "Yes, of course, he did." She pushed herself to her feet. "You have my home telephone number, Pam. If Luke gives you so much as a sneer later, please call me."

"You and Luke mixing it up again?" Dave asked the secretary.

"It's nothing I can't handle," Pam assured him. "Now, when would you like to come back and see us again, Mr. Flanders?"

Catherine went right on out the door rather than set up a schedule for herself, and she was surprised when Dave Curtis came along with her to the parking lot. "How did you and Ron do with the sprinklers?" she asked.

"Pretty good, actually, but I've got a manual with clear diagrams on how to repair damn near everything, and sprinklers aren't all that complicated." He walked her to her Volvo and then leaned back against the fender.

"I'm sure you're wondering what a nice guy like me is doing in a place like this," he began with an easy grin. "I once had a beautiful wife, two cute little kids and a big house in Orange County. Then the bottom fell out of the economy, and the interior design company I worked for went bankrupt. When we had to sell our home, my wife divorced me and took the kids back to Iowa.

"I'd met Luke at a fund-raiser, when I had plenty of funds to donate. He heard about my troubles and offered me a job with living quarters. The apartment is downright cozy, even if it is in the church basement, and I jumped at the chance to work here," he concluded. "Life has a way of throwing us some pretty nasty curves, but I'm surviving."

Despite the offhand way he'd recounted his recent history, Catherine knew having suffered such wrenching losses must still hurt. She'd been burned once today while trying to offer sympathy, but the optimistic glint in Dave's eyes showed he had no need of it.

"We all expect the good times to last forever, don't we?" she asked.

Dave nodded, straightened up and took a step away from her car. "I sure as hell did, but we could talk for hours on that subject, and all I'd meant to say was that even if Luke is having an off day, I sure hope you'll keep coming back."

His smile was very charming, and it suddenly struck Catherine that rather than merely being friendly, he was actually flirting with her. Plenty of men had flirted with her over the years, but they'd all known how devoted she was to Sam, and it had always been playful rather than a sincere effort to touch her heart. She was no longer happily married, however, and didn't know quite what to make of Dave Curtis.

She unlocked her car, then leaned against the door. "Are you coming on to me?"

Dave raised his hands in an exaggerated gesture of innocence and began to back away. "No, ma'am. I saw your wedding ring, and I respect marriage as sacred. Can't help but think that way living here."

His good-natured grin was such a welcome sight, Catherine found it easy to speak the words she couldn't form earlier. "I'm a widow, but I'm not ready to remove my wedding ring just yet."

Dave dropped his hands, and his expression turned to one of genuine concern. "I'm real sorry to hear of your loss, Cathy, but whenever you're ready to start going out, let me know. There are plenty of ways to have fun that don't cost a penny, and I know I could show you a real good time."

He winked again before walking away, and while Catherine couldn't even imagine going out on a date, she was smiling as she left for home.

Luke went running that night. He lived in a condo near UCLA and as usual passed other joggers out burning off the day's tensions. Sometimes he returned home tired enough to sleep, but tonight he could have run all the way to San Diego and back and not outdistanced his demons.

He stood in the shower and let the hot water beat down on his shoulders until the steam eased the soreness in his muscles, but nothing had soothed the ache in his soul since the morning he'd had found Marcy dead. He could block the pain for hours at a time, then something, or some well-meaning fool, would remind him of his daughter, and the excruciating torment would begin anew.

Catherine Brooks had the most beautiful, trusting eyes, but her misplaced attempt at kindness had simply ripped a deeper tear through his heart. He didn't doubt she missed her late husband, but whatever anguish she suffered couldn't even begin to compare with having to live with the senseless suicide of a precious child.

There were nights when he'd done handstands atop the wall enclosing his fifth floor balcony, but it had merely been a dare to fate rather than an attempt to end his own life. Suicide would have been pointless in his case because there simply wasn't enough of him left to kill.

After leaving the shower, he stretched out across his bed and tried to conjure up that peaceful lagoon where one day would blur into the next without a hint of sorrow or pain. He longed for that peace with a desperate hunger, but that night, his only salvation was the memory of the anguish reflected in Catherine Brooks' haunting gaze.

Catherine didn't sleep well, either, that night. While it was often difficult for her to summon the energy to rise in the morning, she got up early to work in the garden. By ten o'clock, she'd been to the Belefontaine Nursery and was busy replanting the flower beds in her backyard. Smoky wound his way through her arms as she packed the dirt around the colorful pansies, but she was more amused than annoyed by his antics.

When the telephone rang, she was tempted to allow her machine to answer, but at the last instant sprinted into the house and tugged off her gardening gloves to get it herself.

"Mrs. Brooks?"

Catherine instantly recognized the caller as Luke Starns. He'd made his feelings so plain the previous day, she couldn't see any need to endure another of his sarcastic lectures and attempted to head him off.

"Dr. Starns, I doubt this is necessary, and—"

"Oh, but it is," Luke countered, but a long, uncomfortable pause followed. "I never discuss my daughter's death because it's simply too painful. I remind myself people mean well, but clearly I don't have to tell you that's not always an effective technique."

Surprised by his candor, Catherine relaxed her grip on the telephone. Luke was probably standing at his office window looking out over the desolate parking lot. The day was warm, and the sun would lend his hair silvery highlights, but she thought he would still be scowling. That he was actually trying to apologize amazed her, but not nearly as greatly as how easily she could picture his expression in her mind.

"Mrs. Brooks?"

"Yes, go on," she responded.

"You're not making this easy."

Catherine could hear a hint of a smile in his voice and felt her own expression soften. "I'm sorry. I tend to weep whenever anyone mentions my husband, but I know men are more likely to respond with anger when someone touches a nerve."

"I don't recall your mentioning that you also have a degree in psychology. Did you simply neglect to list it on your application?"

His tone had deepened slightly, which Catherine wisely interpreted as a warning she'd again overstepped her bounds, or more accurately, his boundaries. "No, but life would be pointless if we didn't pick up any valuable insights along the way."

"I agree, but unfortunately, it's often at too high a price. At any rate, I called to say that I hope you'll overlook my advice to the contrary and still volunteer at Lost Angel whenever you have the time."

The invitation was delivered in such a mechanical fashion, Catherine was tempted to tell him to get a haircut and then go straight to hell, but in the interest of harmony, she restrained herself. "Thank you. I'll try to work it into my busy schedule."

As she hung up, she was uncertain whether or not she would go back to Lost Angel. After all, she could simply substitute in the local high schools to gain experience, but that would require her to take the CBEST test, and she hadn't even signed up for it yet. If she wanted to teach full-time in the fall, however, she would also need the test, and she made a mental note to pick up an application from the school board office.

On Wednesday, she visited the charity thrift shop and dropped off the clothes and shoes she and Joyce had sorted. By Thursday morning, her garden looked beautiful, and she'd run out of excuses to stay away from Lost Angel. She drove on over to Hollywood, but she was determined to avoid Luke Starns and felt certain he would do his best to avoid her.

Pam again put Catherine to work opening the mail, and when she finished, she carried the stack of new flyers over to the hall to post. She'd nearly completed the task when a slender girl in a fuzzy pink sweater and tight jeans came up to look over her shoulder. Catherine turned to smile and found the girl had the remarkable prettiness of Alice in Wonderland, with startling blue eyes and long, blonde hair.

"Hello," Catherine greeted her. "I hope if you recognize anyone, you'll encourage them to call home."

The girl shrugged and slid her hands into her hip pockets. "I don't see anyone I know."

Like so many of the teens Catherine had seen on Friday, the girl looked painfully young. Catherine doubted she would have approached her if she hadn't wanted to talk, but uncertain how best to initiate a conversation, she adjusted the angle of a bright pink flyer and kept quiet.

"You're new here, aren't you?" the girl asked without glancing Catherine's way.

"Yes, I am." Catherine offered her name as she posted another flyer, but she had a lengthy wait before the girl responded.

"My name's Violet. I just come here sometimes to look at the books, but I didn't find anything good today."

Catherine had noticed the sagging shelves which contained the center's paperback library. "I've got quite a collection of paperbacks at home," she said. "What sort of books do you like?"

Violet shrugged again. "The ones with pretty covers." She reached out to finger the rolled corner on a faded orange flyer that had been on display for several months. "You know, the ones where there's a couple dancing or just staring into each other's eyes?"

"Yes. Those are romances. I love to read them too. I'll bring in some of mine on my next visit. Do you come here often?"

Violet began to inch away. "No. Like I said, I just come by to check out the books."

Catherine hadn't meant to frighten Violet away, but as she turned to smile, the girl bolted for the door. When she found Luke blocking the way, she simply turned sideways and slipped by him with a hasty wave.

Luke didn't look pleased, but as he walked toward Catherine, she couldn't imagine what she'd done wrong this time. She inhaled deeply and vowed to hang on to her temper, regardless of how easily Luke Starns lost his. Choosing to ignore him, she admired her neat arrangement of new flyers, which was a vast improvement over the last volunteer's haphazard posting.

Luke stopped so close to Catherine their shoulders were nearly touching. "Thanks for putting up the flyers," he offered in a hushed whisper. "I hope Violet didn't give you any trouble."

It hadn't even occurred to Catherine that Luke could have been annoyed with Violet rather than her. Feeling very foolish,

47

she forced a smile. "Why no. We merely exchanged a few words about books, and I offered to bring in some of mine."

"Oh, great. Come on. I'll walk you back to the office." Luke grabbed the stapler off the adjacent table and gestured for Catherine to precede him.

Catherine moved toward the door with a purposeful stride, but even then she felt as though Luke were rushing her. "Is there something wrong?" she asked as they moved out into the courtyard.

Luke caught her arm and with a gentle tug pulled her to a halt while they were still out in the open. "I'm positive that during the orientation I stressed that we never make promises we can't keep. That goes for something as simple as a few used books."

His chambray shirt had been faded by a hundred washings, but there was nothing soft in his manner, and Catherine found it difficult to look at him. Fortunately, the stone courtyard possessed the tranquility of a cloister, leading her to believe the dull gray granite probably possessed greater warmth than Luke ever did.

"If I tell someone I'll bring in a few used books, or a bucket of dirt, for that matter, I'll follow through," she insisted. "It's a shame you've apparently been disappointed in your other volunteers, but I always keep my word."

Catherine took pride in how positive she sounded, but in truth, she was deeply offended. "Violet is little more than a lovely child. Do you honestly believe that I'd disappoint her?"

Luke swore under his breath. "You mustn't allow yourself to become attached to any of the kids, and that goes double for Violet Simms."

He paused to make certain he had Catherine's full attention. "Violet's father abused her sexually while her mother pretended not to know about it. Violet left home as soon as other men began to notice her. Now she's living with a mechanic who calls himself Ford Dolan. That son of a bitch is as bad as her father, and she comes in here more often than not with a black eye."

"Can't you have him arrested?" Catherine asked.

"There's no point in it when Violet won't swear out a complaint against him. Don't encourage her to depend on you

48

for books or anything else, Catherine, because she'll surely break your heart."

Catherine's heart was already broken, but despite the lack of risk, she couldn't agree. "I'm sorry to argue with you again, but I truly believe it's imperative for these' kids to know someone cares about them."

Luke kept his voice low, but it failed to disguise his irritation. "I didn't say I didn't care. If I didn't give a damn, I wouldn't be here, but there's an enormous difference between a professional offering effective guidance and a misguided volunteer creating more harm than good."

Catherine didn't understand how the man could be so incredibly dense. "I'm not trying to challenge your authority here, Dr. Starns. Do you have an objection to volunteers donating paperback books for your library?"

"No," Luke snorted. "Of course, not."

Catherine waited for him to realize how senseless their latest argument truly was. With his only child dead and his wife gone, she could easily understand why he'd walled up his heart, but she had no desire to emulate his chilling example.

"Are you seeing a therapist yourself?" she asked.

"That's none of your damn business, Mrs. Brooks."

Luke left Catherine standing in the middle of the courtyard and entered the office alone, but she wasn't ashamed to have asked the question. He might have the professional credentials to run Lost Angel, but she considered him pathetically lacking in empathy.

The cloudless sky was the same vivid blue as Violet's eyes, and she stood there a long moment simply to enjoy it. The frantic flight of a hummingbird drew her attention to the honeysuckle growing up the side of the granite church. Since Sam's death, she'd learned to treasure such sweet distractions, and she took it as an omen that any kindness she showed Violet, or anyone else at Lost Angel, would bring only good results.

It wasn't until that evening when she'd sunk down into a hot bubble bath that she recalled the slight break in Luke's voice as he'd spoken her first name. There'd been a whisper of hurt in that instant, but if she wasn't mistaken, there'd also been a husky hint of desire.

Shocked by the discovery, she remained in the tub until the water turned cold. By then she was so thoroughly confused, she couldn't be certain that Luke hadn't really been warning her against caring for him rather than the shy and troubled Violet.

Chapter Four

When Catherine awoke Friday morning, her thoughts immediately flew to Lost Angel, and just as swiftly, she was overcome by a frantic sense of alarm. It had made such perfect sense to volunteer with homeless teens and at the same time hone her teaching skills. Yet the thought of returning to the center filled her with dread.

She'd left—no, fled—yesterday without setting up a schedule. It would be a simple matter to drop by today and take care of that important detail, but she couldn't even bring herself to pick up the telephone and call Pamela Strobble, let alone speak with the charming secretary in person.

"Coward," she muttered under her breath. She was well aware that change could be expected to create discomfort, if not downright terror, but she could handle the shift in her life to accommodate volunteer work. What she couldn't face, however, were the conflicting emotions Luke Starns aroused, at least not that day.

However, she did intend to honor her promise to Violet and deliver some books the following week. While she knew she was avoiding rather than facing the real problem, once up and dressed, she got busy dusting, sorting and boxing the entertaining assortment of paperback novels crowding her bookshelves. As for the hardcover volumes, she would box up all but her favorites and donate them to the annual spring book fair at the public library.

She consoled herself that it was definitely time to make way for the new, but as she placed the books in neat stacks, she kept recalling the frightened faces of the runaways who had witnessed Felix Mendoza's murder. Luke had so easily drawn the girls into conversation that she hoped he'd used equal skill to convince them to return home before they again recklessly risked their lives.

Clearly Luke Starns was a man of many talents and moods, but as she finished packing her books, she began to wonder if, as Pamela had predicted, Beverly Snodgrass really would volunteer that afternoon in hopes Luke would join her for a drink. She didn't want to care, even refused to consider the possibility for a while, but by the afternoon, she finally had to admit how much she truly did.

Because Catherine Brooks appeared to go out of her way to annoy him, Luke half expected her to come in on Friday. Then when she failed to arrive, he was disgusted with himself for missing her.

Beverly Snodgrass worked in the office in the late afternoon, but he was immune to her seductive smiles and offered no more than a hurried hello. He liked to wrap up the week's work and leave his desk clean for Monday morning, but that evening he sharpened pencils and cleaned out drawers until Pam assured him Beverly had gone home.

For a grown man to hide from a woman was absurd, but when he'd taken over as the director of Lost Angel, he'd quickly learned a closed door was the most effective way to discourage a woman's interest without giving offense.

A married couple supervised Lost Angel on the weekends when the center offered prepackaged meals, and hot showers, but no counseling or job placement services. Dave Curtis was always there to handle any unforeseen emergencies, but as usual, Luke had to push himself to plan for the weekend.

He often went on long, strenuous hikes with the Sierra Club. Their members included a great many beautiful women with long, tanned legs, but the rambunctious outdoorsy type simply didn't appeal to him. He'd built houses with Habitat for Humanity, which was exhausting as well as rewarding. On other weekends, he'd driven up to Santa Barbara or down to San Diego simply for a change of scene.

He'd been numb for so long, it didn't really matter how he spent his free time, but that Friday night as he left the office, he felt lonely and wished for a noisy crowd. It might be a good weekend to catch up on laundry and new movies, but rather than action adventure films where he could drown in explosive sound, he thought he might seek out a couple of comedies. It amused him to think how much he might actually enjoy a good laugh, and he hummed to himself as he drove away.

Saturday afternoon, Joyce Quincy again joined Catherine out on her patio. "You have everything looking so pretty. Not that it didn't when I was here last week, but I love pansies' sweet little faces, and they always make me smile."

Catherine propped her feet on the adjacent chair, but she was so restless it was an effort to appear relaxed. She would have welcomed Smoky's calming presence, but he was napping in the sun and apparently too content to move to her lap.

"Thank you, but I still need to make a planting schedule rather than let everything slide again."

"The yard had scarcely slid into ruin," Joyce teased. "I'm almost afraid to ask, but did you actually volunteer at Lost Angel?"

"Yes, I was there twice, in fact," Catherine replied, but she thought better of mentioning a meeting with two eyewitnesses to murder, or the maddeningly perverse Luke Starns. "I was given paperwork to sort, which wasn't at all exciting. Now, tell me what's happening with you."

Joyce shrugged, then toyed with her bangle bracelets. "Nothing spectacular, either, I'm afraid. I've been redecorating an attorney's office in Encino. Unfortunately, his tastes were so conservative that I was limited to forest greens and dark leather, but he was enormously pleased with my work, and there are sure to be several nice referrals."

Catherine knew Joyce too well to overlook her preoccupied frown. "There must be more to the story," she prompted.

Joyce paused to take a deep breath, and her glance again swept the colorful array of pansies bordering the lawn. "The office is in an impressive new building, and I'd hoped to meet a younger attorney, or perhaps a physician, at any rate, someone substantial. Then yesterday, as I was hanging the last of the paintings in the attorney's office, in comes this gorgeous young man with a cart loaded with plants. He explained he had the contract for the building and was delivering the plants to improve the office's feng shui."

Catherine ran her fingers through her hair to catch the sun's warmth and smiled. "Feng shui is popular, and I happen to agree that surrounding ourselves with beautiful living things does promote serenity."

"You didn't see the guy." Joyce fanned her face with her hand. "He had the most beautiful blue eyes and dark, curly hair. He also had a tight, toned body like the men on the UPS calendar. I didn't hear half of what he said about feng shui. Fortunately, we agreed on the placement of the plants."

"Which were?"

"A ficus tree, a philodendron, something else I didn't recognize. They were all big, healthy plants, so he must be a hell of a gardener."

She pulled his card from her blouse pocket and handed it to Catherine. "A nurseryman, he called himself."

"Shane Shephard. What a nice name," Catherine responded.

"Everything about him was nice," Joyce replied. "He probably has a kid brother named Sean and a sister Sharon."

Catherine noted the address on his card. "Oxnard is a prime agricultural region. I visited an orchid grower's greenhouse there once. But clearly your interest wasn't in horticulture."

"Damn right, but I doubt Shane was more than thirty."

"Would a thirty-seven-year-old man balk at dating a thirty-year-old woman?" Catherine asked pointedly.

"Never, but I can't see myself living in the back of a greenhouse in Oxnard with a nurseryman. I'd probably get a striped tan from the building's little slats."

It was an image that made Catherine laugh. "Oxnard is on the coast, and it has a beautiful marina." She was delighted Joyce had been so captivated by Shane Shephard that she hadn't pried into her work at Lost Angel. A scrub jay swooped down to sit on the back wall, and she made a mental note to purchase a new bird feeder.

"Oh, like a nurseryman would own a yacht," Joyce scoffed.

"Stop making excuses. Did he ask you out?"

Joyce brushed a crumb from her blouse and waved her beautifully manicured nails. "Just for coffee, but I told him I was late for an appointment."

"Which you now regret?"

Joyce shook her head. "Regret is too strong a word, but I'm definitely ambivalent."

"I can appreciate ambivalence," Catherine mused quietly without confiding her own dilemma. She handed over Shane's card. "Why not call him?"

Joyce slid the card back into her pocket and gave it a light pat. "I'd be too embarrassed to make any sense."

Catherine shot her a skeptical glance. "Your field is interior design. Tell him you need a variety of plants for a new job."

Joyce took a moment to consider the suggestion. "While it's not very original, I suppose it would work. But still, he's too young and scarcely what I'd call substantial."

"So what? You can provide for yourself, and he might surprise you," Catherine chided.

"Oh, I'm surprised all the time, but it's never good." Joyce sat back in her chair, but she gripped the arms tightly. "Here I am trying to avoid trouble, like Shane Shephard surely is, and you're out looking for it at Lost Angel. One of us has to be misguided."

Catherine considered Joyce a dear friend. She'd been there for her when Sam had died, even slept at her house that first terrible week so she wouldn't have to wake up alone. But there were times, like today, when Catherine wondered if the only thing they truly had in common was an address on the same street.

"Please don't misunderstand me," Catherine warned softly. "I had such a marvelous life with Sam, but now I need to do something that matters on my own. Lost Angel provides that opportunity."

Joyce rose and stretched her arms above her head. "Well, what I need is a man who'll take care of me because I'm sick to death of making ends meet on my own. Why don't we go into Pasadena's Old Town tonight? It'll be noisy and crowded, but it sure beats staying home alone. We can just walk around, eat at one of the new restaurants, maybe go to a movie."

Catherine stood to walk her friend to the side gate. She actually enjoyed being home alone, but her nights were simply a comfortable blur. Perhaps it was time to make some changes in her weekends.

"I remember a place filled with scented candles. Could we go by there?" she asked.

"Of course," Joyce exclaimed. "I didn't mean we wouldn't shop. Walk up to my house at seven and I'll drive."

"I'll see you later," Catherine promised, but as she bathed and dressed that night, she wondered if Luke Starns ever dated any of Lost Angel's volunteers. If so, she sure hoped Beverly Snodgrass wasn't among them.

Monday morning, Luke was back at his desk to tackle a fresh batch of grant applications. At noon, he left his office and purposely ignored the giant calendar where volunteers penciled in their time. While he'd struggled all weekend to suppress thoughts of Catherine Brooks, he'd eventually come to the depressing conclusion that she would probably not be coming back. He just didn't want to verify the fact by searching for her name.

None of their conversations had gone well, and even worse, he'd begun to suspect he might be to blame for discouraging some of the other sophisticated women who'd failed to honor their initial commitment to Lost Angel. It was an uncomfortable supposition, and he did his best to shake it off as he crossed the courtyard and joined the lunch line in the hall.

He ate with the kids several times a week. Mabel usually served spaghetti with a fresh green salad and garlic bread on Monday, and it was one of his favorite meals. As he approached the counter, he joked easily with the kids in line, and then Catherine Brooks handed him a plate and, shocked, he nearly dropped it.

"Mrs. Brooks? I had no idea you possessed any culinary skills," he exclaimed in surprise. With a bright yellow oilcloth apron over a pale green shirt and matching jeans, he thought she looked not merely efficient, but awfully cute as well.

"I can dice fresh vegetables with the best of them," Catherine responded playfully. "Apparently I failed to check that box on my application. Would you please add it for me?"

"Be glad to," Luke replied. Rather than slow the line any further, he hurried away, but as soon as he'd taken a chair at the nearest long table, Nick Bohler dropped down beside him.

"Man, she was flirting with you!" Nick exclaimed. "What'll you do if her husband shows up here looking for you?"

Luke feigned a rapt interest in his spaghetti and twirled it around his fork. "She's a widow, so there's no danger of that."

Nick snorted. "Then you're in more danger than you think. Want to talk about it this afternoon in our group?"

Luke readily grasped Nick's warning, but laughed it off. "No thanks. How's the job search going?"

"Please," Nick groaned, "I'm trying to eat. Everything is especially tasty today, isn't it? Must be the new cook."

Luke could barely contain his smile. "Yeah, I'm sure it is."

Upon her arrival that morning, Catherine had been asked to take the place of a loyal kitchen volunteer who'd called in sick. So it wasn't until after everyone had eaten and the kitchen had been thoroughly cleaned that she went out to her car to bring in books. She'd stopped by Target to buy two sturdy folding bookshelves, and she asked Rafael and Max, a couple of brawny boys, to carry them inside.

"I sorted my books into categories," she explained, "but it looks as though what you have here was simply shoved onto the shelves wherever the books would fit."

Rafael was a Latino who had bleached his jet black hair to a pale orange and wore it teased into spikes. "What's the use of sorting them when most of the kids who borrow them don't bring them back?"

"As long as they're read and passed along, I doubt it matters if they aren't returned," Catherine argued. "They can be replaced easily enough."

"Yeah, like everybody here can read," Rafael muttered under his breath.

"Cut it out," Max emphasized with a shove. "She's trying to do something good here."

"You go on and help her spread sunshine. I'll be outside." Rafael slung his backpack over his shoulder and left Max to deal with the books.

"He's just being a jerk," Max complained. "He only reads comics."

After lunch, the crowd in the hall had thinned, but Nick ambled up to join them, followed by Polly, again wearing her purple high-tops and a print dress. "Need some help?" Nick asked.

Catherine hoped that if she stepped out of the way, they would take the initiative and organize the center's small library. "I brought some new shelves," she said, "but I'm not sure how best to go about using them."

"Why don't we take all the books off the old shelves and make sections for science fiction, true crime and chicks' books," Nick suggested.

"I like science fiction, and I'm a chick," Polly announced proudly.

"Whatever." Max sighed, but he began removing the books from the shelves and scattering them into piles on the floor.

Luke walked up behind Catherine so quietly that she jumped when he spoke her name. "Sorry, I didn't mean to startle you. Where did you get the new bookcases?"

"Target. They're inexpensive and sturdy, and there wasn't room on the old shelves for the books I brought in."

"Get a form from Pam so you can list the donation on your taxes."

"Thank you, I will." Catherine folded her arms across her waist and watched Max, Nick and Polly sort the books into several categories she would never have even considered.

Luke turned his back toward the teens. "It's clever of you to get them to do the work," he whispered.

"It's a technique I found useful as a teacher," Catherine confided softly. "If an adult appears perplexed by a problem, kids will leap in to solve it. Besides, they're the ones who'll be using the books, so they ought to put them where they can find them."

Luke's voice was still low, but his meaning clear. "I won't argue with your strategy, but in the future, make sure you have my approval before you purchase anything for use here at Lost Angel."

Catherine had expected him to thank her for not only keeping her promise about the books, but for providing additional shelves. It would have been the courteous thing to do, but clearly he preferred protocol to manners. She dropped her hands to her sides and turned to face him squarely.

"As I'm sure you'll recall, I received your approval to donate books last Thursday. They couldn't be left on the floor." Out of the corner of her eye, she spied Max, Nick and Polly pretending to sort books while they strained to listen.

"I recall that conversation vividly," Luke replied, "but, Mrs. Brooks—"

"I understand your concern," Catherine interrupted, "but now I have a question about something else."

Luke turned back toward the scattered heaps of books and jammed his hands into his pockets. "I'm almost afraid to ask what it is."

Catherine ignored his sarcasm. "I hadn't stopped to consider this, and I should have, but Rafael just made a crack about some of the kids not being able to read. Is anyone doing any tutoring here to enhance the kids' chances of getting good jobs or a GED?"

"Education isn't our focus. The city libraries sponsor literacy programs, and they're readily available through adult education in many schools."

Catherine watched the muscles tighten along his jaw in a clear warning that she was treading on dangerous ground, but the idea was too good to abandon. "If they aren't filling out job applications, the kids are sitting here all day rapping with their friends and playing games. Wouldn't an opportunity to improve their reading skills be a worthwhile alternative?"

"What about math?" Luke countered. "Hasn't it occurred to you that their academic skills are lousy across the board?"

Before Catherine could respond, Rafael flung open the door and yelled, "Fight!"

Nick, Max and Polly bolted for the door, as did the other teens in the hall, but Luke still managed to sprint by them. Catherine was reluctant to follow, but then, believing the situation might call for a cooler head than Luke possessed, she forced herself to go on out into the courtyard.

Dave Curtis was already there, but he was too busy struggling to keep the fight from escalating into a brawl to break it up. Kids who had been sitting out front on the sanctuary steps were streaming into the courtyard, but the shouts and cries echoing against the stone buildings were already deafening.

Catherine had seen fights at school, but this wasn't a pair of surly boys who had gotten into a scuffle, these were girls. Sheila was a tall, thin African American whose dreadlocks bounced wildly about her head like Medusa's snakes. Frankie was short, but the blonde sporting a buzz cut was solidly built. Both girls wore overalls, and each used the other's straps to haul her opponent close for a vicious slap and then hurl her away.

As the girls pummeled and kicked each other, a red-haired boy near the office building took bets. Other kids were screaming encouragement to their favorite, while some just shouted colorful curses. Volunteers, who had been sorting clothing in the Sunday school building, ran for the parking lot, while Pam Strobble stood on the office steps writing down names in a notebook.

"Break it up!" Luke shouted as he shoved his way through the crowd. He took an elbow to the eye as he grabbed for the back of Frankie's overalls, but he managed to push her away and form a muscular wall between her and Sheila.

"There's to be absolutely no fighting here at Lost Angel," Luke announced in a voice loud enough to carry clear down the block. "Both of you know that."

Sheila raised her fists and danced around like a boxer ready to go another round. "We weren't fighting. I'm just teaching the bitch not to hit on my man, Jamal."

"Liar. Who'd want that creep?" Frankie screamed back.

Polly moved close to Catherine. "We have fights here all the time, but those two are scary. I just keep clear of them."

"Smart girl," Catherine responded. Dave Curtis was on the opposite side of the crowd. He caught her eye and smiled, but she could do no more than nod in return.

Luke called over to Pam. "How many fights does that make for these two?"

"This is the second in two weeks," Pam replied, "and they know our rules."

Luke still looked ready to bite off the girls' heads, but he waited a long moment for the crowd to hush before he spoke. "You go on in and shower, Frankie, then get out of here. I'm suspending you until Thursday, and if you're ever in another fight, you'll be banned from here for good."

Frankie flung an accusing hand toward Sheila. "She started it!"

"I don't care who started it. We have a zero tolerance for fights. Now hit the showers. As for you, Sheila, you'll sit there on the steps and keep Pam company until Frankie leaves. Then you shower and go until Thursday. I don't see Jamal. Where is he?"

"I ain't seen him for days," Sheila replied with an insolent shrug.

"But he's worth fighting over and losing your privileges here?" Luke asked.

"Yeah, he's my man," Sheila insisted. "You keep away from him, you hear me?" she called after Frankie, who ignored her and entered the hall.

"Go on and sit down," Luke ordered. "The rest of you better scatter before I ask Pam to take your names."

"She's already taking names!" the red-haired boy cried.

"Then don't give her the chance to write yours down twice. Can you handle this, Dave?"

"No problem, boss," Dave swore. "Come on kids, let's try out the new soccer field."

With the excitement over, the teenagers left the courtyard in twos and threes. Max, Nick and Polly went back inside the hall to continue sorting the books, while Catherine waited for Luke by the door. As he approached, she could see his left eye had already begun to swell.

"We ought to put some ice on your eye," she offered.

Luke paused on the step below hers and their eyes were level. "Now you're an expert at first aid? I swear our application isn't long enough to list all your skills. I doubt it will help much, but let's go on into the kitchen."

Catherine followed him to the freezer's double doors, then had to wait while he unlocked one. "I hadn't thought about working in the kitchen when you brought us here on the tour, but it was fun."

She turned away to get a bowl from under the counter to hold the ice and then grabbed a clean dish towel from off the stack by the sink. "Mabel has everything so beautifully organized that anyone can walk in and go right to work."

"I'll have to remember that if I'm ever left with time on my hands," Luke replied, his tone teasing.

She waved Luke toward a tall stool next to the kitchen's long preparation island and filled the small aluminum bowl with ice. She wrapped the towel around several cubes, stepped close and leaned her hip against the island as she held it to his eye.

"You just rest a minute," she urged. "I feel shaky, and no one was throwing punches at me."

"I'm not shaken, just disgusted. Did you ever get into a fight over a boy when you were in high school?" he asked.

She adjusted the makeshift ice pack and, thinking it a wonderful excuse to touch him, she smoothed his silvery hair off his forehead. Thick and soft, it slid through her fingers like silk. He didn't seem to notice, but she was embarrassed to be fondling him and quickly dropped her free hand.

"I beg your pardon?" she asked absently. She could hear the water running in the shower in the restroom located behind the kitchen, but Mabel and the kitchen volunteers had left for the day, and they were quite alone.

"Never mind. It always amazes me when girls fight over some guy who's not worth a lengthy argument, let alone a fistfight."

"I imagine when you can carry all you own in a backpack, even a worthless boyfriend takes on immense value. Will you really ban them permanently if they start another fight?"

"We have to have rules here, Catherine, or we'd have chaos. Too many of these kids reject any type of authority, but if they're ever to fit in anywhere, they have to learn to abide by the rules. Even the fast-food places insist upon shoes and shirts."

She added another cube to the ice pack, but he was still going to have a colorful black eye. He had very nice eyes with long lashes any woman would envy. That he was so attractive had always been an unwanted distraction, however, and she focused on making her point.

"I understand that, but these are kids who've run away, or been thrown away, and it seems cruel to ban them from one of the few places they're welcome. Besides, it will be impossible for you to teach them any valuable lessons about getting along in the world if they aren't allowed in the door."

Luke raised his hand to cover hers. "Look, I'm trying to keep these kids safe and well while they gain their independence, and then we build from there. I have to earn their trust, and being consistent is the only way to do it."

His hand provided a welcome heat against the icepack's chill, but she was uncertain whether he was merely attempting to convince her he was right or to thoroughly distract her. She liked the touch of his hand against hers, but in this setting, it was completely inappropriate. Still she couldn't bring herself to pull away.

Then she made the mistake of meeting his gaze, and what she saw was the clear reflection of the desire that deepened his voice whenever he spoke her name. He was no more able to concentrate on their current argument than she, and all she wanted to do was lean in and kiss him long and hard.

"I hate to interrupt such a tender scene," a striking young woman called from the doorway, "but I need to speak with Luke."

Although startled, Luke gave Catherine's hand a light squeeze before he grabbed the now soggy towel and tossed it into the bowl of ice. He shoved himself to his feet and provided polite, if terse, introductions.

"You know the routine, Marsha," he scolded. "Call my attorney and schedule an appointment."

"That will cost us both money, and all I need is a minute. You owe me that much." A petite blonde, Marsha was dressed to absolute perfection in a pale pink suit with a matching handbag and stiletto heels.

"I don't owe you a damn thing," Luke shot right back at her.

All curiosity about Luke's ex-wife satisfied, Catherine moved past her to dump the bowl of ice in the sink. She wrung out the towel and hung it over the side.

"I'm sure you'll excuse me. I have books to sort."

Marsha turned to watch Catherine leave. "Nice clothes. I see your type has changed."

"With good reason. I wish you hadn't come here, but since you have, let's go on over to my office." He walked out and

63

across the courtyard without bothering to look back to see if she was following until he reached the office building and yanked open the door. Unfortunately, she was right behind him.

"Hold my calls, please, Pam."

"Yes, sir," Pam responded without looking away from her computer screen.

Once in his office, Luke leaned against the room's single windowsill rather than take a seat behind his desk. "How much do you need this time?"

"It isn't always about money," Marsha denied hotly. She sat on the side of one of the visitor chairs to face him, crossed her legs and adjusted the drape of her skirt. "It's just that sales have been off at the boutique, and I need a few thousand to tide me over until business improves."

Luke surveyed the parking lot. That he could ever have been married to this soulless bitch filled him with shame, but that was all. "Your own attorney described your divorce settlement as more than generous. I'm no longer obligated to support you. Ask the bank for a business loan, or tap your partners."

"After all the years we were together, I shouldn't have to beg," Marsha cried with a convincing catch in her voice.

Luke straightened up as Catherine crossed the parking lot with a long, sure stride. She slid into her car, and he waited for her to look his way and wave, but she drove off as though she couldn't get away from him fast enough. He tried to believe it was just as well she was gone, but he was disappointed by the abrupt end to their latest exchange.

His head was beginning to ache, and he was in no mood to deal with Marsha's tantrums. "You asked for the divorce. Now you'll have to deal with the consequences of being on your own."

"My field is fashion, not finance, and don't you dare try that tough love stuff on me."

Luke still found it difficult to look at her. "I wasn't. Take a class on money management, hire an accountant, just don't depend on me any longer to bail you out."

Marsha stood and came toward him. "You think I don't know what you're doing? You took this job, which has to pay close to nothing, just to spite me. And look at you! Do you have to let these fugitives from juvenile hall beat you up?"

Luke never explained why he'd taken his job, and he wasn't even tempted now. He turned away from the window. "I'll never do anything simply to spite you. Quite frankly, you're no longer that important to me. Now your minute is up. Good-bye."

"I'm going to call my attorney, and we'll just see who has the last word," Marsha fumed, and she slammed the door on her way out.

Luke had kept his temper, but it was scarcely a source of pride. It was just another day at Lost Angel, and a long afternoon, in which he would have to pull himself together to lead the discussion group, lay ahead.

"I need a strawberry shake," he told Pam as he passed her desk.

"It's a shame about your eye. Better make it two," she advised.

Luke laughed at her suggestion, but he thought if he ran a couple of extra miles that night, he just might slurp down three without swelling up like a balloon. But as he sipped the first a few minutes later, he began to wonder if Catherine Brooks might not also be partial to strawberry shakes. He would have to ask her, if she ever came back.

Chapter Five

Catherine's doorbell rang at 7:00 p.m., and assuming it must be Joyce stopping by, she swung the door open without bothering to glance through the peephole. Then she had to hide her dismay when she found Luke Starns standing on the front porch holding a drink container.

"Dr. Starns?" Catherine didn't wish to appear inhospitable, but she was simply astonished to find him there.

Luke dipped his head and appeared truly contrite. "I'm sorry, I know it's rude to just show up without calling first, but I owe you an apology and thought it ought to be delivered in person."

He'd changed his clothes since she'd last seen him, but he was still casually dressed in a Madras sport shirt and jeans. If he'd gone to the trouble to look his best, even with a black eye, she strongly suspected there was more on his mind than a plea for forgiveness, but she was far too curious to send him away.

"An apology?" she repeated incredulously. "That looks like a milkshake to me."

"Yes, it is. I brought it as a peace offering."

His left eye was nearly swollen shut, but it scarcely diminished his appeal. "Is it strawberry?" she inquired.

"Sure is."

"Then come on in," she invited. She couldn't even remember the last time she'd tasted a milkshake, but it most certainly would have been chocolate rather than strawberry.

Luke handed her the milkshake as he stepped over the threshold. "You have a beautiful home."

"Thank you. We bought it for the family we didn't get around to having. I was just washing my dinner dishes. Have you eaten?"

"Yes, thank you." Luke followed her into the kitchen.

She'd been watching the network news on a small portable television set placed in a convenient alcove between the cupboards in the adjoining breakfast room. She shut it off and pulled out a chair for Luke at the breakfast table.

"Would you like some coffee or tea?" she asked. "Ice for your eye? It must hurt."

"Yeah, it does, but I've suffered worse, and I didn't come here hoping for refreshments or first aid. I'm just embarrassed to look as though I lost a fight."

He scooted out the chair beside the one she'd indicated and waited for her to slide into it before he took his seat. "Now, why don't you try the shake, and I'll make a sincere effort to keep our conversation from deteriorating into an argument."

She slipped the paper from the end of the straw and took a long sip. "Say, this is good." She removed the plastic lid, got up to get a glass, and poured half for him. "Pam swears strawberry shakes have remarkable restorative powers. Drink up."

He shook his head. "Please don't distract me, or I'll make a mess of what I've come to say."

He was frowning as though maintaining his concentration truly were difficult, and her heart sank with the sudden realization that he must intend to ban her from Lost Angel, and not for a few days, but forever. At least he hadn't given her such harsh news over the telephone, but the possibility still stung.

"I know I haven't been the ideal volunteer, but—"

Luke cut her off. "You're not the problem, Catherine. Now please just hush and listen."

Even if his tone was curt, she was relieved, but as usual, she failed to heed his warning. "You sound so serious, but if you're referring to your ex-wife, an apology isn't necessary. Some relationships are difficult, but whatever problems there might be, they're between the two of you."

He forced a dry laugh. "If you really believe that, I shouldn't have come here."

That intriguing remark left Catherine more puzzled than ever, but she nodded to encourage him. "Tell me whatever you wish, then. It'll go no further."

"I'm counting on it." He rested his arms on the table and centered his glass between his hands, but he left the milkshake itself untouched.

"Marsha and I were high school sweethearts. After we graduated, I went to UCLA, and she attended the Fashion Institute downtown. We got married the summer after she'd completed her two-year course, and I'd finished my sophomore year, thanks to our parents, who were horrified by the prospect of our simply living together.

"Marcy was born the next year. Childbirth was such a painful ordeal for Marsha that we didn't try for more children. I know from what you saw of her today, you'll probably find this impossible to believe, but we had a lot of happy years together.

"I received a full fellowship to earn my Ph.D., while Marsha worked part time for a local designer and learned the fashion business. Eventually, she and two partners opened a boutique in Santa Monica, and most years, it's done really well. So we both had fulfilling careers, and Marcy was one of those sweet, sunny girls who are an absolute delight."

Catherine wanted to slip her hand over his and beg him to stop, but he was looking out through the windows to the darkened patio, perhaps relating the story more for his own benefit than hers, and she dared not reach out to him. That he looked so badly abused added to the dark cloud of anguish hovering around him.

"A crisis will reveal a person's true character. When we lost Marcy, Marsha just disintegrated. I was equally devastated, but I did my best to console her." He leaned back and sighed softly. "It was like holding smoke. Sometimes a tragedy will strengthen a couple's bond. Unfortunately, for others, like us, it's the end.

"Marsha cried for weeks. Then she became furiously angry and blamed me for not preventing a senseless accident that no one could have foreseen. Believe me, she turned into a pit bull in a skirt. Still, I understood her despair. One day, we'd had rewarding careers and a bright, beautiful daughter, and the next, nothing mattered, not even each other.

"She demanded a divorce, and I didn't argue. We sold our home in Brentwood. She used her half as a down payment on a condo with an ocean view. I bought a smaller place, and invested, fortunately not all in the stock market. She only turns up when she needs money, and even that hurts."

He picked up the glass and swallowed his half of the shake in two long gulps. "Yes, I've seen a therapist, but no one can raise the dead. Which, sadly, is something you already knew."

He rose and clasped the back of his chair with both hands. "I should have done the gracious thing and thanked you for bringing in the books and new shelves. Let's talk about tutoring the next time you come to the center. Don't bother to get up. I'll show myself out."

Catherine doubted she could stand. She felt sick for the enormity of his loss, but it wasn't pity that made her long to invite him into her bed and make love to him until the ice melted from around his heart. She heard the door close and then finished the last of the shake, but it failed to lift her spirits or erase Luke's disquieting presence from her home.

As she saw it, he'd come to confide something important, and it had had absolutely nothing to do with bookshelves. Instead, he'd wanted her to know that he and Marsha had been happy once, and that she'd been the one to end their marriage. Loyalty was a wonderful trait, but she was confused as to what he now expected from her.

She got up to open the patio door for Smoky. The cat was the one male she understood completely, but he provided surprisingly little comfort on a restless night.

Catherine filled Tuesday with errands to give herself some breathing room, but she returned to Lost Angel on Wednesday with a philodendron in a handsome clay pot for Luke's office. She carried it in and, without asking permission, set it atop the file cabinet nearest the window.

"It was only a strawberry shake, Mrs. Brooks, you needn't have brought me a gift in return."

She adjusted the placement of the plant and brushed off her hands. "Yes, I did," she insisted.

"I should have known we wouldn't agree." Luke left his chair to circle his desk and leaned back against it.

"I'm not thinking only of you, Dr. Starns, but of the numerous visitors who enter your office. It's as inviting as a jail cell."

Luke glanced around as though he'd never given the spartan decor a single thought. His black eye now spread from

69

his brow to his cheekbone like a splash of purple dye, but it effectively enhanced his amused frown. "How could such an obvious point have escaped me?"

"You have other priorities," she responded easily. "If someone were to donate a gallon of paint, I'll bet painters could be found."

He swept her with an appreciative glance. "You wouldn't want to get paint on your pretty clothes."

It had taken her an hour to choose rust-colored slacks that showed off her long legs and a peach blouse that flattered her coloring. Her flats and matching purse were a bronze basket weave leather. She'd wanted to look pretty, but professional too.

"I wasn't referring to me." She knew he was teasing and laughed with him. "You have an abundance of able-bodied men and women here. In fact, with a little experience, the kids might be hired by local painting contractors. I hear the work pays well."

Luke winced in mock pain. "I swear I never know what to expect from you, but I'm tempted to give you the extra desk out front and have a nameplate made that reads Creative Director. That way you could spend your whole day dreaming up perfectly reasonable ideas that would require a genius to implement."

She preferred his sarcasm to anger, but she still hastened to defend her suggestion. "A high school education doesn't guarantee anyone a decent living anymore, and most of these kids probably don't even have a GED." Warming to her subject, she began to pace the small office. "I don't mean to needle you—"

"Needle? Lady, you're wielding a sharpened spear."

"It was only a plant," she pointed out, "but one idea just naturally leads to another."

"In your head, maybe." His voice deepened with sincere admiration. "You must have been one hell of a teacher."

Growing self-conscious, she tucked a wayward curl behind her right ear. "It was a long time ago, and I was probably barely adequate."

"I'll never believe that."

He was smiling now, lounging against his desk in a relaxed pose, but she was growing increasingly uncomfortable and wished she'd been smart enough to prepare an exit line before she'd breezed into his lair. Anxious to leave, she seized upon a plausible excuse.

"Perhaps I should check with Mabel to make certain she has enough help in the kitchen." She turned toward the door she'd left standing ajar, but just then Dave Curtis rapped lightly and looked in.

"Good morning, Cathy. You look awfully pretty today. Luke, I've got all the sprinklers working as well as the old pipes will allow, but it wouldn't hurt to toss around some grass seed and encourage new growth with more than water."

"Take whatever you need from petty cash," Luke responded. "By the way, do you think we could teach some of the kids to paint and hire them out to contractors?"

Dave was wearing a comfortably worn Phish T-shirt and khaki pants. He leaned against the doorjamb and folded his arms across the rock group's rounded fish logo. "I wouldn't trust any of them in an occupied dwelling because the temptation to steal whatever they could sell would be too great. With an unoccupied place, after leaving for the day, they'd probably sneak back in to crash, so that wouldn't work, either. Outdoor murals to cover graffiti are a possibility, though. The kids can't do a hell of a lot of damage to a wall."

Luke sent Catherine a questioning glance, or at least she hoped that was curiosity lighting his lopsided gaze. "You're right, I hadn't stopped to consider the problems associated with putting a homeless teen to work in someone's home, but still—"

Dave straightened up. "Don't you worry, Cathy. I took several art classes in college and while I hadn't thought about it before now, it would be fun to paint a mural. We might even be able to get city funds to buy the paint. Want me to look into it, boss?"

"Sure, thanks, Dave."

"I like the new plant. It gives the place some much-needed class. See you both later."

Catherine responded with a grateful smile, but she felt extremely foolish for being so presumptuous. She hurried to follow Dave out the door, but Luke reached out to catch her arm in a light grasp.

"I'll buy the paint if you'll come in on Saturday and help me redecorate."

He was daring her to put her money where her mouth was, and after she'd been so critical, there was no way to refuse. "You don't think I'll show up, do you?" she shot back at him.

Luke dropped his hand and took a step back. "I know you'll be here if you say you will, so why don't we start at ten. Although I'm sure no matter what color I choose, you'll hate it."

"It's your office," she replied sweetly. "Paint it purple to match your eye if you like, and I won't complain." She left before he could get in the last word, but she doubted they could remain in the same small room long enough to paint it.

Mabel had plenty of volunteers that day, so Catherine decided to walk through the hall and straighten up the books. When she recognized Violet seated on the floor in front of the new shelves reading, she veered toward the wall filled with flyers.

She thumbed through a few that had been added since her last visit and was pleased the volunteer who'd placed them had followed her pattern. She was about to leave when Violet got up and came toward her.

"You brought the books," Violet exclaimed. Her unabashed joy crinkled the corners of her bright blue eyes. "I really didn't think you would."

"I hadn't realized I had so many," Catherine replied, "and I'm happy they'll be read here. Did you find something you like?"

Violet ran her fingertips over the embossed title of a thick historical. "This one looks real good. Is there a limit to how many we can borrow?"

"I don't see a sign with a limit. How many books can you read in a week?"

"A couple maybe, unless this one is as good as it looks and I read it twice." She looked up hesitantly. "Do you ever do that?"

"Reread books? Yes, if I've loved them. It doesn't matter that I know the ending. They're like good friends I'm always glad to see."

"Yes, that's it exactly. Ford doesn't understand why I love to read. He says books are full of make-believe junk."

Catherine wasn't surprised, but she still chose her words with care. "People naturally have different tastes, but a man who claims to care about you shouldn't put down what you love. That's a very good book, by the way, with an exciting love story. While the hero and heroine's opinions often clash, I hope you'll notice how well he always treats her. It's the way you deserve to be treated."

Violet began to back away. "I guess most people wouldn't call Ford much of a hero." She paused briefly as though she wished to say more, then bolted out the door with the book she'd chosen still clutched tightly in her hand.

"Well, I suppose that's a start." Catherine sighed, but she was sorry she lacked sufficient expertise to inspire Violet to want more than the obviously ignorant Ford Dolan could provide.

As soon as she reentered the office, she had an urgent question for Pam. "I meant to ask earlier, but what happened to the girls who'd witnessed Felix Mendoza's murder? Was Luke able to convince them to talk to the police?"

Pam was paying bills and licked an envelope before she replied. "Of course, he's very good at planting a subtle suggestion and making the kids believe it's their own. A couple of detectives came out and took their statements. Then Luke explained the National Runaway Switchboard's Home Free partnership with Greyhound Bus Lines. The girls were from Arizona and were back home by the next morning."

"That's so good to hear," Catherine said, sincerely relieved. "Are there more flyers to post?"

Pam grabbed for the banker's box. "Here you go. Watch out for paper cuts. We had a real sweet lady bleed all over a stack of flyers yesterday. I can't take the sight of blood two days in a row."

"I'll be extremely careful," Catherine promised, and she again opened the drawer of the spare desk to remove the scissors. "I had no idea this would be such hazardous duty."

"That's a good point," Pam replied. "I'll have to ask Luke to add a warning to his orientations. As it is, we've had volunteers trip and fall down the steps, slice themselves up in the kitchen, and get burned ironing clothes, but Luke always takes the worst of it. That's his third black eye in as many months, but this one's by far the most colorful. I keep telling him to use a two-by-four to break up fights, but he just wades right on in without a thought for himself. It's either brave or just plain stupid."

"You're awfully cheeky for a secretary," Catherine offered with an amused smile. "But I bet Luke really depends on you."

"He needs someone he can trust," Pam replied rather wistfully.

"We all do," Catherine agreed quietly, and as she opened flyers, she made a quick reminder on the back of an envelope to bring rubber gloves on Saturday. The mother of a high school friend had painted in an old trench coat and shower cap. Both were splattered with paint to the extent the woman resembled a walking Jackson Pollock painting, but Catherine thought she would stick with merely being practical rather than dare the bizarre.

When Catherine arrived at Lost Angel on Saturday, Luke had already shoved his office furniture to the center of the room and covered it with a tarp. Drop cloths were spread over the floor, and the plant which had inspired the project sat safely out of the way on Pam's desk.

Luke was dressed in a pair of worn jeans. While ripped at the knee, the faded blue denim still clung to his muscular thighs and cupped his backside provocatively. His white T-shirt stretched to fit his broad shoulders and grazed his flat belly.

Catherine's glance lingered over his well-muscled arms, and she thought him so incredibly distracting she doubted she would actually get any paint on the walls. Each time she saw him, she wondered if the subtle changes in his appearance were deliberate on his part, or merely her imagination. Whatever the cause, she wished she knew him well enough to slide a tender caress across his back or along his deeply tanned arm.

She'd dressed in a pair of green shorts she wore to work in the garden and a T-shirt silk-screened with flowers. She'd pulled her hair back in a ponytail and thought with scuffed tennis shoes and an old apron, she was ready for work. She'd failed to consider how sexy the amazingly fit Luke Starns would be, however, and now wished she'd worn something prettier.

She walked back out to store her purse in Pam's desk drawer and made a silent vow to begin thinking with her head rather than a far more neglected part of her anatomy. "What would you like me to do?" she called from the outer office.

He responded with a suggestive chuckle. "Let's concentrate on painting, shall we?"

She stepped back through the door. "That was what I meant. I brought a couple of pairs of rubber gloves. Would you like one?"

"Thanks." He took the gloves and handed her a roll of masking tape. "Why don't you put the tape on the window. I want to patch the nail holes before I start painting."

He grabbed hold of the gallon resting on the covered desk and used a screwdriver to pop the lid. "What do you think of the color?"

Catherine was almost afraid to look, but the paint proved to be a handsome terra-cotta. The large window and overhead light fixture provided the room with ample light, and the vivid hue almost glowed.

"I like it a lot," she replied. "It's warm and yet suitably masculine."

"Well, thank you, ma'am. I tried to match my eye, but by the time I got around to purchasing paint, it had taken on a greenish tinge that I found too nauseating to surround myself with every day."

"Yes, I can well imagine. Terra-cotta is a much better choice."

She slipped on her apron, moved to the window, pulled off a long piece of tape and placed it against the edge of the glass. She knew she would be wise to keep her back to Luke, but he kept moving about the small office prepping the walls. She wondered if he was deliberately brushing against her, or if with the furniture heaped in the center, the office was simply too crowded for them to avoid an occasional bump.

"I want to talk about tutoring," Luke remarked as he did a final sweep for missed holes. "I mentioned it to Ron Flanders, but these kids need to learn basic math, not the trig and calculus he's been teaching."

To provide a sensible response, Catherine had to reel in her wildly straying thoughts. She stalled as she put the last piece of tape on the glass. "So he's not interested?"

"He said he'd help with whatever we need, but his lip curled while he said it. He got me to thinking that you might have the same problem. I doubt many of your students at La Cañada High were unable to read well."

"No, none." Discouraged again, she turned slowly to face him. "I see what you mean. Ron and I would set our sights too high, frustrate the kids, get discouraged ourselves, and no one would be better off."

She was silent a long moment, then offered a new proposal. "What if the kids here were to tutor elementary school students? They surely know more than struggling first graders, and it would give their egos a tremendous lift. Is there an elementary school nearby?"

"Yes, but I'd have to think about your idea before I approached the principal."

"You're being very diplomatic, but I'm simply being presumptuous again, aren't I?"

Luke pried open a quart of white enamel for the woodwork. "The kids who find their way here have mastered how to survive by their wits. Amazingly, some still have good hearts. There are others, however, who'd steal a little kid's lunch money and justify it by insisting they needed it more than he does."

His easy smile was reassuring, but she still wished she'd kept her mouth shut. "I'm sorry. I'm afraid none of my ideas are any good."

"No, they're all good," he argued persuasively. "We just have a difficult situation here." He handed her the white paint and a two-inch-wide brush. "Painting my office was a terrific idea. Will you start on the woodwork?"

"Why? Because I'm the girl?" Catherine challenged.

"Hey, I didn't ask you to bring lunch. If you'd rather use the roller on the walls, I'll do the trim. Or we could flip for it."

"How about rock, scissors, paper?"

"You drive a tough bargain, lady. Three out of five?"

"You're on." She placed the white paint and brush back on the covered desk. Then she shook her hands and took a deep breath as though she were a champion preparing for a big match.

"On three?"

"Fine." Luke laughed as he won the first round with a rock to crush her scissors, but she won the next three pairings, and he had to concede defeat.

"Okay, you win. I'll do the trim."

"Actually, I'd prefer to do the trim myself," she assured him. "Besides it would be a waste of your longer reach to confine you to the woodwork."

He whistled softly. "You just wanted to give me a hard time, didn't you? You're far too clever to be painting offices on the weekends."

She carried the quart of white paint over to the window and dipped in the brush. "I consider it one of the perks of volunteering here."

"At least you've found some advantages. Frankly, I stick around for Mabel's cooking."

They continued their playful banter until the telephone rang, and once Luke had located it under the tarp, he listened only briefly before beginning to swear. He tugged off his glove and covered the mouthpiece.

"Rafael Reynosa has gotten himself arrested for shoplifting." He completed a series of terse commands to Rafael and then slammed down the receiver.

"I never post bail for anyone, and all the kids know it. When Rafael was born, his birth mother tossed him in a Dumpster, and he was found by a homeless man scrounging for food. The story got the usual press coverage, and Rafael was adopted, but by a family who'd lost a child to cancer. Apparently Rafael proved to be a poor substitute for the angelic son they'd lost. He began running away at ten. His adoptive family gave up on him, and he ended up in foster care."

Luke had made a good start, but as he glanced around the small office, he shook his head sadly. "I'd hoped we'd get through this project without being interrupted. Let's just put the lids on the paint, and I'll clean up after I've been down to the LA County Jail to see Rafael."

Catherine had already given the window and door the first coat, and the acrylic paint was dry. "I'd like to finish up the woodwork if you don't mind. I promise not to snoop through your files."

"I appreciate that, but I keep them locked. Don't try to finish the whole room on your own. I'll do the last of the walls later. I really am sorry. I'd hoped you'd at least get a nice lunch for your efforts."

She hid her disappointment behind a friendly smile. "You needn't apologize. This really has been fun."

"Yeah, while it lasted." He tossed his gloves on the tarp and hurried out the door.

Catherine remained by the window and watched him cross the parking lot to a black Subaru Outback. She hadn't known which car was his, but the sporty wagon suited him.

Luke had already unlocked the door when Dave rounded the end of the overgrown shrubbery separating the parking lot from the discount carpet warehouse next door. He was carrying a pair of hedge clippers, and broke into an easy lope when Luke waved him over. Luke jerked a thumb toward the office. Dave nodded, used his arm to wipe the sweat from his brow and broke into a wide grin.

Clearly he was delighted to take over the painting, but the exchange left Catherine feeling as though she'd just been handed off to a fraternity brother. That was even more distressing than Luke's hasty departure, but from what little she'd seen, the unexpected was almost routine there at Lost Angel.

That made it ridiculous to take a sudden change in plans so personally, but the hurt remained surprisingly sharp. She'd had fun with Luke that morning, and she was sorry to see it come to such an abrupt end.

Dave strode through the door and stopped to stare. "Wow. This is a dramatic change, but I really like it. Luke told me he had to leave. Do you mind if I give you a hand?"

He was dressed in khaki shorts and a gray Bob's Dog Otis T-shirt imprinted with their intriguing spiral logo. Perhaps it was merely the name of the rock group, but Dave reminded her of a big, eager puppy, and anything less than a warm welcome struck her as cruel.

"Would you please?" she responded. "I'd love to have it finished today."

"No problem, consider it done." Dave picked up the roller and continued where Luke had left off. "You can tell me it's none of my business, but do you and Luke have something going? Now, don't get me wrong. I'd think it was great if you do. I'm just curious."

Catherine fought to keep regret from coloring her reply. "Quite frankly, the thought of starting all over again and dating simply terrifies me. I've no idea what Luke's feelings are on the subject."

"Well, I sure wouldn't invite a beautiful woman to spend a sunny Saturday morning painting my office," Dave muttered under his breath.

He was teasing her too, but she caught herself before leaping to Luke's defense and promptly changed the subject. "Driving here, I pass several buildings that might be good candidates for murals, but if gangs are responsible for the graffiti, would they hassle the kids who paint it over?"

"Good question." He paused to run his roller through the paint tray; then he tackled the wall with brisk strokes. "We'd have to pick a subject they'd respect."

"Hold a contest maybe?"

He glanced over his shoulder. "Luke's a man who likes to have all his ducks in a row, so he'll insist upon getting an owner's permission before we get the kids all excited about an art contest."

"That's undoubtedly wise, but wouldn't an owner be more likely to agree if he or she had an idea what the artwork would be?"

"Makes sense to me, but I'm going to suggest angels, and not only to honor Lost Angel itself, but as a strong antiviolence message. No one opposes brotherhood, at least not openly."

"Yes, that's a beautiful thought."

"Thank you. I used to be paid quite handsomely for my thoughts. It's nice to know I haven't lost the knack."

Catherine added the last few strokes to the door and stood back to admire her handiwork. The expanse of white brought clouds to mind, and she began to imagine angels, some dipping toward the earth, while others gazed skyward. Their robes would be tinged with gold, and their smiles would offer a glimpse of paradise.

"I do love your angel theme. Do you suppose a space could be left open in the mural's design, not for graffiti, but for people to add names of those they'd lost?" she mused aloud. "That way, it wouldn't only be an inspiring mural, but a memorial wall, as well."

"That's a great idea. That way, the mural would belong to everyone who added a name. That's exactly how it ought to be. Luke will be blown away by your idea."

She doubted it. "He might see it as merely morbid."

Dave gestured with the roller. "No, it's positively transcendent."

"You're the one who suggested angels in the first place," she reminded him. "You deserve the credit." She wiped her brush on the edge of the paint can. "There, that's it for me. Looks like you'll be finished soon too."

"I'll let it dry and check for holidays, or missed spots, before I clean up. Why don't you go on home and enjoy what's left of the day."

"I hate to leave you with this mess."

"It's my job to keep the place neat. Besides, I like being busy."

"Yes, so do I." Catherine put the lid on the enamel, then entered the outer office restroom to clean her brush and rinse out the sink. She pulled off her gloves, washed a spot of paint from her cheek and removed her apron. Ready to go, she was still reluctant to leave and looked forward to a mural project which could well provide a need for a great many volunteer hours.

She couldn't fault Luke for attempting to do whatever he could for Rafael, but damn it all, she wished the day could have ended differently. She retrieved her purse and, carrying her apron and paint smeared gloves, reentered Luke's office to place the brush atop the can of white paint.

"Thank you again, Dave. Good-bye."

"Bye. See you again soon, I hope."

Dave was always so hugely complimentary that it was difficult not to feel encouraged, and she stopped off on the way home to rent a couple of DVDs. She asked the clerk to recommend something hilarious so that night she and Smoky could munch popcorn and have a rollicking good time.

Luke had lost count of how many trips he'd made to the LA County Jail, but this was certainly the most ill-timed. Of course, until recently he hadn't cared where he was or with whom. That day, however, he was deeply frustrated to have to leave Catherine, but at least Rafael had saved them from having to face an awkward good-bye later.

That was pitifully little consolation, however. Catherine was as emotionally damaged as he, and he meant to go slow, not merely for her benefit, but for his own. At least they could laugh together, and that was a damn good sign. Now all he had to do was find the courage to keep making her laugh.

Doubts still clouded his mind whenever he thought of her, and he absolutely refused to contemplate the future, but for now, Catherine Brooks brought a glimmer of hope that his emotions weren't permanently numbed. It was a fleeting glimmer at best, and all too swiftly followed by an icy dread that they were drawn to each other's sorrow when neither had anything left to give.

It was a disastrous combination, and yet one even his broken heart longed to risk.

Chapter Six

Joyce arrived at Catherine's early Sunday morning to provide a ride down the hill to the Rose Bowl for the monthly swap meet staged in the parking lot. Vendors hauling a wide variety of wares in their battered vans and trucks had already set up shop for the day. Much of their merchandise was of dubious value, but Joyce occasionally discovered a treasure. Because she insisted the best bargains were to be found early, she and Catherine were always among the first to arrive.

While Catherine seldom made a purchase, she enjoyed the colorful spectacle and looked forward to spending the morning strolling the crowded aisles. She'd come often enough to recognize several vendors, and understood from their conversation that many spent their other Sundays at similar events scattered throughout Los Angeles and Orange Counties.

"This is an awfully hard way to make a living, isn't it?" she whispered to Joyce. "If these people don't make many sales, it must be tremendously discouraging to have to reload their vans at the end of the day."

"Oh, come on. They're all pack rats who love collecting junk and calling it a business. Now where is that woman with the beautiful old type? I should have bought all of her wood blocks with the italics capital letters. They'll soon be impossible to find. Do you suppose they'll stop calling letters upper and lower case now that printing is done by computer rather than hand set?"

"Frankly, I've never stopped to consider the question, but we're probably stuck with the old-fashioned terms. What do you think of these leather sandals?"

Joyce ran her thumb along a wide strap. "They're good quality leather, but I doubt they'll have my size." She glanced through the rows of neatly stacked boxes and shrugged. "Oh well, there are plenty in yours."

"Are you saying I should be grateful to have big feet?" Catherine lifted a pair of black sandals from their box.

"You don't have big feet," Joyce exclaimed. "You wear an average size, so there're always bargains available, while I've even stooped to shopping in the children's department."

"Clothes and shoes are cheaper there, aren't they?"

"Definitely," Joyce admitted with a satisfied smirk.

"Then there's no reason to complain." Catherine sat on the child's step stool the booth's owner provided for customers and tried on the sandals. They were both stylish and comfortable, and she paid for them quickly so that she and Joyce could move on.

A few minutes later, Joyce plucked an aluminum hair roller from a table filled with knickknacks. "My mother actually had some of these. Do you remember them?"

"Yes, I do. Those are in remarkably good shape. They even have the little rubber disks on the clasps, but would anyone want them?"

Joyce gestured with the little roller. "Movie studio costume departments might, but I sure don't. Now where is that woman with the type? I hope she hasn't sold everything and moved to Florida."

"We'll find her."

As they turned to enter a new aisle, Catherine paused to study some hand-woven rugs. They were colorful and well-made, but she had no use for one. Unless...

"Wait a minute, Joyce, I want to look at these rugs."

"Do you need one?" Joyce raised her hand to shade her eyes and scanned the surrounding vendors for the woman with the type.

"I took some books into Lost Angel, and kids were just sitting on the floor to read them. There's a carpet store next door, but remnants would be difficult to keep clean, and these are small enough to go into the large washers at a Laundromat."

"Good lord, when was the last time you visited a Laundromat?"

"College, I suppose," Catherine replied. "Do you like this one with the rust and black bands?"

"Now you're buying rugs for Lost Angel? Can't you just write them a check if you're in a generous mood?"

A Latino clad in western apparel complete with cowboy boots and a wide straw hat approached them. "You like the rugs? I give you a bargain price on two."

"How about three?" Joyce asked. "Or four?"

The man broke into a wide grin. "Six, eight, whatever you want, pretty lady. Make me an offer."

With no interest in the striking area rugs, Joyce turned her back and scanned the crowd while Catherine debated which to select and then purchased three. "Oh, great," Joyce grumbled, "now we'll have to lug those things out to my car."

"May I leave the rugs with you until we're ready to go home?" Catherine asked the friendly vendor.

"I will be happy to watch them," he replied. He rolled each rug separately, then ripped masking tape from a large roll, slapped it around the rugs, and wrote sold in black marker. "Be sure to come back by three."

"We'll be back before noon," Joyce assured him. She hurried Catherine through the crowd. "Is there anything else Lost Angel needs? What about big pillows to make lounging on the rugs more comfortable? Someone must be selling them here."

Catherine tried to imagine Luke's objection to pillows and immediately found one. "No, I'm afraid they'd be seen as an invitation to lie down and sleep rather than a comfortable place to choose a book."

"Do those kids actually know how to read?"

While Catherine frequently made allowances for Joyce, she was fast becoming annoyed with her relentlessly negative attitude. "Is there a reason you're in such a bad mood today? If so, I'd like to hear it rather than more biting sarcasm."

"Me, a bad mood? What other kind is there?" Joyce protested, but she swiftly gave in. "Oh hell, if you insist. I meant to tell you about it after we got home, but we might as well talk while we walk."

Catherine shifted the shoebox containing her new sandals to her other arm, then had to dodge a woman barreling down the aisle pulling a cardboard box filled with antique iron toys strapped to a set of luggage wheels.

"If it's something serious," Catherine cautioned, "perhaps you should wait until we're not surrounded by a noisy crowd."

"No, it's the same old problem. I went out with a new guy last night, but he bored me witless. He was nice enough, but all we had in common was a love of movies, so I won't date him again.

"The problem is, I've been invited to the opening of a spectacular new art gallery on Main Street in Santa Monica next weekend. The invitation includes a guest, and if things had gone well last night, I would have asked the guy. But I won't lead him on just to have an escort for a party and then dump him."

"That's very considerate of you."

"Thanks, but I've already considered every other man I know who's even a remote possibility. I finally remembered an artist who's kind of fun. He's a little old for me and certainly not the man of my dreams, but at least he'd enjoy the party."

Catherine nodded. "Sure, you'd go as friends."

"Precisely, but I couldn't bring myself to give him a call. The funny thing is, I ran into him in Trader Joe's on Friday. As soon as he'd said hello, he flashed a photo of this dimpled twenty-something and announced they were getting married this summer."

"So you were right not to call him," Catherine complimented. "I've found it's wise to trust my instincts."

"True, but here I was afraid of looking pathetic, and sure enough, had I called him, I would have. I just can't imagine why such a young woman would want to marry a man nearly old enough to be her father."

"Maturity appeals to some women, but why didn't you call the gorgeous nurseryman if you need a date?"

"Shane Shephard?" Joyce gazed toward the foothills. The morning was so clear the craggy mountains looked close enough to reach out and touch. "Because if he'd said no, it would've been worse than pathetic. It would've been humiliating."

"Then call him about plants," Catherine urged.

"He'd see through it."

"So what? The object is to connect with him. What does it matter how you do it?"

Joyce glanced away. "Please. I still have a smattering of pride."

"Well, Shane risked his pride and took the initiative to ask you out for coffee."

"Maybe he just needed a caffeine fix."

Catherine studied her friend's downcast expression with sudden insight. "I do believe I've just been hit by a blinding glimpse of the obvious. You're afraid you'll hit it off with Shane, aren't you? Your fear isn't of being rejected but of being loved."

"When did you start writing an advice column? I don't see you dating any handsome young men," Joyce shot back at her.

When Luke chose to, he had a very charming grin, and before Catherine could suppress it, an incriminating smile brightened her expression.

"Are you holding out on me?" Joyce gasped. "If you've met someone, why haven't you mentioned him?"

"I'm not dating anyone," Catherine replied truthfully. "I was home last night cuddling with the cat."

"That was a guilty grin if I ever saw one. You've met someone," Joyce persisted. "Now spill it."

"Sorry, but the subject under discussion is you and Shane."

"Is not," Joyce cried.

Catherine took her friend's arm to direct her toward the right at the intersecting aisle. "There's a white van. Could it belong to the woman with the type?"

"Yes!" Joyce exclaimed, "But you're going to tell me all about this mystery man just as soon as we get home."

"I won't say a word until you call Shane," Catherine promised, and she meant it.

Catherine went into Lost Angel on Monday morning. Pam was away from her desk, but Luke's door was open, and he waved her on in. With the furniture back in place, the freshly painted office looked quite handsome, but Luke wore the same guarded expression she'd seen on their initial interview.

"The office is beautiful, but clearly something's wrong," she greeted him. "What happened with Rafael, or aren't you at liberty to say?"

"That's what I like about you, Mrs. Brooks. You never waste a moment in idle chatter. Please sit down, and forgive me, but I haven't the energy to rise."

Catherine chose her usual chair. There was a coffee container on his desk, but she thought he would be better off sipping Celestial Seasonings' Tension Tamer Tea. She didn't make the suggestion aloud, however.

"Since you're so curious, let me begin where we left off." Luke leaned back in his chair. "That Rafael was arrested for shoplifting was the least of his problems. The police found a few candy bars in his backpack, which he swore he'd purchased earlier in the day.

"The real problem lay in the hunting knife he'd stowed in the bottom of his pack. He claimed it's a dangerous world and that he owned it for protection. The police had a different view and regarded him as a likely suspect in a string of unsolved stabbings."

Alarmed, Catherine sat forward in her chair. "Do they believe that he killed Felix Mendoza?"

"No, apparently not, but there are plenty of other crimes."

"Then he'll need an attorney. There are several at my husband's firm who do excellent pro bono work. Would you like me to call one?"

Luke cocked his head slightly. "You don't know Rafael. Why are you so eager to come to his defense?"

"Well, someone has to," Catherine responded.

Weary, Luke rubbed his right eye. His left was no longer swollen, and the deep bruising had begun to fade. "Have you always just jumped right into things?"

"If they're important, yes. Granted there's a time to be thoughtful, reserved, deliberate, but not when some poor kid is accused of multiple stabbings. You thought so too last Saturday, or you wouldn't have left here to run down to the County Jail."

"True. You've made your point, but you needn't worry about Rafael. Lost Angel has all manner of volunteers, from those you might meet here at the center, to those who pick up food from supermarkets and restaurants that would otherwise be discarded, to several highly skilled attorneys. They're taking care of Rafael and assure me the police don't have enough evidence to hold him for shoplifting, let alone murder."

Despite his earlier protest, he hauled himself to his feet. "I'm late for a community resources meeting that might last the whole day, so I probably won't see you before you leave."

When he paused, Catherine tried not to stare, but he sounded as though he was working up his courage to ask her out, and she wanted to savor every second of it. She licked her lips and offered an encouraging smile.

"From what Dave told me," Luke continued, "you two are running with the mural project. I don't want to discourage you, but let me line up a suitable building before you begin any preliminary drawings."

That wasn't what she'd expected him to say. No, she corrected herself silently, what she'd hoped he would say. She made an attempt to shrug off her disappointment and rose to precede him into the outer office where Pam was now working at her computer.

They exchanged quick greetings, and then Catherine turned toward Luke. "You needn't worry, I understand that you make the decisions here," she assured him.

"That I do, but please don't look so unhappy. I didn't forbid you to do a mural, but we need to take our time and do it right."

"Of course," Catherine agreed, but she wished he was referring to something more personal than an art project.

Luke had left the center before Catherine realized that she'd neglected to ask his permission to place the new rugs in the hall, but when she again found kids seated on the cold floor by the bookcases, she felt justified in acting on her own. With so many hanging around idle, she easily enlisted some help.

Nick was performing tricks on his skateboard out front when Catherine went by with Polly and a tall boy with a wild mop of red curls who called himself Spike. Nick grabbed up his skateboard and followed.

"Where are we going?" he asked.

"Just to my car," Catherine explained. "I found a good buy on some rugs, and they aren't too heavy."

Nick flexed his biceps. "So what if they are? I've got muscles."

"Yeah, in your head," Spike scoffed.

"You think you're so smart? What's fifty-six times twenty-eight?" Nick challenged.

"Hell, I don't know."

"It's 1568," Nick announced proudly.

"What is that, the one answer you know?"

"Gentlemen, please," Catherine scolded softly. "If you can't get along, Polly and I will carry the rugs ourselves, won't we, Polly?"

"We sure will." Polly twisted around to make a face at Nick, but he just laughed at her.

Catherine unlocked the back of her Volvo, and Nick slipped past Spike to grab the first of the rugs. He took a step back and rolled it up on his shoulder. "These going to Luke's office?"

"No, the hall, but his office floor could sure use some help, couldn't it?" Catherine glanced toward the nearby carpet warehouse. Luke's office was a neat rectangle, so it wouldn't be much of a challenge to purchase and install a remnant while he was away. She wondered if they had anything in a deep russet that would complement the walls.

She waited until Spike and Polly had picked up the other tightly rolled rugs, then slammed the rear door shut. "Have any of you seen Dave Curtis this morning?" she asked.

Spike shook his head and started off toward the hall with Polly and Nick trailing. "He's got to be around someplace," Nick answered. "You want me to find him?"

"Yes, please," Catherine replied. She was sure Dave would think it a fine idea to carpet Luke's office while he was away for the day. As soon as they had the rugs scattered in front of the bookcases, she explained her idea to Pam and then went to the carpet warehouse to survey the possibilities.

Dave Curtis had been every bit as enthusiastic as Catherine had anticipated, but with padding, the carpet project had taken longer than either had expected, and it was nearly three o'clock before she was ready to leave for home. When she entered the parking lot, she was amazed to find a slender young man leaning against her car. With long, black hair and sideburns, he resembled an Elvis impersonator, and it was all she could do not to laugh.

He was older than the homeless youth frequenting the center, and when she came within five feet of him, she noticed the name Ford embroidered above the left pocket on his blue work shirt. Immediately understanding who he was, she greeted him by name. "Good afternoon, Mr. Dolan."

Ford shoved away from her car. He laced his hands together, showing off nails ringed with grime, and cracked his knuckles menacingly. "So, you've heard of me."

He appeared to be immensely flattered, but Catherine wouldn't repeat what she'd heard. His eyes were a pale watery blue that reminded her of a Weimaraner's, except they lacked the big gray dog's intelligent sparkle.

"Did you wish to speak with me?" she asked, but she remained at a wary distance.

"You could say that." Ford reached into the pocket of his oil-stained jeans, withdrew a handful of shiny pink paper scraps and tossed them into the air. "Quit giving Violet your silly books, or I'll just rip them up like I did the last one. Then I'll come looking for you."

As a large scrap drifted toward Catherine's feet, she recognized an embossed letter from the title of the book Violet had been so thrilled to find. As much as she abhorred violence, she was sorely tempted to kick Ford in the balls for not only abusing Violet but good books as well.

"You're an ignorant punk," she exclaimed, "and while your pathetic threats might work on Violet, you don't frighten me. If you really cared about Violet, instead of just your own miserable self, you'd be taking her to bookstores and buying her what she loves to read. You're not clever enough to understand that, though, are you?"

Ford hunched his shoulders as he took a step toward her. "Are you calling me stupid?" His upper lip twitched, as though he had yet to master Elvis's classic snarl.

"No, I'm calling you ignorant, and deliberately so, which is infinitely worse. Now get out of here and don't come back."

Ford clenched his fists at his sides. "I go where I choose, and if you know what's good for you, you'll stay away from Violet."

Catherine wished she knew how to spit on the ground, but unfortunately, it was a skill she'd neglected to learn as a child. She was about to spray Ford with the fiery string of obscenities he so richly deserved when Luke drove into the parking lot. Ford recognized his black Subaru and took off at a run.

Catherine's anger had fueled a brave front, but now her hands began to shake so badly she was unable to unlock her car. Embarrassed to be so stressed, she leaned back against the silver Volvo and made a concerted effort to gather her composure.

Luke sprang from his car and slammed the door. "Was that Ford Dolan?"

Catherine waited until he was beside her to reply in a husky whisper. "Yes, but I had things under control." Yet even as she made that claim, tears stung her eyes. She quickly brushed them away. "He tore up the book Violet took with her. How can anyone be so mean?"

While she'd stubbornly denied it, she was obviously shaken, and Luke slipped his arm around her shoulders to offer an encouraging hug. "I warned you not to become involved with Violet, but I'm sorry Ford caught you out here alone. I swear I could kill that sorry son of a bitch."

Catherine relaxed against him. Lean and tough, he was as solid as a concrete wall, and yet she could feel the anger coursing through him. There were a few cars in the parking lot, but she wouldn't be embarrassed if one of their owners found her in Luke's arms. Still, she wasn't so lost in romantic daydreams that she could ignore the bitterness of his tone.

She glanced up and recoiled at the dark threat glowing in his eyes. "Forget Ford," she advised, "and concentrate on teaching the young men you can reach how they should behave toward women, and teach the girls what every woman has a right to expect."

"You know where kids are supposed to learn that wondrous ideal?"

Catherine nodded. "At home with loving parents, and these kids have neither."

Luke sucked in a deep breath and released it slowly. "Right, and that's a lot to overcome. Fortunately, snakes like Ford Dolan have a way of coming to a very bad end on their own, so I won't go looking for him. But the next time you're here, let me walk you out to your car.

"Brooks is a common enough name that I doubt Ford can find your home telephone number, but if you receive any threatening calls, let me know immediately. I won't let him intimidate you. Now are you sure you feel well enough to drive yourself home? I could drive your car and have Dave follow in mine."

While it was a thoughtful offer, Catherine knew he would do the same for any volunteer. Determined to look out for her own welfare, she took a firm grip on her keys. "Thank you, but I'm fine."

This time, she succeeded in unlocking her door. Luke swung it open for her, then closed it and waved as she drove away. She'd reached the freeway before she remembered the new carpet in his office. With the confrontation with Ford to distract her, it was no wonder she'd failed to mention it, but she hoped he would laugh when he saw it rather than call her to complain.

Luke cursed as he crossed the parking lot. He was furiously angry with Ford Dolan for daring to upset Catherine, but he was even more disgusted with himself for not being there to prevent it. As he entered the office, he paused at Pam's desk to explain what had happened.

"If Ford Dolan comes around here again, call the police."

"I'll be real happy to," Pam replied. "Your messages are on your desk."

"Thanks." Luke took a couple of steps toward his office, then stopped to stare. "What the hell? Where did the new carpet come from?"

"It was on sale next door," Pam informed him with a beguiling grin. "It's woven from synthetic fibers and designed for use in high traffic areas, so it should wear like iron. How do you like it?"

The rug was a deep russet that blended perfectly with the newly painted walls. "I like it fine, but how did it get from next door in here?"

"Half a dozen of the boys carried it over. They looked like ants stealing peanut butter logs from a picnic. You know how they're made with celery? Then Dave installed it."

Luke nodded. "I know what peanut butter logs are. You can add raisins and call them frogs on a log if you like, but since when does Dave know how to lay carpet?"

"Since today, I guess. It looks like a professional job to me."

"That it does, but I think you're leaving out a significant detail. Was Mrs. Brooks behind this?"

Pam fluttered the papers on her desk in an apparent search for a missing document. "Nick said it was his idea, but she paid for it. She picked up a donation receipt just as you'd suggested. And by the way, she brought in a few other rugs for the hall."

"What will the woman think of next?"

"Well, since you asked, now that you've classed up your office, mine could sure use a coat of paint. Shall I suggest it to her?"

"No, I'll pencil it in on my calendar for the weekend." Luke entered his office and then called over his shoulder. "Now the furniture in here looks like hell."

"It always did, you just didn't notice. If you like, I'll keep an eye out for something better at a yard sale."

"You do that." Luke thumbed through the stack of messages piled on his desk. Several were from generous, but talkative, contributors, and he was in no mood to chat with them now.

"No mayhem to report?" he asked.

"None, sir, it was a remarkably calm day, as it always is when you leave me in charge," Pam claimed smugly.

Luke glanced up at the clock. He had only a few minutes before the afternoon group session began, and he doubted he would be very effective. He scrubbed his hands through his hair and decided it needed to be cut, but he just never seemed to have the time.

"One final point of curiosity." Luke slowed his pace by Pam's desk on his way to the sanctuary. "Did anyone stop to consider it might be a good idea if I were consulted before purchasing carpet for my office? After all, it is my office, and I would swear that only this morning, Mrs. Brooks acknowledged the fact I'm paid to make the decisions here."

"Everyone knows that," Pam agreed. "But you've got too much to do, and carpet is such an insignificant thing. Besides, you always tell me to use my own judgment when you're away. I thought it was a nice surprise."

"It is, but...oh hell, never mind. I'm going to lead the group, then go home and run."

"If you don't mind my saying so, you look as though you ought to go home and take a long nap."

"I do mind," Luke replied, but when he walked into his condo, his bed looked a whole lot better to him than his running shoes. He meant to lie down for a few minutes, then call Catherine Brooks to make certain she'd made it home safely, but when he awoke, it was six o'clock Tuesday morning.

When Luke did call Catherine, it was late Tuesday afternoon, and he asked if he might stop by to see her that evening. Certain he must be upset about the new carpet, she tightened her grip on the receiver.

"You needn't come all this way to yell at me. Everyone thought the carpet was a fine idea, and with you away, it seemed the perfect time to install it."

Luke chuckled softly. "I hadn't planned on yelling at you."

"You hadn't? Then why did you want to see me?"

"That's an excellent question. Let's just say we need to talk."

She caught herself before again asking why, but as much as she would enjoy seeing him, she was still concerned something was amiss. Then she began to worry that something wasn't. The last time he'd been there, she'd wanted him to stay, even if she hadn't dared say so. What if the suggestion came from him this time?

She quickly slid into a chair at the breakfast table and tried not to choke. She wondered if she should invite him to come for dinner, but fearing that would be offering too much, she decided against it. She was just so dreadfully out of practice when it came to men, but if there was practice to be had with Luke, she definitely wanted it.

"Seven o'clock would be fine," she managed smoothly, but as she hung up, she thought of Joyce's continuing anguish over men and made a firm promise not to be as great a fool.

There was no milkshake in Luke's hand when he arrived, and Catherine quickly offered coffee or tea. "I have soft drinks as well, and while I'm not sure what's left in the liquor cabinet, there must be something."

They were standing in the living room, a remarkably cheerful room decorated in shades of yellow and blue. She drew on its sunny mood now. Not wanting to look as though she'd gone to great lengths to look nice, she'd dressed casually in a flared deep green skirt and matching knit top.

"I don't need anything now, thank you," Luke responded. "You look awfully pretty in green. You could promote tourism for Ireland."

Surprised by that unexpected compliment, she blushed. "My family traces its roots to Scotland, but thank you. Won't you sit down?"

He waited for her to settle herself at the end of the sofa, then chose the wing chair at her right. He sat forward and clasped his hands between his knees. "I meant to call you last night to make certain you'd gotten home safely, but unfortunately, I got distracted."

She couldn't help but wonder just who had provided that distraction. "It happens, but thanks for the thought."

"I thought you might come in today, but when I checked the master schedule, I couldn't find your name anywhere. I'm sure I emphasized how important it is to make a schedule and keep it when you attended the training session."

She'd been so nervous, but now she just wanted to laugh and had to bite her lip to stifle the impulse. "Is that what this is about? You're annoyed because I failed to sign up on the master schedule?"

Giving up all pretense of calm, Luke rose and began to pace in front of the coffee table. "No, I'm annoyed because I keep waiting for you to come through the door, and I can't handle the disappointment when you don't. If I'm completely wrong about this, I'll save us both any further embarrassment and get out of here, but if there's a chance that you'd like to see me outside of Lost Angel, I'm all for it."

The sleeves of his white dress shirt were rolled on his tanned forearms. His Levi's were neatly pressed, his loafers polished, and with his hair still too long, he called to mind a very charming college professor. Fortunately, she knew there was far more to the man.

She rose gracefully and came toward him. She hadn't been this frightened with Ford Dolan, but she liked Luke too much to hide what she felt. "Yes, I'd love to see you, anytime, anyplace."

She held her breath as he moved close, but he kissed her cheek and then her earlobe before trailing a tender caress along the curve of her jaw. She'd expected him to kiss her with a thorough passion, but instead, he moved with a disarming stealth.

"You have to remember to breathe," he whispered against her hair, "or you'll miss all the fun."

She drew in a quick breath. "You wouldn't take advantage of an unconscious woman."

He smiled. "Certainly not, but with you, I'd sure be tempted."

She raised her arms to encircle his neck. He smelled delicious, and he felt so good to touch. As his heat melted away her fears, she slid her fingers through his hair. When he leaned in, she pressed his mouth close for a near endless kiss to prove quite emphatically just what a temptation she really could be.

Chapter Seven

Catherine found him so incredibly appealing, and it was no mere trick of great chemistry. He had a manic charm, and yet there was a darkness to him even beneath the luscious kisses. He was undoubtedly more than most women could handle, and yet she relished the challenge.

When she could bear to pull away for a breath, he had her wrapped so tightly in his arms that even if she'd fainted, she wouldn't have fallen. The man certainly knew how to kiss, and from the sly smile tugging at the corner of his mouth, it appeared he also wanted more. Desire coiled low in her belly, and she felt more alive than she had in months.

"We probably shouldn't rush things," she whispered against his lips.

A deep chuckle warmed Luke's reply. "I'm not sure I can."

She could feel the erection straining the front of his Levi's, leaving no doubt as to his capabilities. She ground her hips against his.

"God, woman, what are you trying to do to me?"

She brushed his mouth with a light kiss. "You came here tonight knowing I'm the impulsive sort. Did you really expect to be turned away?"

He rested his forehead against hers and sighed softly. "I didn't expect anything at all."

His unexpectedly poignant reply tugged at her heart, and she leaned back and framed his face between her hands. His black eye was fading to an unattractive green, but his gaze held a fascinating array of emotion. There was a sparkle of desire as well as a lingering hint of the despair he'd shared on his earlier visit. She knew which she wished to encourage.

"You still have a pocketful of condoms?" she asked.

"I might," he admitted with a grin that revealed he'd indeed come prepared.

She reached back to take his hand from around her waist and laced her fingers in his. "Let's go up to my room." With an easy tug, she led the way up the stairs and down the hall to the master bedroom. Rather than flip on the wall switch, she turned on the small pink-hued lamp on her dresser.

She dropped his hand to slide her fingertips up his chest and began to unbutton his shirt. "I like the way you dress, and yet I can't help but feel clothes mean nothing to you."

"Less than nothing," Luke murmured against her hair. He yanked off his shirt and flung it toward the wing chair placed near the window. "Now kiss me again so I won't forget why we came up here."

She was only too happy to oblige. She ran her hands over his muscular back, then up between them to comb the springy curls swirled across his chest. The wiry hair was dark like his lashes and brows and wound easily around her fingers.

She might have teased him about her impulsive nature, but despite his delicious taste, she was drawn to him by something far more powerful than mere whim. He simply felt right, and that he was in no hurry to bring their extraordinary attraction to its natural conclusion made his slow, deep kisses all the more tantalizing. She could have kissed him all night and well into the next day.

He unhooked her bra, and she quickly pulled it along with her top off over her head. He rolled her nipples between his index fingers and thumbs, but the tips were already puckered into rosy buds. He bent to lick one and then the other while she ruffled his hair.

"The silvery cast to your hair is very handsome," she almost purred.

He gave her a last playful nip before he straightened up. "I'm pushing forty, but you don't think it makes me look old?"

"Not at all, and it's striking, like the rest of you."

He laughed. "How long have you thought that?"

She bounced her knuckles down the hard planes of his belly. "Since the first time I saw you, but now I've discovered you also have great abs."

He caught her hands. "So it's just a physical thing?"

The question caught Catherine off guard, and for one painful instant, the memory of Sam's loving threatened to overwhelm her in a tumbling wave of sorrow. She pressed against Luke to keep her husband's ghost at bay.

"Chemistry is a wonderful thing," she began hesitantly, "but I hope there's more between us."

He slid his hands through her hair to tilt her mouth up to his. "I can't find the words to describe this magic," he whispered, and his deep kiss made further speech irrelevant.

She drank in his affection and returned it eagerly. She loved his strength and the sinewy feel of his well-toned body. She was naturally slender, but he'd run the last ounce of fat from his muscular frame. She slid her fingers into his pocket to withdraw several condoms and set them on the nightstand beside a box of tissues. She unbuckled his belt, then unbuttoned his Levi's to free his sex. He was hot and heavy in her hands, and she dropped to her knees to taste him.

Luke could stand only a few seconds of her provocative kiss before he had to pull her up into his arms. "Any more of that, and you'll push me over the edge."

"You won't fall far," she promised.

"I still want to take you with me." Luke had already kicked off his loafers, and he sat on the side of the high brass bed to remove his pants. He was wearing black knit boxers, and he peeled them off and tossed them on the growing heap of clothes strewn across the convenient chair.

She was so intent upon watching him, she failed to discard the rest of her clothing until he looked up to send her a questioning glance.

She didn't feel the least bit awkward with him, merely fascinated to have him there and find him such a warm and tender lover. She stepped out of her skirt and slip, and he reached out to grab the waistband of her panties. With an easy tug, he coaxed the satiny pair down her thighs. She quickly stepped out of them.

"Had I known you'd be in such an affectionate mood," she confided in a sultry whisper, "I wouldn't have bothered with underwear."

"Mrs. Brooks," Luke scolded, but whatever else he'd meant to say was lost in a roll of deep laughter.

She pushed him back on the bed and crawled up over him to brush the tips of her breasts across his chest. "Don't we know each other well enough for you to call me Catherine?"

Rather than reply, he slid his hands around her waist and rolled over with her clutched tightly in his arms. He kissed her until she was again breathless, then licked a meandering trail over the soft fullness of her breasts and down across the inviting hollow at her hipbones. He combed her soft bush, then shoved her legs apart with his shoulder. He slid his tongue along her moist cleft, then with a graceful precision found her clitoris.

He eased two fingers inside her and stroked in time with his slow, sweet lapping until her inner muscles began to spasm. Deliberately leaving her on the brink of release, he raised himself up to slip on a condom and positioned himself between her thighs.

"Now I know you well enough, Catherine."

His first thrust was shallow, but she rolled her hips to take him deeper, and his next thrust stretched her with an intoxicating warmth that he stoked with each successive lunge. Once buried deep within her, he stretched out, and with his weight balanced on his elbows, he remained perfectly still.

She wrapped her legs around his thighs to bridge the last separation between them. Close in height, she savored the feel of his hair-roughened skin along the whole length of her body. He dipped his head, and her own exotic taste flavored that kiss and the next, and then she was so lost in him she could only moan as he began to move with a slow, slyly teasing rhythm.

She clung to him to encourage more, and as his breathing grew ragged, he quickened his pace to fill her with a fiery heat that sent her spiraling through a climax so intense it bordered pain. Their passions perfectly matched, she uttered a joyous cry as echoing waves of pleasure coiled through her and tore through him.

Awash in bliss, she floated down from their tangle of shared ecstasy and fell asleep with her head cradled on his shoulder. When she awakened hours later, he was wrapped around her still and gently combing her hair through his fingers.

Unable to devise a compliment that would do him justice, she was satisfied to simply snuggle deeper into his embrace. "Do you suppose we could go out on a date sometime?"

Luke yawned sleepily. "I remember dates. I'd have to wash my car, iron a shirt, buy you flowers. Do you like holding hands in the movies?"

"Hmm, I sure do."

"How about romantic dinners in candle-lit restaurants where we'd eat each other's entrees without noticing the waiter has mixed up our orders?"

"I've done that," Catherine recalled dreamily.

"Moonlit drives along the beach?"

"That would be nice too."

Luke hugged her tight. "For now, I just want to lie here and pretend nothing else matters."

She understood him completely. "It doesn't," she assured him, and when he turned toward her, she expected the loving to be even better the second time, and incredibly, she wasn't disappointed.

The first faint rays of dawn had just begun to lighten the room when Smoky's insistent meow woke Catherine from an exhausted slumber. The irate tomcat was outside on the roof, peering through the window to noisily protest the fact he'd been forgotten. Chagrined to have completely overlooked her beloved pet, she slipped from Luke's embrace to feed him.

She pulled on a silk robe, then paused at the doorway to appreciate just how comfortable Luke looked in her rumpled bed. The tension that so often marred his expression had been soothed away, and he appeared years younger.

Believing sex was most definitely a delicious fountain of youth, she went downstairs to feed Smoky, brought in the *Los Angeles Times*, and made coffee before she ventured back upstairs. When she found Luke had already gotten dressed and made her bed, she forced a smile and handed him a mug of coffee.

"I didn't know if you took cream or sugar."

"No, thanks, black is fine." Luke nodded toward the framed photograph atop her dresser. "Is that your husband?"

Sam had been tall and blond with a grin that never failed to melt her heart. It had been months before she'd been able to glance at the precious photograph without sobbing. Now, she strove to remember the love rather than the eventual pain.

"Yes, that was taken in Las Vegas on our wedding day. My parents were nearly forty when I was born. My father was a history professor at USC and my inspiration to become a teacher. He was a wonderful man, but he had a weak heart. By the time Sam and I became engaged, he was quite ill, and we didn't want a big showy wedding when neither of my parents would have been able to truly enjoy it. So, with their blessing, Sam and I eloped.

"I wanted an Elvis impersonator, but Sam insisted upon a much more tasteful ceremony." She adjusted the placement of the photograph and wished with all her heart she'd known how brief their time together would be. "We had a wonderful marriage."

"You were lucky, then." Luke sipped his coffee, but his eyes were on Catherine rather than the charming photograph. He had shaved before coming to her house last night, and his beard barely shadowed his cheeks.

He seemed ready to go, but Catherine would have preferred to keep him in bed all day. "Would you like some breakfast?" she asked.

"You're undoubtedly a marvelous cook, but I need to go home, clean up, and get to work. Are you coming in today?"

"Looks like we're right back to where we began with my schedule." She led the way downstairs, then took his mug and set it on the table in the entryway. She still felt warm all over and much too lazy to leave home. She could barely find the energy to swing open the front door.

"No, not today," she replied. "After last night, I'd be too distracted to get anything done."

Luke leaned in to kiss her good-bye. "I'm going to take that as a compliment."

"Good, it was meant to be."

She remained at the open door until he'd driven away, but after closing it, she leaned back against the polished wood and slid down to the floor in a disjointed heap. She was happy clear to her toes, but while Luke had been quite pleasantly relaxed that morning, he'd left without expressing any hope of seeing her outside of Lost Angel.

Perhaps he'd forgotten their late night conversation about dating, or maybe her wistful memories of Sam had put him off, but he'd soon wear out his welcome if all he wanted was sex. Joyce dismissed such rude men as "Midnight Creepers", and while her friend had run into more than her share, Catherine wouldn't tolerate even one.

While Luke certainly had a healthy appetite for sex, so did she, but she'd never trusted condoms. She wondered if it wouldn't be wise to go back on the pill. But after all the years of avoiding pregnancy, the possibility of an unplanned baby was almost irresistibly sweet. She harbored little hope that Luke's response would be as positive, however, for after losing his only child, she doubted he'd welcome another.

It was a wrenching thought, but Luke was simply too vulnerable for their future to be forecast with any accuracy, and yet she felt a compelling need to know just what was possible. She'd prided herself on learning to live in the moment; but while it brought fleeting comfort, after one night with Luke, she needed more.

Embarrassed to feel so pathetically needy, she shoved herself to her feet and tightened her belt. One wild night didn't mean Luke and she would fall in love and remain together, but that she could even entertain such an intriguing possibility gave her hope that one day Luke could too.

The heavy volume of commuter traffic demanded Luke's complete attention on the way home, but once he'd stepped into his shower and turned on the water full-blast, he began to shake. Grief had numbed his emotions for so long, but last night he'd felt a hell of a lot more than mere lust.

Catherine had such a deceptively innocent gaze, he'd never expected her to be so abandoned in bed. Nor had he displayed a shred of reserve himself. And now what? he agonized. Seize the moment, or back off before it was too late?

"Oh, hell, it's already too late." He propped his arms against the tile and let the water pound down on his shoulders, but all he got for his efforts was wet. He might be able to wash off the lingering traces of Catherine's seductive scent, but her endearing presence remained coiled around his heart. He could still feel the sweetness of her caress and hear her soft moans of surrender. Best of all was the memory of how gracefully she'd welcomed him into her bed.

Stubbornly refusing to allow his thoughts to drift in that enticing direction, he shut off the water and grabbed a towel. Catherine Brooks invited all manner of entertaining daydreams, but he resisted making plans for the real world beyond a single day. She deserved better. Hell, so did he, but he no longer trusted life to be good.

The problem was, now that he'd tasted Catherine's delicious affection, he ached for more, but it disgusted him to offer no more than eventual disaster in return. If he possessed an ounce of character, he knew he should be brutally honest with her now.

He didn't want another wife, nor could he bear to father another child who might go skipping off to school one day and never come home. He could see it all so clearly. It might take a year or even two before his refusal to consider marriage and family would force Catherine to end their affair with pain-choked sobs, but the day would surely come.

It would be better to blow it all apart right now. He wiped the fog from the mirror with a hand towel and stared at his reflection, but all he saw were eyes so shadowed by loss that he wondered if Catherine hadn't already guessed the truth he'd kept so well-hidden last night.

In his present dark mood, he'd be lucky to shave without cutting his throat, and it was a damn good thing that Catherine wouldn't be volunteering today. He'd barely lathered his cheeks, however, before the brief sense of relief turned to despair. He missed her already, but he was determined to do the honorable thing just as soon as he could speak the words.

Catherine was weeding the backyard flower beds when Joyce knocked lightly on the gate. "Are you busy?" she called. "I need help."

Catherine stood, brushed off her knees and yanked off her gardening gloves. "Come on in. The weeds will wait. What's the problem?"

Joyce reached over the gate to flip up the latch and let herself in. "It's Wednesday, and I still haven't called Shane. If I wait any longer, it'll look as though he's my last resort."

"God forbid. Would you like some lemonade?"

"Thank you, I sure need something." Joyce flopped down at the patio table and waited for Catherine to bring the refreshments. The flavorful beverage was as cold and sweet as expected, but when Catherine raised her glass, Joyce noticed a purple smear on her middle fingernail.

"I've always admired your poise. Please tell me that you didn't slam your finger in a door."

"Sorry, but that's exactly what I did, and it wasn't only stupid, but painful."

"I'll bet, but where's your wedding ring?"

A white band marked its usual place on her finger, and suddenly self-conscious, Catherine dropped her hands into her lap. "I decided it was time to remove it, and as I left the bedroom, I pulled the door shut behind me and caught my finger."

"Sounds like a cosmic message to me," Joyce exclaimed. When Catherine responded with a puzzled frown, she sat forward in her chair. "You made the decision to take off your ring, enter the next phase of your life, if you will. But part of you, perhaps subconsciously, clings to the past, and wham, you're given a painful reminder that every choice has its price."

Because Catherine had already linked the two events in her mind, Joyce's comment made perfect sense. "Frankly, I thought it was Sam. Even if I can let go, it might be too soon for him."

"I hadn't considered Sam," Joyce admitted, "but I'll concede the possibility. Now tell me who prompted you to remove your ring."

"First call Shane," Catherine directed smoothly. "Use your cell phone."

Annoyed to be reminded of the man, Joyce began to rummage in her oversized purse. "That's why I'm here. I need you to tell me what to say."

"This is scarcely a challenge. You'll probably get his service or answering machine. Just give your name and number, invite him to the opening, and wait for his response."

Joyce fumbled with his card then set it on the glass-topped table to dial with a fuchsia-tipped nail. "Hello, may I please speak with Shane?"

Catherine flashed an okay sign and sipped her lemonade. Joyce appeared to be handling the call calmly, but Catherine understood her apprehension and hoped Shane would be pleased to hear from her.

After a brief exchange, Joyce ended the call and slapped her cell phone shut. "That was his mother." She moaned. "If she actually gives him the message, what are the odds that he'll return my call?"

"If she answers his business telephone, she must be capable of forwarding a message. At any rate, I'm proud of you for trying. If Shane doesn't respond, go to the opening alone. Maybe you'll meet someone interesting there."

Hunched over her purse, Joyce looked utterly crushed. "I should have kept count of the times I've done that and found every man in the room with his wife." She consoled herself with a long sip of lemonade before she recalled Catherine owed her an answer.

"So, what's his name?" she asked.

Catherine had already decided just how little she wished to reveal. "Luke Starns, he's the director of Lost Angel, and I wouldn't have met him had I not been so insistent about becoming a volunteer."

Joyce's gaze narrowed slightly. "Can you describe him in a single word?"

"How would you describe Shane?"

"Hot!"

Luke was definitely hot, but Catherine believed he deserved more than the provocative adjective implied. "Intense," she said instead.

"Oh, lord. Please tell me he's not one of those dark, brooding types."

That was part of Luke too, but Catherine shook her head. "He's complex, but he knows how to laugh."

"And from the width of your enigmatic smile, he knows a lot more. I don't suppose he's in his twenties, is he?"

"No, late thirties. Now don't you have appointments to keep or fabric to order this afternoon?"

Joyce checked her watch and leapt from her chair. "Damn, I procrastinated longer than I'd thought. I'll let you know what happens with Shane."

"Please do."

Catherine finished her lemonade before going back to work on the flower beds. When she next took a break, she carried her book on CBEST test preparation outside to study. She wasn't worried about passing the sections of the exam devoted to reading and writing skills, but it had been quite awhile since she'd taken a math class.

She'd just begun to study the book's chapter on algebra when the telephone rang, and she hurried inside to answer. When she heard Luke's voice, she leaned back against the kitchen counter and crossed her legs.

"How are things at Lost Angel today?" she asked.

"Pretty good, actually. If you're free Saturday night, I'd like to take you out to dinner."

"Are you suggesting a real date?"

"That's my intention."

"Then I'm most definitely available." She glanced at the calendar on the counter and wished he'd wanted to see her that very night rather than wait until the weekend.

"If you'll come in tomorrow," Luke coaxed, "we can tour the neighborhood. I'd like to show you the most promising possibilities for the mural."

"You needn't offer enticements for me to visit the center." Delighted he was more anxious to see her than it had first appeared, Catherine licked her lips.

"That's good to hear, but I don't want you to think I'm not interested in going ahead with the mural. There are too many kids sitting around here all day with nothing to do except get into trouble, and an ambitious mural would keep them occupied a long while."

Catherine waited for him to say something more personal, then realized he must prefer to keep his office conversations focused on business. "I'll be there in the morning. Sweet dreams," she couldn't resist adding before hanging up.

Thursday morning, Catherine wore tan slacks and a sunny yellow sweater into Lost Angel. Luke's door was open, and this time it was Pam who waved her on in. Luke left his seat to close the door, and then he leaned back against his desk and pulled her between his splayed knees.

He kissed her lightly, then whispered, "I'll always be glad to see you walk through my door, but we'll have to be discreet. Whatever relationship we might have outside Lost Angel has to remain a closely guarded secret."

She slid her arms around his waist. "You're giving me a decidedly mixed message here, Dr. Starns, and as I recall, body language holds more truth than words."

A warning flash crossed his gaze, but it faded before she could be certain she'd actually seen it. Still, she felt uneasy. "What's the matter? Have I strayed into your area of expertise?"

He responded first with a reassuring kiss. "No. You're an intelligent woman, and you have every right to your opinions. You're also correct about my body language. It's appalling."

"I'm not appalled." She ran her fingertips under his collar and leaned close to kiss him.

He sent that single kiss into a dozen before he found the presence of mind to ease her back a step. "We better get out of here, now."

Amused by his haste, she remained where she stood. "Are you worried the kids will tease you unmercifully?"

"They already have. That day you served the spaghetti, Nick swore you had a crush on me."

"Really? Did I give you extra spaghetti?"

"No, but you were flirting with me. So we'll have to be more careful. I'm a father figure here, but I'm also the resident psychologist. It's already a struggle to keep our group sessions focused on problems and solutions, but if the kids mention you to divert the attention from themselves, then my leadership will be severely compromised. I can't allow that to happen."

He was wearing a soft chambray shirt, but it was his heat she felt, not the smoothness of the fabric. He was holding her in an easy embrace and seemed sincerely pleased to see her rather than torn by regret. That was reassuring, but she doubted they could keep their budding romance a secret for long.

"While I can certainly be discreet," she confided, "if the choice is seeing you or volunteering here, then you win in a heartbeat. After all, you have to be here. I don't."

"I appreciate that, but I haven't dated any other volunteers, so maybe I'm just being overly cautious. I definitely want you to head up the mural project. Now come on, let's go scout the neighborhood."

She stepped back as he eased off the desk. "I've never made love on a desk, have you?"

He attempted an exasperated frown, but it was swiftly erased by laughter. "Is that your idea of discretion?"

She drew herself up into a prim and proper posture. "Sorry. I'll give it more effort," she promised, and she preceded him from the office with a purely professional nonchalance.

"Let's use my car. We'll be back within the hour, Pam."

Catherine caught Pam's wink and knew at least one person was already in on their secret. Pam would probably tell Dave, and he might mention it to Mabel, and before long, all the kids and volunteers would know they were seeing each other.

She waited until they were seated in Luke's Subaru to speak. "I hope you've already had a talk with Pam, because if that sly wink meant anything, it's that she already knows about us."

"She knows, but she won't cause either of us any trouble." He pulled a hastily drawn map from his pocket. "Now let's get to work. Here are the buildings I'm considering."

Catherine scanned the map and the surrounding neighborhood. As Luke turned from the parking lot out onto the side street, she checked his notations. "Lost Angel is on the southwest corner. An automotive supply store is directly opposite us on the northwest corner. I never even noticed what it was, but with no windows facing the side street, it's a possibility, but I wish it weren't just one story."

"Let's circle the block. There's a Ninety-Nine Cent store next to the auto supply. It has a graffiti-covered exterior wall facing the next side street, but I'd really like to do our first mural on a wall the kids could see from Lost Angel."

"I would too." She observed the buildings closely as Luke drove down the main boulevard. "We need a corner, don't we, but that sleazy bar opposite the auto supply won't do."

"I agree, but it does have a suitable wall. Let's just go a couple of blocks in each direction and see what strikes us."

"Fine." Other than visiting Lost Angel and the carpet store, Catherine was unfamiliar with the neighborhood, but she was unimpressed with what she saw. There were lots of little shops with dingy displays, fast-food restaurants, used car lots, apartment buildings with aluminum foil covering many windows, and a few single family homes that had seen far better days.

Finally, Luke parked his car on the side street next to the bar, and gazed across the street at Lost Angel. "Not much promising real estate around here, is there?"

"No, but what about Lost Angel itself? Would the owners object to a mural decorating the front of the church?"

Luke drummed his fingers on the steering wheel. "I called them right after Dave suggested a mural, and while the building no longer serves as a church, they like the look of the weathered granite and don't want it, 'defaced'. That was their exact word."

Catherine stared past Luke to the Victorian home on the corner opposite the bar. She checked his map, where it was noted simply as a house. "It looks as though someone is working on the Victorian right here. They're often painted in fanciful colors. Do you suppose the owner might consider a mural?"

Luke was so startled by her suggestion that he opened his car door and got out to look. It was a three-story house with all the gingerbread and curlicues that made the style so distinctive. He leaned into the window to respond.

"I can see a ladder and paint cans on the porch, and someone's been watering what's left of the lawn, but that's someone's home, Catherine."

"That's no reason to eliminate it from consideration," she argued. "The Germans and Austrians decorate private homes with colorful murals. Other cultures probably do too. Maybe we could start a trend here."

"It's not really a trend I'm trying to set."

She hurriedly left the car. "I realize that, but would you mind terribly if I introduced myself to the owner and described the idea?"

"Yes, I would," Luke responded crossly. "It's probably some dear little old lady who'd agree to a mural just to have some company."

"Then we'd all benefit, wouldn't we? Besides, with three stories, an angel mural would soar toward the heavens."

He stared at her a long moment and then shook his head regretfully. "You're not going to give in on this are you?"

"You asked me to head up the mural project. What are my responsibilities if you insist upon making all the decisions? Will I have to get your approval before I select the paint?" She knew she was pushing him, but if he were really the control freak he appeared to be, she wanted no part of the mural.

Luke rested his hands on his hips. "I thought we'd work together, cooperatively. I didn't intend to micromanage every brushstroke."

"Good. Now it'll only take a moment to introduce ourselves and pose the question."

Pushed into an uncomfortably tight corner, he appeared angry enough to spit. He glanced toward Lost Angel, where the kids seated on the steps were watching their every move. He turned his back toward them.

"We have quite an audience, so I'll have to do it, but I'm hoping some grouchy old man lives here, and he'll shoo us off the porch without hearing what we have to say."

Delighted to have her way, Catherine would have reached for Luke's hand as they started up the cracked concrete walk, but with Lost Angel right across the street, she squelched the impulse. "We could invite him to volunteer. Maybe he'd find Mabel's cooking every bit as delectable as you do."

He paused at the bottom on the front steps. "This is a crazy idea. Are you absolutely sure you want to do this?"

"Quit stalling." She nodded to encourage him, and they climbed the steps.

Luke knocked at the door. Expecting an elderly woman, if not a cantankerous old man, he took a cautious step backward, but the door was opened by a young man clad only in low-slung jeans.

He had dark curly hair, green eyes, and an engaging grin, but those assets weren't his most remarkable attributes. His upper body was covered from his collarbones out to his wrists and down to his waist with colorful tattoos. The exotic array of dragons, Samurai warriors, cranes, chrysanthemums and kimono-clad ladies spread over his shoulders and appeared to plunge down his back. While the whole staggering display was interrupted at his waistband, it certainly didn't appear to end there.

Astonished, Luke nevertheless recovered sufficiently to introduce himself and Catherine. He pointed across the street. "We're from Lost Angel. We're considering a mural project and thought this house might make a suitable location. Are you the owner?"

"Sure am. Name's Toby McClure. You want the kids to paint a mural here? That's cool. You've got some real tasty chicks over there. Not that I'm into underage babes. I like real women, myself." He swept Catherine with an appreciative glance and extended his hand.

He was a handsome man despite his zest for decorative art, but Catherine wasn't certain she wanted to touch him. Good manners indicated she ought to at least shake his hand, and surprisingly, his skin was warm and his touch quite pleasant.

"I'm pleased to meet you, Mr. McClure," she said. "You have such stunning tattoos. Are you a tattoo artist?"

Toby gave her hand an affectionate squeeze before releasing it. "No, I'm a collector," he replied with a conspiratorial wink. He turned back toward Luke. "When do you want to start?"

"We're still in the planning stage," Luke explained. "But it was good to meet you, and I'll let you know what we decide."

"Stop by any time. I'm a sculptor and work out of the garage in back. A fancy mural might be a real good backdrop for my work."

"It just might," Luke agreed, but he hurried Catherine out to his car and quickly returned to the Lost Angel parking lot.

"What an extraordinary character," she mused aloud. "While I still like the house, you were right to be concerned about the owner. I'm surprised some of the Lost Angel girls haven't found Toby already, but I sure don't want to invite any to meet him."

"Neither do I," Luke replied. "I had no idea you were fond of tattoos."

She opened her purse to repair her lipstick before they left his car. "We don't know each other well yet, do we?"

"You want to warn me now so I'll be prepared for the next surprise?"

She rested her hand lightly on his knee. "I like a bit of mystery, don't you?"

He shot her a darkly skeptical glance. "Just how mysterious do you plan to get?"

"I don't know. I'll let you know if I'm hit with a sudden inspiration."

"Oh yeah, you do that. Now the purpose of this little expedition wasn't to cultivate the friendship of bizarre neighbors, but to select a building for the mural project."

She gave his knee a playful pat, then forced herself to be serious. "I'd prefer a two-story building, but the auto supply store is at least convenient. Do you think the owner will be receptive to the idea?"

"He will be when I finish with him."

"Yes, you can be very persuasive, Dr. Starns."

Her glance was slyly seductive, but he was still curious. "If you're really fond of tattoos, perhaps I should go out and get one."

"I wouldn't rush," she advised. "Now hadn't we better get back to work?"

He shoved open his car door. "You go on in. I want to visit with the owner of the auto supply."

She stepped out of the car and carefully closed the door. She waved and started toward his office. "Don't worry," she called in a stage whisper. "I'll be excruciatingly discreet."

Luke offered a grateful nod, but as he walked away, he turned back to watch her enter the office. She moved with the lithe grace of a gazelle, but nothing was ever going to be easy with her, and that was truly excruciating.

Chapter Eight

Luke walked over to the auto supply store, but now that Catherine had pointed out how much better a two-story building would be for a mural, he had second thoughts about approaching the owner. The bar was definitely out, because he refused to place the kids so close to beer-guzzling lowlifes.

He discounted Toby McClure's Victorian for much the same reason. The Ninety-Nine Cent Store looked damn good by comparison, but it faced the wrong direction. He usually had no difficulty coming to a swift decision on matters concerning the center, but the mural project wasn't nearly as simple as Dave had originally made it sound.

Then there was Catherine, who took great delight in complicating everything. He jammed his hands in his pockets and walked around the block, but the only inspiration that came to him was to hand the mural right back to Dave and Catherine and let them choose a site which he would then approve or veto. Dave lived at Lost Angel and knew the neighborhood, so he ought to be able to suggest a better site than Luke had been able to find on his own.

Pleased to have found a way to sweep the mural project off his desk, Luke returned to Lost Angel, but as he walked into the office, he found Nick sprawled across one of the guest chairs. The kid was a bloody mess, and Catherine was kneeling at his feet, playing paramedic. There was a bloody handprint on her yellow sweater, and for one terrible instant, he feared the blood was hers.

"Good God, what happened?" Luke cried.

Nick shifted in his chair and winced. "I was skateboarding down the sidewalk, minding my own business like I always do, when this little old lady came barreling down her driveway in her Buick. She knocked me right out into the street, but because I'm such a lucky dude, no one was driving by to smear me into the asphalt."

"Thank God. Did you call the police to report the accident?" Luke asked.

Nick sneered at the suggestion. "No. She was somebody's grandmother, like the ladies who volunteer here, and you know the cops would have blamed me rather than her."

"I don't know anything of the kind. Now, this is clearly more than we can handle here. You belong in an emergency room. Can you make it out to my car?"

Nick made no effort to rise. "They'll make me wait for hours for a couple of Band-Aids and an aspirin. I had a tetanus shot last year, and Mrs. Brooks is fixing me up just fine."

Luke couldn't meet Catherine's gaze, but the sight of Nick's scraped and bloody hands and knees didn't seem to bother her nearly as much as it did him. He felt shaky and leaned against Pam's desk for support. "Where's Pam?"

Catherine continued to clean Nick's torn knees with a wet towel and spoke without looking up. "She'd already gone to lunch when Nick stumbled in, and I knew you'd be back soon."

Before Luke could reply, Rafael burst through the door, followed by Polly. "Shit man, what happened?" he yelled.

Nick provided a flippant summary of his ordeal. "It's worse than it looks, but I'll need some new clothes. You'll help me out there, won't you, Luke?"

Clothes were about all Luke could replace, and he swallowed hard before he spoke. "Sure. When you feel up to it, Pam will open the clothes lockers. Take whatever you need."

"Thanks, man." Nick winked at Polly, but she was so badly frightened, she collapsed in the chair at his side and began to moan softly.

Luke still felt uneasy, but he was satisfied Nick had no deep cuts that would require stitches. "Mrs. Brooks, when you can spare the time, I'd like to speak with you in my office. If you change your mind about going to the hospital, Nick, let me know."

Nick gave a jaunty salute, then rested his bloody hand palm up on the arm of his chair. "What do they call these scrapes, abrasions?"

"Nasty abrasions is what I'd call them," Luke countered, "but that's scarcely a medical term."

"Whatever. I'll survive. It'll take more than a Buick to do me in."

"Try and be more careful in the future," Luke cautioned. "I'd like to report the woman who hit you even if you wouldn't. Did you notice her address?"

Nick shook his head. "It was only a couple of blocks away, but I was just watching the blood drip off my hands, not the house number."

"Want me to go look for blood in the street?" Rafael offered eagerly. "Maybe I could find the house."

"No," Luke ordered. "You'd be more likely to be hit by a car yourself." With a last anxious glance toward Nick, he entered his office and closed the door.

"I think I'm going to be sick," Polly whispered.

"Rafael, will you please help her into the bathroom?" Catherine asked.

Rafael offered Polly a hand but clearly wasn't happy about it. "Just don't puke on me," he warned, but he got Polly across the office to the bathroom without mishap. He came back, picked up Nick's skateboard and turned it over.

"At least your board wasn't ruined."

Catherine hadn't seen Rafael since his run-in with the police, but his orange hair was still spiked, and he looked none the worse, or better, for the experience. Still, she couldn't help but wonder if the police had returned his knife. Because she would want a weapon if she were ever forced to live on the street, she hoped his was tucked away safely in his backpack.

A few minutes later, Polly came weaving out of the bathroom, but she was still pale. "I'll wait for you guys on the steps," she murmured softly. "Come get me when you go to look for clothes."

"Will do," Nick assured her. He leaned over to gauge the damage to his knees. "Are there any of those big, wide Band-Aids in the first-aid kit?"

"Yes, just let me sponge off the last of the dirt, then I'll apply a layer of antibiotic cream and cover it with the largest bandage. As for your hands, maybe the cream and a gauze wrapping would be best."

Nick flopped back and drew in a deep breath. "It was such a nice day too. I was just cruising along and then, wham. That's the way life is though, isn't it?"

"It sure is," Catherine agreed, but she was very sorry he was so cynical at such a young age. It took her a few more minutes to complete what treatment she could offer, and then she removed the disposable rubber gloves. "Wait here for Pam," she suggested.

"Don't worry. I'm trying hard not to move," Nick promised and Rafael laughed as though greatly amused by his friend's sense of humor.

Catherine tossed the gloves into the trash then went into the bathroom. When she discovered Nick's bloody handprint on her sweater, she considered changing into the spare clothes she kept in her car for emergencies. This certainly looked like a good day to use them, but she hated to keep Luke waiting and decided against it for the moment.

She rapped lightly on his door and waited for his call to enter. She found him standing by the window, arms braced against the sill, his head down in a dejected pose that didn't invite conversation. It upset her not to know if he was angry with her, or frightened by what had happened to Nick. She'd learned not to second-guess him and waited patiently for him to speak.

Before the wait grew uncomfortably long, Luke drew in a deep breath and straightened up. "I wasn't gone for more than thirty minutes. I walked through the door thinking about a mural, but blood sure has a way of reordering priorities. Frankly, I don't know which is worse, that Nick was struck by a car on his way here, or that you're covered with his blood."

He sounded furiously angry, but his caustic rebuke wasn't mirrored in his eyes. He had chosen sarcasm over the truth, but Catherine could see he was frightened for her. He'd lost everyone he loved, and he had to be terrified some tragedy would befall her as well. That she couldn't promise that it wouldn't made her ache for him.

"I saw the film on blood-borne pathogens years ago, and I wore a pair of the rubber gloves kept in the office first-aid kit. So you see, I avoided any needless risk."

"That's not much comfort," Luke complained, his tone still bitter.

"Perhaps not, but it's all I have to offer. You know what Nick told me when he first got here? He said he'd refused help from the woman who'd struck him because he just wanted to get home. That's how he thinks of Lost Angel, and you deserve the credit. Just as you'd hoped, the kids feel safe here."

"But none of them truly is safe," Luke countered darkly.

"Sometimes the belief is enough," she offered. "Often it's all we have." When he clenched his jaw rather than voice his disgust, she took another tack. "Perhaps it's time I told you what happened to Sam."

Taken aback, Luke frowned slightly, then gestured toward a chair. "If you feel you must."

She sat, and rather than take the chair behind his desk, Luke dropped into the one at her side. His gaze, while still guarded, held a sparkle of curiosity now, which she considered a great improvement. She folded her hands in her lap, but it was an effort not to wring them pathetically.

"We were scheduled to leave on a trip to Scandinavia the next day, and Sam went into his office to clear up some last minute detail on one of his cases. He thought he wouldn't be gone long, and then we planned to finish packing, eat an early supper, and be ready to fly out of LAX first thing the next morning.

"He'd been gone about an hour when I got a frantic call from one of his partners. He told me Sam had been rushed to Huntington Memorial Hospital, and that I should get there just as quickly as I could.

"I was at the hospital within ten minutes, but it was too late. Sam had suffered a massive coronary, and the paramedics had been unable to revive him. The doctors at Huntington had worked on him too, but he was gone.

"He'd always been so healthy, and it'd been several years since he'd been to his doctor for a physical. A simple stress test would have revealed the problem and saved his life, but he'd never had one. I blamed myself for not taking better care of him."

A painful lump closed her throat, and she coughed to clear it. "The hospital staff was wonderful and let me sit with Sam for as long as I needed."

That precious hour belonged solely to her and Sam, and she would never share the details with anyone. "You will probably find this impossible to believe, but I'm grateful that if Sam had to die, he'd died here, where I'd be surrounded by our friends rather than a day later in Copenhagen where I'd have had to rely on strangers to help me fly his body home in a coffin.

"That's the real difference between us, Luke. I can find a glimmer of hope in a puddle of ink, while all you'd see is the spreading blackness."

Luke was silent for a long moment, but rather than argue, he reached for her hand and ran his fingertip across her blackened nail. "What happened here?"

She told him. "It was stupid, like most accidents are."

"Did it happen right before or just after you removed your wedding ring?"

She wasn't surprised he'd noticed the gold band was gone, but she didn't like where his question was leading. "After, but that's merely a coincidence I'm sure."

Luke drew her hand to his lips and kissed her fingertips tenderly. "No, it wasn't. Freud believed there are no accidents, and most of the time I agree."

His touch sent a shiver of desire clear to her shoulders, and she left her hand resting in his. "But wouldn't that mean Nick was deliberately ignoring the dangers while he rode his skateboard? Courting disaster, if you like. That doesn't make any sense."

"Doesn't it? He received a whole lot a concerned attention from you, and that looks like a big plus to me."

She pulled away from him. "That's sick."

"No, it isn't. As I'm sure I pointed out during your training, we keep first-aid kits in all the buildings to tend the cuts and scrapes the kids receive nearly every day. Some are self-inflicted, but once I've hustled a kid off to the emergency room for stitches, that's usually the end of it, for him, at least."

"You can't imagine that Nick threw himself into the street in hopes of winning a little sympathy and some new clothes."

"No, the scrapes were too deep, but the fact he can't tell us where it happened or the name of the woman who hit him makes me wonder if he told us everything. Nick is a good kid, but that doesn't mean he's above bending the truth to his own advantage."

Catherine sat back to consider that possibility, but what struck her as odd was how Luke had reached for her hand rather than murmur a comforting comment about Sam, or dispute her observation on their differing views of life. He had simply changed the subject to brush both aside. Because each disclosure had been important to her, she now regretted confiding in him.

"I was going to change my clothes, but I think I'd rather just go on home." She stood and repositioned the chair in front of his desk. "But before I go, what did the owner of the auto supply say about the mural?"

Luke nearly leapt to his feet. "I decided you were right about the need for a two-story site and didn't talk with him. I'll assign Dave the job of finding us a better location."

While she was surprised he now agreed with her, the brightness had already faded from the day, and she took no pride in it. She wore a preoccupied frown as she hurried for the door. "That's a good idea. Maybe he'll see something we didn't."

"Catherine? Wait a minute. Have I upset you?"

She rested her hand on the doorknob and shrugged. When he'd confided his painful losses, she'd been unable to speak. Perhaps he was equally at a loss for words and had seized upon her bruised nail to distract them both. It was logical but failed to supply the reassuring affection she truly needed.

"Maybe it's just a delayed reaction to Nick's injuries, but I need to go home."

"All right then. Take tomorrow off, and I'll pick you up at seven Saturday night."

Catherine had been looking forward to their date, but now she was relieved it wasn't until Saturday. "Seven's fine. Goodbye."

After she'd closed the door, Luke looked around for something to throw, but other than the philodendron, which would create a dirty mess on the new carpet, nothing lay within reach. Still, he felt as though every word out of his mouth had been wrong, and he was sick to death of feeling guilty.

Friday, Catherine read, worked in her garden and bought groceries. On Saturday she went into Pasadena's Old Town to shop for something new to wear that night. Not that she needed anything new; she simply didn't want to wear a dress Sam had selected or that she'd worn with him, and that eliminated everything she owned.

She was uncertain what to purchase until she found an apricot sand-washed silk sheath and jacket in a trendy boutique. The flattering outfit was casual in style, and the soft sensuous fabric was a joy to wear. She then needed shoes, which were more difficult to find. By the time she'd completed her shopping, it was late afternoon, and she had to rush home to get ready.

There was a message on her answering machine from Joyce. She hadn't heard from Shane, but she was going to the party alone to look for artwork for future decorating jobs. She sounded resigned rather than happy, but Catherine was too nervous about her own evening to take the time to call and offer encouragement.

She loved to scent her bath water with bubble bath, soak and read, but that night she was too nervous to relax, let alone read. She was dressed and ready to go forty-five minutes early, but her heart was in her throat as she paced from the entryway to the kitchen and back again.

She'd never been so anxious before a date. Despite their tendency to disagree, she liked Luke enormously, but she was beginning to fear that either she was too much for him, or sadly, not nearly enough. It was an awful thought either way, and when the doorbell finally chimed, she had to run all the way from the kitchen to the front door. Then, before she welcomed Luke, she took a moment to gather the composure she certainly didn't feel.

Luke was dressed in a charcoal gray suit, white shirt and maroon and silver striped tie. He looked so handsome it hurt, but it was the fragrant spring bouquet he carried that proved to be her undoing.

A colorful mix of yellow roses, purple iris, sparkling white daisies, sprigs of pussy willow and tendrils of ivy, it was delicate and utterly enchanting. The instant she took it from him, she dissolved in tears.

Luke closed the door behind him and took her elbow to guide her toward the living room sofa. "You don't like flowers? When your yard is so pretty, it didn't occur to me you might not want any."

Horribly embarrassed, she fought to control her sobs and began to hiccup. "I love the flowers. It's so sweet, and completely unexpected."

He was positive he'd mentioned buying her flowers when they talked about going out on a date. Perhaps her memories of that night were blurred by the pleasure they'd shared, but he recalled every minute in exquisite detail. He leaned over to kiss away a tear rolling down her cheek.

"You look so pretty, and I didn't mean to make you sad."

"I'm not sad," she insisted, "just overwhelmed."

He sat back slightly. "You're not usually so easily overwhelmed. In fact, you're often downright obnoxious."

"I hope you're just trying to make me laugh." But the playful insult really did make her feel better. "I'll go and wash my face, then I'll be ready to go." She left the sofa carrying the flowers, but he rose and caught her arm.

"Why don't you tell me where I might find a vase, and I'll put the flowers in water."

"Oh, yes, of course, I wouldn't want them to wilt. Here, let me do it."

He followed her into the kitchen, where she quickly produced a crystal vase from a high cupboard. She filled it with water, then trimmed the stems before placing the flowers in the vase. As he watched her, he ran his hand up her back and rubbed her shoulders gently.

"It's no wonder you're nervous, but I haven't been out on a date recently, either. I hope we'll have a good time."

"Yes, so do I." As soon as she had the bouquet artfully arranged in the vase, she turned to hug him. "You cut your hair," she exclaimed.

"I thought it was about time, but did it look that bad?"

"No, in fact, I liked it long, but it's still feathered over your ears, so it's not really that short."

"I hope not. I made a dinner reservation, but I don't mean to rush you. Would you like to make yourself a cup of tea and rest a minute before we leave?" he suggested.

"No, really, I'm fine. I just need to touch up my makeup. Would you like anything to drink while you wait?"

"No, but while you're repairing your mascara, you ought to remove the price tag from your jacket. That's a gorgeous outfit, but there's no need to advertise it's new."

Her eyes widened in surprise. "Oh no." She slipped off her jacket, and there was the tag dangling from the side seam. "I should have noticed this, but thank you for saving me from any further embarrassment tonight. I'm so sorry. What must you think of me?"

He leaned over to smell the flowers. "I think you either like me an awful lot, or not at all."

"And you can't tell which?" she asked incredulously.

"I'm a psychologist, not a mind reader," he replied, and he drew her into his arms for a lengthy kiss that removed all doubt as to her affection for him. "I should have done that before giving you the flowers. Now go on and fix your makeup. I'm getting hungry."

"For something more than me?" she teased.

He laughed. "There's the Catherine I know."

She felt like herself now too, but it was difficult to reapply her makeup when she couldn't stop smiling.

Pasadena was filled with fine restaurants, but Luke took the freeway for the short trip to China Town. Delighted by his choice, she reached for his hand as soon as his car was safely parked.

"I came here with my parents when I was a little girl. I loved the food, but tossing dimes to the organ grinder's monkey and dropping pennies into the wishing well were what really made the evening fun for me."

"We used to come here too. So much is new now, but I think you'll like this place." He grabbed for the dragon door handle and ushered her inside. Dimly lit, the elegantly appointed restaurant was scented with sandalwood incense and boughs of fragrant jasmine.

"Everything smells delicious. If the food tastes half as good, I may not want to leave."

As they approached the hostess, Luke slid his arm around her waist and pulled her close. "Don't worry, I'll offer an irresistible incentive to return home."

"I'll look forward to it," she responded softly.

He gave his name, and they were shown to a red leather booth in a secluded corner. Catherine slid in first, and Luke followed. He reached under the table and laced his fingers in hers. "This is the most romantic restaurant I know. I hope you'll like the food."

"I'm sure I will." She left her hand in his as she perused the menu with an eager gaze. "I love wonton soup, and walnut shrimp, beef and broccoli, spareribs, and oh, I'll bet their green beans are perfectly crisp and delicious."

Luke closed his menu. "Why don't we just order one of everything?"

"That would be way too much food," she cautioned. She loved seeing him in a lighthearted mood and decided right then to do her best not to mention Lost Angel all evening.

"Then we'll just take home the leftovers in those cute little cartons," Luke promised, "and you'll have enough food for a week. Although you don't look as though you eat more than a few spoonfuls a day."

"I'm blessed with a fast metabolism, but even with that advantage, I haven't really been hungry in a long while."

"Well, you certainly sound hungry tonight, but be sure to save room for your fortune cookie."

Catherine responded with a knowing smile, but he was all she wanted for dessert. "Thank you for bringing me to such a special place." Their waiter arrived before Luke could respond, and he ordered all her favorites plus spring rolls and fried rice.

She poured their tea from the warm ceramic pot into the matching cups. She raised hers in an affectionate toast. "To good evenings with good friends."

Luke took a small sip, then set his cup aside. "I hope I'm more than a good friend."

"You're on your way, but I'm trying not to be presumptuous again. Besides, I believe lovers should also be friends. Are you worried that we're not?"

He looked away for a moment. "Let's not worry about anything tonight."

"That sounds ominous. Do you recommend taking life one night at a time?" Catherine feared she knew where his thoughts were leading and held her breath.

"No, but it's a practical approach," Luke insisted. "It's an effective way to beat an addiction, and it might not be such a bad way to look at life in general."

She saw their waiter coming toward them with their soup balanced on his tray and hurried to respond before they were interrupted. "I happen to believe the whole point of life is growth, and that requires an openness to the future beyond what a single day, or night, might bring."

Luke sat back while their waiter placed steaming bowls of wonton soup in front of them. "There's a great deal to be said for living in the moment, especially when confronted with something as delicious as this."

Disappointed he was again sidestepping an important issue, she released his hand to pick up her spoon. "I can't wait for the fortune cookies," she exclaimed, but while she could understand his desire to avoid contemplating the future, it didn't make it any easier for her.

Love was widely believed to conquer all, but it had not been enough to preserve Luke's family, and Catherine preferred silence to a debate on the subject. Either a person was open to love or he wasn't, and in her view, it was plain were Luke stood. He was an extremely attractive man, even with his emotional scars, but she wasn't so foolish as to believe she could ever change him. He would have to want to change on his own.

The wonton pillows were stuffed with shrimp, and Catherine savored every bite. "I can't even remember the last time I was hungry, but then I eat so many meals alone, that one blurs into the next. I used to plan our meals for the week, but now, more often than not, I just open a can of soup."

"You need to take better care of yourself," Luke scolded gently.

"If one lives in the moment, there's no reason to worry about health. After all, I'm perfectly fine tonight, and that's all that really matters."

He sipped the last drop of his soup and set his spoon aside. "You've made a good point, if we don't look after our health today, we may have no marvelous moments to enjoy tomorrow."

She nodded thoughtfully, and having scored a point for her side, she wisely smiled and waited silently for the rest of their meal to be served. When their waiter placed all the delicious dishes on their table, she blotted her mouth with her napkin rather than drool.

"I don't know where to begin," she murmured.

"What about alphabetical order?" Luke teased. "We could begin with the beans and work our way across the plates to the walnut shrimp."

"A logical plan, but I love the walnut shrimp and don't want to postpone it another minute."

"Then you've answered your own question. I'll begin with the spareribs."

The walnut shrimp was so incredibly good, she took two servings before moving on to the bright green string beans. She picked up one in her fingers and bit off the tip. "Crisp perfection, just as I predicted."

Luke waited until she'd finished that bean, and then before she could wipe her hand on her napkin, he licked off her fingers. "I don't know. These spareribs are awfully good, but you taste even better."

Catherine leaned over to kiss him. "I wonder if they have apartments available for rent upstairs."

"They might. Are you thinking of moving in and ordering take-out every night?"

"Well, it would certainly beat a can of soup."

"Maybe it's the company," he replied.

They teased each other throughout the meal, licked each other's fingers, and sat for a long time just sipping tea rather than open their fortune cookies. Finally Luke broke his with a loud snap. He read his fortune but refused to share it until Catherine had read hers.

She broke open her cookie and then smiled. "Your fondest hopes will soon be realized."

Luke tossed her his. "That's inspiring. Mine claims recognition comes through hard work."

"What?" Catherine read it for herself. "That's almost snotty."

"Yeah, but it happens to be true. Are you ready to go? I thought we might walk around a while and soak up the atmosphere."

"I'd like that." She took his hand again, and in the other he carried the bag containing the cartons of leftovers neither had expected to have. They peered in shop windows and admired the ornate architecture that gave China Town its magical flair. The night was clear, and the stars sparkled brightly overhead, while an occasional firecracker popped in the distance.

"Thank you again. This really has been a perfect evening," Catherine exclaimed. "But didn't you promise an incentive to leave?"

"How could I have forgotten?" Luke leaned close and kissed her ear, then the smoothness of her cheek before his mouth found hers. Oblivious to the others out enjoying the evening, he kissed her until she was so unsteady, she had to cling to him for support.

As they broke apart, Luke spoke to the middle-aged couple strolling past. "Sorry, I can't take her anywhere."

"Me? You started it."

"I'd swear you requested an incentive all on your own."

"A minor point," she conceded. "Come on, let's find the car."

"Yes, ma'am, whatever you say."

Catherine stopped while she was ahead, but once they reached her house and had stowed the leftovers in the refrigerator, she had another request. "Let's dance. Do you mind?" She walked ahead of him into the living room, opened the cabinet containing the sound system and turned on the radio.

"I haven't danced in years," Luke responded.

"I'm not expecting Dimitri from *Dancing with the Stars*. Just dance with me."

He sloughed off his coat and loosened his tie. "As long as you don't have high expectations, find something nice and slow, and I'll do my best not to trip over my own feet or yours."

Catherine kicked off her new pumps and slowly turned the dial. When she found a Spanish language station playing a sweet, romantic ballad, she glanced toward him. "Will this do?"

"*Sí, gracias,*" Luke replied, and he drew her into his arms. She snuggled against him, swaying in time with the music, and he sighed softly against her hair. "This is indeed the perfect LA evening—Chinese food and mariachi music."

"Sounds like paradise to me," Catherine cooed softly. Despite his protest, he danced as gracefully as he moved, and she was having a marvelous time.

At that song's end, the announcer broke in with a long string of dedications but they kept right on slow dancing into the next song and the next. Catherine's hair slipped through Luke's fingers in a silken shower, but she was almost too pliant.

"You falling asleep on me?" he asked.

She smiled up at him. "No, I was just enjoying the moment."

"I'm glad, but I'd like to go on upstairs before they play *La Bamba* and I make a complete fool of myself."

"Oh, Luke, I doubt that's even possible."

"Let's not take the risk."

He'd just given her the perfect opening to discuss the real risk of the evening, but when they'd had such a good time together, to voice her fears on a condom's effectiveness struck her as absurd. It wasn't deceitful, she swiftly convinced herself, it was simply too soon for "what if" discussions when they might cause Luke needless pain. She also knew the best time to discuss sex was when it wasn't the immediate option.

Her decision reached easily, she made a mental note to call her doctor first thing Monday morning and request a new prescription for birth control pills. Then any child they might conceive would have been planned by them both. Relieved to have found such a sensible solution, she laced her fingers in Luke's, shut off the radio and turned toward the stairs.

"The cat," she recalled suddenly. "I need to put the cat to bed." Smoky appeared the instant she opened the back door, but he stopped there and eyed Luke suspiciously. "Do you like cats?" she inquired.

Smoky's whiskers were twitching and Luke swore the little beast was sneering at him. "Yeah, I like them fine, but yours doesn't appear to think much of me."

"I once owned a marvelously affectionate tomcat who would climb into a stranger's lap and make himself at home, but Smoky is a bit more reserved. He'll get used to you soon enough."

She took a can of cat food from the refrigerator and spooned out Smoky's dinner onto a paper plate. With Smoky dancing around her feet, she carried it out onto the back porch and then closed the door to shut Smoky in for the night. She washed her hands and winked at Luke as she dried them.

"Now I'm ready for dessert," she nearly purred, and he followed most willingly. As they moved up the stairs, she peeled off her jacket, tossed it over her shoulder, and he caught it.

She was ecstatic they'd been able to converse the whole evening without once mentioning Lost Angel. She'd hoped Luke would relax and enjoy himself, and it certainly appeared he had. She was the first one to disrobe that night, and he stopped so often to kiss her that it took him a very long time to remove the last of his clothes.

He wrapped his arms around her and pressed her close. "I'd forgotten how warm and soft a woman feels."

She bit her tongue rather than ask if he were recalling a variety of women, or only Marsha's petite figure. "As long as you remember me, I'll be content."

"Good, now let's make love for hours, and then get up and eat Chinese food, and then take a bath together."

"A bath? That sounds wonderful. Do you like bubbles?"

"Of course, gobs of them." He tightened his hold to lift her off her feet. "Do you need a nap first?"

She licked his shoulder. He wore only a subtle trace of cologne, but it was an incredibly seductive scent. "No. Do you?"

Luke answered with a playful growl and pulled her up onto the bed. They stretched out, their arms and legs tangling as he kissed her with a passion that deepened with each hastily drawn breath. When the telephone on the nightstand rang, it was a jarring reminder of the real world, and Luke pulled back slightly.

"Do you want to answer?" he asked.

"No, you're here, and there's no one else I'm even remotely interested in speaking with. I'll let the machine answer, but could it be for you?"

"No, I'm not on, on the weekends."

"Then come back here." She laced her fingers in his hair to lure him back into another lengthy kiss.

The answering machine gave a soft click and whir, and then Joyce began to speak in a frantic whisper. "It's late, and there's a strange car in your driveway. I don't know what to do, call the police or send over a bottle of champagne."

Highly amused, Catherine reached over to pick up the telephone. "Thank you for the Neighborhood Watch alert, but I'm fine and need neither the police nor champagne. I'll call you tomorrow. Good night."

Catherine hung up before Joyce could reply and ran her fingertips down Luke's side. "It's nice to know the neighbors are watching out for me."

He slid over her. "Yes, but what about your reputation, Mrs. Brooks? Should you be entertaining gentlemen callers overnight?"

She spread her thighs to welcome him. "Only one gentleman," she stressed. He began to tease her with his fingertips and lips, and she was lost in a grateful surrender.

Chapter Nine

Joyce scooted her chair closer to the patio table. "Tell me more, tell me more," she begged, singing the tune from "Grease".

It was Sunday afternoon, and Catherine was comfortably seated with Smoky napping in her lap. She tickled his ears, and he stretched to encourage more lavish attention. "It was a memorable evening from beginning to end."

"It must have been, and yet when I went out to get my paper early this morning, Luke was already gone."

Catherine was deliciously sore, but she wouldn't confide such a trifling consequence of Luke's tireless loving. "We had a great time together. There was no need for him to hang around until noon."

Joyce sat back and toyed with her beautifully manicured nails. "Perhaps not, but it says something about a man when he splits at dawn."

"I'd say it's what happened before he left that counts."

"That's obvious from the width of your smile, but be careful. Don't let him take advantage of your good nature."

"Hasn't it crossed your mind that I might be taking advantage of his?"

Joyce nearly bolted from her chair. "You wouldn't!"

"No, but when I doubt there's much hope of a future with Luke, maybe I'm the one who's leading him on rather than the other way around."

"Do you want a future with him?"

Catherine dipped her head. Her passion for Sam had never waned, and she had no reason to believe it would ever fade with someone as affectionate as Luke. That wasn't the issue, however.

"After a couple of dates, most people can tell if there's any potential for more than a casual friendship. It's definitely there with Luke. From what I've seen, he's a man of character and depth, but I'd like a baby or two, and he might not."

"Did he actually say so?"

"No, and it's not a line of questioning I care to pursue just yet. We haven't known each other long, and it's much too soon to begin talking about marriage and children."

"You don't have to say, 'Let's get married and have a couple of kids.' You can always just ask if it's something he'd like to do someday with the right woman."

Catherine nodded, but she hadn't told Joyce how Luke had lost his daughter, nor did she intend to share his confidence with others. "Thanks, I'll try and work it into our conversation soon. Now tell me about your night. How was the gallery opening?"

Joyce reached up to fluff her curls. "I'm so glad you asked. It was very nice, but there was such a huge crowd that it was difficult to get close enough to appreciate the artwork. Then I rounded a corner, and there was Shane Shephard, sipping a Perrier."

"You're kidding, Shane was there?"

"He sure was. He was dressed in a black silk shirt, black slacks and loafers, and he looked even better than he does in shorts. Someone had mistaken him for one of the artists, and he was laughing as he explained he'd merely provided the profusion of plants.

"Then he glanced my way and responded with a startled expression. He came right over to me and said if I'd been the Joyce who had called him, he was sorry he hadn't gotten right back to me immediately. It seems he'd had several jobs that had kept him so busy he'd let his messages pile up, but he'd planned to answer all of them on Monday."

"What did you say?"

Joyce shrugged. "My initial reaction was to deny I'd called him, but because he had my telephone number, he would have caught me in an obvious lie."

"Please tell me you went with the truth."

Joyce giggled. "Part of it, at least. I said what we'd rehearsed, that I wanted to begin incorporating plants into my decorating jobs."

Catherine took a sip of iced tea and swore she could still taste Luke. It was such a distracting thought, she sat up and jarred Smoky out of his sleep. He leapt off her lap and went strutting away toward the camellias.

"He bought the story, didn't he?" she finally had the presence of mind to inquire.

"Of course, although there was a hint of suspicion in his eyes. Did I mention he has the most beautiful blue eyes?"

"Yes, you did. Now go on. What else happened?"

"He complained the place was too crowded to talk and asked if I'd like to go down the street to get a cup of coffee. This time I said yes, and we sat at a tiny corner table at Starbucks for hours. They make a delicious Chai iced tea, by the way."

"I'll remember that, but I know you wouldn't have stayed for hours if you hadn't liked what you heard."

"No, I wouldn't. Cut your losses and escape the losers I always say. But while Shane may be young, he's one of the most focused individuals I've ever met. His dad died when he was in his teens, and he took over the operation of his family's nursery business before he'd graduated from high school.

"He earned a college degree in business by attending classes at night, and his firm is doing so well that his younger brother and sister, a set of twins, are at the University of California at Santa Cruz, also majoring in business. He believes a concern for the environment, as well as our own well-being, just naturally increases everyone's desire to fill their homes and offices with healthy plants."

"He discussed the nursery business all evening?"

Joyce shook her head emphatically. "No, that was merely the beginning. We talked about all sorts of things, politics, world problems, where we wanted to be in five years. He's such an open man, it was easy to confide in him."

She hesitated briefly and with a small sigh grew thoughtful. "He said he hoped to marry soon and have at least two children. When I admitted I was afraid I might have missed my chance to have a family, he assured me that I hadn't. He seemed so sincere, but it will take awhile to discover if that's merely a pose, or the way he truly is."

"What does your intuition tell you?" Catherine inquired.

"That he's real, but that doesn't mean he'll fall madly in love with me."

"It doesn't mean that he won't either. Did he ask to see you again?"

"Yes, he walked me to my car, kissed me good night, and I mean really kissed me, and said he'd like to take me to dinner tonight. I usually make a man wait a few days, but I didn't even consider it with Shane. I just blurted out, 'Yes!', and thank God, he didn't appear too startled."

"He must have enjoyed talking with you and expected you to accept his invitation."

"I suppose. Now all I have to do is hold myself together until tonight. Maybe I should suggest we go to China Town. When are you seeing Luke again?"

"I'll see him Monday morning at Lost Angel. We hope to get the kids involved in painting a mural, and I'm really looking forward to it."

"Wonderful, but didn't he want to make plans for another date?"

"Frankly, I think he was too tired to plan more than driving home, but you needn't worry. We'll go out again."

Joyce studied her friend's confident smile. "I hope you're right, but I've found if a man really likes me, he'll ask me out again when he brings me home. It's always the guys who say they'll call, who vanish without a trace."

"Luke can't disappear. I know where he works," Catherine insisted, but it was yet another reminder of how unsettling it was to be with someone who preferred not to plan. It was a way to avoid disappointment that was true, but it seriously hampered delicious anticipation.

First thing Monday morning, Catherine called her gynecologist and requested a new prescription for birth control pills. She'd recently seen her, and the conscientious physician agreed to call her pharmacy so that she would be able to pick up the prescription that same day. While Catherine would have to wait until after her next period to begin taking the pills, she was relieved just to have put her plan in place.

When she arrived at Lost Angel, Dave was in Luke's office, and from the volume of their voices, she doubted it was wise to disturb them and hung back.

"Go on," Pam encouraged with a bracelet jingling wave. "Luke will be glad to see you."

Catherine hoped he would be, but rather than intrude, she settled for a quick peek in the door. "I just wanted to let you know I'm here, but I'll come back later."

Luke stood. "No, come on in. This concerns you as well. It seems after taking the weekend to check out the neighborhood, Dave chose Toby McClure's Victorian."

She was enormously pleased and beamed her approval. "You like it too?"

Dave took a step toward her. "I sure do. It has three stories, it's right across the street, and Toby's eager to do it."

"Too eager," Luke interjected.

"He moved in about a year ago, after some relative died and left him the place," Dave said. "He makes huge metal creatures out in his garage, and I believe he's even sold a few. If he were inclined to hit on the girls, he would have done it a long time ago. It'll take some effort to rig scaffolding, but it'll be worth it."

Luke appeared decidedly skeptical. "Let me think about it a while longer. In the meantime, keep looking."

"Fine, but what do you say to starting the art contest? That way, when a site is chosen, we'll be all set to begin."

Luke glanced from Dave to Catherine. "As long as all you request are preliminary sketches. I don't want the kids disappointed if we can't pull this off."

"We'll find a way," Catherine insisted.

"Do you have any idea how to paint a mural?" Luke shot back at her.

She wondered if he was being curt for Dave's benefit, but she didn't appreciate his tone. "As a matter of fact, I do. We just need to work out our design on a grid and then enlarge the grid on the building. Then the drawing is transferred to the larger grid and painted in."

While Luke didn't appear reassured, he gave in. "All right, I'll make an announcement at noon. We have plenty of white paper, but you probably ought to walk down to the Ninety-Nine Cent Store for some colored pencils."

Phoebe Conn

"Will do," she replied. "We want angels, but we could have as many different kinds as there are kids who care to submit a design."

Dave moved toward the door. "If we go with Toby's house, then he ought to be on our committee too."

Luke raised his hand. "Didn't I just tell you to keep looking?"

"That you did, and I'll be on my way just as soon as I finish my chores. See you at noon, Cathy?"

"Yes, see you then." Catherine waited for Dave to leave and then carefully closed the office door behind him.

She could appreciate Luke's concerns, but that didn't mean she would accept his surly attitude. She lowered her voice to a near whisper to avoid being overheard. "I didn't argue when you said we had to keep what happens between us outside the center a secret, but you needn't bark at me to keep Dave from becoming suspicious."

"I didn't bark," Luke complained too loudly.

"All right, then you're tired and forgot to eat, whatever the cause of your foul mood, you still need to be nice to me. Pretend I'm one of the other volunteers, like Alice Waggoner and Betty Murray who help Mabel. I've seen them here often."

Exasperated, Luke shoved his fingers through his hair. "I didn't mean to be rude. I was just hoping Dave would come up with a viable alternative rather than provide another vote for Toby's house."

She wished he weren't so dead set against it. "I really do like the Victorian."

"Well, I don't. I don't think much of Toby, and three stories of scaffolding will make accidents, and serious ones, inevitable. I'll grant you the mural might be spectacular, but I don't want to lose any of the kids in the process."

"Neither do I. I want to go take another look at the house. Maybe we can lean out the windows to paint rather than use scaffolding."

"Do you plan to paint, yourself?"

He appeared incredulous, and she much preferred the warmth passion lent his gaze. "No more than a brushstroke here and there. We want this to be the kids' project, remember?"

136

"Only too well."

She walked over to the window. Dave had trimmed the weeds creeping up through the asphalt, but it was still a desolate sight. "Is something else bothering you? I know I had a great weekend, and I'm sorry it didn't leave you happier."

Luke circled his desk and came up behind her. He slid his arms around her waist to pull her back against his chest and nuzzled her nape. "I had a wonderful weekend too, but this morning a letter arrived from my ex-wife's attorney. They're going back to court to ask for more money."

She turned slowly in his arms. "Marsha's actually done that?"

He nodded. "The judge will probably review our initial settlement and laugh in her face, but still, it's another problem I don't need."

"No, of course not." Catherine longed to kiss him, but waited for him to make the first move. When he did, the first brush of his lips was tender but so incredibly enticing that she could barely contain the enthusiasm of her response.

Luke finally had to set her back a step. He sent a playful glance toward the desk. "You better leave now," he warned, "before things really get out of hand."

For a second, she couldn't recall where she was supposed to go. "Oh, yes, the Ninety-Nine Cent Store. I'm on my way."

It took her a moment to realize nothing had actually improved, but that Luke was smiling as she walked away was all that really mattered. As she left the office, she was startled to find Dave waiting for her right outside.

"Do you have a minute to look at Toby's house again?" he asked.

"Sure. We ought to take some before pictures of whatever site we choose. I'll have to remember to bring my camera."

"Good idea. You could photograph the entire process. If the mural is any good, it will generate some interest from the media, inspire some new volunteers, and even better, create a flood of donations."

Catherine had been concentrating on the mural itself rather than the results from the community. She was now struck with the belated realization that reaping the benefits of the project would surely be Luke's chief concern. She didn't want to let him down, and that increased the pressure to achieve a good result enormously.

When they reached the corner, she was planning more logically and took note of the window placement. "It's a beautiful house, isn't it?" she said.

"If you look beyond its present faded glory to its potential, it surely is. I can already see the angels flying upward. The kids are going to love this."

"I hope so, but I wish Luke were more inclined to agree."

Dave laughed and rocked back on his heels. "If you put your mind to it, I'll bet you could sweet talk him into accepting Toby's house."

His teasing jest had struck too close to home, and she ignored his suggestion and turned away. "I need to get those colored pencils."

He hurried to catch up with her. "I'm sorry. That was a stupid thing to say. Luke's ex is giving him such a hard time that he probably wouldn't notice if you walked through his office naked."

"There's no danger of that," Catherine assured him.

"You're right. He wouldn't ignore you."

"That wasn't what I meant," she was quick to point out.

"I know. Do you mind if I walk to the store with you?"

"No, of course not." Dave was a flirt, but in no danger of succumbing to his charms, she felt safe with him. She sent a brief glance toward the auto supply as they passed and hurried on. "I guess I'm just anxious to get started."

"Me too. There's always plenty to do at Lost Angel, but not much of it is fun. I think the mural will be a hoot from beginning to end."

"I hope you're right. I happen to believe having fun is an important aspect of life."

"Damn straight it is, especially for the kids. Luke does a hell of a job, but no one would ever hire him to be the activities director on a cruise."

She kept quiet rather than agree, but she was surprised after all Luke had done for Dave, that he would be so disloyal. "I thought you two were friends," she offered and pushed open the door of the Ninety-Nine Cent Store.

Dave caught the door and followed right behind. "We are, but that doesn't mean we don't butt heads occasionally. I think the art supplies are over here."

Catherine quickly gathered up a dozen boxes of colored pencils. "We'll need the little sharpeners too."

"Here they are. The metal ones are best." He grabbed a handful.

She paid for their purchases, and they walked back to Lost Angel with Dave again doing most of the talking. When they arrived, he went out to work on the grounds, while she stayed in the office to sort through the latest mail.

Shortly before noon, Luke produced a three-foot-wide roll of white butcher paper from the office supply closet, and walked Catherine over to the hall. "I thought I'd catch the kids while they're lining up for lunch rather than when they're full of spaghetti and yawning," he explained.

"Good plan." She swung the bag of pencils and sharpeners in rhythm with her stride. "I just hope there are a couple of artists in the crowd. I'm sorry I don't have any examples to show. I should have gone by the library and checked out some art books."

"You're expecting a Renaissance masterpiece?"

She hated to admit that was precisely what she'd envisioned. "That's unrealistic, isn't it?"

"Wildly," Luke stressed. "Think Colonial folk art, and you won't be so badly disappointed."

The kids were already streaming into the hall, and Catherine moved aside to allow Luke to pass through the open doorway with the heavy roll of paper. They hadn't once discussed how they would present the project to the kids, but she trusted him to make it sound appealing.

He set the roll of paper against the wall and then asked for everyone's attention. "I promise not to slow down the lunch line," he began, "but we're seriously considering painting a mural on a building owned by one of our neighbors. We're hoping for angels to honor the center, but it's your call as to how you portray them. We've plenty of white paper and colored pencils, so after you eat, try your hand at working up some preliminary sketches."

"Is there a deadline?" a feminine voice called from the far side of the hall.

139

Luke turned toward Catherine. "How's Friday?" he asked.

"It's fine," she assured him.

"Friday it will be, then. Are there any other questions?"

"Is there any money in this?" Rafael sauntered up to ask.

Luke shrugged. "It's difficult to say. If you submit a spectacular design, for a single angel or the whole mural, then I just might be inspired to offer some prize money."

"Might?" Rafael pressed.

"Yeah, I might," Luke replied.

Tina Stassy wove her way through the crowd. "How are we supposed to know what angels look like?"

When Luke appeared perplexed, Catherine stepped forward. "They'd look like all of you. Have any of you ever watched figure skating on television? The skaters' poses are so graceful they often appear to be flying. While that may be beyond our capabilities to achieve, I'd like for you to try."

Dave had entered the hall in time to hear Luke's remarks, and he pushed off the wall and came forward. "If I lift you, can you show everyone what you mean?"

"That's not a good idea," Luke cautioned under his breath.

"No, I'm serious," Dave insisted. "I know exactly what Cathy means, and I think we ought to provide a quick demo."

Several boys began to stomp and clap sending a chorus of encouragement echoing throughout the hall. When Mabel began to pound a spoon against a pot lid, Catherine couldn't help but laugh.

"The skaters are moving, spinning, dancing across the ice," she reminded Dave. "Their speed is part of the magic."

Dave motioned with his hands. "I'll turn. Come on, let's feed their pitifully starved imaginations."

Perhaps it was the bold graphics of his Rolling Stones T-shirt, but his proposition suddenly made perfect sense. Catherine laid her hand on his shoulder. Dave dipped slightly to grasp her knees and, seemingly without effort, raised her aloft. She arched her back, gazed up and lifted her arms in an elegant gesture that would have done an Olympic gold medalist proud.

Dave turned in a slow circle and then set Catherine down to thunderous applause. Slightly flustered, she took a quick bow. "It's merely a suggestion. Many of you must have better ideas of how angels might return to heaven. Now isn't it time for lunch?"

Luke had been right beside her moments before, but when she turned toward him, he was no longer there. Startled by his unexpected absence, she scanned the hall, but he'd simply disappeared as though he'd dropped through a trapdoor. Before she could make sense of that puzzling happenstance, Polly rushed up to her.

"That was so beautiful," Polly gushed. "You make me wish I could ice skate."

"I can't skate either," Catherine readily admitted. She tried to smile, but Luke's abrupt departure had thoroughly dampened the exhilaration she'd felt in Dave's arms. Clearly Luke had shown his disapproval of their stunt with his feet, and she couldn't have been more insulted.

Polly, however, was staring up at her with an awestruck admiration, and she refused to be as rude as Luke had just been to her. "Do you like to draw?" she asked.

"I love it, but all I've ever been good at is flowers. My people don't look much better than stick figures."

Catherine took Polly's elbow and urged her toward the lunch line. "I'm sure we'll need decorative elements. Draw your best blossoms, and I'll find a place for them."

"Oh, thank you, I will."

"Where's Nick?" Catherine asked. She looked around but saw no sign of him either.

"He's limping around somewhere," Polly replied. "He'll be along soon. Spaghetti is his favorite meal."

"Mabel's is awfully good, isn't it? Excuse me, I want to make certain she has plenty of help to serve."

Catherine sidestepped the line to enter the kitchen where she'd hoped to find Luke, but again met with disappointment. Only the best magicians could vanish with the speed he'd displayed, and she feared he must have left the hall at a run.

Whatever appetite she might have had for lunch had fled with him. Alice and Betty were there again so Mabel had volunteers to serve and Catherine took cleanup. Scrubbing pots and pans proved to be positively therapeutic and by the time the lunch hour was over, she'd paved over Luke's haughty rejection with the determination to create the best mural the citizens of Los Angeles had ever seen.

In the hall, Dave had laid the roll of butcher paper at the end of a long table, and he was tearing off generous sections. Several kids were already seated at the tables, either arguing about where to begin, or like Polly, who had found Nick, doodling with the new colored pencils.

Catherine walked around to offer words of encouragement, but she was shocked to find Sheila, the black girl with the dreadlocks, blocking out a design with Frankie, whom she'd accused of plotting to steal her boyfriend Jamal.

"Have you two become friends?" she asked.

"Sure, why not?" Frankie replied, and the buzz-cut blonde went right on sketching an angel with enormous purple wings.

If they'd forgotten all about Jamal, Catherine chose not to provide a reminder and promptly moved on. When she returned to the table holding the supplies, Rafael was leaning against it and arguing with Dave.

"What's the problem?" she asked.

"He claims he needs twice as much paper as everyone else," Dave replied. "Naturally, I don't agree."

Rafael leaned close to Catherine and whispered, "I'm twice as good as everyone else, so I deserve more paper." He straightened up, and his spiked hair made him Dave's equal in height. "Give me two sheets if you have to."

Catherine doubted Rafael was as good as his boast, but she hated to discourage anyone on the first day of the project. "Let's give him whatever he needs, Dave. We'll just buy another roll of butcher paper if we run out, which I doubt."

Dave still appeared skeptical. "Are you really that good?" he asked.

Rafael responded with a wicked grin. "I'm a fucking Picasso. Give me the paper, and you'll see."

"Watch your language," Dave scolded, but he tugged on the roll, drew out at least three times the length he'd given everyone else and handed it over. "I can't wait until Friday."

"Me neither." Rafael grabbed up a box of colored pencils and walked out of the hall in a cocky strut.

"Do you suppose he's any good?" Dave inquired softly.

"For all our sakes, I certainly hope so," she responded, but she wondered if Rafael's angels wouldn't be holding knives. Luke had not placed anything off-limits, but when she found

Tina Stassy drawing an angel and a winged cat scrounging through garbage cans, she thought he might be real sorry he hadn't.

She remained in the hall all afternoon. Dave cruised through every half hour or so sometimes toting a mop, hedge clippers, or broom. When Luke failed to put in an appearance before the time his afternoon group was scheduled to begin in the sanctuary, she called it a day. She congratulated everyone on their progress, went straight to the parking lot without stopping by the office and drove home.

The telephone was ringing when she unlocked the door, but unwilling to listen to Joyce's ecstatic praise for Shane, or Luke's excuses, she let her machine answer. She fed Smoky his afternoon snack and took her time before she finally checked her messages.

The first call was from a firm offering to reduce her mortgage payments. The next message was from Joyce, who claimed her dinner date with Shane had gone amazingly well and that she would see him again over the weekend. The last was from Luke, who said only he was sorry to have missed her.

Catherine played that one twice, but she found it impossible to believe Luke actually cared. She took her mail outside to sort on the patio, and when the telephone rang again, she ignored it. She got up to make herself a cup of tea, then later went inside to watch the network news, but she still had no interest in food.

When the doorbell rang, she feared it would be Luke and took her time answering. "My, what a nice surprise," she exclaimed without any hint of joy. "I haven't seen you in ages."

"I was afraid there might be a problem." He stepped over the threshold and jammed his hands in his pockets as he turned to face her.

"How perceptive of you. Frankly, I'd say you created it when you walked out on me at noon, and don't you dare blame me for not dealing well with abandonment issues."

While startled by that accusation, Luke quickly recovered. "I wouldn't dream of it. Why don't we make some tea and see if we can't straighten this out?"

"Do you actually drink tea?"

"Sure, on occasion, and this seems like a good one."

She simply stared at him a long moment. His smile wavered with what she hoped was acute embarrassment. He'd come straight from the center rather than clean up first. A day's growth of beard shadowed his cheeks, and his clothes were slightly rumpled. She supposed that was some measure of his sincerity.

"Fine, we'll have some tea," she agreed, "but I'm on to you, Dr. Starns, and if you careen off the subject the way you usually do, you're out of here."

He appeared aghast. "I might stray, but surely I don't careen."

She refused to quibble and led the way into the kitchen. She turned on the burner beneath the teakettle and opened the cupboard containing several boxes of tea. "Do any of these appeal to you?"

"Tension Tamer might be nice." Luke surveyed the spotless kitchen. "Did you have dinner?"

Catherine leaned back against the counter and folded her arms across her chest. "I wasn't hungry."

"Well, Mabel's spaghetti is filling."

"I didn't feel like eating at noon either." She glanced toward the wall clock and wished she'd set a time limit on his visit. Now it was too late.

"You have to eat," Luke argued. "Let me fix you something."

"You like to cook?"

"I like to eat, and I don't think it's fair to make women do all the cooking. After all, anyone who can read can follow a recipe."

"There, you just careened right off the subject."

"Did not." He glanced toward the cupboards. "You must have something, soup, a can of chili. Don't you have earthquake supplies?"

"Sure, a package of beef jerky I keep in the car."

Luke winced. "I'd rather not chew off a hunk of jerky, and I haven't eaten today either."

"Why is that? I thought you loved Mabel's spaghetti, or was it merely the company you couldn't stand?"

He raised his hands in a gesture of surrender. "Let's talk about it after dinner." He began opening cupboards. "Hey, you've got Tuna Helper. I love this stuff."

"You can't possibly be serious."

"Why are you making fun of me? It's on your shelf, isn't it?" Luke grabbed the box and a can of tuna and set them on the counter. "Do you have some onion, bell pepper, maybe celery we could add?"

While she was still thoroughly annoyed with him, she went out to the closet on the back porch for the apron Sam had worn to barbecue. There was a chef roasting wieners over a campfire silkscreened on it. That had been the extent of Sam's interest in cooking, but she didn't think he'd mind if Luke wore his apron.

"Here, you'll need this." She handed it to him and stepped out of his way.

"Thanks. I hate wearing those little frilly things."

"You've borrowed a lot of aprons, have you?"

He winked at her. "I'll admit to a few."

Catherine tried not to laugh. "You realize this is surreal, don't you?"

"Not at all. We're just cooking dinner." He walked by her and began to search the vegetable drawers in the refrigerator. "You've got all we need right here and strawberries. Could we eat the strawberries for dessert?"

He glanced over his shoulder to gauge her response. He looked completely at home in her kitchen, as though they'd cooked dozens of meals together.

"Sure. The water's hot, so I'll make the tea and then sit down and get out of your way." She took a couple of mugs from the cupboard and filled them with hot water. She flipped the Tension Tamer tea bag into Luke's mug, but took orange spice for herself.

Luke emptied the entire contents of the crisper drawer out on the counter by the sink. "Why don't you make us a salad?"

"You're the one who volunteered to make dinner," she reminded him pointedly, and she moved into the breakfast room and sat.

Luke put a skillet on the stove and sprayed it with Pam. He soon had the onion, bell pepper, and celery browning, and the kitchen filled with their delicious aroma. He took a sip of his tea and watched Catherine stare out into the patio. Her tea sat untouched on the table, and he walked around the cooking island to join her.

"Catherine?"

"Hmm?" She finally recalled her tea and took a small sip.

"When I left the hall at noon, I didn't think it would be such a big deal. Obviously it was. I'm sorry. I hope you'll feel better after supper."

The man had buckets of charm when he wished, but she needed more than slick apologies. "You're being excruciatingly nice. Do you really feel that guilty?"

"Give me a minute." He got up, checked the Tuna Helper box and then had to search for a measuring cup for the water and milk. Once he had that in hand, he tossed and poured the rest of the dinner ingredients into the skillet, plunked on a lid, set the timer and started on the salad.

"All right, it's plain you won't wait until after dinner, so here's my best shot." He paused to gather his thoughts while he tore the lettuce into bite-size pieces, and the effort furrowed his brow. "I just had to get out of there. Please don't press me for more. I'm sure there'll be times when you'll lose it and prefer not to leave me to pick up the pieces."

Catherine regarded him with a suspicious stare. "That's it, you just lost it?"

"Big time," Luke claimed, and he sliced a tomato into chunks.

"You'll have to be more specific," she prodded.

Obviously reluctant to say more, Luke added avocado to the salad. "Look, I'm not proud of the way our first few conversations went, and I chose to leave rather than blow up again."

"So whenever you disappear, I should assume you're too furiously angry with me to stay in the same room?" It made her mad all over again.

"No. I wasn't running from you but from myself."

She gaped at him. "Even if you weren't a psychologist, you ought to know you can't escape yourself."

"That doesn't mean I can't try."

Growing wary, she sat back in her chair. "Does that mean I'm merely an escape?" she asked softly.

He responded with a rueful laugh. "Hardly. Just give me a chance. That's all I ask."

"What sort of chance? Are you referring to time, or until we've had X amount of arguments?"

"I'll be damned if I know. Will you set the table, please?"

Catherine still had no real appetite but returned to the kitchen to take out plates and silverware. "Fine, we'll eat, but as soon as you swallow the last strawberry, I want you to leave. I won't sleep with you again until I can trust you to be there when I turn around."

"Is that why you think I came here tonight?"

"Don't push your luck, buddy, or I'll boot you out now." She placed the plates by the stove and carried the silverware to the table and took out napkins. He'd used a wooden salad bowl, and she found the matching wooden serving forks.

"While I think of it, you put me in charge of the mural project, which you didn't explain to the kids. So if I want to stand on Dave's shoulders half the day while I direct the work, why should you care?"

"Because I do!"

She responded with a wicked grin. "Now we're getting somewhere. Are you jealous of Dave? He's cute, but I've always preferred you."

"I didn't say it was a rational response." He stirred the tuna mixture another time and adjusted the heat on the burner. "Now will you just let it drop? If I have to leave the room, just let me go."

"If you can't be charming, then you'll hide?"

"I prefer to regard it as a strategic retreat."

She leaned against the cooking island. "Do you actually expect me to accept temper tantrums as normal behavior?"

He shot her a darkly threatening glance. "Don't push me, Catherine. It won't be worth it."

"You think I don't know we're both damaged goods? I'm more than willing to be careful of your feelings, but you'll also have to take better care of mine. Now if you can't agree to that, you don't have to wait for an excuse to walk out on me for good. Get the hell out now."

"After I've gone to all this trouble to cook such a nice dinner? No way."

"You may be stubborn, Luke Starns, but I'll warn you now that after being married to an attorney for ten years, I know how to argue for days without repeating myself once."

Luke spooned the bubbling tuna mixture onto their plates and carried them over to the table. "I'm actually looking forward to it," he replied.

His rakish smile added to the challenge, but Catherine still sent him home with nothing more than strawberries for dessert.

Chapter Ten

With pitifully few prospects in Tennessee, Bobby Clyde Flowers had hitched a ride to California with the Tuttle twins, Nadine and Wayleen. While neither was a beauty, each possessed a remarkable talent for attracting men and a limitless appetite for sex.

Whenever their travel funds had run low, Bobby Clyde had arranged a party in a roadside motel and made certain the twins were well paid for their favors. It was the easiest money any of them had ever made. While they often had to crawl out a bathroom window before dawn when word of their exotic brand of entertainment reached the ears of the local sheriff, it had made for an exciting trip.

Upon their arrival in Hollywood, the twins had swiftly scored a contract in the burgeoning porn video industry. With their flaws masked by expertly applied makeup and curly wigs, they were free to indulge themselves with whomever a director invited onto the garish set. The proud owners of a brand new Chevy convertible, they had hired Bobby Clyde as their driver.

An ambitious young man, he'd soon discovered he could boost all their incomes by hosting private parties to showcase the twins' unique brand of charm. In less than a year, the ungrateful pair had run off with an oilman from Texas, but Bobby Clyde had had no trouble procuring fresh talent.

Tonight he was hosting a party where the highest bidder would claim an eager young virgin for the night. At the first such event, the bidders had been skeptical that Bobby Clyde could even find a virgin in Hollywood, but the winner had provided such convincing testimony that Bobby Clyde had had to turn away men at his next such party.

Bobby Clyde handed out bite-size candy bars and made friends easily with the starry-eyed teenagers pouring into Los Angeles. The girls were often quite pretty, and fortunately for him, pathetically easy to seduce with a tempting taste of chocolate and a whispered promise of fame.

He munched a tiny Snickers bar as he closed the front door behind him and glanced up and down the street. He never gave a party in the same house twice. His clients frequently complained he was too damn hard to find, but he intended to keep right on moving to elude the vice cops and their tedious concept of what constituted legal entertainment.

As he saw it, he was merely supplying what every man wanted: an opportunity to enjoy pretty young girls, while the teens were equally grateful to have the money. In his opinion, it was a satisfactory exchange, and the one time he'd been arrested for pandering, he'd hired an attorney from among his regular clientele and beaten the rap.

With an adorably innocent virgin tucked away inside, he was just waiting for the last of his guests to arrive when a blonde in a tight red dress rounded the corner. She was wearing platform heels and walked with an appealing sway, but Bobby Clyde's guest list was entirely male. When she started up the walkway, he moved to block the door.

"Sorry, sweetheart," he offered in the thick Southern drawl he strove to maintain, "this here's a private party, but you'll sure be welcome tomorrow night."

The blonde didn't slow her pace, and arriving at the steps, she reached around Bobby Clyde to ring the doorbell.

"Hey, baby, don't force me to play rough."

The blonde shrugged, and turned as though she were giving up, but then with a quick flip of a switchblade, she leaned in and gutted Bobby Clyde with a single savage jab.

He grabbed for his torn intestines as he fell down the steps and died with his own frantic scream still echoing in his ears.

After a sleepless night, Catherine had avoided any further confrontations with Luke by remaining in the hall to dispense art supplies and offer advice on the mural designs. He never left her thoughts, however, and at noon, she spotted him the instant he came through the door. He was walking with Nick, who was holding his skateboard in his right hand and gesturing wildly with his left.

To avoid being seated together, she'd planned to allow them to join the lunch line ahead of her, but Nick curved away from Luke and came straight toward her. When, after a brief hesitation, Luke followed Nick to her side, her smile wavered.

"Did you hear there's been another murder?" Nick asked breathlessly. "That blonde chick in the red dress has struck again."

Catherine glanced past him to Luke who shook his head in warning, but she already knew better than to encourage the teenager's interest in such a distressing subject. "Why no, I hadn't heard."

"Yeah, some pimp called the Candyman got his guts ripped out last night. How many do you think the blonde can off without getting caught?"

"I've really no idea. Why don't you try today's lunch? Mabel's made tuna melts."

"Great." Nick strolled away and cruised the tables checking out the mural designs on his way.

"Let's go to my office," Luke suggested softly.

"With tuna melts?" she countered. "I thought you'd want to be at the head of the line."

He responded with a good-natured chuckle. "Mabel knows I like them, and she'll save me a couple. All I need is a minute."

"A minute it is, then," she accepted, and they left the hall, crossed the broad courtyard and entered the office. Pam was just going out the other door for her lunch break and waved good-bye.

Luke led the way into his office and then gestured toward a chair. "I have a few thoughts I'd like to share. Make yourself comfortable."

Catherine slid into the closest chair and crossed her legs. "The mural project appears to be going well. The kids are excited, and some of the artwork is actually good."

"I'm glad to hear it, but I didn't invite you in here to make a progress report."

She glanced down at her sandals. She wore a fine gold anklet, and it sparkled as she bounced her foot. "No, I didn't really think so."

He leaned against his desk and folded his arms across his chest. "There are certain predictable patterns in relationships," he began. "Couples get together, and while they might each be happy, one or the other might pull away to create distance. It's almost a dance that expands and contracts. I want to take you out this weekend, but if you'd rather be by yourself for a while, I'll understand."

Catherine hoped he was attempting to be considerate of her feelings, which was what she'd asked of him, but his observation on the dynamics of romantic relationships sounded as though it had come from one of his university lectures rather than his heart.

"I'm not the one who staged the retreat," she reminded him.

"True, but I'm just saying it's natural for people to be drawn together and then become wary, and I won't fault you for it."

"Thank you, I'll attempt to be equally generous." She reached for the LATEXTRA section of the *Los Angeles Times* laying open on his desk. The murder was above the fold. She scanned the article briefly and looked up. "Have you read this?"

"Just enough to know the Candyman won't be missed any more than Felix Mendoza."

She slid her nail rapidly down the printed column. "It appears this Bobby Clyde Flowers, aka the Candyman, was hosting a party attended by approximately a dozen men and one underage female runaway. I sure hope she wasn't one of ours."

"So do I," Luke agreed.

"One of the few men who didn't flee before the police arrived said he answered the doorbell and found Bobby Clyde dying on the front steps. He reported seeing a woman with long blonde hair walking away, but was too horrified to pursue her. Who do you suppose rang the bell, Bobby Clyde, or the blonde?"

"Bobby would have had a key, wouldn't he?"

"Probably, but if he'd already been stabbed, he must have been in too much pain to press the bell. I can think of only one reason why the murderer would have rung it."

"Which is?" he asked.

"She wants to be seen."

"Why?" Luke prompted.

She paused a moment to consider her answer. "She could be taunting the police, or she could be deliberately misleading them. With such a flamboyant appearance, I can't help but wonder if the dress and hair aren't part of an elaborate disguise."

Luke appeared incredulous. "You think someone is disguising herself as a hooker to off pimps? I think legitimate hookers, if they can even be described as such, would have excellent reasons of their own."

"They undoubtedly do, but let's think about this a minute." She hoped she wouldn't sound as intrigued by the gruesome murders as Nick and took a breath to slow down. "Felix Mendoza preyed on runaways, and if Bobby Clyde's idea of a good time was watching one underage girl entertain a dozen men, then he was no better. That means a runaway might have felt justified in killing both men, and it could just as easily have been a boy as a girl. In fact, a boy would have greater need of a convincing costume."

"A guy in drag?" Luke scoffed. He glanced toward the philodendron which was doing nicely atop the file cabinet. "I don't even want to go there. Besides, my job is to protect the kids who come here, not conduct witch hunts."

"I'm aware of that, but Nick appears to be fascinated by the crimes, and he has a slim build."

"Oh Christ," Luke swore. "Why stop there? Three quarters of the boys who come through here are painfully thin. There's no fat on me either, and I'm sick to death of the bastards who prey on vulnerable teens. Maybe I ought to be the prime suspect in the murders."

There was a dangerous gleam in his eye, and for one terrible instant, she believed him fully capable of murder. His daughter's tragic death had filled him with a seething fury. Could he have unleashed it upon the despicable creatures who used homeless teens as sex toys? she agonized. Unable to meet his accusing gaze, she glanced away.

"Catherine, look at me," Luke ordered, his tone harsh.

It took her a moment too long to comply. "Yes?"

"My God, you actually believe I'm capable of it, don't you?"

She fought to make herself understood. "Please don't consider it an insult when in the case of Felix and Bobby Clyde, it would have been a heroic deed."

153

"You think vigilantes are heroic? I don't. I'm trying to set an example here of how a responsible adult handles his life. It would defeat my whole purpose to step outside the law."

"I didn't actually accuse you of murder," she stressed with forced calm.

"Fine." The muscles clenched along Luke's jaw as he pushed away from his desk. "But if I were going to do it, I'd gather a group of men who share my commitment to troubled youth. That way, none of us would have to handle more than a single killing, and it would be nearly impossible to link any of us to the crimes. But I sure as hell wouldn't squeeze myself into an eye-catching red dress to commit murder."

When he put it that way, Catherine had to laugh. She rose and reached for his hand. "That's a convincing argument right there, but something very peculiar has to be going on for the woman in the red to want to call attention to herself."

"I agree, but let's let the police work it out." He drew her close and dipped his head.

She reached up into the kiss, then regretfully broke away. "Lunch," she reminded him. "You'll be missed."

"I miss you," he breathed out against her lips. As he kissed her a second time, he hugged her tightly and lifted her clear off her feet. A loud knock at the door jolted them both.

"We were discussing the mural," she whispered anxiously. She smoothed her hair with her fingertips and backed out of his embrace.

Luke shook his head. "This is my office, and I won't make excuses to anyone." He crossed to the door and pulled it open. When he found a pair of detectives flashing their brightly polished badges, he gestured for them to enter. "Let me get us another chair."

"That won't be necessary. We won't stay long." A handsome Latino walked into the office and nodded to Catherine. A neatly trimmed mustache set off his smile, and his dark eyes shone with a teasing sparkle. "I'm Gerry Garcia, but before you ask, I was named for Geronimo rather than the star of the Grateful Dead. This is my partner, Detective Salzman."

Garcia was dressed in a tan suit, white shirt and gold patterned tie reminiscent of a Gustav Klimt painting, while his partner, a petite brunette, wore a severely tailored navy blue suit and the sturdy black heels worn by women in the military.

Startled by their arrival, Catherine responded as warmly as she could. "I'm Catherine Brooks. If you'll excuse me, I'm sure you'd rather speak with Dr. Starns privately."

Luke swung the door shut. "You're one of our most trusted volunteers, Mrs. Brooks. I'd like you to stay. These are the detectives who came to take the girls' statements after Felix Mendoza died. What progress have you made on that murder?" he asked them.

Chagrined, Garcia cleared his throat noisily, while his partner flipped open a small notebook and scribbled the date.

Catherine moved to the chair nearest the window and gestured for Detective Salzman to take the one closest to the door. After a slight hesitation, she sat on the edge of the seat, but her posture remained perfectly erect.

"You needn't point out that Bobby Clyde Flowers wouldn't be dead if we'd solved Felix Mendoza's murder," Salzman chided.

Luke slid into the chair behind his desk. He grabbed up the LATEXTRA section of the *Los Angeles Times* and flung it down on the desk top. "We were just reading about it. Do you believe it's the same woman?"

Garcia jammed his hands into his pants pockets and began to pace the narrow space in front of the door. The new carpet swallowed the sound of his footsteps. "Frankly, I thought the witnesses to Felix's murder were too rattled to provide an accurate description, but apparently they did."

"Or some copycat killer was inspired by the news coverage to adopt a similar disguise," Salzman murmured almost to herself.

"Do you regard that as a serious possibility?" Catherine inquired.

"Not really," Garcia replied. "But it was no accident that the witnesses to Felix's murder came here; and the girl meant for the main course at last night's party had one of your cards listing your programs. I'd say that's two important links to Lost Angel and the murders."

"We work awfully hard to get word of our services out to the kids who need them," Luke responded. "You can't blame us if we succeed."

Salzman tapped her pen against her notebook in a nervous beat. "Let's cut to the chase. The killer must have had a good reason to despise Mendoza and Flowers. They won't be missed, but we really dislike unsolved crimes. As we see it, the killer will continue her brutal attacks unless she's stopped cold. Because the dead men were known to traffic in young girls, and you've plenty passing through here, we need you to provide us with the names of all those with long blonde hair."

"No way," Luke swore. "We keep no records of who visits Lost Angel. We tally the numbers to be certain we'll have enough food, but that's it."

Garcia waved aside that objection. "Even if there are no written records, you must know the names of your regulars."

"Sure," Luke replied with a shrug.

"Well?" Salzman persisted, pen at the ready.

"Well, nothing. If I begin giving names to the police, the kids will scatter faster than cockroaches at dawn, and unlike those hideous insects, they won't return. I always encourage the kids to contact you if they have knowledge of a crime, but I won't rat them out."

"Harboring a criminal is in itself a crime," Garcia interjected.

"I'm not harboring anyone," Luke assured them. "I have absolutely no information on either pimps' death."

Catherine watched the detectives' expressions harden and couldn't help but think of Violet, who had the requisite long, blonde hair, but who didn't appear to be strong enough to even slap a man, let alone plunge a knife into his guts. She raised her hand. "If I might be permitted to ask a question?"

"Yes, of course," Detective Salzman responded defensively.

"You described the crimes as brutal. I thought the men were simply stabbed."

Garcia rocked back on his heels and smoothed out the ends of his golden tie. "There are stabbings and there are stabbings, Mrs. Brooks. An enraged killer can murder a victim several times over with multiple stab wounds. The woman in red is so calm and cool, she uses a single deep thrust to the belly to slice through the aorta, and then widens the wound when she withdraws the blade."

"That must take considerable force," Catherine offered.

"Definitely," Salzman agreed, "to say nothing of a vicious lust for blood."

"Would a teenage girl possess that kind of strength?" Catherine asked pointedly.

"She must," Garcia replied.

Luke knew where Catherine was heading and stepped in. "Mrs. Brooks believes your killer is a man in drag. He could be a rival pimp or someone who lost a daughter or sister in the flesh trade."

Garcia and Salzman exchanged startled glances. "What an interesting theory, Mrs. Brooks," Garcia responded. "Do you consult with many of the police departments in the county, or do you usually keep such imaginative thoughts to yourself?"

Clearly he believed that's what she ought to be doing now, but Catherine refused to give in. "Sometimes the obvious is overlooked, but clearly the killer wishes to be seen. I'd love to hear your theory as to why."

Salzman snapped closed her notebook and rose to her feet. "We'd really hoped you'd be more cooperative, Dr. Starns."

Luke stood as she did. "Believe me, I'm the very soul of cooperation when it comes to the police, but there's no evidence to convince me there's even a tenuous link between the stabbings and Lost Angel."

"You're being deliberately obtuse, Dr. Starns," Garcia shot back at him. "And don't think we don't recognize a diversion when we hear one. Most of the drag queens in Hollywood would faint at the sight of blood, so Mrs. Brooks' theory makes as little sense as your refusal to help."

Neither Luke nor Catherine responded before the detectives left the office. "I really thought detectives would be more open to a variety of possibilities," she mused aloud.

"I'm sure they are when it's their own ideas they're considering. Come on let's forget them and get some lunch."

She preceded him through the door. "I doubt they'll just disappear. Do you suppose they'll keep Lost Angel under surveillance?"

Luke cursed under his breath. "Probably, which means I'll have to discuss the murders at this afternoon's counseling session."

As they crossed the courtyard, she drew to an abrupt halt and tugged on Luke's arm. "You'd know this. Aren't the overwhelming majority of serial killers male?"

He nodded. "Yeah, they sure are. The next time Garcia and Salzman appear, and they will, I'll remind them of it. I'll also give you the credit for the thought, since they seem to be particularly incensed by your observations."

"Why was that?"

"You made them appear incompetent, which is easy enough to do. What did you think of Garcia's flashy tie?"

"I thought it an odd choice. Shouldn't a detective strive to blend in rather than stand out in a crowd?"

Luke glanced toward the hall's open doorway. He could hear laughter and the scraping of chair legs as kids got up to go back for seconds. His stomach growled, and he urged Catherine on toward the entrance. "They weren't on a stakeout, so their clothes probably don't matter."

"Not yet, maybe, but are they likely to park across the street and watch for blondes?"

"Maybe I ought to ask Toby to entertain them," Luke countered.

"Are you speaking to him?"

"No, not really, but I doubt he'd enjoy having the police hanging around either."

Catherine entered the hall first, but she went to check on the pencil supply before joining the line and let Luke get ahead of her. The police visit had left her feeling vaguely unnerved, as did the prospect of those coming to Lost Angel being under surveillance.

In mid-afternoon, Catherine was sharpening colored pencils with a small battery-operated sharpener she'd brought from home, when Tina Stassy slumped into the chair opposite hers. She set her canvas bag on the floor, and her cat bounded out and made a dash for the door.

"Charlie has to go pee," Tina explained. "He'll be back in a minute.

"He seems very attached to you," Catherine observed, although she thought the attachment mutual.

Tina shrugged, then yanked her overall strap back up on her shoulder. "He's loyal 'cause he's well-fed. I should have thanked you again for the money for cat food. That was real nice of you."

"You're welcome." Catherine watched Tina pick up her bag and hug it to her chest as though the cat were still snuggled inside. She doubted Tina really wanted to discuss cat food and continued sharpening pencils. The soft whirring sound broke the silence while she waited to hear what was really on the girl's mind.

"I met the Candyman once," Tina whispered. "You won't tell Luke, will you?"

Catherine laid the newly sharpened pencil aside and waited to pick up another. "No, not if you'd rather I didn't."

"I like Luke an awful lot, but he'd never understand." Tina sent an anxious glance toward the door and was clearly relieved when she saw her cat wandering back her way.

"Understand what?" Catherine asked.

"Let's just say the Candyman, and he did pass out candy like it was Halloween, he said, well..." She dipped her head to hide a brightening blush. "He was looking for virgins."

Catherine was appalled. "Just like that? Any virgins in the crowd?" she inquired softly.

"Sort of, except he talked like a hillbilly. He said, 'you all', and stuff like that."

"He was a Southerner?"

"Yeah, but no Southern gentleman. The guy creeped me out. He offered $2,000, though, and swore no one would have to sleep with him unless they wanted to."

Catherine was glad she'd eaten only half a tuna melt for lunch and swallowed hard to keep from losing it right there. "Apparently that wasn't enough for you."

Tina raised her hands to smother her laughter. "Oh, I would have grabbed for it, but I haven't been a virgin since I turned twelve." She welcomed her tattered cat onto her lap, slipped the bag around him and stood. "Thanks again for the cat food."

Catherine tried to continue sharpening pencils, but she felt more like breaking them all in half. Finally, she grew so angry she had to leave the hall to find Luke. Pam was on the telephone and waved her on in.

She knocked lightly before peering in Luke's door. "Do you have another minute?" she asked.

He checked his watch. "I have a couple. Come on in and sit down."

Too restless to sit, Catherine moved to the window instead. "I just heard from a reliable source that the Candyman was paying $2,000 a head for virgins. What kind of a miserable human being would stoop that low? These kids are little more than children, and all they have to sell is themselves."

"Catherine," Luke murmured. He left his chair and came up behind her. "That's not even the worst of it. There's plenty of porn on the Internet, and I've heard the horny teen sluts are real popular."

"Yeah, I know. I only check my email about once a week, and there's always several of those ads even more disgusting than the previous week's crop."

Luke slid his arms around her waist and pulled her back against him, but she remained as tense as a broom handle. "Maybe we ought to post explicit warnings in the hall, but I do all that I can to discourage the kids from taking money for sex or porn."

"I'm sure you do." She tried to draw on his strength, but failed. "I don't want the blonde blamed for another's crimes, but what if I bought a black satin dress and a long red wig? Could you point me toward a pimp who deserves to die?"

"Catherine!" Luke scolded. "You might have the makings of a spectacular slasher movie, but I can't see you stabbing anyone."

"Maybe not, but I could sure swing a baseball bat with deadly force and smash heads like spoiled melons."

Alarmed, he tightened his embrace. "Go on home and take the nice, long bubble bath we never got around to the other night."

"What makes you think I take bubble baths?"

"There's a big bottle of vanilla-scented bubble bath beside your tub, and your skin always has a delicious hint of vanilla."

"Are you trying to distract me?"

"Completely," he admitted.

She turned in his arms. "Well, it won't work. We aren't doing nearly enough here to protect these poor kids."

He rested his hands lightly on her waist. "I know, but it'll take a lot more in grant money to expand our services, and I've nearly exhausted every source."

"I'm not criticizing you," she stressed. "But the kids need tutoring, GEDs, the chance to join the Merchant Marine, to go to beauty school, whatever. They just need a whole lot more than lunch and a sympathetic ear."

Luke dropped his hands and stepped back. "You bucking for my job?"

"No, I just want Lost Angel to offer more than pimps."

"So do I. The awful reality of the kids' lives grinds up the majority of our volunteers to aching little bits. I don't want that to happen to you. Now, please go on home. We'll work on broadening our services just as soon as we get the mural started."

"Promise?"

He raised his hand. "Scout's honor."

"What about scouting?" she asked. "How many eagle scouts come through here?"

Luke opened his door. "Go."

"I'll be back."

He laughed. "I'm counting on it."

She closed the door on her way out and smiled as Pam winked at her. "How can you stand working here?" she asked.

"I came with Luke, and I'll leave when he does. You ought to hang in there too, girl. He's worth the trouble, and I know he thinks the world of you. He's even come into work smiling a time or two lately, and that didn't happen before you arrived."

Catherine had not viewed Luke and Lost Angel as inseparable entities, and it startled her to think that maybe she should. She planned to volunteer only through the summer, and yet she'd made demands Luke couldn't easily fulfill. Embarrassed now, she left for home burdened by the weight of a guilty conscience.

That evening, Luke stopped by Catherine's house on his way home. "You didn't list your email address on your application," he told her.

161

He actually appeared perplexed by the oversight, but she doubted he truly was. "You have an amazing array of excuses for making house calls, Dr. Starns, but come on in. Would you like something to drink?"

He followed her into the kitchen. "No, thanks. I'm serious, Catherine, I really should have your email address."

She'd just finished her dinner dishes, and she folded the dish towel over the rack before she replied. "It was Sam's, and I still think of it as his. I seldom access it and then only to dump the spam."

"I might want to send you a message," he coaxed.

Because that was no motivation, she couldn't help but laugh. She moved close to loop her arms around his waist. "The answer's no, then, because I like having you deliver your messages in person."

After a small shrug of defeat, he drew her closer still for a soft, yet increasingly luscious, kiss. He slid his fingers through her hair, then ran his hands down her back as though he wished to absorb her right through his skin. That first kiss slid into a dozen before they finally had to draw back to breathe.

Then he managed only a sad, sweet smile. "Are you seeing anyone else?" he asked.

Catherine couldn't have been more astonished had he slapped her. "What?" she gasped. "Do you think I'd welcome you through the front door while another man snuck out the back?"

"Just answer my question."

She shoved away from him. "No, Dr. Starns, I'm not, which should have been obvious from my kiss just now. What about you? Am I merely one of the stops on your route?"

"No," he swore. "I didn't mean to upset you, but it's never wise to rely on assumptions, and I just wanted to get things straight between us."

"Did you? Do you ever stop to analyze your own motives as thoroughly as you study everyone else's?"

"You've lost me." He propped his hands on his hips, clearly annoyed with her.

"What a shame. I was trying to find the real man beneath the layers of professional expertise." She grabbed one of the glasses she'd just washed and filled it with water from the tap.

After taking a long drink, she replaced the glass on the counter and turned back toward him.

"You might have said you cared about me and hoped I wouldn't want to see other men. You might have suggested we agree to date exclusively, you might have asked..."

He took a step toward her. "All right, I get it, but when it comes to dating etiquette, I'm dreadfully out of practice."

He looked sincerely pained, and she regretted having been so curt with him. "It isn't practice that's needed, Luke, it's simply heart."

"Then we have a problem," he replied, "because I don't have one anymore. I'm just as hollow as the Tin Man."

She watched him walk out and made no move to stop him. It wasn't until she began to prepare for bed that she realized something must have prompted Luke to ask if she were seeing other men. His ill-timed question had actually revealed a great deal. His heart might be badly bruised, but clearly, he still had one.

Chapter Eleven

After being away all day, Luke returned to Lost Angel with only a few minutes to spare before his afternoon counseling session. When he dropped off his briefcase in his office, he found Sam Brooks' business card on his desk. He carried it out to Pam.

"Was Catherine Brooks here all day?" he asked.

Pam glanced up at the clock. "Yes. She left about half an hour ago. She's real excited about the mural."

Luke nodded thoughtfully, then handed Pam the card. "Please make a note of her email address for our files."

Pam read the name on the embossed card. "Is it current?"

"Apparently so, even if Sam Brooks isn't."

Pam studied Luke's pensive frown and chose the safest conclusion. "The meeting didn't go well?"

"They never do, and it's my fault because I hate to beg for money. Unfortunately, I've no other choice when we need the donations and grant dollars so badly."

"True, but it must have been a tough day. You look as though you could use a nice evening. Maybe you know someone who'd care to join you for dinner?"

Luke's preoccupied frown deepened to a threatening scowl. "My personal life is off-limits. Back off."

Undeterred, Pamela tidied up her desk as she offered another unsolicited opinion. "You didn't think Catherine would be here today, did you?"

"Frankly, no, I didn't."

"Well, she was here, and she seemed real disappointed when you weren't."

"That's wild speculation on your part. If you don't have anything more important to do than obsess over my social life, go on home."

Pam picked up Sam's card. "I'll just enter this email for you, and then I'll be on my way, but it doesn't take a degree in psychology to know a woman who'd pass out her late husband's business card needs to be shown some tender concern."

"Are you saying I'm too great an oaf to recognize such an obvious fact? Do you think I drag women off by their hair?"

"No, of course not," Pam responded with an amused giggle. "Although it would be something to see. I'm just urging you to be careful. Catherine's a treasure, and the timing might be wrong for both of you, but don't let her slip away."

"That's it. You're fired. Clean out your desk."

"Yes, boss," she replied agreeably, but they both knew she would be there tomorrow morning. She made a mental note to bring him some coffee and a danish in hopes it would keep him from being grumpy two days in a row.

Catherine found an invitation to have dinner at Joyce's house on her answering machine, and she was delighted to accept. Joyce had furnished her stark modern home with an abundance of leather and chrome. Catherine admired the simplicity of the striking decor, but she much preferred her own far more colorful and comfortably appealing furnishings.

"Thanks for coming over." Joyce fussed with the single blue-violet hydrangea bloom she'd chosen for a glass beaker as a centerpiece. "How's the salmon?"

"Delicious, but what's the occasion?"

"It's nothing special. I'm just trying to keep my feet firmly planted on the ground, and cooking does it for me. I could also use some advice."

Catherine felt confident it would be related to Shane Shephard, and between bites of salad, she nodded to encourage her friend.

"I had the best time with Shane Sunday night. He came to get me in a Porsche. It's from the sixties, but I've forgotten just which year. He restored it himself. It's a pumpkin color and so pretty it looks new. He took me to a nice steak house, but I can't even tell you where it was or what I ate. Isn't that awful?"

"No, it simply sounds as though Shane is an extremely charming man."

"Yes, he is, and he told such amusing stories that my sides ached by the time he brought me home. I had absolutely no idea that growing up in Oxnard would provide such a wealth of ridiculous situations, but he appears to see everything in a humorous light.

"I invited him to come in, but he said he had to get up early Monday morning for a big job. He kissed me again, and my God, does he know how to kiss, but I sure didn't want him to leave."

Joyce paused for a quick sip of Chablis. "Then he told me if I really intended to incorporate plants in my interior design work, I ought to come up to Oxnard and tour his nursery."

"Why not? Did he give you a specific time?"

"No, and that's what worries me. I'm trying to believe that he'll call, but get this, he said he wants me to meet his mother."

"Don't you regard that as a good sign?"

"I suppose it could be construed as such, but I'm sure she won't like me. The problem is, if I refuse to visit the nursery, then Shane will think I don't like him. What am I going to do? I'm dead if I go, and dead if I don't. Then I keep wondering why he didn't come in Sunday night. Do you suppose he waits for his mother's approval before he sleeps with a woman?"

"That's a little bizarre, don't you think? He probably did have a job scheduled for early Monday morning and thought you deserved more than a quickie. As for his mother, he might want to show you off."

"Oh yeah." Joyce rolled her eyes. "She'll surely notice I'm on the wrong side of thirty and convince Shane he can do a whole lot better."

"Do you really believe that?" Catherine inquired softly.

Joyce raised her napkin to brush away the threat of tears. "Shane looks like a model. He owns his own successful business. He can tear apart a car and put it back together again. How many men do you know who can build anything, even a birdhouse, anymore? He doesn't need an older woman."

"Please, you're not his grandmother's age. Besides, I don't really believe we can choose whom to love. But rather than rush things, try and take them one step at a time. When Shane calls, make plans to visit the nursery. Take a notebook and write down the names of the plants as though you had a place to put them next week. Then find one, of course.

"As for Shane's mother, she may be delighted you have a career which dovetails so neatly with her son's. You also have a natural style I doubt they see much in Oxnard, and she might be impressed with your artistic flare. At least give her the benefit of the doubt. If she's nasty, then you wouldn't want her for a mother-in-law anyway."

"That's where you're wrong. I could tolerate some pretty awful in-laws to have Shane," Joyce mused wistfully.

"Relax and get to know him, Joyce. Give it at least a year before you start making wedding plans."

Joyce appeared crushed by that prospect. "If I wait a year, I'll be thirty-eight before we could marry. That means I probably wouldn't have a baby before I was thirty-nine. I'd be forty or forty-one before I could have a second child."

Joyce slumped back in her chair. "The years are just flying by, and what do I have to show for them? Nothing at all."

"All that self-pity is beginning to annoy me," Catherine warned. "You have a beautiful home. You're a wonderful cook, a great friend, and a damn good interior designer. Now stop worrying about Shane, hurry up and eat something, and then I'll help you with the dishes."

Joyce sighed sadly. "You're right, of course. That's why I invited you over. Whatever happens will happen whether or not I cry myself to sleep, won't it?"

"It sure will," Catherine confirmed.

Joyce paused with her fork poised over her salmon. "So how are things with you and Luke?"

Catherine scarcely knew where to begin. "We butt heads so often that I'm reminded of the bumper cars they used to have at amusement parks."

"I remember those," Joyce cried. "In fact, I once dated a man who had one he'd bought from the Newport Beach Fun Zone. It made a nifty little couch in his bedroom."

"I'll just bet it did."

"At least he didn't live with his mother."

"And Shane does?"

"I don't know, but it wouldn't surprise me."

167

"Will you please stop looking for trouble?" With a concerted effort, Catherine kept their conversation light for the remainder of the meal. Then as she left Joyce's, she saw Luke's car parked in front of her house and hoped she could take her own advice. But it was a challenge to remain calmly optimistic rather than desperately eager for love.

Luke had been sitting on the porch steps and leapt to his feet as Catherine came up the walk. He brushed off the seat of his pants and raked a hand through his hair before greeting her. "I swear I'm not stalking you."

"That's a relief. How long did you plan to wait?"

He shrugged. "As long as it took."

She slipped by him to unlock her door. "Come on in. What's happened, has another lowlife been murdered?"

"I don't know, maybe. We can always hope."

Catherine left her keys on the table beside the door and held up a plastic storage bag filled with cookies. "I had dinner with my Neighborhood Watch buddy, and she makes great cookies. Would you like some?"

"Do you have any milk? I haven't had milk and cookies in years."

She wished all his requests were so easy to fill. "Sure, I have milk."

Luke sat at the breakfast table while she turned on the fire under the teakettle and poured his milk into a glass. She got out a plate for the cookies and brought them to the table with the milk and napkins.

"Thanks," Luke said. "I just came by to say that I was wrong, yet again. I do have a heart, but it's shriveled to the size of a raisin."

She sank into a chair, slid her hand over his and gave his fingers an affectionate squeeze. "From what I've heard, milk and cookies are the recommended treatment for shriveled heart syndrome."

He laughed in spite of himself. "I'm trying to be serious, Catherine."

"So am I, but not too serious, and it's far easier to relax here than at Lost Angel."

"Yes, it sure is." He grabbed a cookie with his free hand and took a bite. "Say, these are good."

"Joyce swears she just uses the recipe on the bag of Nestle Toll House Morsels, but somehow her cookies are always especially good."

"That's a gift, isn't it?"

"I suppose. She's frantic a certain man's mother won't like her, and it just occurred to me that you haven't mentioned your parents other than to say they insisted upon a wedding. Are they still living?"

He swallowed a gulp of milk before replying. "I'll say. They're in their mid-sixties and still have more energy than most people half their age. My father's a geologist, and he and my mother travel a good part of the year. Their home is in Tucson now, where he does some work for the University. Arizona is a great place to study rock formations."

"If you're into that kind of thing," Catherine amended.

"Right, and I wasn't. Not that I didn't love dinosaurs as much as any other boy, but people were always more interesting to me than fossils. So I became a psychologist and swiftly learned the more I studied, the less I knew. I'll try to find time to look up some statistics on serial killers, though, so we'll be ready for Garcia and Salzman the next time they show up at our door."

At the teakettle's whistle, she got up to make her tea and brought it to the table. "If it weren't for Lost Angel, we wouldn't have met, but I'm afraid the tensions there will make everything doubly difficult for us."

He reached for another cookie. "That's just modern life. It's complicated everywhere."

"Please don't be flippant."

"I wasn't," he denied. "It's the truth."

"I've heard truth described as a matter of opinion."

"Well, in many cases it is," he agreed with a deep chuckle. "You're a dangerous woman, Catherine Brooks. You have an eye for the heart of any matter, and I'll bet that makes most people damn uncomfortable."

"Yes, frequently with disastrous results, but life is too short for evasion and pretense."

His expression darkened, and he sat back to regard her with an accusing gaze. "I explained why I don't want the kids to know we're seeing each other."

She was surprised by his curt rebuke. "I wasn't referring to you."

"I think you probably were, so I better get out while the getting is still good."

Before he could stand, Catherine reached out to coil her fingers around his arm, and his skin held an inviting warmth. "Wait. I wish you'd stay."

"Why, do you have some old *National Geographics* you need to sort?"

She was glad she hadn't just taken a sip of tea, because she would have blown it all over him. "What a goofy idea, but that's what I like best about you."

He rose and pulled her from her chair. "You think goofy is appealing?"

"Not in anyone else, but you can be so delightfully playful at times that I wonder if that isn't the real you."

"You want to see the real me?"

A daring gleam had entered his eye and when Catherine nodded, he grabbed hold of her waist and, with a seemingly effortless lift, set her atop the nearby counter. She was wearing a skirt, and between deep kisses, he peeled off her panties and ran his fingertips up her thighs to trace teasing circles along her cleft.

She was amazed he could move with such astonishing speed from a wary skepticism to a heated hunger, but she welcomed his affection gladly. She was already wet and spread her legs wide to encourage him to delve deeper. She reached for his belt and quickly unfastened it and his zipper. She slid her hand over his erection, fondling, enticing, guiding him, until he drew back to yank on a condom. For one dreadful instant, she feared the counter was too high for what he intended, but then he moved back between her legs and, with an easy jab, slid right into her.

With his next lunge, he stretched her depths, and she rocked forward to lock her legs around his hips and created a perfect fit. When he quickened his thrusts, she gasped way back in her throat in a low, keening purr. She ran her hands through his hair to gather him close and clung to his shoulders. Awash in desire, she rode him, bucked with him, and finally joined him in an explosion of pleasure that tumbled them both crazily to the floor.

When she could again draw a deep breath, she rose up slightly and was astonished to find her whole kitchen wasn't in complete disarray, but except for a pair of tangled lovers, nothing was out of place. The width of Luke's smile convinced her he was feeling no pain, and she leaned over to whisper in his ear.

"Will you still have time to sort *National Geographics*?" she asked.

The provocative question was so surprising, he laughed until tears rolled down his cheeks, and in an instant, Catherine fell in love. She enjoyed prompting his laughter almost as much as sating his passion. He didn't laugh nearly enough, and she vowed to remedy that sad situation as often as humanly possible.

Eventually they were able to pull their clothes back into place and feed the cat. They climbed the stairs and found her bed far more comfortable than the kitchen counter, but as Catherine fell asleep in Luke's arms, his unrestrained laughter still echoed in her heart.

Luke was away from Lost Angel for much of Thursday and again missed seeing Catherine, but he was there bright and early Friday morning ready to help her and Dave judge the mural contest. Too curious to remain in the office, Pamela walked over to the hall with him.

"What is it you're looking for in the winner?" she asked.

"Damned if I know, but I imagine we'll recognize it when we see it," Luke answered. He had the sinking suspicion he and Catherine would never agree on the winner, but because they still hadn't chosen a site, he refused to be overly concerned.

Dave had on a colorful Aerosmith T-shirt that day, and he'd already pinned up most of the drawings on the long bulletin board reserved for flyers. "I'm particularly fond of Tina's trash cans and cat," he remarked. "Let me know when you find one to your liking."

Luke spotted Catherine talking with Nick, but he cautiously remained beside Dave while Pam began perusing the drawings. "I hadn't thought we'd get so many entries."

"Neither did I," Dave responded, "but interest just sort of mushroomed during the week. Looks to me like we have enough ideas here for a dozen murals. Have you made up your mind about Toby's place yet?"

"No, but I'm praying something more suitable will occur to me in the next few minutes." He jumped when Catherine brushed against his side.

"I'm sorry, I didn't mean to startle you," she apologized. "What do you say to having the kids sit down while we study the entries? If we start at opposite ends, and Dave begins in the middle, we won't constantly be in each other's way."

"Good plan," Luke said, and he strode off toward the kitchen end of the bulletin board to wait while Dave pinned up the last few drawings. "Do you want to help judge, Pam?"

The secretary backed away. "No, thanks, now that I've seen everything, I don't believe I could choose. I better just get back to the office. Good luck, kids."

Dave turned to Catherine and dropped his voice. "I don't think Luke is much interested in this, so it'll be up to us to pick the winner. I sure hope we agree."

Catherine noticed Rafael standing with Tina, and he still had a long roll of paper in his hand. "Do you want to put your entry up on the board?" she called to him.

"No, I don't want to spoil it for everyone else. I'll wait until you've seen the others," he replied.

Catherine didn't care for his confident smirk but nodded and walked down to the far end of the bulletin board where she stole a quick glance at Luke. He was looking her way with an equally appreciative expression, and certain the whole room must know they were lovers, she hurriedly focused her attention on the artwork.

Because she'd observed the drawings as they had progressed during the week, there were no real surprises. Several of the kids had complained they just couldn't get what was in their imagination down on paper, but she'd encouraged them to keep trying. Now, looking at their completed drawings, she was delighted that even the most frustrated of the teenagers had wanted to display their work.

She was also impressed by the incredible variety to the angels posted along the wall. Some possessed a whimsical charm, while others, like Tina Stassy's, were drawn in a darker, more impressionist style. "I'd like to choose them all," she whispered as her path crossed Dave's.

"We could make a collage," Dave replied.

Catherine rather liked that idea, but she stood for a long moment in front of Tina's design. The drawing itself wasn't as polished as some, but the idea of a homeless angel and cat scrounging through trash was infinitely appealing.

"What do you think?" she asked Luke as he stepped around her.

"I think we might choose several of the designs and have a set of greeting cards made. The volunteers would all buy them, and it might be a good publicity tool."

"That's a wonderful idea," Catherine exclaimed. "It'll be so much easier to select several winners rather than one."

"Are you finished yet?" Rafael called to them. "I don't want an unfair advantage, but if you've seen all the other drawings, then you ought to take a look at mine."

"Come on down," Luke instructed with a wave. "We're dying to see your work."

When Rafael chose the center of the board, Catherine had to step back out of his way. She couldn't help but fear he might have drawn a tasteless orgy rather than an angelic scene, but when he unrolled his artwork, she was absolutely stunned.

His angels were drawn in exquisite detail, and not only did he possess an impressive knowledge of anatomy, he'd also dressed his heavenly creatures in pastel robes whose hems were ruffled by a graceful breeze. Alone, in pairs, and groups of threes, the angels were climbing up the front of a Victorian house easily recognizable as Toby McClure's. Not merely a hazy background, the historic structure was rendered with a draftsman's skill.

That would have been enough to win the contest right there, but Rafael had also given each angel the beautifully expressive face of one of his friends.

The drawing brought tears to Catherine's eyes, but Dave had an entirely different reaction. "I think we ought to get Toby over here right now," he stressed to Luke.

The teenagers had responded with hushed amazement, but Luke just shrugged. "Go on and call Toby. I'd value his opinion, but I don't for a minute believe this is your work, Rafael."

Dumbfounded, Catherine shook her head in disbelief. On more than one occasion, Luke had shocked her by going off on an absurd tangent, but this was simply too much. "Then whose work is it?" she asked.

"I have no idea," Luke replied, "but did you see Rafael draw even a corner of this?"

"No, I haven't seen him all week," Catherine admitted, "but that doesn't mean the drawing isn't his."

"I don't believe it," Rafael swore. "You didn't accuse anyone else of stealing someone else's work, but you don't believe I'm capable of turning out anything good?"

Catherine was as disgusted as Rafael. "Look at the angels' faces," she implored. Stepping close, she recognized Violet's shyly averted gaze in an angel scaling the porch roof. "This was obviously drawn by someone who knew the kids who come here. Why do you doubt it was Rafael?"

"It might just be a hunch, but I do," Luke stated calmly. "Here's Toby, he's a professional artist. Let's see what he has to say."

Catherine turned toward the door, but in jeans and a black long-sleeved turtleneck jersey, none of the flamboyant artist's tattoos was visible. He had pulled his long curls back into a ponytail and looked quite respectable. Then he winked at her, and she knew, regardless of his more conservative attire, he was the same sly flirt she'd met.

Toby scanned the long bulletin board, then paused to study Rafael's drawing and let out a long, low whistle. "Who did this?" he asked.

"I did," Rafael almost shouted. "I'm Rafael Reynoso."

Toby glanced over his shoulder. "Toby McClure. Where have you studied?"

Rafael appeared flustered by the question. "Nowhere. I just like to draw."

Toby caught Luke's eye. "Dave said you needed an artist's opinion, but any man off the street would recognize this much talent. If you want a scholarship to Art Center, kid, we could probably get you one by this afternoon. Do you have a portfolio?"

"What's that?" Rafael asked.

"Some nice samples of your work," Toby explained.

Rafael fell back on attitude. "Hell, I don't have anything saved. I just draw on scraps and throw them away."

Toby winced, then looked back at the magnificent drawing. "My house is the perfect background, and I'd like to see you get started on the mural just as soon as you can. When you're through here this morning, Rafael, come on over to my place, and I'll help you get some sketches together for a portfolio."

"Wait a minute," Luke cautioned. "The drawing's good, I'll grant you that, but you haven't proved who did it. I'd like to see you draw something right here, Rafael."

Tina Stassy had worked her way to the front of the crowd. She had a firm hold on Charlie so he wouldn't bolt if he became frightened. "Go on, Rafael, I've seen you draw. Show Luke how it's done."

After returning with Toby, Dave had hung back out of way, but now he began to laugh and was his usual helpful self. "We still have plenty of paper and pencils."

Rafael's chin was tucked close to his chest as he addressed Luke. "What is it you want me to draw?"

"Why not a sketch of Mrs. Brooks?" Luke suggested. "She'd make an interesting subject."

Catherine didn't dare look at Luke when she was so angry with him, but she was too eager to help Rafael to refuse his surprising request. She swept her hair around her ear and moved toward the closest chair. "Will this be all right?" she asked.

"Wherever," Rafael grumbled. He took the paper and pencils Dave offered and sat opposite her. When the kids began to press close, he waved them off. "Give me some room or I'll suffocate."

Once his request was honored, Rafael stared at Catherine a long moment and then gestured for her to tip her head slightly. "Yeah, that's it."

Catherine held still, but she was acutely aware of the kids' comments all around her. Some really did admire Rafael's artistic ability, while others complained their drawings were just as good as his. Adding to her discomfort, she could feel Luke watching her, but fortunately, Rafael worked quickly, made a show of signing his drawing and then rose to hand it to Luke.

It was a simple pencil sketch with a minimum of shading, but Rafael had captured not only the sweetness of Catherine's features, but also the subtle force of her personality. Luke compared it briefly to the climbing angels and then gave a reluctant shrug.

"I'll accept this as proof the drawing is yours, but I need to confer with the other judges before we announce a winner. Mrs. Brooks, Dave, let's talk outside."

Eager to speak with Luke where the kids couldn't overhear, Catherine followed him into the courtyard. After he'd questioned whether Rafael had actually produced the best drawing, she wondered if he might not continue to be perverse and select another entry as the winner. She glanced toward Dave, counting on him to be an ally, but he was waiting for Luke to speak rather than looking her way. She widened her stance and hoped she wouldn't have to talk until sundown to hand Rafael the honor he'd earned.

"There was a vague reference to a prize," she reminded Luke. "The winner ought to receive something more than recognition."

Luke rolled up the drawing of Catherine and held it in a loose grasp. "As I recall, Rafael made it sound as though he wouldn't pick up a pencil if there weren't a cash prize. I didn't want the kids working for the money rather than for the challenge of the mural itself."

"While that might have been a worthy goal, the drawing is a masterpiece, and Rafael deserves a prize," Catherine insisted.

"Do you suppose Toby actually believes Rafael might receive a scholarship to Art Center? Wouldn't that be enough of a prize?" Luke replied.

"No," Catherine was quick to argue. "The prize has to come from you."

"Children, please, let's play nice," Dave cautioned. "First we ought to choose the winner, then we can hand him, or her, the prize."

"I'm voting for Rafael," Catherine announced quickly. "What about you, Dave?"

Dave hunched his shoulders and looked down at his scuffed boots. "I'm mighty partial to Tina's work, or the idea of it at least, but I can see Rafael's is far more polished. The angels are almost floating up the front of the house, and it's an image that would play well on TV. That's what we need, isn't it, Luke, a mural that will draw people into Lost Angel rather than send them scurrying away?"

Luke nodded. "We'll go back in and tell everyone we came to a unanimous decision. I'll award Rafael a hundred dollar cash prize. Then I'll explain I'll have some blank greeting cards made to use as many of the other entries as we can. Will that make you happy, Mrs. Brooks?"

The question caught Catherine off guard, but she had an immediate comeback. "I didn't know that pleasing me was one of your priorities here, Dr. Starns."

"Let's just say I try not to alienate too many of our loyal volunteers," Luke replied in a perfect imitation of her barely civil tone.

"Now I still expect you to head up the mural project, Mrs. Brooks. While you're figuring out how much paint you'll need and choosing the colors, I'm going to have our attorney friends draw up a contract for Toby. I can't risk having him balk in the middle of the project, or God forbid, having him change Rafael's design to advertise his own work instead of Lost Angel's needs."

Catherine had to admit that was an excellent idea, and it proved just how thoroughly Luke had considered the mural project. That care to detail made her suspect that he'd deliberately meant to provoke Rafael. He certainly possessed a stunning aptitude for stirring up trouble, and it hadn't even occurred to her until that very moment that he wasn't merely thoughtless nor clumsy with words.

No indeed, he expressed himself with a cautious precision. That had to mean he deliberately posed provocative questions and at the precise instant when they could do the most damage. Did he actually enjoy creating discord, simply so he could take credit for minimizing the damage? she wondered.

It was a chilling thought and not one she would keep to herself Saturday night. Luke might believe he was a master at the barbed question, but she would give him a taste of his own medicine and laugh if he couldn't choke it down.

Chapter Twelve

When Luke announced that Rafael's design would be used for the mural and that he would indeed receive a cash prize, the young artist fought to maintain a studied indifference, but a boyish grin quickly overcame his sullen frown. Nick, Tina, Polly and most of the kids slapped him on the back and offered teasing congratulations, but there were a few who, obviously badly disappointed, hung back from the crowd.

Catherine hated to see any of the teens feel slighted. "Does the center have access to a digital camera?" she asked. "I'd like to photograph all the entries now for the greeting cards."

Luke nodded, then called to Dave. "Mrs. Brooks is going to have her hands full with the mural. So I'll need you to get the camera to record all the entries, load the photos into the Mac and oversee the artwork for the cards."

"Sure, I'll get on it this afternoon." Dave raised his voice slightly to make an announcement. "Make sure your names are on your drawings, then leave them where they are so that I can take photos. Each one has something we can use to promote Lost Angel's cause, and I know Mrs. Brooks will expect all of you to help paint the mural."

"I most certainly will," she promised.

"Come on back to my office," Luke murmured. "I need to give you the center credit card to pay for your supplies."

"I could hand in receipts and be reimbursed," Catherine replied.

"No, let's keep things simple for Pam and use the card."

"All right, then, I don't want to create bookkeeping problems." She followed Luke to his office, but on the way, it was all she could do not to tell him exactly what she thought of the shabby way he'd treated Rafael.

"Were you able to pick a winner?" Pam asked as they entered the office.

"Yes. Rafael turned in an incredible effort after you left," Catherine responded. "You'll have to go over and see it."

"I'll make a point of it," Pam promised before reaching to answer the telephone.

Luke drew Catherine into his office, and the instant he shoved his door closed, he grabbed her in a boisterous hug and lifted her clear off her feet.

"I may have insisted that you not argue with me over how I run the center, but we couldn't have played that scene with Rafael any better had I written a script."

He was about to dance her around the small office, but she put her hands firmly on his chest to discourage the idea. "Wait a minute, are you admitting you intended to humiliate Rafael?"

Shocked as much by her question as by her accusing tone, he released her and took a single backward step. "I wasn't out to humiliate him. Like a lot of the kids here, he gives up on things too easily and then claims he didn't care about them in the first place. I wanted to shake him up a bit to inspire him to stand up for his artwork. There was a risk he'd shrug off my challenge and walk away. But my ploy worked, and he fought to win."

That Luke could so easily justify his actions didn't surprise her, but it also failed to impress her. "You played him," she insisted, "and because I had no idea you weren't sincere, you played me as well."

His lighthearted mood burst like a soap bubble, Luke retreated behind his desk and dropped into his chair. "I didn't play anyone," he swore. "Look, my job is to help these kids become responsible citizens. Sometimes they need to be jarred out of their indifference, and I do it gladly."

Her voice was honey-smooth. "So you manipulate people for a just purpose, is that it?"

"No!" he shot back. "Is that what you think I'm doing with you?"

His threatening scowl was all too familiar, and she just shook her head. "I don't know. You have a way of asking odd questions, and now I wonder if it isn't just for effect."

He leaned back and propped his hands behind his head. "I already apologized for asking if you were seeing anyone else. It was a stupid question, and I'm sorry I let my fears get the better of me."

Intrigued, Catherine propped her hip on his desk. "What fears?"

He appeared startled to have spoken the word aloud. He sat up and yanked open his top drawer to find the credit card he'd mentioned. After a quick search, he handed it to her.

"We all have the same fears. That we'll always be alone, or God forbid, we'll be with the wrong person and wish we were.

"Had I realized Rafael was such a talented artist, I'd have warned you I was going to hassle him. As it was, I was as surprised as everyone else when he turned in such a stunning design. I saw an opportunity to make a point and seized it. If Toby doesn't take Rafael over to Art Center for a tour, then I will. These kids have such slim hopes for success, I sure as hell won't let Rafael waste his."

Up to a point, his righteous indignation was convincing, but Catherine still harbored the suspicion she'd been used. It was an uncomfortable sensation, as though she'd worked in her garden all morning and left home without rinsing off the dirt.

"Do you have any other especially effective techniques you'd care to warn me about now?" she asked.

He considered her question a long moment and then shrugged. "You saw me ban the girls for fighting. Being tough in enforcing our rules earns the kids' respect, but no one thinks I'm a mean, manipulative bastard."

She took exception to his tone. "I didn't use such derogatory terms."

"My mistake. We still on for tomorrow night?"

He was pretending to sort the papers on his desk. Catherine saw through his feigned nonchalance, but she remained hopelessly confused about his motives. He struck her as a man of principle, but how he put those principles into practice was something else entirely.

"Yes," she assured him. "Why don't you come to my house for dinner? We can go to the movies later, if you like." She pocketed the credit card as she straightened.

"I don't want you to go to a lot of work," Luke protested.

"It's not much fun cooking for one, and I'd enjoy it." Before he could argue, she crossed to the door. "How's six o'clock?"

"Fine, I'll be there."

He didn't look real pleased about it, but Catherine was still glad she'd confronted him about Rafael. Luke provided such a perplexing mixture of stubborn masculine pride and what she hoped was sincere concern that she made no effort to predict what his mood would be on Saturday night. All she could do was bake one of her favorite recipes and hope the gesture touched his heart.

Joyce had been watching for Catherine's arrival, and when she saw her Volvo pull into the driveway, she sprinted down the street and beat her to the front door. "Please, I already know I'm an idiot, but today was such a disaster that if I don't tell someone about it, I swear my head will explode."

Joyce was dressed in a baggy pair of faded jeans. The buttons on her lavender shirt were misaligned, and there was a hole in the toe of her left tennis shoe. Catherine needed only a single glance to understand something alarming must have happened to her usually impeccably dressed friend.

"Come on in," she invited. "It's still warm. Let's go on out to the deck."

Joyce followed right behind her. "I went up to Shane's nursery today, and I swear every word of this story is true, although I'm embarrassed to admit that even a minute of it happened."

Catherine carried a pitcher of iced tea out to the patio, while Joyce brought the ice-filled glasses. She sat, propped her feet on the adjacent chair, and after a long sip of tea, encouraged Joyce to continue. "Why don't you begin at the beginning?"

"Yeah, right, as if I could think straight." She held her icy glass to her cheek and struggled to compose herself.

"Shane called me last night, and when we discovered neither of us had any appointments for today, it seemed like a good day to visit Oxnard. I must have changed my clothes half a dozen times before I decided to wear my pink linen sheath. It's business-like and yet feminine."

Catherine had had a rather trying day herself, but just coming home relaxed her enough to attend to Joyce's rambling tale. "I've always liked that dress."

"Thank you, but I was going to Oxnard after all, so I wore pink flats rather than heels. I took the notebook I use on all my jobs, and thinking we'd be outdoors, I brought along a straw hat.

"Shane's directions were superb, and his nursery is just beautiful with a huge variety of plants all arranged in orderly rows. He has several employees who maintain the place and take care of walk-in customers while he handles big jobs and deliveries.

"We actually talked about plants, but there was a teasing sparkle in his eye the whole time."

"And probably one in yours as well," Catherine suggested.

"Please, I was doing my best to appear attentive and take notes, but I doubt they'll make any sense. Anyway, the morning went really well. Then Shane invited me to lunch and said on the way, we'd stop by his mother's hair salon so I could meet her."

"She owns a hair salon?"

"Well, that's what he called it, but it's a small-town beauty parlor just like the ones that always turn up in movies. Apparently it's been called the Curlicue since the fifties, and when Shane's mother bought the place ten years ago, she kept the name. It was really cute and quaint, and his mother was exactly what you'd expect: a bleached blonde with a generous bosom."

"I get the picture. Did you two hit it off?"

Joyce almost moaned. "Not really. Her name's Marion, and she was giving a sweet little old lady a perm when we came in. When she barely glanced our way, it made me think Shane must bring in a new girlfriend every other day."

"You don't know that," Catherine cautioned. "Perhaps she was preoccupied by something that had happened earlier in the day."

"Maybe, but after being so worried about meeting her, it was insulting. After that awkward minute at the Curlicue, we went on down the street to this really nice Mexican restaurant. Then things really started going downhill."

"What could go wrong at a Mexican restaurant? Was the salsa too spicy?"

"I didn't have a chance to taste it. Shane was being his usual charming self, but after a couple of sips of lemonade, I excused myself to use the restroom. We were in the central patio, and Shane pointed me toward the rear of the place. When I got to the kitchen, I thought I must have taken a wrong turn, but a waitress waved me on. There was a door just past several racks of dishes, and I thought the restrooms must be through it. Anyone would have assumed so."

Catherine could easily imagine what was coming. "They weren't?" she asked.

"No. I ended up out in the employees' parking lot and the door swung closed and locked behind me." Joyce pulled a tissue from her pocket and blew her nose.

"Well, surely someone in the kitchen must have seen you go out the wrong door."

"That's what I thought, so I waited, and not all that patiently mind you, when I really did need to use the restroom. Then I began to worry Shane might think I'd slipped out a side door and ditched him. I'd left my cell phone in my car, so I couldn't call the restaurant and tell them to let me in."

"Were you gone that long?"

"I don't know, five minutes, ten. Believe me, it was uncomfortably long, so I began to pound on the door, but kitchens are always so noisy that either no one heard me or no one cared. At least I had the straw hat so I wasn't getting sunburned, but that was a slight consolation, believe me."

"Well, you're here now, so how did you get back to Shane?"

Joyce choked on a gulp of tea and lapsed into a coughing fit. When she recovered, she looked thoroughly dejected. "I thought I'd just walk around to the front of the restaurant and go in, but there was a high fence around the parking lot and the gate was locked.

"I wish you'd been there. You're always so sensible, but here I was trapped alone in the parking lot. I had no idea what time the luncheon shift ended and people might begin to leave, but I doubted it would be before two, and Shane would have been gone long before then."

"Where was Shane while you were pounding on the kitchen door? Didn't he send a waitress to look for you in the restroom?"

Smoky wound his way around Catherine's chair and jumped into her lap. She gave her darling cat a quick snuggle but kept a concerned glance on her friend.

Joyce waved off the question. "I'll get to that later. Anyway, there was a small mountain of broken chairs piled against the fence beside the Dumpster, and with no other choice, I hiked up my dress, and climbed up. I thought I'd just climb over the fence, but once I was clinging to the other side, I realized I was a lot farther off the ground than I'd anticipated."

"You scaled the fence in your pretty pink sheath?" That preposterous sight was easy enough to visualize, but Catherine still couldn't believe Joyce had actually done it.

"By that time, my dress was the least of my worries, but things just continued to get worse."

"How? Did you fall?"

"Right on my ass, which was not only painful but humiliating. But at least I was out in the alley where I could walk to the end of the block and get back in the restaurant. Only by that time, I was such a mess I didn't think I could face Shane. I was trying not to cry and look even more pathetic when I slipped on an oil slick, fell again, and skinned both my knees."

"Oh, Joyce, how awful."

"You are so wonderfully sympathetic. That's why I knew I could tell you what happened. There was a construction project midway down the alley, and by that time there was no way I was going to leap a ditch, so I had to go back and walk the long way around the block. The Curlicue was on that corner, so I went in, and asked Marion to call Shane to come and get me, if he were still at the restaurant, that is."

Catherine knew without being told that the Curlicue's patrons must have all been gaping bug-eyed at Joyce. "Well, I certainly hope that Marion was helpful."

"Oh, she was. She showed me right to her restroom and went to call Shane. By the time I got myself pulled together enough to face him, he was there. He and his mother didn't see me standing at the back of the shop, but I heard Marion laughing about how stupid I was not to ring the bell by the service entrance.

"Now I swear to you, there was no bell to ring, but that's really beside the point. I'd arrived a disheveled mess, and she was laughing at me. When Shane began to chuckle right along with her, I'd had it with him."

"Was he still at the restaurant?"

"Oh yes, he'd thought I hadn't liked Oxnard and had just gone home. So he canceled my order and was enjoying his when he got the call from his mother. It hadn't even occurred to him I might have become ill and he ought to send a waitress to check on me. He had just assumed I'd left without telling him good-bye. Although I've no idea how he thought I'd get home when my car was parked at his nursery."

Catherine knew how much Joyce had liked Shane, and she was shocked his affection for her hadn't been deeper. "That was a strange way for him to behave."

"That' s exactly what I told him, but I put it in a lot more colorful terms, which I won't repeat, but they won't soon forget me at the Curlicue."

Catherine had heard Joyce fume about suppliers and clients often enough to understand the petite blonde had thrown in every curse word she knew. She thought of the dear little old lady getting the perm and winced. "Oh no."

"Oh yes, but I don't care. Shane apologized the whole way back to the nursery, but it was too late. If he'd rather eat lunch than investigate what might have happened to me, then he wasn't the man I'd thought him to be."

Catherine felt sick with disappointment for her friend. "But you really liked him."

"No, I liked what I imagined him to be. It turned out they were two entirely different men."

"What are you going to do?"

Joyce blew her nose again. "Swear off men, I suppose. I'm so damn sick of being betrayed in one awful way after another that I'm tempted to just give up hope of ever finding a soul mate."

"That's understandable, but Shane must also feel terrible about this. I'll bet he'll send you flowers tomorrow and beg your forgiveness."

"He owns a nursery," Joyce sneered. "So he'd send a potted plant with the care instructions attached."

"Wallowing in pity won't help," Catherine scolded. "Come on, let's make some grilled cheese sandwiches with lots of butter." It was therapy Joyce had insisted upon after Sam had died. Catherine hoped it would help Joyce to cope now.

"Why not?" Joyce replied. "I was too nervous to eat breakfast, missed out on lunch, and I'm too tired to cook anything for myself."

Catherine deposited Smoky on the ground and gave Joyce a hug to start her toward the backdoor, but for her friend's sake, she sure hoped Shane found a way to redeem himself over the weekend.

Saturday night, Luke brought a phalaenopsis with lovely white butterfly blossoms to Catherine's house. "I'm hoping an orchid won't bring on more tears," he quipped.

Catherine greeted him with a quick kiss and accepted the pretty plant with unabashed delight. "They won't, and this one is gorgeous. Thank you so much, but you needn't bring me presents."

"I wanted to," he assured her. "Whatever you're cooking smells delicious."

"So do you," she replied in a throaty whisper. She found it so easy to tease him outside Lost Angel. She was sorry they had to spend so much time there.

"Come on in the kitchen and help me finish the salad." She placed the orchid on the coffee table and led the way. "Would you like a drink?"

"No, I'm fine."

"All right, then, will you peel the carrots for the salad while I grate the mozzarella to top the chicken?"

"I'll be right happy to, ma'am. You know how much I like to cook." He stepped up to the sink, grabbed the peeler, a carrot, and got busy.

Quickly assured he was happy about taking on the chore, Catherine worked beside the stove to grate the fist-size hunk of mozzarella. "How was your day?" she asked.

"Busy. I'd let my usual weekend errands pile up, but at least it was a nice day to be out. How about you?"

"I gardened a bit and had lunch with a friend who's nursing a broken heart. I realize you're not Dr. Phil, but would you mind terribly if I asked you a relationship question?"

"For your brokenhearted friend?" he asked in a decidedly skeptical tone.

She took a quick step to give his shoulder a playful shove. "Yes. I wouldn't ask you for advice and then use it against you!"

He laughed at her promise, but he still appeared unconvinced. "Go ahead, but you already know I lack Phil McGraw's charm."

"You have plenty of your own, Dr. Starns. Besides, what I'm really after is some insight, a man's perspective, on a difficult situation."

"Well, at least I qualify in that regard," he replied with another burst of hearty laughter.

She savored the magical sound to the last resonant note. Sam had filled the house with such joyous noise, and it was far too quiet now. "Fine. Let's say you and I are in that wonderful restaurant in China Town. If I went to the restroom and didn't return within a reasonable amount of time, what would you do?"

He grabbed another carrot. "Knowing just how long women can spend in restrooms, I'd wait awhile longer. Then I'd go and check the bar to make certain you hadn't run into an old boyfriend or someone else you liked better than me and forgotten that I exist."

"And if I weren't in the bar?" she coaxed.

"I'd ask our waitress to check the women's room to make certain you weren't ill."

"And if I weren't there?"

Luke glanced over his shoulder. "Is this some kind of test?"

"No, I'd just like to know how an intelligent man might behave if his date disappeared."

"Right. Okay, if the waitress couldn't find you, I'd speak to the manager and ask him to conduct a discreet search. Should I consider the possibility of an alien abduction?"

"Aren't people usually alone when that happens rather than in a popular restaurant?"

"Yes, I believe so, but it still might be too soon to rule it out." He began slicing the peeled carrots into neat chunks as he continued. "Let's say the manager searched the kitchen, pantry, employee bathrooms, under all the tables, and still didn't find you. Then I'd suspect foul play and call the police."

"Really?" She donned a pair of oven mitts and opened the oven to remove a baking dish filled with chicken breasts in a bubbling tomato and onion sauce. She sprinkled the grated cheese on top, returned the dish to the oven, and yanked off the mitts. She set the timer for five minutes.

"Wouldn't it cross your mind I might have simply walked out on you?"

"No way. I know you, Catherine. You're not the type to ditch a date. Even if I were the world's biggest loser, you'd spare my feelings and concoct some believable excuse to return home early."

He tossed the carrots into the salad bowl heaped with mixed greens, then grabbed a paper towel to dry his hands, and turned to face her. "Why don't you just tell me what happened to your friend?"

"You understand this conversation goes no further?"

"Of course, if you should ever introduce us, I'll feign complete ignorance of her romantic history."

"Thank you. While we might not always agree, I trust you to keep your word."

"That's very generous of you, but quit stalling. Tell me about your friend."

Despite his encouragement, Catherine doubted she could make him appreciate Joyce's awful sense of betrayal. She needed a moment to gather her thoughts and then provided a condensed but highly dramatic version of her friend's lunchtime ordeal.

He leaned back against the counter, listened attentively, and shook his head. "And her date just went ahead and ate lunch?"

The timer sounded and she again pulled on the mitts to remove the baked chicken from the oven. "Yes, although I don't understand how he could have swallowed a bite."

Once she'd closed the oven, Luke stepped up behind her. "And then he laughed about what had happened?"

"Along with his mother," she stressed.

"So he's an insensitive jerk," he announced.

"Is that a question or a professional opinion?" She removed the lid from the pot of rice on the back of the stove and stirred it with a long-handled spoon.

He moved even closer to nuzzle the tender hollow behind her left ear. "This is why I don't do couple's therapy," he whispered, "But I'll give it my best shot. The guy made a major blunder, but maybe he's been ditched a lot and just couldn't deal with it. It's possible he's well-known at that restaurant was just trying to save face when his date disappeared."

Catherine leaned against him. "Are you taking his side?"

"Absolutely not. His actions were unforgivable, but sometimes guys screw up."

"That's precisely what my friend told him, but in more emphatic terms."

"I'll bet. What does she want to do now, rehabilitate him, or continue her search for Mr. Perfect?"

"She feels betrayed and is too hurt to think. There's a great line from a Phish song: every betrayal begins with trust."

"She'd naturally feel betrayed, but what does she intend to do about it?"

"Other than cry?" His kiss tickled her ear, and she couldn't suppress a giggle.

He slid his arms around her waist. "A lot of women don't realize that even good-looking young men might not date that often. Most days they work long hours, order a pizza and fall into bed, or they hang out with their friends, have a few beers and shoot pool.

"Then along comes a woman they just have to pursue. Unfortunately, they don't go about it very well. They make some colossal gaff, the woman won't speak to them again, and they're right back to the pizza and pool. Until another irresistible young woman appears, only they haven't learned a damn thing about themselves or women, and they make the same pitiful mistake again. If they're lucky, eventually a smart woman will gently nudge them in the right direction."

They were having a serious discussion, but with him pressed so close to her back, she found it difficult to think at all. Being sandwiched between his seductive heat and that of the stove was almost more than she could bear.

"You make it sound so simple." She sighed.

189

"Nothing is ever simple. Didn't Sam ever do anything to disappoint you?"

"Other than to die, you mean?"

Luke released her instantly. "God, I'm sorry. I wasn't trying to provide a demonstration of how stupid men can be. But I shouldn't have asked that."

She was more appalled by her own flippant response than by his question. When she turned toward him, he looked so angry with himself that she raised her hands to frame his face and kissed him soundly. She wasn't certain when it had happened, but she could talk about Sam now without dissolving in tears. That it might be due in part to the healing nature of Luke's affection wasn't lost on her.

"I don't compare the two of you," she stressed. "But we can't pretend I wasn't married to Sam, or that Marsha wasn't your wife. But those days are over. You may ask me about Sam whenever you like, but frankly, I don't give a damn about whatever Marsha might or might not have done."

Luke still looked mortified. "I am sorry, though. It was a thoughtless question."

"No, it was a logical one. Upon occasion, Sam and I did argue. I recall throwing a bright red shoe at him once, but I always knew he'd be there for me if I needed him. That's why Joyce is so upset. Shane didn't merely disappoint her. He abandoned her when she needed him."

"So he's toast," he offered.

"Looks like it, but I'm hoping Joyce means so much to him that he'll fill her house with roses and convince her to forgive him."

He'd relaxed enough to lean back against the counter, but he pulled her along with him. "I was in junior high when I learned not to meddle in my friends' romantic adventures. It always backfires."

"Was asking you for advice meddling?"

"It could be considered borderline, Mrs. Brooks, so be careful."

She slipped from his grasp and moved back to the stove. "I will. Come on, let's talk about something else while we eat. I know a little about you, but tonight I want you to tell me about an embarrassing incident, or even a scandalous one, if you like.

It could even be something stupid you did as a child and lived to tell about."

A slow smile tugged at the corner of Luke's mouth. "I wouldn't want to shock you and ruin your dinner when you've gone to so much trouble preparing it."

"Yes, do, please," she begged. "What's the most shocking thing you've ever done?"

"There's only one thing that comes to mind, and you'll have to wait until after dinner for me to show you."

She waved the rice spoon at him. "Oh, no, I already know what a wild man you are in bed. You'll have to use something else."

"I wasn't talking about sex," he promised.

His sly grin was so charming, she gave in. "All right, that means I'll have to go first, but I'll warn you right now not to laugh."

"I wouldn't dream of it," he promised, but his smile was too wide to be convincing.

With his help, she served their dinner outside on the patio table, and she gratefully acknowledged each of his compliments. "It's a very simple recipe, and one that always tastes as though I spent days preparing it."

"Well, whatever you do, this is the best chicken I've ever tasted." He scooped up another mouthful with rice and closed his eyes to enjoy it fully before he swallowed. "If you've taken the edge off your hunger," he then suggested, "go ahead and tell me something you wouldn't list on your resume."

She finished a bite of salad first. "It's funny you mentioned junior high, because it brought back the memory of one of the worst days of my life. Now you might describe this as a trivial incident, but it left me scarred."

"I assume these are metaphorical scars?" Luke asked.

"Definitely. Now, I've been this tall since the summer after seventh grade, and the boys I'd always thought were cute were suddenly no taller than my shoulder. I felt as clumsy as a newborn giraffe. I even began to collect little giraffe figurines."

He took another slice of garlic bread from the wicker basket. "I can't even imagine your being clumsy. You move like a dancer."

191

"That's my mother's influence. She insisted tall girls needed ballet lessons, and I actually enjoyed them. But junior high isn't really about the facts of the situation, is it? It's about how it feels."

"That's not only junior high, but you're right, feelings are much more intense then, and even the slightest hurt can be excruciatingly painful."

With a sudden appalling clarity, Catherine realized that by talking about an unhappy school experience, she might have unwittingly reminded him of his daughter's anguish. She wished she hadn't begun the story now, but it was too late to switch topics. All she could do was rush through it and hope for the best, but she made a mental note not to stray into such dangerous territory ever again.

"Somehow I managed to survive until graduation. It was held in the afternoon of a scorchingly hot day. The band played. A couple of students delivered earnest speeches about the future, and then the principal spoke and began to hand out diplomas.

"When it came my turn to receive mine, I walked across the outdoor stage and shook the principal's hand. But when I reached the steps to return to my seat, I tripped and fell."

"Oh no!" Luke cried. "I've never seen that happen. Were you hurt?"

"Not physically, but whatever poise I'd managed to affect was completely shattered. The P.E. teacher was standing at the bottom of the steps, and he picked me up and set me on my feet before the boy following me in line started down the stairs. The whole incident took no more than a split second.

"I was too horrified to get back in line, though, and hid behind the potted plants at the edge of the stage. There was a dance afterward, but I told my parents the heat had given me a horrible headache and didn't go. They'd taken a picture of me as I received my diploma, and they were looking down at the camera when I fell, so they had no idea what had happened.

"I spent the whole summer in absolute dread that come September, I'd be known as the girl who'd gone bumping down the stairs like Winnie-the-Pooh."

"And in September?" he prompted.

"The first day, I wore my hair in this wild punk ponytail hoping no one would recognize me, but of course, everyone did and they all told me that my hair looked really weird. I kept waiting for someone to yell they'd seen my underpants when I'd fallen down the stairs, but thank God, no one did.

"After a few days, it finally occurred to me that everyone had been watching the student receiving his diploma rather than me. So I'd wasted a perfectly good summer agonizing over what others thought of me when I hadn't even entered their heads. That was a valuable lesson, but I sure wish it hadn't been so painful to learn."

"Yeah, I know exactly what you mean," he replied. "But falling at a graduation ceremony would upset anyone. After all, there you were, proud of your accomplishments, and wham, you landed in the dust."

She was grateful he'd remarked on the incident rather than become maudlin over teenage angst. "I'm sorry, that story wasn't all that entertaining, was it?"

"I thought the idea was to share something new. Anyone who meets you now would never guess you were once painfully shy. I'm afraid my transformation may have gone in the opposite direction, but you'll have to wait a while longer to see what I mean."

He winked at her, and she sighed with relief. She could taste the remorse he'd felt when he'd asked about Sam, and it tied her stomach in knots. Unable to eat, she rearranged the food on her plate into scattered lumps. She smiled often to distract him, and even after he'd eaten a second helping, he didn't realize her appetite had failed to match his.

"The next time I speak with Joyce, I promise not to mention your name," she confided, "but I did appreciate your insights. Shane became the head of his family in his teens, and I'll bet he hasn't dated much. He wouldn't have intentionally abandoned Joyce, and I'll encourage her to give him a second chance."

"As long as you merely plant the idea, it's not really meddling now, is it?"

She knew he had her there. "No, it is, but it's for a good cause."

"Now where have I heard that one before?" he teased. "But if Joyce and Shane don't get back together, do you think she'd like Toby McClure?"

"My God, what a thought," Catherine exclaimed, but after a moment, she nodded. "An artist and an interior designer would have a great deal in common. But I've no idea what she thinks of tattoos."

"She might like Toby's as much as you do."

She wasn't taken in by his teasing grin. "You're stalling, but I don't distract that easily. It's time for your shocking confession."

"Hey, I just ate. You'll have to let me sit out here under the stars for a while or I won't do it justice."

"You are a terrible tease, Dr. Starns."

"I know, but thank God, you have a forgiving nature."

"I've obviously conditioned you to believe that's true, but it can change," she warned.

She sat back and listened to the crickets' insistent chirping, but it took a long while to relax. She felt as though she'd danced through a veritable minefield with her stupid story about junior high. She might have gotten away with it, but her remorse had yet to completely fade.

"How long do you suppose it takes to really get to know someone?" she asked.

"It depends on the person. After five minutes you know all you'll ever want to know about some people, but with others, a lifetime might not be long enough."

"Hmm," she murmured agreeably, but she wisely didn't comment on how tragically brief some lifetimes were.

Chapter Thirteen

The evening had grown cool before Luke rose to his feet and, with an easy lift, helped Catherine to hers. "I could sit out here all night with you, but I ought to get on with my part of the evening while I still have the courage to go through with it."

"No matter what it is, I swear I won't laugh," she vowed as she began to clear the table.

"Here, let me take the dishes," he insisted, and he carried them into the house while she held the door. "We can load these into the dishwasher later after dessert." He washed his hands, then laced his fingers in Catherine's and led her into the living room.

"First, I'll need some music." The entertainment center held a CD player and an ample collection of CDs, as well as the radio they'd danced to and a television. He thumbed through the CDs, set a couple aside as possibilities, and then chose the Blues Brothers. "*Soul Man* will do."

"It'll do for what?" She sat on the end of the sofa, slipped off her sandals and pulled her feet up under her cinnamon-colored gauze skirt. The neckline of the matching peasant blouse slid down over one shoulder with a charming nonchalance.

Luke paced as he replied. "This is the most shocking revelation I can come up with on such short notice, and I'll admit it was a brief stint, but for a while, I was one of the Chippendale dancers."

Catherine responded with a delighted shriek. "You weren't, not the staid Dr. Starns!"

He halted in front of her and rested his hands lightly on his hips. "I was a college kid and not in the least bit staid. It paid really well, but Marsha didn't like my being gone at night or the fact I was dancing half naked for screaming women who'd crawl all over each other to shove ten dollar bills into my satin underwear, what little there was of it."

"I know I promised not to laugh, but that's just too much." She gasped amid a burst of musical giggles.

He kicked off his loafers and began to unbutton his shirt. "Now, this isn't Chippendale's, and I don't have the pants with Velcro down the sides, or the black satin bikini briefs, so you'll have to use your imagination. Of course, I'm no longer in my twenties and didn't have time to shave my chest, but I trust you to be kind."

She raised her hands to stifle her laughter. "Please don't apologize. If you were any better looking, I'd swoon right here!"

He shook out his arms and ran his hands through his hair in an excellent imitation of Elvis. "Thank you, ma'am."

She howled again. "I'm not sure I can stand this."

He placed the CD in the player and pressed the button for *Soul Man.* He turned up the volume on the driving beat and then glanced over his shoulder and winked.

Catherine had expected him to relate some silly adolescent adventure, perhaps involving an English teacher, not launch into a pulse-pounding performance, but as he began to dance, it was all she could do not to scream with the same frenzy that had rocked Chippendale's. It might have been more than a dozen years since he'd been paid for the provocative routine, but he still had every suggestive step down cold, complete with sly winks, and sex-charged pelvic thrusts.

He peeled off his shirt, teasing her every inch of the way. By the time he tossed it into her lap, she was weak from appreciative laughter and used it to dry her happy tears. Even when he was standing still, she'd always considered his lean muscular build handsome, but now every ripple of lightly tanned muscle called her name. Her cheeks filled with the heat of desire, and she wondered what she would have to promise to inspire him to dance for her again.

Luke flipped open the top button on his Levi's, but he went no farther with his tantalizing striptease. But when he ground his hips with the music, he left so little to Catherine's imagination that he might as well have been naked. When the lively song came to an end, he quickly shut off the CD, then dropped to his knees in front of her and rested his arms across her lap.

"I'd ask if you'd like to take me home, but luckily we're already here."

Catherine ruffled his silvery hair, then leaned forward to give him a long, slow kiss. "You needn't worry I'll ever tell a soul what I've just seen. No one would believe me."

"Damn, I should have sworn you to secrecy first."

"And to think you once claimed you didn't dance well."

He shrugged. "True, but I was referring to dancing with a woman, not doing a solo act. Although when you mentioned Dimitri, I'll admit to feeling a twinge of guilt."

His pulse throbbed at the base of his throat, and she swept her hair aside to lean down and press her lips against his heat-moistened skin. She was tempted to leave her mark on him but instead moved up to kiss his lips.

"You taste every bit as good as you look." After brushing his arms aside, she slid off the sofa to join him on the floor. "You don't know how glad I am that my living room is so much more private than Chippendale's." She combed the coarse hair circling his nipples, then bent to lick the tender buds.

He caught her in his arms and leaned back to bring them both down into the soft, cool carpet. "Let's not take the time to go upstairs," he begged between fervent kisses.

She slid down his chest and buried her tongue in his navel. "What stairs? You're all I need. Although the pants with Velcro sides would be nice."

He chuckled through her tickling kisses and eased his hips out of his Levi's. "I've never danced for such a small audience, ma'am, but you're easily the most appreciative."

She helped him discard his jeans, then slid her hand into his briefs and wrapped her fingers around his rock-hard penis. "Did dancing always turn you on like this?"

"Hundreds of screaming women will turn on any man."

She leaned forward to draw him deep into her mouth, sucked lightly, and then paused to whisper, "I had no idea. I thought it was just a hoot to guys."

"That too," he admitted in a gruff whisper. He wound his fingers in her hair and pulled her back down onto his shaft.

She listened to his breathing quicken and changed positions slightly to lap at his balls. She adored him and liked everything about his body, the width of his shoulders, the flatness of his belly, and the musky scent of his desire. She thought him a perfect male specimen and enjoyed pleasing him with her hands and lips. She teased him too, her touch light and slow, and then hard and fast until, desperate to remain in control, he shoved her away.

"You are too damn good at that," he vowed in a husky moan.

Rather than admit how thrilling a tutor Sam had been, she helped him remove her clothing with sufficient haste to keep them both on the sizzling edge of release. He fumbled with the condom, so she rolled it down for him. She straddled him then and slowly slid down his cock to take him deep. She rocked her hips to find the perfect fit, then rode him with a rolling insistence that quickly had him bucking beneath her.

He found the sweet spot where their bodies met and rubbed in time with her graceful lunges. Their eyes held through the mist of soaring rapture, but then neither could see nor hear but only feel the shattering descent into the utter madness of perfect bliss. Lost in their shared climax, Catherine collapsed in Luke's arms, and too content to move, she welcomed sleep.

He fought to float with her, but his conscience speared him with anguishing doubts. He had again taken more than he had any right to ask and rather than pleasant dreams, he lay on a bed of his own sharply whittled spikes. That he needed Catherine's intoxicating affection so badly made him want to shout and curse; but unable to murmur even the softest word of endearment, he lay awash in a painful pool of regret.

The sweet sound of guitars gradually invaded Catherine's dreams. Enchanted by the stirring music, she yawned lazily and stretched, then recognized the contours of Luke's muscular body and rolled to his side. "Sorry, I didn't mean to crush you."

"Hush. You don't weigh enough to crush me, and your skin is so soft it feels incredibly good against mine. I'm sorry the mariachis woke you."

Half expecting to find them in the room, she sat up and looked around. "I thought it was the radio, but they're live, aren't they?"

"Sure are. Someone must be serenading his lady love."

"How wonderfully romantic, but I have to see who it is." She pushed herself to her feet, felt dizzy and swayed a bit, but made it to the front window.

"They're across the street and up a way. Their black suits melt into the shadows, but I can see the silver buttons on their trousers in the moonlight. They're in front of Joyce's house. Do you suppose Shane sent them?"

Luke propped his head on his hand to improve his view. She was silhouetted against the moonlight, and her gently rounded figure was as exquisitely beautiful as any marble goddess gracing the world's finest museums. When he could catch his breath, he gave a low appreciative whistle.

"Maybe, but I sure hope he was smart enough to come along."

She remained at the window for a long moment. She couldn't catch the words of the mariachis' song, but the haunting melody tugged at her heart. "He was smart enough not to give up, which ought to count for quite a bit."

She came back to him and offered him a hand up. "I have strawberries for dessert if you like."

He took her hand but rose only as far as his knees and nuzzled her soft, silken bush. He gripped her thighs lightly and licked. "You taste better than strawberries. Do you like this?"

She rested a leg over his shoulder to invite more. "You know I do. Don't make me beg."

"Never," he promised, and he lost himself in pleasuring her while the mariachis strummed their love songs on her neighbor's lawn.

She slid her hands through his hair to hold on, but his tender invasion made it difficult to stand. He slipped two fingers inside her to deepen the thrill, and she angled her hips to press against his mouth. She tried to remember to breathe, but his delicious tonguing made coherent thought impossible. Then, with a sweet, gasping moan, she found paradise again in his arms.

After midnight, they fed each other plump strawberries and, still sticky with the juice, fell into her bed and made love again. She kissed him good-bye when he left for home before dawn, and, drugged with his good loving, she didn't wake again until mid-morning.

Smoky was asleep on the foot of her bed, and thinking Luke must have let him in, she sat up to cuddle her pet. Her stomach then objected so violently to being jerked upright that she barely made it to the bathroom before becoming ill.

After the last painful retch, she sat on the floor and leaned back against the cool porcelain bathtub. Smoky had followed her into the bathroom, and she raised a shaky hand to tickle his ears. "Just give me a minute, fella, and I'll serve your breakfast."

Yet the mere thought of cat food sent her stomach into another heaving flurry. She was never sick and couldn't understand why she was so ill now. She'd baked the chicken thoroughly, but perhaps she hadn't rinsed the strawberries as carefully as she should have. Of course, Luke was a terrible distraction, but she refused to blame him for the carelessness that must have caused her illness.

She hoped he hadn't spent the morning with his head in a toilet, but she didn't feel up to calling him to inquire as to his health. Instead, she stretched out on the bathroom floor and closed her eyes. Smoky nudged her arm, and satisfied she would stay put, he lay down beside her.

When she awoke from a brief nap, she felt well enough to stand and brush her teeth. She splashed water on her face and ran a quick comb through her hair. She stared into the mirror above the sink and decided she still looked a bit green, but perhaps she'd merely become overtired.

When the queasiness suddenly returned, she sank down on the edge of the tub and attempted to ignore Smoky's insistent meow. She had to rest before risking a trip downstairs to the kitchen. Once there, she held her breath as she opened the can of cat food, but the aroma of tuna got to her anyway, and she vomited in the sink.

She made it back to bed with a wobbly, lurching gait and didn't awaken again until noon. Fearing the nausea would return, she rose slowly, but after taking a moment to assess the situation, she felt fine. Certain Joyce would come by soon, she made her bed and opened her lingerie drawer to grab underwear.

She kept her personal calendar in that drawer, and the birth control pills she'd yet to resume taking. Her period wasn't due for another couple of days, but a quick count revealed she and Luke had made love for the first time at the exact mid-point in her cycle. It had been the optimum time to conceive, but Luke had been so careful to protect her, she refused to believe that she'd been hit with a bout of morning sickness.

Still, that the awful possibility might exist terrified her. She sat on the side of her bed and fanned herself briskly with the calendar. It had to have been a bad strawberry, she insisted to herself, but even a believable excuse failed to dispel a growing sense of dread.

Once she'd filled the prescription for the pill, she'd ceased to worry about a condom's effectiveness, but could she have gotten pregnant that first time they were together? she agonized.

It was simply too horrible a thought to entertain, and not because she didn't want Luke's child, but only because she didn't want it as an accident. That would be like stealing something precious from him that he hadn't freely given. How could she ever make it up to him? It made her head ache to consider what his reaction would be, but it couldn't possibly be good.

Since she'd gone off the pill after Sam died, her period was often a day or two late, so it might be a week before she knew if she truly had a reason to worry. That it promised to be a very long and anxious week made her shudder.

She gritted her teeth. "It was a bad strawberry," she swore darkly, "nothing more." But she was still shaken. She would have to tell Luke the instant she was sure she was pregnant, but she already knew his eyes would darken with an indescribable pain. He was too fine a man to blame her, but things would never again be the same between them, and they had been so good that she couldn't bear such a dismal future.

"Bad strawberry, bad strawberry, bad strawberry," she repeated as she ran a bath, but as a mantra, the phrase didn't hold nearly enough power to erase her mounting fears.

Catherine dressed in an old pair of shorts and faded T-shirt to work in her garden, but Joyce arrived before she'd pulled more than a half dozen weeds. "That was an excellent troupe of mariachis on your lawn last night. Did you invite them in?" she asked.

"I offered them refreshments," Joyce explained, "but they were in an awful hurry to get home to Oxnard." She was dressed in white cropped pants and a lavender sweater and again looked her best.

"I've never had a man make such an extravagant gesture to impress me, and I'm not just referring to the cost." Joyce took her usual place at the patio table and waited for Catherine to take hers.

"That's pitiful, isn't it? Whenever I've gotten pissed at a guy and told him to go to hell, he's disappeared with his tail between his legs, never to be seen again. Or he's told me off, and I've been grateful to be rid of him. I've just never had a man apologize with a musical accompaniment. After Shane had gone to all that trouble, I couldn't stay mad at him. Do you think I let him off too easy?"

"Don't second guess yourself," Catherine advised. "It sounds as though Shane's apology was sincere, and you were right to accept it. It can't hurt to have a forgiving nature."

"It can if he takes advantage of it," Joyce complained.

"I doubt that he'll disappoint you again."

Joyce swung her foot, bouncing her lavender sandal. "Well, he was very sweet last night, and we talked a long while, but we still didn't make love. So in a way, he's already disappointed me, but just in a different way."

"You've complained so often of men who've rushed you into bed, I'd think Shane would be a refreshing change. Besides, it's always wise to build a strong friendship before you go any further."

"Is that a fact? And what were you and Luke doing last night?"

"I'll not deny that passion was a part of the evening, but we're also getting to know each other better. Barring unforeseen catastrophes, we should do all right." Yet even as she spoke the upbeat prediction, Catherine feared the very worst sort of disaster might have already befallen them.

Joyce frowned slightly as she studied her friend's faint smile. "If everything's going so well, where's that sappy grin you usually wear after a date with Luke?"

Catherine shrugged off the surprisingly insightful observation. "I had another great time with him, but I must have eaten a bad strawberry, because I threw up all morning. I'm just not up to full speed yet. That's all."

Joyce's eyes narrowed slightly. "You were sick this morning? I'm the one who wants a family, and I swear if you've gotten pregnant without even trying, I'm going to leap off my roof!"

That Joyce had immediately zeroed in on such a dire possibility brought incriminating tears to Catherine's eyes. She quickly blinked them away. "You live in a one-story house, so you'd probably just break your ankles. Let's not jump to any other ridiculous conclusions, either.

"Luke is an incredible lover, athletic, graceful, and endlessly inventive in his approach. He simply wears me out, but I refuse to believe that I'm pregnant."

Joyce sat forward. "Let's go buy one of those home pregnancy test kits."

"It's much too soon for that," Catherine insisted, too great a coward to chance learning the truth that day. "Now, when are you seeing Shane again?"

Joyce opened her mouth to argue, then apparently thought better of it and sat back. "He has a job in Burbank on Tuesday, and we're meeting for lunch. I don't ever want to go back to Oxnard, so it's a good thing Shane's down here fairly often."

"Oxnard's his home. You'll have to go there eventually."

Now it was Joyce's turn to shift uncomfortably in her chair. "I suppose, but I'm going to put it off just as long as I possibly can."

Catherine could easily understand that sentiment, but she thought Joyce could probably avoid going to Oxnard longer than she could withhold the truth from Luke.

Sunday night, Catherine was outside savoring the twilight when the telephone rang. Certain it was Luke, she dashed to answer before the machine caught the call.

"I knew it was you," she greeted him breathlessly.

"Am I that predictable?"

"No, not at all, and after seeing you dance, no one would accuse you of it."

He chuckled along with her but then added a caution. "Whatever talent I might have as a dancer really does have to be our secret."

"Well, when no one knows we're seeing each other, why would they care what we do?" She held her breath. She'd thought he'd missed her and wanted to hear her voice, but perhaps he was simply concerned with maintaining his extremely proper image.

He was quiet a moment too long. "I don't even want to go there. I just called to say I was thinking of you."

"Thank you." She'd been thinking of him too. "You needn't worry, Luke. All your secrets are safe with me." As were her own, she didn't dare add.

Monday morning, Catherine reached over to shut off her alarm, and then sat up slowly. She took a deep breath and released it gradually; then, having suffered no ill effects, she risked swinging her legs off the bed to stand. She waited a moment, but still felt fine and went on into the bathroom.

Despite having gone to bed early, she still looked a little tired, but her skin no longer held a peculiar olive tinge. She leaned closer to the mirror and blinked. "It was a bad strawberry after all," she concluded, but the words were easier said than believed.

Expecting to spend the day buying paint and working at Toby's house, she dressed in jeans, an aqua T-shirt with a purple cat across the front, and tennis shoes. She remembered to take a hat, but when she arrived at Lost Angel, the mural project had already progressed further than she could have imagined.

Over the weekend, Toby and Dave had erected a scaffold and begun to trace the outer borders of a grid on the Victorian. She walked across the street to join them. Rafael and a dozen other kids were seated along the porch, eager to begin painting, while Nick did skateboard tricks on the sidewalk.

"You'll all need clothes to paint in," Catherine suggested. "Let's have Pam unlock the clothes lockers so that you can find something to work in while I go and buy the paint."

Rafael rose and took a step toward her. "It'll be a real pleasure to get paint on some of the awful rags people donate. In fact, it would only be an improvement."

"Hey, when we're finished, maybe we can sell the stuff as Jackson Pollock's old clothes," Tina Stassy urged.

"That would be fraud, Tina," Catherine warned. "Let's just concentrate on painting the mural."

"You're all business, aren't you?" Toby observed.

Catherine shot him a dark glance rather than reply.

He had his hair pulled back in a ponytail, but he was clad in jeans and a T-shirt which left his colorfully tattooed arms on full display. "Let's take my truck," he said. "We'll need tarps, scrapers, sandpaper, brushes, rollers, masking tape, gloves, buckets to mix the paint in. It won't all fit in your Volvo."

"What makes you think I drive a Volvo?" Catherine asked.

"You just drove into the center parking lot," Toby pointed out. "I'm an artist and observant. Now you take that convertible cruising by now. Someone's spent a lot of time and money to restore that '50's Ford. I noticed them driving by several times over the weekend, and they're up to no good."

Catherine turned to watch the dark green car roll by. It had been lowered to suit the owner's definition of cool. The cream-colored top was up and obscured her view of the occupants, but she thought Toby was probably right about their motives.

"Dave, what kind of car does Ford Dolan drive?" she asked.

Dave had been trimming the scraggly bushes at the front of the house to clear the way to paint. "He has a battered old truck. What made you think of him?"

"Just the mention of a Ford, I guess."

While she was relieved Ford Dolan didn't own the convertible, Toby's slow, sexy smile convinced her she didn't want to ride anywhere with him, either. Her own shopping list was tucked in her pocket, but his sounded more complete than hers.

She cleared her throat nervously. "We'll be buying a lot. Maybe we should take two cars."

Toby looked surprised but finally nodded. "Okay, if that's what you want. Let me get you the address of the place where I've been buying my paint. I talked to the manager on Saturday, and he's giving us a good price in exchange for allowing him to post a sign advertising his store."

"Really? And just how large is this sign?" Catherine inquired.

Toby gestured. "Not big. It's about the size of a realtor's for sale sign. Let's just call the paint store our first corporate sponsor and hope to attract others."

"Sounds good to me." Dave looked up from his work and winked. "Lost Angel sure needs the money."

"I know it does," Catherine answered, "but that doesn't mean we ought to have product endorsements all over Toby's lawn. They'll only distract from the beauty of the mural."

"You are so damn cute," Toby said. "Do you ever stop worrying long enough to have fun?"

"I saw her first!" Dave shouted. "When she's ready for fun, I'm her man."

The kids found that exchange hilarious, but Catherine certainly didn't. She'd been sure Pam would have told Dave that she and Luke were dating, but apparently, Dave hadn't a clue. It was even more disappointing that Luke hadn't confided in Dave. She looked down at the patchy lawn to focus her thoughts and then up at the ornately decorated Victorian home.

"I expect painting the mural to be lots of fun," she interjected, "but we need to buy the supplies. Now where's that store, Toby?"

"Hang on, sweetheart, it's only a couple of blocks away. I'll give you the address."

She wasn't his sweetheart and never would be, but she bit her tongue rather than provide another belly laugh for the teens.

Luke forced himself to concentrate on the center's budget until well past eleven o'clock, but he couldn't put off seeing Catherine a minute longer. He crossed the street to Toby's house, then had to mask his disappointment when Dave reported that she'd gone shopping with Toby.

"They should be back any minute," Dave explained. He wiped his forehead on his sleeve and then gestured with his clippers. "I hope you don't mind if I split my time between here and the center. I'm sure I can get everything done, and we really ought to dress up the yard here to frame our mural."

Luke jammed his hands in his hip pockets and rocked back on his heels. "Go ahead and help out all you can here. If you're needed at the center, we'll know where to find you. Besides, Mrs. Brooks will probably appreciate your help with supervision."

The kids were back at Lost Angel searching the clothes lockers, so Dave and Luke had the front yard to themselves, but Dave still took the precaution of lowering his voice. "I'll do all I can to help Cathy, and I'm sure you know how I'd like to be repaid."

Luke instantly grasped Dave's meaning, and he had to swallow hard to find his voice. "It would be better to keep your relationship strictly professional," he advised.

Dave responded with a derisive snort. "That will be a challenge with Toby drooling all over Cathy."

Luke had already known he'd have to keep an eye on Toby. "I'll have the contract ready for his signature this afternoon, and I'll speak to him then. I don't want anyone spoiling the mural project for Mrs. Brooks, least of all him."

"Yeah, I understand what you mean, but I really like Cathy, and I think she likes me too. I'm getting myself together, and I'll go back out into the real world soon. The economy may have changed, but I can still be a success, and Cathy provides a hell of an incentive. I just don't need any competition from a guy who looks like a rock star."

Luke couldn't encourage Dave in what he sincerely hoped was a losing proposition. Neither could he admit how close he and Catherine had become when Dave would angrily demand to know what his intentions were.

Unfortunately, intentions required a belief in the future, and Luke had lost all hope for anything more than what he could see or touch in a single day. That meant he had no intentions other than to make love to Catherine as often as he possibly could. That dark realization forced him into a bitter silence, and all he could offer Dave was a perfunctory nod.

Chapter Fourteen

Luke was seated on the Victorian's porch when Catherine drove up and parked on the adjacent side street. As he and Dave approached her Volvo, Dave was grinning happily, but Luke wore a preoccupied frown. By the time she'd left her car to open the rear door, however, his expression had cleared.

Her initial glimpse of him had signaled something was amiss, but she hoped it had absolutely nothing to do with her and greeted both men with a smile. "Toby had already calculated how much paint we needed. I was very careful about what we bought. Rather than have custom colors mixed, we're going to do it ourselves. That way we can return any unopened cans of paint."

"You needn't worry so much about the cost," Luke assured her. "The mural itself will generate new donations."

Catherine leaned close to whisper, "If not the expense, then what is worrying you?"

With a quick warning frown, Luke shook off her question before Dave took note of their exchange.

Dave had already pulled the canvas tarps out of the Volvo and hefted them over his shoulder. "You want these on the porch?"

"Toby wants to store everything in his garage for the time being," Catherine directed.

Before the three of them had rounded the house, Toby drove his Chevy truck into the driveway. He jumped out of the cab and swung open the garage doors. He had been working on a giant cat sculpted from scrap metal and the head loomed eight feet above them.

"I love it!" Catherine cried. "Do you find many buyers for such heroic cats?"

"You'd be surprised by how many people want them. Let's stack the paint cans and supplies along the wall, and the kids can tote them out front when they're needed."

When they'd finished unloading the Chevy, Toby yanked over a battered wooden stool and sat down to speak with Luke. "Do you have any objection to Rafael mixing the colors? He has the best eye for subtle shadings I've ever seen."

"He's the artist," Luke replied, "but I doubt he knows much about mixing paint."

"Fortunately, I do. Once Rafael sketches in the figures, I'll block out the whole mural as though it were a paint-by-numbers kit."

As Luke listened to Toby describe the steps he intended to take, his gaze followed Catherine as she circled the whimsical feline. Her whole expression glowed with delight, but that she might also admire the cat's flamboyant creator increased Luke's dislike for the artist tenfold.

"It sounds as though you have a good game plan," Luke said, eagerly edging toward the door, "but I want your name on our contract before the work begins. I'll bring it over as soon as it arrives by messenger."

After Luke returned to Lost Angel, Catherine was left to contend with Toby and Dave, who were eyeing her much too appreciatively. She made a mental note to wear a less formfitting T-shirt the next day. The men helped her organize the painting supplies in the order they would be used, but if there were a chance to slide a hand across her shoulder, or brush close with their whole bodies, each made the most of it. At another time, she might have thought their antics amusing, but she was far too tense to be more than deeply irritated that day.

She was relieved when she checked her watch. "It's time for lunch, and I want to make certain the kids have the clothes they'll need. I'll see you later, Toby."

"I doubt there will be much to do today," the sculptor complained, then his expression softened. "You come on back anyway, and I promise to keep you entertained."

Dave laughed at Toby's suggestive invitation. "She'll never be that desperate for entertainment. Come on, Cathy, I'll walk you back to Lost Angel."

She debated a quick moment, then left her car parked beside the Victorian. "It's another beautiful day," she exclaimed as she and Dave crossed the street with the light. She hoped if she always kept their conversation focused on the mural or Lost Angel, he would eventually perceive her lack of interest.

Dave swung the hedge clippers up to rest on his shoulder. "It sure is. I hope you won't mind my saying this, but I think you ought to see if Toby actually delivers on a few of his endless boasts before you trust him with much."

"It is his house," she pointed out.

"Yeah, and he'll remind us of that fact every chance he gets. Luke was smart to have a contract drawn up so there will be no misunderstandings. But then he is terrific with details. Of course, thinking is about all the guy does do."

Catherine knew without glancing up that Dave would be wearing his usual affable grin and hoping she would laugh right along with him. She wasn't even tempted. "If I were you, I wouldn't make fun of Luke. He could just as easily have nixed the mural project, but he's been very supportive."

"You call doubting that Rafael did his own drawing being supportive?"

She hesitated a moment but decided against revealing Luke's reasons for appearing skeptical. "No, but generally, he has been very helpful. Did you have any time to work on the greeting cards?"

"Sure, there isn't much happening here on the weekends. Come on in the office, and I'll show you."

Catherine needed to turn in the paint store credit card receipt to Pam and followed him. It was time for the secretary's lunch break, and after accepting the receipt, Pam happily relinquished her seat at the computer and grabbed her purse.

"Wait until you see what Dave has done," Pam enthused. "Rather than use whole drawings, he selected the most meaningful part of each. The cards will be spectacular, and I bet all of our volunteers will want them for Christmas.

"Our would-be painters chose some clothes, although I swear they made such awful choices, they'll resemble clowns when they paint."

"I don't care how they look. I just don't want them to worry about ruining what few clothes they do own," Catherine replied.

"Well, don't you worry another minute over that," Pam advised. "We've got a mountain of clothes best used for painting, and I'll see they get every stitch."

As soon as Pam had left the office, Dave laid his hedge clippers aside and slid into her chair. He quickly opened the mural file. "Rafael's design will be the big seller, but take a look at these others and tell me what you think."

Catherine knew all the designs well enough to appreciate how skillfully Dave had cropped his photos to give the artwork the maximum impact. As he clicked through them, she was amazed. "You've improved them all," she complimented sincerely. "Even Tina's trash-sorting angel and winged cat look better with a tighter focus."

"Focus used to be one of my favorite words. It's time I started using it again. Speaking of which, do you have a minute?"

"Sure, what is it?" She crossed to one of the visitor chairs. She liked Dave but not in the way he liked her, and she didn't want to give him any false hopes by remaining close while they talked.

"I've still got a couple of my good suits, and with a little work on my résumé, I might actually get some interviews. Of course, I'll have to cut my hair to pass for the corporate type again, but that's a small price. What I'm trying to say is that I intend to win back everything I've lost. I may have wandered a while, but it won't be much longer, and I'll have my life back on track."

"I know you will. Although you'll surely be missed here."

Before Dave could respond to her encouragement, Detectives Garcia and Salzman came through the door. That day Salzman was dressed in a tan suit and Garcia in navy blue, as though they had swapped outfits to double their wardrobe options. Salzman was carrying a lumpy black shoulder bag which looked as though it might contain hand grenades.

Catherine immediately leapt to her feet and hurried to knock at Luke's door. "The detectives are here," she announced.

Luke mouthed a most uncomplimentary term but immediately left his office to greet them. "How nice to see you again. Have you arrested a suspect?"

211

"Not yet," Garcia replied. "But we wanted you to know how popular red satin dresses and blond wigs have become among a certain element of our population."

"You're kidding," Luke scoffed.

"I assure you we're not," Detective Salzman replied. "We heard you provide kids with clothes here. I don't suppose you've noticed a run on red cocktail dresses?"

"We don't accept donations of party clothes, so if red dresses are now a trend, they aren't from here. Try the Goodwill, Out of the Closet, or Salvation Army thrift shops."

"We intend to, but we thought you might have heard something," Garcia pressed. His paisley tie in wines and blues was remarkably subdued compared to the golden brilliance of the one he'd worn on his previous visit.

"I haven't heard a peep," Luke assured them. "How about you?"

"No," Salzman claimed with an exasperated sigh. "But we will. Even if it's the Lady in Red's dry cleaner, someone will talk soon."

"I'm surprised you're so optimistic," Dave commented from his seat behind the computer. "From what I read in the *Times*, more than fifty percent of the homicides in Los Angeles remain unsolved. So it stands to reason that a lot of people aren't talking."

Neither detective had taken much notice of Dave, but obviously peeved at the lack of efficiency his comment implied, they turned toward him with the precision of synchronized swimmers.

"That's due in part to gang killings where the murderer didn't know the victim," Garcia emphasized. "Clearly, the Lady in Red targeted her victims."

"Excellent point," Dave conceded. "I wish you good luck."

"We make our own luck," Salzman insisted, her mouth drawn as tight as a drawstring bag. "Let's keep in touch." She led the way out the door, and with a disgusted grimace, Garcia followed.

"Charming pair," Dave noted. "Maybe I ought to consider a career in law enforcement. Do you suppose I'm too old to enter the police academy?"

"Call them and ask," Luke replied. "Now, this is Monday, and I don't want to miss out on Mabel's spaghetti. Let's go have lunch."

Dave walked over to the hall with them robbing Catherine of the opportunity to speak with Luke privately, but she hoped he could suggest a diplomatic way to discourage Toby and Dave without alienating either one. As if that were her only worry, she mumbled under her breath, but the thought of facing a plate of spaghetti wasn't welcome, either.

To elude Dave, she slid into the last place at a table and sat directly across from Polly. "Did you find an extra pair of shoes? You won't want to get paint on your purple hightops."

"Yeah, I thought of that and found some jogging shoes that look brand new. I guess somebody must have given up on jogging awfully quick. I picked up a baseball cap too. I sure don't want to get paint on any of my good hats."

"No, of course not." Catherine twirled her spaghetti on her fork but guided none to her mouth.

"I'm glad you're working on the mural," Polly offered softly. "All the volunteers here are nice, but you're my favorite."

"Thank you, Polly." She was pleased, but attempting to follow Luke's advice, she was determined to be a friend to all the teens and not make favorites of any.

Luke was seated at a table near the door to the courtyard, and when he finished his lunch and left the hall, Catherine followed. She caught up to him just as he reached the steps leading up to the office.

"I need your help with something," she began.

"Sure, if you have a problem, I want to know." He held the door open for her.

Pam wasn't back yet, and the outer office was cool and quiet. Luke escorted her into his private office, but she left the door standing open. She had to force herself to sit down, but even then she perched stiffly on the edge of the chair. She hadn't been this nervous on her first visit to Lost Angel, and she slid her hands between her knees to suppress her jitters.

"You can pretend we're not well acquainted, but you don't have Toby and Dave constantly hitting on you. I'm hoping they'll back off once we're working on the mural and surrounded by kids, but if they don't, I'll be forced to tell them

I'm dating an insanely jealous trucker from San Bernardino. Unless, of course, you can come up with a better story."

Luke leaned back in his chair. He was so pleased she had no interest in Toby, it was difficult for him not to gloat. "I'll speak with Toby when I take him the contract. Let's hope that cools him off. San Bernardino is a nice touch, but before you go making up any stories, let's think them through. After all, a trucker would be likely to drive by to check out the mural, wouldn't he?"

The office's warm terra cotta walls and deep russet carpeting formed a soothing cocoon, but Catherine continued to fidget. "I suppose, but just what is it you plan to tell Toby?"

Luke knew precisely what he'd like to say to the tattooed freak, but for her benefit, he modified it considerably. "I'll just point out you're a lady and unaccustomed to having to fend off guys on the make. I'll say you're too polite to complain to him, but that you're deeply insulted by his more or less constant stream of sleazy sexual innuendoes. That ought to work."

She had a sinking feeling such a tasteful request might have no impact whatsoever on Toby's behavior. "I can handle Toby," she said confidently. "It's Dave I'm more worried about. You're right, of course, a trucker would be sure to show up here. Who wouldn't? What about an airline pilot who flew European routes?"

"That's good," Luke agreed, "or maybe an acrobat with *Cirque de Soleil*. Perhaps a rock musician on tour?"

"Right, as long as I'm going to lie, it might as well be a whopper," she murmured to herself, but her pensive frown warned him his efforts at humor were misguided at best.

"I know you don't want to hurt Dave's feelings and this is my fault. I'm sorry, but I'm not just being a selfish bastard here, Catherine. I've a damn good reason for keeping my private life out of the center."

"Yes, I understand, but for how long? Weeks, months, years?" She bit her lip, but the complaint had tumbled from her mouth before she could catch it.

Her emotion-laced question caught him off guard, and he shrugged wearily. "Right now, I can't think past this afternoon." He didn't mean to mislead her, but neither could he do the courageous thing, the right thing, and send her away. At least not when Toby and Dave would be so eager to console her, he couldn't.

He cleared his throat and pressed on as though her problem were easily solved. "If you like, I'll tell Dave you're seeing someone. There's no reason to go into imaginative detail when it's plain you don't want to lie."

Catherine felt sick to her stomach, and it wasn't because she was worried about lying to Dave, but to Luke. "It would still be a lie, though, wouldn't it?" she cautioned. "It would be meant to spare his feelings, but when Pam knows, why haven't you told Dave the truth?"

In hope of ushering her smoothly out of his office, Luke rose to his feet. "I'm providing Dave not only with a job and a place to live, but psychological counseling as well. That means I listen to his problems and guide him toward solutions, but I don't confide in him. Does that make sense to you?"

"Of course, it's the same as a doctor-patient relationship," she replied. At least she understood that much. She rose and took a step toward the open doorway. "I really don't know what to do until that contract arrives and we can begin work."

She appeared so uncharacteristically befuddled that he couldn't resist the impulse to give her a hug. The instant she was tucked neatly into his arms, however, it wasn't nearly enough. He breathed in her delicious vanilla scent and then regretfully released her.

"Why don't you go on home? When you come in tomorrow, we should be all set."

"All right, I'll go. See you in the morning." Catherine was now sorry she'd left her car parked beside Toby's house, but because she would walk right by the hall, she decided to make a quick check of the center's library.

Violet was kneeling on one of the new throw rugs placed in front of the bookshelves. She smiled happily as Catherine walked up. "I've got Ford fooled into believing I've quit reading, but I've just been reading here rather than taking books home."

Violet looked very pleased with herself for being so clever, but Catherine wasn't impressed. She sat on the adjacent rug and began to straighten the books in one of the new bookcases.

"I suppose that's one way to deal with the problem, but it isn't the best."

Violet shrugged her thin shoulders. "I think it's a pretty good way," she argued. "If Ford doesn't know what I'm doing, then he can't throw a fit over it."

"True, but there must be a limit to how much a woman can sanely hide." Catherine feared she was close to discovering her own limitations in that regard. "Have you seen Rafael's drawing for the mural? One of his angels looks an awful lot like you."

Violet caught Catherine's wrist with a frantic grip. "Oh no, he can't use me. Ford would know I've been over here, then."

Violet's eyes were filled with stark terror, moving Catherine to cover the girl's small hand with her own. "Perhaps he won't notice."

"Oh, he'll notice, all right. That man can almost see through walls. I better go." She quickly released her hold on Catherine, turned down the page in the book she'd been reading and shoved it back into the bottom shelf.

"Tell Rafael not to use me. He just can't."

Catherine watched Violet sprint from the hall and thought if any of the girls deserved a guardian angel, it was Violet. She was uncertain what to tell Rafael. After all, Violet made a stunning angel, and he might not want to paint someone else in her place.

"Damn, if that isn't another prickly problem I don't need," Catherine moaned to herself, but by the time she had the bookshelves looking as neat as any library's, she still lacked a viable solution.

Later that afternoon, Luke carried the contract over to Toby's along with a pen to make certain the artist would have no excuse not to sign. Toby was at work in his garage welding hubcap eyes on his huge cat. When he spotted Luke at the doorway, he climbed down off the ladder, extinguished his torch and raised his protective visor.

As he stripped off his gloves, he looked Luke up and down with a disdainful glance. "You don't like me very much, do you?"

"I don't like you at all, but we don't have to be best friends for the mural project to go well."

"Right, my sentiments exactly. An artist has to learn to deal with all types of humanity, and I can deal with you." Toby used the toe of his boot to yank his stool close and sat down. "I intend to read every word of that contract, so I hope you don't mind hanging around for a while."

"Not at all." Luke handed it over with the pen still clipped to the front. "My signature is already on it. It's a straightforward agreement. You're granting us permission to paint a mural on your house, but we'll own the mural and all rights to reproduce it by whatever means currently in existence or might be invented."

"Okay," Toby offered agreeably, but he still reviewed the multi-page document thoroughly. "Looks like all you want is the exclusive right to reproduce the mural."

"That's correct. Even if it's one of your favorite art magazines, we'll have to give permission. But we want the image everywhere, so we'd be unlikely to withhold it."

"There's no mention of my maintaining the mural, so if the paint starts to peel—"

"Then it peels," Luke stated for him. "It won't last forever, but our photographs of it will."

"I might sell the house next year," Toby warned.

"It's your house; you have that right."

Toby looked torn momentarily, then used his thigh to steady the contract and scrawled his name on the appropriate line. He shook the pages into order, and handed the contract and the pen back to Luke. "You'll give me a copy?"

"Of course," Luke refolded the contract and slid the pen into his shirt pocket. "Now that's out of the way, let's talk about Mrs. Brooks."

Toby responded with a taunting grin. "One of my favorite subjects."

Luke hated Toby's smirk, but he succeeded in fighting back his temper. "I can see that, but you're definitely not one of hers. You're embarrassing her, and you can't keep coming on to her, especially not in front of the kids. She deserves your respect as well as theirs, and I intend to see that she gets it."

"Cut the bullshit," Toby responded angrily. "You want her for yourself. Now, access to my studio wasn't part of your contract. Get out."

Luke turned on his heel and left rather than risk having Toby relight his torch and use it as a flamethrower. He wasn't surprised the artist had guessed the truth. He'd bluffed a professional detachment he didn't feel, and Toby had seen right through it. For some bizarre reason, that actually made the guy a lot more likable.

Tuesday morning, Luke was waiting for Catherine when she drove into the center parking lot. "I just wanted to encourage you to use the same technique you used on the bookcases to make the kids believe they're running things."

"They will be," she insisted. As always, the first time she saw him each day, she was struck by how handsome he was when he smiled. The affection brightening his gaze was most welcome as well.

"I'll be manipulating them just as deftly as you, though, won't I?" she asked.

He was relieved she appeared to be in better spirits that day. "I always think of it as guiding them toward independence."

"Which is merely a rationalization, as I'm sure you know. Did Toby sign the contract?"

"Yes, and if he so much as winks at you today, come and get me." He paused to reroll the left sleeve of his Madras shirt, but his gaze remained locked with hers.

"And just what is it you plan to do? I think you could take him in a fair fight, but he doesn't strike me as a man who'd fight fair."

"I'll bet you'd like to see it, though," Luke teased.

"I've seen you with a black eye, and it sure wasn't pretty, so no, I don't want to ever see you fight anyone, and most especially not over me. Now let's attempt to be more professional, Dr. Starns, or I'll be tempted to turn around and drive right back home."

He squared his shoulders as though he'd been properly chastised. "Yes, ma'am, I'll be as professional as possible. Are you free tonight?"

"Better ask me after I've spent the day supervising the work on the mural. I may not be able to do more than float in my tub."

He made no effort to contain his smile. "I could go for that too."

"Quit distracting me." She plunked on a straw hat and forced a businesslike demeanor. "I've got my clipboard to make notes of who's working so that everyone will have a turn. I plan to take photos with my camera in addition to whatever photos Dave might take with the center's digital. Will I need your written permission?"

"No, of course not. Get doubles when you have your photos developed, and we'll post them in the hall. Nobody photographs these kids, and they ought to get a real kick out of the pictures."

"I hope so. I brought some bottles of water, but I'll have the kids carry them across the street."

"That's very thoughtful of you. They might need snacks too. I'll buy some protein bars. I should probably go on over and have another chat with Toby. I don't want the kids in his house for anything other than to lean out the window to paint. If they need to use the john, then they'll have to come back here. I don't want them to depend on Toby for anything."

"I can tell him that," she offered. "I thought I'd warn him not to serve anyone beer, or any illegal substances, either. I know you were worried he'd be a bad influence when we first met him, but I really think he's more talk than trouble."

"Then we've got some kids who might corrupt him, but for the first few days, anyway, keep an eye on the guy. If he's flirting with the girls the way he does with you, then I'm going to banish him to his garage while the kids paint."

"Does the contract give you that right?"

"No, but I'm going to take it."

"I love it when you talk tough." She giggled. She had to restrain the impulse to throw her arms around his neck and kiss him, but she managed to walk away with a brisk stride as though work were her only concern.

Indeed, that was all she wanted on her mind for the next few days. There was a chance her life had already been irrevocably changed. But there was also the chance it hadn't. All she had to do was survive the next few days without suffocating on anxiety, and then she would deal with whatever future her passion for Luke had created.

She crossed the street to Toby's followed by Sheila and Frankie, who carried the water. She directed them to place the bottles in the shade at the side of the house, then had to move quickly to avoid colliding with Toby, who had snuck up behind her.

When he dipped beneath the brim of her hat to kiss her cheek, it was abundantly clear Luke's efforts to restrain the amorous artist had met with failure. She conjured up her most evil stare and fixed him with it.

"I'm looking forward to painting the mural, but that's the extent of my interest here, Mr. McClure."

Toby responded with a smart salute. "Aye, aye, Captain. We're almost finished with the base coat. When it's dry, we'll draw in the grid." He handed her a copy of Rafael's drawing with the grid superimposed. "Dave did that on the computer, and it should be pretty easy to follow."

"Let's hope so. Other than to make certain we have the necessary supplies, I plan to stay out of everyone's way."

"Hey, come on. You're more than welcome in mine." He spread his hands wide and swept her with a suggestive gaze.

It was still early, but Toby had exhausted the last shred of Catherine's patience and, desperate to be rid of him, she seized upon the perfect threat. "Do you ever watch the WWE?" she asked.

Surprised by her question, Toby laughed before he replied. "Maybe once, why?"

"Because my boyfriend is one of the stars." She was surprised she hadn't thought of the WWE sooner. After all, the heavily muscled wrestlers were huge, and she assumed they must have some kind of professional tour; at least her sweetheart would.

Stunned by that news, Toby's mouth fell agape. "My God, which guy is he?"

Catherine savored his fright for a long, delicious moment. "Believe me, you don't want to know. Now I need to take some photographs to document the initial stages of the work. I'm sure you'll excuse me."

"Yeah, sure, I'll be around if you need me."

During the rest of the morning, Toby occasionally regarded her with a skeptical stare, but he kept a respectful distance, for which she was most grateful. At noon, the whole crew trooped back to the center for lunch, and Dave hurried to her side.

"What's with the guy from the WWE?" he whispered.

"Hush," Catherine ordered. "The story worked well, and don't you dare tell Toby otherwise."

"I don't need any competition, so you have my word on it."

He began to whistle happily, and Catherine wished she could think of something as menacing as the WWE to use on him.

Luke arrived at Catherine's that night carrying a half gallon of lime sherbet and a two liter bottle of grapefruit soda. "Come on, let's make some floats, sit out on the deck and watch the moon rise."

It sounded like the perfect evening, and Catherine quickly provided tall glasses and iced tea spoons. She even found some fluorescent straws. As soon as they were seated outside, she took a long sip.

"I keep telling you not to bring me presents, but when they're this delicious, I'll make an exception."

"The orchid was a present; refreshments don't count, but while you're moaning so contentedly, let me congratulate you on your close contact with the WWE."

"Dave told you?"

"He sure did. He was so happy you'd found a way to discourage Toby that he could barely contain himself. I'm sorry Toby didn't take my complaint more seriously, but apparently you handled him well enough on your own. I don't want Dave to be your problem now though. You've inspired him to apply for work elsewhere, but—"

"But what? Don't you want him to get back on his feet?"

"Yes, of course, but not until he can handle the pressure." Luke took several sips of his frosty drink as he searched for the means to make her understand.

"I won't violate Dave's trust, but just let me say he's got to put himself back together before he can tackle the world again. Lost Angel is the perfect haven for him, and he does more work than I would have imagined he'd tackle, but please be careful not to be anything more than a friend."

She saw straight to the bottom of his warning and sighed softly. "If Dave's ego is as fragile as you suggest, isn't there a danger he'll see simple friendship as something more?"

"Yes," he admitted, "the danger exists. But each time he brings up your name, I'll do my best to lessen his expectations. It'll be a delicate balancing act, but I think we can pull it off."

She would have preferred to tell Dave the truth, but she could scarcely lecture Luke on the danger of harboring secrets. She was tired and would rather do anything than argue.

"I'm going to adopt your policy and not think beyond tonight," she vowed.

She left her chair to kneel in front of his. She rested her arms across his thighs and slid her thumbs along the inseam of his jeans. "Now I'd like to try something, and I'll need your promise that you won't scream and frighten the neighbors."

"Just what is it you intend to do?"

She began to unbutton his fly. "Where's your spirit of adventure?"

When her fingers encircled his shaft, he was already hard and chuckled way back in his throat. "I think you've found it."

She paused to take another sip of her icy cold drink, then tasted him and, with a soft, sucking hunger, took him deep.

Luke was used to the heat of her exotic kiss, not this stunning chill. His legs tightened around her convulsively, and he buried his fingers in her hair. Before the frozen thrill had even begun to thaw, he was lost, but she'd been wrong; he had no breath to scream.

She knew exactly what she was doing, and it eased her conscience to know she wasn't the first woman to escape her fears with a lover. She quickly enticed Luke out of his clothes, and they were soon naked on the lawn, as playful as pagan gods who lived only for pleasure. She gave as much she took, and the enchantment lasted until dawn.

Chapter Fifteen

With such enthusiastic workers, progress on the mural was swift. Content to supervise from a distance, Catherine brought a low aluminum beach chair from home and parked herself near the sidewalk. Occasionally someone would wander by on their way to the neighboring bar and pause to comment, but otherwise foot traffic was scant.

Out on the street, however, cars had begun to slow as drivers gawked at the kids climbing the scaffolding. She couldn't help but notice how pleased the teens were to attract so much attention, but she warned them all to keep their wits about them to avoid a fall.

She took lots of candid photos and even managed a few of Luke while he toured the project Thursday morning. When he caught her and smiled, she simply took another shot, but she intended to keep that photograph for herself rather than post it on the bulletin board.

The previous afternoon, Toby had taken Rafael to Pasadena's Art Center College of Design. Now the spike-haired artist was excitedly recounting his tour of the campus to Luke, but it was plain he was even more excited by the prospect of impressing Art Center's professors with his spectacular mural.

Rafael had used charcoal to block in all the figures, but none had distinct features as yet. Catherine knew if she were going to raise Violet's objection to appearing in the mural, it would have to be soon, but she hated to mention the girl's name in front of Luke. She also knew better than to try to work around him.

She waited for a break in Rafael's animated conversation and then approached the young man and Luke. "In your drawing, one of the angels resembles Violet. I think she's a perfect subject, but she's afraid Ford Dolan will object. I couldn't bear it if he took his anger out on her."

Luke responded with a bitter curse, then addressed his comment to Rafael rather than Catherine. "I refuse to allow a bastard like Ford Dolan to force us to change so much as an eyelash, but it's your call, Rafael. What do you want to do?"

Rafael shook his head in disbelief. "I don't know what Violet's doing with that asshole, but she's much too pretty to tack on a witch's crooked nose to keep Ford from recognizing her."

"It's just a thought," Catherine offered, "but we don't have signed releases from the kids who'll be portrayed in the mural, so maybe she really does have the right to object."

"Whose side are you on?" Luke asked pointedly.

"Lost Angel's, of course. The other teens are all so proud to be appearing in the mural, but there might be consequences for them as well. Christmas cards are mailed to distant friends and passed around at work. It's possible some abusive parent might recognize one of the kids from our cards and come after him."

"It's just as likely some parent who has been worried sick will at last discover where their child is through the mural or cards," Luke posed.

"That's true," Catherine granted easily. "And now I think about it, if any of the kids are underage, they can't legally sign a release anyway."

"You're just all kinds of help today, aren't you, Mrs. Brooks?" Luke jabbed the toe of his loafer in the sparse grass. "What you don't understand," he softened his tone to explain, "is that if Rafael were to take Violet out of the mural, Ford would just pick something else to rag on her about. That's why it never pays to give in to bullies, because it just inspires them to increase their demands."

"Look," Rafael interjected, "even if I just made up faces rather than used the kids here, someone somewhere would think one of the angels looked exactly like them. I'm using Violet, and if Ford gives her any grief over it, she can send him to me."

Catherine admired his jaunty walk as he headed toward the porch. He was dressed in bright red polyester pants and a purple T-shirt, both of which clashed with his orange hair. "At least Rafael never lacks for confidence."

"Frankly," Luke whispered, "I think we've created a monster. He had an attitude problem before, but now he's become insufferable."

"Cheer up. He sounds impressed with Art Center, so maybe he'll attend in the fall."

"Only if they come through with a full scholarship, but let's hold that thought. Now, how are you doing over here?"

"Fine really. Toby's behaving, and so is Dave." She turned toward the sound of a car horn just as the dark green Ford convertible rolled through the intersection. She had her clipboard and made a quick notation of the license number.

Luke moved to read what she'd written. "What are you doing?"

"That '50's car cruises by here rather often. It could be members of a gang, or just a car buff who goes home for lunch, but it can't hurt to make a note of the license number."

"You want to keep track of license numbers, what about the tan sedan parked across the street in front of the auto supply?"

There were two people in the car, and while they were too far away to be recognized, she had a good idea who they were. "Garcia and Salzman on patrol?"

"Looks like it to me. I can't decide whether to ignore them or go over and chat."

"Let's not tip our hands," she whispered, "or they might resort to strange vehicles and bizarre disguises."

"They could," he agreed, and there was a twinkle in his eye he usually took care to hide when others were around. "I'll get back to work without speaking to them, but I wish I could hang out here with you."

"So do I, but there's the grave risk I'd be so distracted that I wouldn't watch the kids properly."

"Now I really don't want to leave." He spent a few more minutes talking with the kids, then surveyed the scaffolding with Dave before he returned to Lost Angel.

Getting back to work, Catherine took a few photos as Toby and Rafael mixed paint. Much of the mural would be done in grays that ranged from a deep charcoal to a pale smoke. On the angels' robes, the same grays deepened to a rich berry or lightened to sky blue. Some angels would have a peach-toned skin while others would be a burnished bronze.

Catherine still felt uneasy about Violet until it occurred to her that Ford's absurd objection to the mural might finally inspire the pretty blonde to leave him. "And not a day too soon, either," she muttered to herself.

"You talking to me?" Dave asked. He'd been helping to carry paint and was walking by with a bucket of sky blue.

"No, but you seem to be enjoying yourself, and the mural is going well."

Dave left the paint on the porch for the teens to grab and knelt beside Catherine's chair. "There are several places to eat within walking distance of here. When the kids break for lunch, instead of going to Lost Angel, why don't we go elsewhere for a change?"

He had glanced back toward the mural as he spoke and merely made a casual suggestion rather than ask for a date, but she doubted that was his true intention. "The WWE doesn't frighten you?" she teased.

"Not when the guy isn't real." Dave rose with an easy stretch. "What do you say? It's just lunch."

She would have twisted her wedding band had she still been wearing it, but it struck her as ridiculous to retreat behind her widow's pose now that she was seeing Luke. "That's sweet, Dave, but I really need to keep my focus here. If we were ten minutes late getting back and someone starting throwing paint, I'd never forgive myself."

"Maybe when it's finished, then," Dave replied, his gaze again averted.

"Maybe," she responded playfully, but she knew it was a lie and that hurt. "Say, are you any good with algebra?"

"Sure, but I don't think we'll need it here." Dave shoved his hands into his hip pockets and regarded her with an amused smile.

Catherine had finally mastered the art of rising from the low chair smoothly and did so. "No, not here, but I want to take the CBEST test so that I can teach again, and I don't remember enough about algebra to work the problems in the book I bought to help me prepare."

"We could do algebra problems over lunch," Dave offered, his grin spreading wide.

"I'm so slow we'd never get back on time, but if I brought the book tomorrow, could you give me a couple of tips while we're here?"

Dave appeared intrigued, but still a bit puzzled by her request. "You're serious. You really want help with your algebra?"

She'd been hoping for a way to be friendly without offering anything more, but now thought perhaps the whole idea had been stupid and began to back away. "I taught English, Dave, and I've never needed algebra to balance my checkbook."

"Hey, that's all right. I'll be glad to help you. Let's get everyone working in the morning, and then we can hit the math. If it looks like we're having fun, it might even interest the kids."

"The Tom Sawyer approach," she mused, but if she were going back to teaching, someone else would have to set up the tutoring program at Lost Angel.

She angled her hat to better shade her face as she studied the mural. The big bold patches of color were going up today, and each day the design would become more refined until it reached the perfection of Rafael's drawing. She could hardly wait to see it.

Joyce urged Catherine to try a brownie. "I added some peanut butter. How do they taste?"

Catherine took a bite and responded with a contented sigh. "Heavenly. What are you doing, whipping up treats for Shane?"

Joyce responded with a sassy shrug. "They say the way to a man's heart is through his stomach, and Shane's coming here for dinner Saturday night. I don't want to obsess over the menu, but a crisp roasted rosemary chicken followed by a damn good brownie ought to help my cause."

"Do you have a frilly apron?"

"Battenberg lace, and I look adorable in it, if I do say so myself." She refilled their iced tea glasses and then sat opposite Catherine.

"Now, it's been days since we've talked, and I'm dying to hear your news. Did you buy the pregnancy test, or is there no longer any need for one?"

Catherine scrunched down in her chair. They were in Joyce's breakfast room, and the late afternoon sun lent the pale gray walls a pearly luster. She took another bite of brownie rather than reply. "These really are extraordinarily good."

"Catherine," Joyce coaxed. "What's up?"

"I'm only a couple days late. Give me another week."

Joyce leaned back and fixed her friend with a decidedly skeptical gaze. "Rather than stall, you ought to make an appointment with your gynecologist. If it turns out you don't need one, then cancel it, but if you do, you'll have plenty of options. The French pill is supposed to be relatively painless."

Catherine understood Joyce's line of thinking, but still had to wash down her last bite of brownie with a long swallow of tea before she found her voice. "I really don't want to think about this now."

Joyce slapped her palm on the table. "You're acting like some naïve teenager who believes if she refuses to think about babies, they'll just go away. Well, if you're pregnant, girl, you'll have to deal with it like an adult, and you better get used to that idea right now."

Catherine didn't appreciate being lectured to, but she couldn't deny Joyce had a valid point. "It's just that I didn't expect this to happen."

"Didn't your mother warn you it only takes once?"

"Oh yes, when we had the birds-and-bees talk, I believe she threw in every single warning her mother had given her, but knowing how sperm and egg meet doesn't mean I expected to conceive the first time I slept with Luke."

"Stand up guy that he is, he used condoms, didn't he?"

"Yes, but you're entirely too curious about this, Joyce."

"I am not, but cut me some slack. Until I can get Shane into bed, I need a vicarious thrill from your romance. When do you plan to tell Luke he might become a father?"

"Oh lord." Catherine sat forward to prop her elbows on the table and rest her head in her hands. "I'm not going to torture him with that possibility until I absolutely have to."

"So, despite my suggestion, you never had that little abstract chat about marriage and children?"

"No, and I'm not going to, either." She sat back and swept brownie crumbs onto her plate. "I'm not refusing to think about being pregnant, Joyce, in fact, I've thought of little else since waking up sick Sunday morning. Sam and I missed our chance to have children, and if I have a chance this time, I'm going to grab for it."

"What if Luke says no? Men insist they have rights too, you know."

"Which they do," Catherine agreed, "but if Luke can't face fatherhood again—"

"Again? You mean the guy has other children?"

Catherine licked her lips. She could hear Luke yelling about her lack of respect for his privacy, but when she was so closely involved, she thought she deserved some consideration too. Believing it was time Joyce learned the truth, she provided what few facts she knew about Marcy's death.

"Oh my God! Why didn't you tell me that sooner? That's awful. No wonder you're so reticent to confide in Luke, but you can't wait to tell him the truth until it's too late for him to have any input."

Catherine knew that too. "That's what you don't understand. He doesn't have any choice. If it turns out I really am pregnant, and I might not be, then he can either be thrilled and be a real father to our child, or walk. I can raise a baby alone, and I'll tell anyone who's rude enough to ask about the father that I used a sperm bank."

"Well, if Luke walks, then that's all he was." Joyce shook her head sadly. "Now that you've told me his story, I feel just sick over this, so I can imagine how you must feel."

"Please, I don't even want to go there."

Joyce nodded thoughtfully. "You're slender. A pregnancy might not show on you for four months, but you won't make it past five without Luke wondering what's happened to your svelte figure. Of course, if he's as great a lover as you say, he'll notice that first sweet swell of your belly, and if the baby shows before he knows, I sure wouldn't want to be there."

"Nor would I. I know I'll have to tell him, but if I were to lose him and then miscarry—"

Unable to sit still another second, Joyce stood and began to wrap up the remaining brownies. "You can't hedge your bets on something like this. A couple is either a team or they're not. I've always thought you had it together, unlike me, who can't seem to cook up anything worthwhile outside of the kitchen, but keeping secrets from a man you care about, a man who has every right to know, is so damn stupid I can't even believe you'd seriously consider it."

"Neither can I," Catherine admitted, "but thinking of Luke's feelings makes this so much more difficult."

Catherine left without giving her friend a hug, but she felt sick too, and every choice she had seemed to be the wrong one.

Dave had gotten a haircut, and when Catherine first saw him Friday morning, she failed to recognize him. Then she noticed the Phish T-shirt that was one of his favorites and realized who he was.

"You look completely different, Dave. Really good too, by the way."

No longer pulled back in a ponytail, his light brown hair dipped over his forehead in soft waves that enhanced the blue of his eyes. The stylish cut had made such a dramatic difference in his appearance that he'd gone from looking like a handyman who loved the outdoors to a model for *GQ* between wardrobe changes.

"Thank you, but I've been working on my résumé and don't want to waste any time getting a haircut should I actually receive a request for an interview."

"It's always good to plan ahead," she complimented, "although I hope you won't be disappointed in the response you receive."

"Oh, I'm sure to be disappointed. I know guys who've sent out hundreds of résumés and not received a single reply. The postage alone can be heartbreaking, but I'm going to do as much as I possibly can through the Internet. Luke's been cool about letting me log on after Lost Angel closes."

When Catherine found herself unable to offer a coherent comment about Luke's generosity, she excused herself to make certain the necessary supplies were on hand. She'd had to make a couple of extra runs to the paint store earlier in the week, but everyone had what he or she needed that morning.

It was nearly ten o'clock before she and Dave could sit down to study. In his usual easy manner, he reviewed the problems that had confused her and provided solid instruction on how to go about solving the rest. Catherine was quite pleased with the way the day was going until a dark shadow fell across her book. She knew without looking up that it would be Luke.

"Are you cramming for an exam, Mrs. Brooks? You never cease to amaze me."

Dave stood and brushed off the seat of his khaki pants. "It never hurts to hone your math skills," he muttered. "You'll have to excuse me. I need to get back to work across the street."

"Go right ahead," Luke encouraged, but he waited until Dave was out of earshot to kneel down beside Catherine. "I don't really care what it is you're doing," he whispered. "But you can't complain that Dave is bugging you one day and pal around with him the next. It's a mixed message that'll drive any man crazy."

Catherine slammed her CBEST review book closed and jammed her pencil behind her ear. "I wasn't flirting with him and don't believe I gave him the wrong impression."

"Did you leave the house without glancing in the mirror?" When he saw he'd merely confused her, Luke tried again. "You're a beautiful woman, Catherine, and Dave's lonely. The other day you understood how easily he could misinterpret your actions. What happened today?"

That she'd needed help with algebra struck Catherine as too silly an excuse to offer. Feeling trapped, she tried not to get angry, but her nerves were too frayed for her to be mellow. "I wish you wouldn't scold me as though I were one of the kids. You didn't stumble onto a tryst."

She sprang from her chair, her book clutched to her chest, and then had to wait for Luke to rise. A hot lick of tears blurred her vision, and she feared hormones might be to blame. She'd once been such a calm, easy-going person, but that was before she'd met Luke.

"I'm sorry," she apologized quickly. "I shouldn't have been so snotty."

"No, you're right, I do tend to lecture at times. I'm on my way to my attorney's office for a meeting with Melissa, so I'll blame my foul mood on her. Maybe I'll see you later."

"Yes, I want to hear what happened."

"I can tell you that now," Luke joked. "She'll weep into a lacy handkerchief and insist she deserves more money. I'll disagree. The attorneys will argue as if they actually cared which side won, and we'll either end up in court or arbitration. Still, I have to show up and play the bad guy."

"You're not the bad guy. Why would you say that?"

Luke offered a sad, sweet smile and shrugged. "Don't get me started. I've already spoken with Melissa once this morning, so I know my role."

He left her to swing through the yard and admire the mural. In less than five minutes, he'd crossed the street and was gone, while she was left behind to wish she could have gone along with him.

Work on the mural ended each day at four o'clock to make certain there was time to clean brushes and put everything away for the next day. Several of the kids were regulars at Luke's afternoon session, and Catherine didn't wish to interfere with his schedule, either. She covered a wide yawn as she leaned her beach chair against the house, and she was moving too slowly to avoid Toby when he came her way.

"The mural looks great, although it's easier to appreciate from across the street than my front yard. The kids are really getting into it. I hope you can find other projects for them when they're finished here."

"So do I, but I'll bet they'll miss working with you."

"They'll know where to find me," Toby reminded her with a mischievous wink. "I'm sorry, but I keep thinking about you and some overgrown lump of muscle from the WWE, and it just doesn't compute. Why don't you tell me the truth? I can stand it."

"I wish it were that simple," Catherine replied. She removed her hat and used it as a fan. "It's plain you're not used to being turned down, but my affections lie elsewhere. Whether or not my honey is a hunk with the WWE or not, really doesn't matter."

"It matters to me. Come on, I'll walk you to your car." Toby kept to a respectful distance as they crossed the street to the Lost Angel parking lot. Then he stepped close, and his tone became intimate.

"Now, as I see it, if you're in love with the guy and he's treating you well, then I'll stay out of your way. But there's something in your eyes that tells me things aren't right. If I have to start taking karate lessons to defend myself, then I'll do it, but please come to me if you have problems with your love life you can't handle on your own."

His sleeves were rolled up, and for a brief instant, Catherine was sorely tempted to reach out and trace the delicate scales of the dragon's tail curling around his forearm. "That's very nice of you, but really, whatever problems we might have can't be solved with karate, although I do understand it's very good exercise," she added flippantly.

Toby raised his hands and backed away. "Fine, I get your message, but you remember what I said. If someday you need me, I'll be there for you."

Completely overwhelmed by that thought, Catherine managed only a faint smile. She'd wanted to talk with Luke, but he'd be busy for the next hour or two, and she was too tired to wait.

"I better go, Toby."

He waved and strolled off toward his house with a swaggering gait that wasn't all that different from Rafael's.

Before leaving his office to conduct the afternoon session, Luke had glanced out the window to check if Catherine's Volvo were still in the lot. When he saw her and Toby standing by her car with their heads together, he was so shocked he had to stay to watch. They appeared to be discussing something more serious than the mural, but he couldn't even imagine what that might be.

Catherine was undeniably lovely, but that she attracted such devoted male attention without the slightest bit of effort on her part annoyed him no end. He wasn't used to feeling jealous, and yet he couldn't rationalize it away. Then he began to worry Catherine might look up and catch him watching her.

Here he'd thought Melissa was his problem for the day, but with Dave and Toby circling Catherine like sharks, it was clear his real problem lay far closer to home.

Catherine already had the Tuna Helper cooking when Luke rang the doorbell. She welcomed him with a kiss and then took his hand. "Come on in the kitchen and tell me what happened with Melissa."

While Luke usually refused a drink, he poured himself a scotch before sitting down at the breakfast room table. "It went exactly as I predicted. Melissa even wore a misty blue suit to highlight her deeply depressed mood. She had the linen hanky with the lace border and sobbed into it the whole time.

"To hear her tell it, I tossed her out in the snow without so much as a threadbare blanket. I did my best not to let her pathetic charade make me angry, but—"

"You failed?" She continued to rip lettuce into bite-size hunks and tossed them into a salad bowl.

"Spectacularly," he admitted sheepishly. "I even threw my chair across the room."

She began to chop a bell pepper. "Wonderful. Is Melissa now calling you not only cheap but abusive?"

"You got it, but thank God we weren't in court. Unfortunately my attorney was ready to deck me for it, so we're lucky the meeting didn't end in a brawl. In a couple of days, the attorneys will meet and see what they can work out by themselves, but with neither of us willing to give in, we're sure to end up in court."

"While it's little comfort now, I'm sure it'll all work itself out in time. You look tired. I was hoping you'd come by for dinner."

"Thank you, but I should have called."

"Yes, that's always nice, but I still like finding you on the doorstep."

"Yeah, but for how long?" He nearly snorted. He downed his scotch in a quick swallow and then set the glass on the table with exaggerated care. "I didn't really come here to talk about Melissa."

Catherine had just reached for the celery but paused to give him her full attention. "What have I done wrong now?" she asked hesitantly.

He left the table and came forward to give her a reassuring hug. "You see, you expect me to lurch around in attack mode, and that's not good for either of us. Hell, I might as well be with the WWE."

The image of him strutting around a wrestling ring screaming insults to another wrestler was so absurd she couldn't help but laugh. "What would you do, call yourself Dr. Fist?"

He laughed, hugged her again and lifted her clear off her feet. "Say, I like that. Maybe I'll wear black leather into court and tell them to call me Dr. Fist."

He kissed her lightly, then still laughing, stepped back. "You distract me every damn time, lady, and you do it on purpose too."

"Well, of course, I enjoy your laughter a great deal more than your shouting fits."

He leaned back against the counter. "That's reasonable. Now what I intended to say before you got me sidetracked, was that maybe I've been too tightly focused on my job as director of Lost Angel and lost sight of how my decisions affect you."

She tried to smile, but her lips froze in a questioning pout. "Oh?" Was all she could manage, but none of his decisions compared with the one she'd already made for him. He was serious now, all trace of laughter erased from his expression, and it only served to frighten her.

"Yeah, and while I can still justify not telling anyone that you and I are a couple, you were right about my choice putting you in too awkward a place. I'm going to come clean with Dave and Toby and tell them you're seeing me. No, that's still too damn arrogant, isn't it? I'll say we're seeing each other. Is that better?"

When she couldn't find the words to respond, she kissed him instead, but it was a desperate ploy rather than sincere affection. She'd disliked having to be evasive at the center, but now Luke had seen his way to tell the truth, she hated herself for not being able to do the same.

Chapter Sixteen

"You're not eating," Luke observed between bites of his second helping of Tuna Helper.

With her stomach twisted in knots, Catherine had found it next to impossible to swallow, but she hadn't wanted him to notice how little she ate. "I'm not very hungry."

"Come on, I'm not going to force you to eat, but you're putting in pretty long days with the mural, and I don't want you to get sick."

She was extremely uncomfortable under such close scrutiny but tried to remain civil. "Is there any real scientific evidence that people with little appetite fall ill more often than those who gobble up everything in sight, or is that just an old wives' tale?"

"Catherine," Luke cajoled. "What's wrong? If something's bugging you, tell me about it rather than go on a hunger strike."

She searched her mind for some problem, no matter how minor, to avoid mentioning her true concern. At the point of desperation, something of real significance finally occurred to her. "Now that you mention it, I was studying for an exam this morning. I plan to take the CBEST test and look for a full-time teaching position for the fall."

He paused in mid-bite. "Really? When did you make that decision?"

She twisted her napkin in her lap. "Actually, I'd made it before I met you at Lost Angel. I was afraid I wouldn't be able to relate to teenagers anymore, and if my volunteer work there had been a disaster, I wouldn't be thinking about teaching again."

Luke laid his fork very carefully on the side of his plate and sat back in his chair. "Wait a minute, let me see if I have this straight. When you came to Lost Angel, you weren't interested in volunteering with us per se but simply in working on your rapport with teenagers?"

His expression wasn't nearly as harsh as his question, but Catherine could see he was disappointed in her. "No, my motives weren't entirely selfish. I really did want to volunteer with homeless teens. It's a huge problem, and I believed I might be able to help. The fact that I had to fight you for the privilege should convince you of my sincerity."

"Yeah, you convinced me, all right. When did you plan to tell me about your plans for the fall?"

Again, the sarcastic edge to his voice sliced her sore conscience, but certain she deserved worse, she shrugged. "I don't know, after the mural is finished I suppose. Of course, if I don't pass the CBEST test, and Dave was helping me with the algebra portion, then I won't be going anywhere until I do. Besides, it's a long time until fall, so I'll still be volunteering for several more months."

"Well, it's nice to know we'd still fit into your plans."

"Luke, I'm not leaving you, but I would like to teach again, and as you pointed out, there would be enormous problems associated with setting up a volunteer tutoring program at Lost Angel."

"True, but rather than discuss this with me," he asked pointedly, "you went to Dave for help?"

"You're awfully busy, and I was just trying to be nice to Dave. But you were right, I probably gave him the wrong idea. He was very helpful, though."

Luke stood and rested his hands on the back of his chair. "Well, that's just great. I've already told you this wasn't the best day of my life, but I try not to get into more than one fight per day with a woman, and Melissa used up my quota. Now I'm going to be really rude and walk out without helping with the dishes, but I'll see you tomorrow morning. I've got the day off, and there's nothing I'd rather do than work on the mural."

Catherine left her chair with sufficient speed to overtake him before he'd left the kitchen. "You invited me to confide in you, but now you're angry. I have every right to plan for my future. I haven't done anything wrong."

He nodded thoughtfully. "Fine, you got me, but I'm not your therapist, Catherine. You're not paying me to respond with sympathetic questions, and I gave you my honest reaction. We've got nothing if we can't be honest with each other, and springing a major decision on me like that wasn't fair. After all, if you're teaching, we'll have a lot less time to spend together, and that will affect me too."

The knot in her stomach tightened to a gut-wrenching clench. "I know, but I'm trying to get my life together. Going back into teaching will be a big step for me. I need your support."

He leaned in to kiss her forehead. "Sure, I'll write you a glowing reference. But the next time you go off in some new direction, will you please signal to warn me first?"

She let him walk out of her house without begging him to stay. Considering what she'd witnessed of Luke's temper on previous occasions, his reaction to her news had been mild, but she'd still hurt him, and that increased her own anguish tenfold.

When Catherine arrived at Toby's Saturday morning, Rafael had already been at work several hours painting the angel who had resembled Violet in his drawing. Now she was complete to the last meticulous detail, and the resemblance was strikingly accurate. He climbed down from the scaffold to observe his work and greeted Catherine warmly.

"Good morning, Mrs. Brooks. What do you think of my angel?"

"She's very beautiful, but I wish Violet could be proud to appear in the mural rather than frightened witless."

"That's her problem," Rafael exclaimed. "Now the light is perfect this morning, and I want to take advantage of it. Got your camera?"

"Yes, I'll get one of the angels right now." Catherine was still seeking the best angle to shoot through the scaffolding when Luke walked up behind her. She went ahead and took the photograph before he distracted her completely, but unwilling to apologize, she waited for him to speak.

"Did you sleep well?" he whispered.

She turned around slowly. His sunglasses obscured his expression, but the sly smile which had always been her undoing tugged at his mouth.

"That's classified information," she responded coolly, "and to renew your security clearance, you'll have to reapply."

"That bad, huh?" Luke shook his head. "I didn't sleep well, either. I kept thinking about how much you like to plan ahead while I don't. I imagine we're going to run smack into that difference over and over again. Unless, of course, one of us changes his point of view."

"Is that even possible?" she asked.

He was dressed in the same tattered Levi's he'd worn the day they'd painted his office, but his T-shirt was a souvenir from a beach city's ten kilometer run. "I'd like to believe anything is possible," he hedged, "but that would be admitting a better future might exist."

"Careful, Dr. Starns, you're straying dangerously close to my side."

Again Luke dropped his voice. "I'm interested in a hell of a lot more than your side. Let's try to make it to a movie tonight so we'll have an excuse to hold hands."

"I'd like that. Maybe we could just go into Old Town, stroll around until we find a place to eat and then see what's playing in the theaters."

"Are you suggesting we plan not to plan?" Luke teased.

"For the moment, yes." She enjoyed this playful banter so much more than the unavoidable confrontations which constantly sprang up between them. "Now we better get to work before the kids start pointing and giggling at us."

"Maybe we ought to just get that over with now." Luke slid his arms around her waist and kissed her so soundly all the kids scattered around the porch and scaffolding began to hoot and holler.

Toby and Dave, who had just rounded the house carrying paint, nearly dropped their buckets in surprise. "What the hell are you doing, Luke?" Dave called to him.

Luke laced his fingers in Catherine's and drew her along with him toward the house and the two men. "Catherine and I have been seeing each other almost since her first day at Lost Angel. I asked her to keep it quiet, but I should have been up front about it with you."

Toby just laughed. "I knew it, but you remember what I said, Catherine. It still goes."

Dave, however, regarded Luke with a darkly threatening glance. "You knew what my feelings were."

"Yes, I did, but the choice was hers, Dave, not mine."

Rather than reply, Dave left the yard and returned to Lost Angel before Catherine could say anything to ease his shock. Clearly he was furious with them both for carrying on right under his nose and lying about it.

"I hate secrets," she blurted out. "Now, Rafael says it's a great day to paint so let's get to work."

"Yes, ma'am," Toby replied. "Just point me in the right direction."

"We don't need you out here," Luke said. "Go pound on some metal in your studio."

"That okay with you, Catherine?"

"Sure, Toby, we'll call you if we need you."

"You do that," Toby called over his shoulder, and he left them to attend to his own work.

Catherine turned and nearly bumped into Tina Stassy. "Oh, Tina, I'm sorry. What do you need?"

"Those guys in the tan car over there are creeping me out. Why are they watching us?"

"They're looking for suspects," Luke responded, "but they're in the wrong place, so they're wasting their time and the taxpayers' money. Now, what would you and Charlie like to paint?"

"We're just hanging out here. I'm going to help Polly when we get to the flowers at the bottom. Polly's real good with flowers."

"Is that a fact?" Luke grabbed Catherine's beach chair and carried it across the yard to where she usually sat. "Just make yourself comfortable, and I'll try and stay out of your way. I brought donuts for the kids. Who's ready for a break?"

Catherine watched as Luke produced a couple of cardboard boxes filled with donuts, and the kids all gathered around to grab one. Nick slapped Luke on the back and leaned close to whisper something that made Luke laugh, and Catherine was certain it must have been about her. If she knew Luke, which she did, he would tolerate such playful teasing today, but on

Monday, it would be business as usual, and he'd demand the respect they both deserved.

The weather was beautiful, clear and yet not too warm, and if she just admired the mural and the kids' ambition to complete it, it was a perfect morning. It was only when her glance drifted toward Luke, which was often, that she longed for so much more.

That night Catherine and Luke ate a mesquite wood-fired pizza and went to an off-beat romantic comedy which had gotten excellent reviews. It was a lighthearted evening, and she wanted it to end that way. She kissed Luke as soon as they'd come through her front door and did so with an enthusiasm that convinced him he'd been missed.

He ran his fingers through her hair to hold her close and returned her kiss with equal fervor before pulling away. "Hey," he whispered. "I'm sorry about last night, but you must have learned by now I'm never angry for long."

"True, but I don't like your being angry at all. It frightens me."

He rested his forehead against hers. "Don't forget that upon occasion, you've been equally angry with me."

"True, but that's different."

"Why?"

"I don't know, it just is." She began to unbutton his shirt, and just as she'd hoped, one luscious kiss swiftly followed another. She leaned into him, savoring his every caress, as though love were a spell to be woven with pleasure, while he'd already captured her heart.

She ran her hand over his hairy chest and circled his nipples with her fingertips. "You have a handsome build, much better than those muscular monsters on the WWE."

"What if I hurt a knee, couldn't run and pudged up to two hundred pounds?"

She slid her hands around his waist. "We'd have to find another exercise to keep you in shape, maybe Pilates or yoga."

"You'd keep me company?"

"Hmm. It might be fun, if you made it worth my while."

"If I started now, could I build up some credits?"

"Are you suggesting a Sex Bank?" She muffled her giggles against his shoulder.

"Why not?" He dipped his head to nibble her earlobe.

She quickly removed her hoop earrings. "Too much paperwork."

"Not if we kept a tally on the computer."

She was quiet a long moment. "As goofy as it sounds, with the right infomercial, we might be able to sell a Sex Bank program on late night TV."

Luke laughed so hard he had to cling to her to keep standing. "God, woman, I thought I'd forgotten how to laugh, but you're a hell of a lot better than a therapist."

She gave him a playful punch to the gut. "Hey, I'm serious here. Let's go upstairs and work on ideas for the infomercial."

He kept his arm around her as they climbed the stairs. "Who's going to take notes?"

"Too early for that yet. Now I'm thinking a kiss ought to be worth only a point or two, while going down on a woman could have a sliding scale."

As they entered her bedroom, Luke nearly tore off his clothes and hers too. "Do I get points for effort?"

"Bonus points?" She loved being able to make him laugh and tickled him as she pulled him down on the bed.

He sucked her toes, tickled her foot and sent kisses slowly up her calf. "Anticipation is such a great part of sex."

"Won't get you any points," she warned in a husky whisper.

He slid his fingers into her and spread tender kisses up her thigh. "I should never have walked out of here last night."

She moaned way back in her throat. "If you'd had any points, you would have lost them."

He moved up and swept his tongue into her cleft. "You're too wet to play hard to get."

"No, I'll leave being hard to you." Their playful game blurred by desire, she raised her arms above her head and slid her legs over his shoulders. He created the most luscious warmth that rolled down her legs and left her too lazy with joy to offer another teasing word. When he crawled over her to claim her for himself, she welcomed him into the last quivers of her orgasm and sought the joy of his. He pushed the night into a magical realm, and when he left with the dawn, she uttered a small sigh in protest.

Luke seldom went into Lost Angel on Sundays, but he did that day. He checked his messages, then went looking for Dave. When he found him sitting on the front steps reading the comics with the kids, he nodded for him to follow.

Dave handed the newspaper to Polly, then caught up to Luke. "You got something for me to do, boss?" he asked.

"No, I just want to talk with you. Come on in my office."

"I'd rather stay out here. The grass is doing pretty well, don't you think?"

The side yard did look a whole lot better than it had just a few weeks prior and Luke nodded to acknowledge Dave's work. "Fine, let's talk out here. Catherine Brooks is a remarkable woman—"

Dave began to back away. "If that's all you've got to say, then we're through."

Luke swore under his breath. "She can't be the first woman you've wanted who liked someone else better."

Abruptly ending his retreat, Dave came back toward Luke with a long, menacing stride. "No, but she's the first woman since my life went to hell who looked at me as though it didn't matter. She claimed she wasn't interested in dating anyone, but I sure as hell thought that when she was, it would be me."

"I'm sorry you were hurt. Neither of us meant for that to happen."

"You and Cathy talked about me? What did you do, laugh about how stupid I was to dream of dating someone like her?"

"No, of course not." Luke shut his mouth before admitting that he couldn't have successfully fought his attraction to Catherine had he tried. "Look," he began again, "Catherine is not only beautiful but bright as well, and any man would be interested in her. Had she wanted you, she'd be sharing your basement apartment, but damn it all, she chose me."

"Yeah, like she had a choice," Dave shot right back at him. "Well, what are you going to do now? Do you plan to marry her and have some little red-haired kids, or will you just brush her off once you've had your fill?"

Luke couldn't even think of marriage without feeling sick to his stomach, but he couldn't imagine his life without Catherine either. Torn, he feared Dave was uncomfortably close to the truth.

"We haven't been dating long," he said. "It's too soon to make plans for the future."

"Like hell. At least I'm open to marriage and kids, and when Catherine realizes you're not, I may be her choice after all. Now, I won't be coming to you for therapy any longer, and unless you've got work for me, stay out of my way. A job offer should come through for me soon, and I'll move out the very next day."

Dave's hands were clenched in tight fists, and Luke could see he was close to taking a swing at him. While they might be an even match, Luke didn't want to fight him when it would prove nothing and provide the very worst kind of lesson for the kids. He walked away rather than argue, but Dave had forced him to consider what he did have to offer Catherine. Afraid it wasn't much, he drove down to the beach, yanked on his jogging shoes, and ran until he was too tired to do more than sleep.

Monday morning, Violet hid in the bushes until she saw Catherine drive into the Lost Angel parking lot. Then she came stumbling out into the sunshine, a heavy backpack slung over her shoulder.

Had it not been for her flowing blonde hair, Catherine wouldn't have recognized Violet when her blackened eyes hid their pretty blue color and her mouth was too swollen to smile. "Oh, my God," she cried.

Violet raised a hand to keep Catherine from coming too close. "Please, I've got bruises all over and if you touch me, they'll just hurt worse."

Catherine took the backpack as a hopeful sign Violet had left Ford Dolan, and she gestured toward the office. "At least come inside and sit down. Luke will know what to do."

"That's what I'm hoping," Violet mumbled.

Pam Strobble took one look at Violet's battered face and hit the intercom to summon Luke. "We need you out here."

Luke immediately came through his door, but he stopped when he recognized Violet. He watched as she slowly eased herself down into a padded chair, then sent Catherine a questioning glance.

"She was waiting for me outside," Catherine explained. "But I knew you were the one who'd know what to do."

"How many times have we gone through this, Violet?" Luke asked wearily. "I've lost count."

Violet pulled a tissue from her pocket and made a fluttering attempt to dry her tears. "Too many, but I've left Ford for good this time. I'm not going back, not ever."

"Fine, let's call the police." Luke came on out into the office and leaned back against Pam's desk.

"No, I just want to get away. I don't want to have to tell my story over and over and then just have Ford laugh at me in court. He saw my angel yesterday and called me a lying whore for hanging out here when he'd forbidden it. He screamed at me that I wasn't no homeless teen, my home was with him. But not anymore it isn't. You got some place for me to go?"

Luke stared at her and shook his head. "I won't waste a bed in a shelter unless you're finally serious about leaving Ford."

Violet's eyes were swollen to mere slits, but she returned Luke's skeptical stare. "It frightened me at first, but I love being one of Rafael's angels. There's no way I'm going to let Ford take something that special away from me."

Dave came in the door in time to hear the last of Violet's comment. Stunned she'd been so badly beaten, he looked toward Catherine, who just shook her head sadly. "Shouldn't we take some pictures?" he asked. "Isn't documentation important?"

"Yes, it is," Luke said. "But before we do anything, I need your word, Violet, that you'll stay at the shelter until they find you work and a home, and you'll attend their therapy sessions for as long as it takes for you to learn to avoid abusive men like Ford Dolan."

"I've already learned that," Violet murmured.

Apparently unconvinced, Luke waited a moment longer, but when Violet remained silent, he gave in. "All right, I'll call the shelter. Take a couple of photos, Dave, but if you have other bruises you'd rather not show him, Mrs. Brooks could take photographs of those."

"I've got bruises all over," Violet admitted shyly. "So maybe Mrs. Brooks ought to do it."

"Fine," Dave agreed. He had entered the office to grab a pencil from Pam's desk. He got one and left without again glancing Catherine's way.

"I may have to call several shelters to find a place for you, but I want you to sit right there and wait."

"I understand," Violet replied. "I'm not completely stupid about everything, you know."

Luke caught Catherine's eye before returning to his office, and it was plain he doubted Violet knew anything at all worth knowing.

Pam left her chair to open the restroom door. "Why don't you come on in here, Violet, and strip down to your underwear. Catherine can take the photos through the open door so no one else will see you. Then if you change your mind about pressing charges against Ford, you'll have the necessary evidence."

"Okay," Violet reluctantly agreed. She left her backpack on her chair and then shuffled into the restroom.

"I feel sick," Catherine whispered. "What kind of a monster gets his kicks from beating up such a beautiful child?"

"Ford Dolan's a pathetic excuse for a man, all right, but this isn't the first time Violet has shown up here with a split lip or black eye. She's always refused Luke's help, but she needs it as much as Ford does. Let's hope she finally gets it in a battered women's shelter."

When Violet opened the restroom door, Catherine took the photographs, but the girl's arms and legs were covered with so many bruises she looked as though she'd fallen down a flight of stairs. It truly did make Catherine sick to think how Violet must have cried and begged for Ford to stop before he'd finally vented his foul temper.

While Violet was getting dressed, Catherine whispered to Pam. "Luke swore to me that men like Ford Dolan usually come to a bad end, but clearly it hasn't been nearly soon enough."

"I hear you, girl. At least Violet came to her senses before she was injured more severely, but for some women, anything short of death doesn't faze them. At least now domestic violence is treated more seriously, but Luke swears no one is doing enough to prevent it from happening in the first place."

"He's right too." Catherine really did feel unsteady and sat down to rest a moment. "What a way to start the day."

Pam raised her brows. "Doesn't bode well for the week, does it?"

"No, it sure doesn't." Come tomorrow, her period would be a week late, and she would have no excuse to avoid taking a pregnancy test. It was time, and Luke deserved to know the results just as soon as she had them. Just imagining that conversation truly made her ill.

She pushed out of her chair. "I think I need some fresh air. I'm going to go on across the street. Will Luke need me to ride to the shelter with Violet?"

"No, the fewer people who know its location, the better," Pam said.

Catherine stood on the steps and took in several deep breaths, but she still felt far from well. When Dave joined her at the corner, she didn't feel up to arguing with him and quickly said so. "I'm sorry, Dave, I know what you must think of me, but—"

Dave hit the button for the light. "Don't apologize. Just ask Luke what his hopes are for the future. We eat dinner together a couple of times a week, or at least we used to, and I can guarantee that he's not interested in having a wife and more kids. You just think about that, because there are a lot of guys, me included, who'd like nothing better than to come home to you and some cute little red-haired kids."

He wasn't telling her anything she hadn't agonized over herself, and her smile was faint. "Thank you, Dave."

"You're welcome. I'm just going over to check the scaffolding, and then I'll stay out of your way. If you need another algebra lesson, Pam can find me."

"Thanks, but I understand so much more than I did, I think I'll be okay."

Catherine found her beach chair and sat down to observe the day's work on the mural. Rafael was painting in the features on another angel while the rest of the kids were still working on the angels' flowing robes and wings. The whole mural was coming along nicely, and best of all, the kids were working together and getting along well.

The other Lost Angel volunteers were crossing the street more regularly now to gauge the mural's progress, and

Catherine enjoyed their friendly company, but whenever she was alone, she shifted uncomfortably in her chair.

Having had one horrible encounter with Ford Dolan, she didn't want to see him ever again, but she doubted it would take him long to discover Violet was gone. Then he was sure to come to Lost Angel. She'd stood her ground when he'd warned her away from Violet, but he'd be in a terrific rage now.

At noon, when Luke came to walk her to Lost Angel for lunch, she knew no matter how delicious Mabel's spaghetti was that day, she wouldn't be able to eat a bite.

"How long do you think it will take for Ford to show up here looking for Violet?" she asked.

"I expect to see him this afternoon," Luke replied, apparently not in the least bit concerned.

Catherine gripped his arm. "What are you going to do?"

"Nothing. I'll just give him a blank stare and swear I've not seen Violet today. It's the best way to protect her."

"Fine, I'll remember that if he confronts me in the parking lot again."

"Don't worry. I'll come and get you at four o'clock and make certain you reach your car safely."

They had just crossed the street and started down the sidewalk when Ford Dolan drove his truck up over the curb to block their way. He jumped down from the cab screaming obscenities, and Luke took a protective step in front of Catherine.

"What the fuck have you done with Violet?" Ford yelled at them, shaking loose his carefully styled pompadour. Part of his shirttail hung over his belt, and his pants were stained with grease. "That slut ought to be home. Where is she?"

"I've no idea," Luke replied, "but I'm real pleased to learn she's left you."

Catherine turned in hopes Garcia and Salzman might be observing them, but their sedan was parked around the corner. She was tempted to run and get them, but she was unwilling to leave Luke alone with Ford. Most of the kids had crossed the street to go to lunch ahead of them, and the few stragglers still in Toby's yard were all girls.

"You're lying," Ford swore, "you and the book bitch hiding behind you. You know where Violet is, and if you know what's good for you, you'll tell me right now."

Luke remained calm and shrugged off Ford's threat. "I can't tell you what I don't know. Maybe Violet took a bus to San Diego, or San Francisco. My guess is that she'd want to be a long way from you."

"That's crazy. Violet loves me." Ford spit in the street. "She's my woman, you hear, and you tell her she better get herself home by tonight."

"Do I look like your secretary? I'm not relaying your messages. Maybe Violet left you a note. Did you look for one?"

"No, but—" Ford stammered a moment and then fell into another long string of expletives, got back into his truck and, with screeching tires, careened away.

Catherine sagged against Luke. "What did Violet ever see in that oily slug?"

"I told you she was an abused child. Healthy relationships are completely foreign to her, and that made Ford irresistibly appealing."

"But still—"

Luke hugged her. "Hush. Don't try and get in her head, but you'll be pleased to learn Violet took a whole bag of books with her. At the shelter, she'll be able to read without anyone criticizing her taste."

"It wasn't her taste in reading material Ford objected to. He just didn't want her to read period. Makes me rather proud to be the book bitch, though."

"That's the spirit. Now let's have some spaghetti."

"How can you think about food?"

"How can you not? Ford will probably go home and tear up the place looking for a note. Then he'll be back, and I want to be ready for him. I need food for energy. I can't fight punks on an empty stomach."

"Are you serious?"

"No, I'll just call the police if he shows up here again. Now, sit with me today. I'm tired of pretending you're just another volunteer."

She was still trembling. "I don't understand how you can remain so cool."

"Look, I'm playing Ford. I want him to flail around in his own misery for a few days. Then when it finally hits him that Violet is gone for good, he'll either come back in a rage I'll let the police handle, or he'll cry, bitch and moan that no one understands him. I might be able to convince him to get treatment then. That's my goal, not just to punch him out and send him on to abuse another poor girl. That won't help anyone."

"Well, at least you have a plan."

"Of course, my life isn't completely aimless."

"No, I didn't mean that. It's just that Ford scares me. When he actually believes he has the right to beat up Violet, how can you predict what he'll do next?"

"I can't, but psychology would be a really dull field if human behavior were always predictable. People tend to follow certain patterns. Those can be observed, and I doubt Ford is so creative he'll go off on some new tack of his own."

"Still, I wouldn't put anything past him. Do you consider me predictable, by the way?"

Luke laughed and hugged her as they passed through the office on their way to the hall. "Never, but that's the challenge. Now let's eat."

"Easy for you to say." She trusted Luke, and his years of experience had given him a confidence she would never attain. Still, there was a wild gleam in Ford's eye that had been truly terrifying.

Chapter Seventeen

On the way home from Lost Angel on Tuesday afternoon, Catherine stopped by a drugstore and bought a pregnancy test kit. She followed the directions with meticulous care, then couldn't bring herself to check the results. She wished Luke were there to do it for her, and in the next breath, was relieved that he wasn't.

"Courage, Catherine." She finally forced herself to look, and just as she'd feared, the result was positive. She had already known the truth in her heart, but holding the scientific proof was still daunting.

It was dusk before she walked up the street to tell Joyce. Her friend welcomed her with an ecstatic cry and then took note of her somber expression. "I'm pregnant," Catherine blurted out.

"I knew it. Come on in. Let's have a drink to celebrate, or bemoan the fact, whichever, but I guess alcohol isn't recommended, is it?"

"No, it isn't. But I stopped by to let you know you've convinced me to tell Luke right away. He's a stickler for honesty, and waiting will only worsen his reaction."

"That's a big plus right there. At least split a soda with me. Have you planned what you'll say?"

"No, but I'll try and sneak up on the subject rather than pummel him with it."

"You might as well try to sneak up on the Matterhorn. What can you possibly say?"

"I don't know yet, but I'll wait until we're away from Lost Angel and he's in a real mellow mood."

"Sleep with him first, you mean? That could work, I suppose." Joyce pulled a can of diet 7UP from the refrigerator, poured two glasses and added ice.

Catherine carried her glass to the breakfast table and sat. "Sleeping with him would be too devious, but he's always more relaxed away from the center."

Joyce joined her at the table. "Maybe you've got him all wrong. He might be thrilled at the prospect of fatherhood."

Catherine took a sip of her drink. "Not a chance. The very best I can hope for is stunned silence. Now how did Saturday's date go with Shane?"

Joyce's expression lit with a happy glow, but turning shy, she ran her fingertip around the rim of her glass. "It went exceptionally well, but that's trivial compared to your news."

"No, it isn't. I want to hear all about it," Catherine encouraged, but as Joyce described how affectionate Shane had become, her mind drifted away. Her whole life had changed since meeting Luke, but she had little hope he'd welcome those same changes in his neatly ordered world.

She glanced up and found Joyce had fallen silent. "I'll tell Luke tomorrow," she promised. "I'll invite him to come over for dinner, and then I'll break the news."

"You go, girl. I'll be home tomorrow night, so give me a call if you need reinforcements."

"I just might," Catherine admitted, but this was one thing she was determined to do on her own.

Despite Catherine's resolve, she found it difficult to approach Luke Wednesday morning. She avoided the Lost Angel office and went straight to Toby's. The kids were fooling around, not ready to get to work yet, while Rafael was already busy painting in the features of another angel.

Nick was out on the sidewalk with his skateboard doing tricks, but when he saw Catherine, he yelled to his buddies, "Hit the brushes, Mrs. Brooks is here."

"Thanks, Nick, maybe we should let you foreman this project."

Nick spun in a tight circle, then stepped off his board and picked it up. "No, thanks, this is enough work for me. Where's your honey?"

Catherine rested her hand lightly on his shoulder. "I'm not the director of Lost Angel, so I won't ban you from the site for that remark, but please don't say that kind of thing to Luke."

"Are you kidding? He's already warned us to watch our mouths. But you do make a hot couple." Still carrying his skateboard, he walked across the yard to join Polly and his buddy, Max.

Catherine was relieved Nick hadn't inquired into the more intimate details of their relationship, but she still feared he might be giving Luke a hard time. "Luke can handle it," she mumbled under her breath.

"Handle what?" Luke asked.

Surprised by his sudden appearance, Catherine fought to find a smile as she turned to face him. "Lost Angel, of course. If you've no plans for the evening, I'd like you to come over for dinner. There's something we need to discuss."

"That sounds ominous. Should I be worried?"

She was already frantic enough for the both of them and glanced away. "You asked me to signal before I make a turn. That's all I mean to do."

He reached out to lift her chin. "Now I'm intrigued. I have a meeting that'll take most of the afternoon, so I might be a little later than usual, but I'll be there for dinner."

"Thank you." She attempted to sound delighted rather than apprehensive. When he kissed her cheek before returning to Lost Angel, she was pleased to have succeeded.

She glanced up the street, but Garcia and Salzman were no longer parked in front of the auto supply store. She supposed that meant they'd given up on their ludicrous theory that one of the teenagers was the Lady in Red. She hoped they'd gone snooping in a more appropriate direction.

She wandered around the yard encouraging everyone to get busy, but with a project they cherished, it didn't take much to inspire them. When Rafael came down off the scaffold to refill his paint containers, she approached him.

"Do you think another week will do it?" she asked.

"Maybe, but what's your hurry? We've all got plenty of time."

"That may be true, but this beautiful mural may very well lead to others, and I'd like to be ready for the next opportunity."

Rafael wiped his forehead on the sleeve of his chartreuse T-shirt. "Toby says Art Center is cooking up a scholarship for me. What do you think of that?"

"I think it's great, but there's a lot of talent out here."

"Maybe, but I'm definitely the best."

Catherine refused to argue with him, but it annoyed her he was right. She took her beach chair out to sit and observe, but even with the colorful project to supervise, she feared it was going to be a very long day.

After the afternoon meeting ran even longer than expected, Luke still took the time to go home to shower, shave, and change clothes before going to Catherine's. He was more curious than worried about the evening, but believed it couldn't hurt to look his best. He wanted to take her something, and decided upon a box of chocolate turtles.

"Thank you, I love these," Catherine exclaimed after kissing him hello. "You've spoiled me terribly, Luke, and I keep telling you not to bring me presents."

"Those aren't a present; we can eat them with dessert. Now what can I do to help with dinner?"

"I thought we'd barbecue steaks. Will you light the charcoal?"

"Sure, where's the apron?" He followed her into the kitchen and promptly began to swear. He yanked his pager off his belt and checked the number. "Lost Angel doesn't page me at night unless there's a real emergency. I left my cell phone in the car. May I use your telephone?"

"Of course." Catherine gestured toward the one on the kitchen wall. She turned away to give him some privacy, but she was concerned too. She couldn't follow the gist of the conversation from Luke's comments, but rather than continue to prepare dinner, she sat at the breakfast table to wait.

When Luke hung up, he remained by the telephone for several seconds before relaying the bad news. "I'll have to take a rain check on dinner. There was a drive-by shooting half an hour ago. The mural was sprayed with bullets, and a couple of the kids were hit."

She leapt to her feet. "My God! Have they been taken to a hospital?"

"Yes, I'm going there now."

"I'll come with you." She grabbed her purse from the entryway table and followed him out the front door. "Was it a gang shooting?"

"Sure sounds like it." Luke started his Subaru, then paused before putting the car in gear. "Dave said it was bad, and it might be a long night. Maybe you should reconsider and stay home."

She buckled her seat belt. "No, I want to be with you. Drive."

"All right, but don't say you weren't warned."

"I won't. Did Dave tell you who was hurt?"

"Nick and Max. Hang on, I'll try and beat the ambulance to the County/USC Medical Center."

She'd ridden with him before and assumed he must be exaggerating, but he wasn't. They sped from one freeway to the next, zipping in and out of traffic, and pulled into the County/USC parking lot in what she was convinced had to have been record time. She grabbed his hand as they headed for the Emergency entrance.

Dave and Toby were in the waiting room, along with Polly, whose dress was splattered with blood. Dave got up and came to meet them. "We were just standing in Toby's yard when we heard what sounded like firecrackers. Max screamed and grabbed his leg, but Nick just fell. That's his blood all over Polly, rather than hers, but she was standing right next to him, and it's a wonder she wasn't hit too."

"Take care of Polly," Luke urged. "I'll check with the doctors."

Catherine nodded, but she hadn't realized how quickly visiting an emergency room would bring back painful memories. Suddenly light-headed, she sat beside Polly and took her bloodstained hand.

"Polly, let's find a restroom, and I'll help you clean up."

Polly turned toward Catherine, but her gaze was blank. "The bullet tore off the side of Nick's head. He's dead."

Catherine would have begged her not to give up hope, but Toby caught her eye and nodded. The waiting room was crowded, and she could hear someone crying softly in the row of chairs behind them.

"We still need to clean up." She rose and, with a gentle tug, raised Polly from her chair.

Catherine found the nearest women's room, led Polly over to the sink and eased her backpack to the floor. "Take off that dress, and we'll rinse it out. You have other clothes in your backpack, don't you?"

"There's no point in washing my dress when I'll never want to wear it again," Polly insisted.

Polly removed her hat, then yanked off her badly stained dress, wadded it up and shoved it into the trash container. Underneath, she had on a tank top and shorts, so she was still fully clothed.

"That's fine, as long as you have something else to wear." Catherine held the faucet to keep the water on as Polly began to scrub her arms. Two other women came in, appeared unconcerned by Polly's gruesome appearance, and entered the stalls.

Catherine felt sick clear through. She'd wanted to be there, indeed, was convinced she should be there. But after they'd all had such a good time painting the mural, to have a tragedy like this strike was nearly unbearable. She tore off several towels and handed them to Polly.

"I don't expect you to feel any better, but you look far more presentable now," Catherine told her.

"That's 'cause all people can see is the outside." Polly unzipped her backpack, and after a quick perusal of her choices, she drew out another gauze dress in a tiny floral print. She slipped it over her head, fluffed out her hair, and added her hat.

"Let's go see if there's any news about Max," Polly suggested. She slung her backpack over her shoulder and led the way to the waiting room. A little child was screaming in the corner, but she went straight to her chair without glancing his way.

Even with the bright splashes of color on his tattoos, Toby looked pale. "Maybe the mural wasn't such a good idea after all," he whispered as Catherine sat down.

"No, it was a wonderful idea," she argued. "The city is filled with crazy people who get their kicks shooting off guns. It doesn't matter what you do or where you go, anyone can become a target of random violence."

Dave was slumped back in his chair. "I didn't see the gunman, did you, Toby?"

"I was too busy grabbing for dirt, and all I saw was blood." Toby shuddered and rubbed his arms. "Is it freezing in here, or is it just me?"

"It's cold," Polly agreed, "probably to keep the bodies from rotting."

"They'd be in the morgue," Dave said, "not here."

Catherine put her arm around Polly and hugged her, but the girl was sitting so stiffly, she doubted the sympathetic gesture was felt. An ambulance cut its siren as it drew up outside, and she tried to imagine spending a whole shift flying from one ghastly accident or emergency to the next. Faced with that horror, she didn't understand how paramedics remained on the job for more than a day or two.

When Luke finally rejoined them, his expression was grave. "Max lost a lot of blood, so they're keeping him overnight, but he'll be all right. Nick didn't make it."

Of all the kids at Lost Angel, Catherine had known Nick the best. He had teased her only that morning, and she could still recall the sound of his infectious laughter. "Could we see Nick?" she asked.

Luke appeared incredulous. "Why would you want to?"

"I'd like to say good-bye."

"Me too," Polly said. "Will you ask them, Luke, please?"

Toby stood and took a shaky step. "I'm not up for viewing a body. You'll have to excuse me. I'm going to be sick."

Dave came up out of his chair. "I'll see you make it to the restroom."

Luke watched the pair make their way down the hall before turning back to Catherine and Polly. "They asked me if someone was here, so I think they're cleaning Nick up. Give me a minute to check."

Polly whispered as Luke walked away, "He isn't crying, but he looks like he lost his own kid."

"In a way, he did," Catherine responded. "All of you at Lost Angel are his children."

But it looked to her as though Luke had simply detached from the unexpected sorrow. He was taking care of the necessary details, doggedly doing his job, she supposed, but he'd cut himself off from the pain. Rather than merely sad, to her he looked hollow and completely spent.

When they were able to see Nick, Luke hung back by the door. Catherine took Polly's hand as they approached the treatment table where Nick still lay. His head was bandaged to hide the wound, and he appeared to be only sleeping. Polly leaned over to kiss his cheek and burst into tears.

"Nick always watched out for me," she cried. "What am I going to do now?"

Catherine hugged her rather than answer. "I'll miss him too, sweetheart. We all will."

Tears stung Catherine's eyes, but she forced them away for Polly's sake. She reached out to touch Nick's shoulder and gave him a tender squeeze. He had not deserved this, but then no one did.

"It's time to go," Luke called softly from the doorway.

Polly kissed Nick a last time, wiped away her tears and followed Luke out into the hall. "What about Max? Shouldn't we visit him too?"

"Maybe tomorrow. Tonight he needs to rest," Luke replied. "Toby and Dave will give you a ride back to Lost Angel."

Catherine had another concern. "Wait a minute, Luke. We aren't Nick's parents, but can we claim his body?"

"I already did. That's what took me so long, but we needn't go into details here."

"Fine, I didn't want to abandon him."

Toby and Dave were waiting for Polly, and Dave dropped his arm around her shoulders. "Let's go on back to Lost Angel. Everyone will be waiting to hear what's happened."

"They're not going to like this," Polly said.

"No, I imagine not," Toby added, and the three of them huddled close as they walked out into the night.

Luke didn't speak until they got to his car. "I can't go back to Lost Angel tonight. I'm taking you home."

The evening Catherine had planned forgotten, it didn't occur to her that he meant his place rather than hers until he got on the freeway and headed west. That he would want to take her to his home was a relief, however, for she hadn't wanted him to grieve alone. She didn't care if his anger spilled over into tears; she just wanted him to react rather than withdraw any further.

There was underground parking at Luke's condo building, and he rolled the Subaru into his space, then held Catherine's hand as they walked to the elevator. He didn't speak as they waited for it to arrive, nor did he comment as they rode up to the fifth floor. He unlocked his door and drew her inside, where the light in the entryway was dim.

Rather than break his silence to welcome her to his home, Luke abruptly shoved her against the door and kissed her with a near brutal passion. After her initial shock, her choice was made in an instant. She clung to him rather than struggle to tame his agony. She returned his fevered kisses and encouraged him to exhaust his heartache on her.

He drew back slightly to strip away her clothes, and to hasten their joining, she helped him with his. She braced herself against the door for support and hooked a leg around his hip to ease his way. Mindless of her brazen invitation, he thrust into her to begin a forceful coupling, fast, hard, and she fought to hold on and ride the force of his despair.

Ablaze with his own inner heat, he held her pinned in his arms, prey to his need, and poured his grief into her. He twisted and ground his hips against hers to pound her against the cool flatness of the door.

With her hands in his hair, she took each plunging thrust deep, then at last surrendered to a violent climax that caught and swept through him as well. Exhausted by his strength, she remained coiled around him even as she sagged back against the door and fought to catch her breath.

When he picked her up and carried her into his bed, she slid under the covers beside him and drew his head down upon her breast to sleep. He had not uttered a single sob, but she felt the unshed tears splash deep in his heart to mix with her own.

The evening's tragedy invaded Catherine's dreams, and she slept fitfully, but each time she awoke, she found Luke's arms still wrapped tightly around her. When he left the bed at the first light of dawn, she sensed his absence almost immediately.

He had pulled on a pair of Levi's before stepping out on the balcony, but even in profile, he looked haunted. Head bowed, he grasped the cement wall enclosing the balcony, and the muscles across his shoulders and back flexed in an uneasy rhythm. He might have been in bed several hours, but he didn't appear to have slept any better than she had.

She grabbed an oxford cloth shirt from his closet and joined him on the balcony. She knew how rotten he felt, and rather than offer sympathy he'd surely refuse, she stood silent beside him and waited for him to speak. She rolled up her shirt sleeves, but the garment was still much too large. It was a comfort, however, just to wear his clothes.

He shuddered and closed his eyes as though the sight of her actually hurt. "I'm sorry about last night. It won't happen again. I can't take anymore, Catherine, I'm finished."

She reached for his shoulder, but he pulled away. "Don't touch me. I can't bear it. I've known all along we'd end badly, and the fault is all mine, not yours. You're a wonderful woman and deserve a man who can love you. That won't ever be me."

She'd always feared he would cut and run rather than share her dreams, but not like this when he was hurting so badly. "You're not the only one who was devastated by Nick's death. Let's wait a few days before we make any decision about us."

"It won't help," he swore, "and I won't give you false hopes. Whatever there was between us, it's over right here and now."

She drew in a deep breath. She had the advantage of knowing they had a lasting link, but this was no time to reveal that precious tie. "All right. Now what about a memorial service for Nick? Even if it's no more than having the kids share their thoughts and sing along with Eric Clapton's 'Tears in Heaven', we ought to do something."

"I've buried other kids," Luke snapped. "I know what to do. I'll wait a day so Max can attend, but I don't want you there. I don't want you to come back to Lost Angel ever again."

She recoiled from him. "You're not only shutting me out of your life, but Lost Angel as well?"

He shook his head. "You're not usually so incredibly dense."

"You think I'm dense?" Catherine peeled off his shirt and threw it at him. "I said I'd supervise the mural and I will. I'll park by Toby's rather than curse Lost Angel with my presence, but I won't let some low-riding sleazebags chase me off. Nor will I allow you to scare me away.

"Now, unless you plan to give me cab fare to get home, you better get dressed and take me there yourself. One last piece of advice. The next time you break up with a woman, put on a shirt, because you look sexy as hell without one."

He was used to her temper, but clad only in righteous indignation, her beautiful auburn hair tousled, her doe eyes flashing with fury, she was the most delicious distraction he'd ever seen. She made him ache for all he'd just thrown away, but when it was all he could do to hold himself together, he had nothing left to give for her.

"Wait," he offered wearily, "I didn't use a condom last night, and if I've gotten you pregnant—"

"Don't worry," she interrupted before he made an offer she refused to hear. "The timing wasn't right."

She left him on the balcony, gathered up her wrinkled clothes by the front door and went into the bathroom to shower. He had a handsome home decorated in shades of charcoal and rust, but she saw little through her tears. By the time she left the bathroom to him, however, she'd dried her eyes and was anxious to get home.

He said not a word to her on the painful trip to her house, but when they arrived and she opened her car door, she gave him one final warning. "I know what's happened to you, because I'm fighting so hard not to slide down into the pit of grief I dug for myself after Sam died. Deal with whatever you must, then remember where to find me. I'll never turn you away." She took care to close his car door rather than slam it, but he sped away as though he were overjoyed to be rid of her, and that made her heart ache all the more.

She made her way up the walk and with every step became more convinced she would never spend a more remarkable night nor ever love a more challenging man. Worn out in both body and spirit, she apologized profusely to Smoky for not having fed him his dinner, then fell across her bed and slept until noon.

Positive no one would feel up to working on the mural that day, she stayed home, but she wandered aimlessly from room to room without hope she would find anything compelling to do.

Late that afternoon, Joyce came through the side gate and found Catherine seated at her patio table cuddling Smoky in her lap. One look at her dear friend's downcast expression was enough to convince her that things had not gone well with Luke.

"It's plain Luke didn't take your news well, and I can't believe any man you cared about would be that great a fool."

Catherine waited until Joyce had slipped into the chair opposite hers before she recounted how the evening had gone so dreadfully awry. She said only that she'd spent the night with Luke, without revealing any of the lurid details.

"Nick was a popular kid, and his death hit Luke hard. My news will just have to wait until he's pulled himself together."

"You're being awfully considerate of his feelings, but that's got to be damn hard on yours," Joyce exclaimed. "I thought being abandoned at a restaurant was bad, but this is so much worse. Couldn't Luke have taken a moment to consider your feelings?"

"Actually, I think he did, but there's no point in my brooding over it. In time, Luke will either choose love or he won't, but with any luck, I'll have a child to raise. I'll always be grateful to him for that."

"Grateful?" Joyce gasped. "How can you put such an optimistic spin on what was obviously a disastrous affair?"

"It's easy. I know just how rotten it feels to lose someone you care about, so I don't blame Luke for being overwhelmed with grief when he was already carrying too much."

"You'll still have to tell him about the baby one day, though."

Catherine nodded thoughtfully. "Yes, but it doesn't have to be any time soon."

Joyce leaned across the table. "You want me to do it? I can look up Lost Angel's address and pay Luke a real informative visit."

"I imagine you would, but no, don't you dare. I don't want him hurt."

"Well, it sure looks to me like you're hurting, and you don't deserve to be thrown away."

Catherine glanced around her beautiful yard. "I've scarcely landed in a trash heap."

"No, but even a palace could be as dismal as a prison when you're all alone."

Catherine didn't argue, but she didn't really feel alone. She was sad, for Nick and for all the kids who'd loved him. Her sorrow for Luke ran deeper still, but she wasn't ready to give up on him.

"Luke's built his own prison," she murmured, "but I trust him to break out before long."

"If Shane were to give me that old, 'it's not you, it's me, baby,' good-bye speech, the only thing I'd trust him to do is get lost. Men," she fumed. "I've a Wolfgang Puck pizza in my freezer that's calling my name. You want to eat with me tonight?"

"Sure, that's the best offer I've had all day." Catherine set Smoky aside before leaving her chair, and determined to inspire Joyce to talk about Shane all evening, she walked home with her friend.

Catherine couldn't bear to wear black to the memorial service and instead chose a lavender two-piece dress she usually saved for summer. When she arrived at Lost Angel, the sanctuary was nearly filled. Volunteers were seated in folding chairs toward the back of the room, while the kids were seated cross-legged on the floor at the front.

She'd bought flowers and carried the basket of white chrysanthemums, iris and daisies to the front and placed it at the foot of the podium. Polly, who was weeping softly into Tina's shoulder, moved over to make room for her in the front row. She was about to sit down, when Dave brought her a chair. She thanked him and placed it at the end of Polly's row so she wouldn't block anyone's view.

Max then moved into a chair behind her. He was wearing baggy shorts, and his right leg was heavily bandaged. When he dropped his crutches, the thud echoed throughout the room. Catherine turned to smile at him, but he managed only a nod in return. He'd carried bookshelves for her, but she didn't know him well.

Catherine caught only snatches of the whispered conversations of those seated near her, but she overheard enough to learn many thought the mural would remain unfinished. She hoped Luke hadn't stopped the mural project simply to be rid of her, but it wouldn't have surprised her if he had.

When he entered with Pam, she was saddened to see he looked no better than when they'd parted. His posture was still proud, but he moved slowly, as though he'd been unable to sleep and were desperately tired. She expected him to begin with a Bible verse or perhaps poetry, but instead, he spoke from his heart.

"This is the most difficult part of my job, and I'm going to need your help to carry it off well. We all loved Nick. He always had a joke or something amusing to say regardless of the situation, and it's his laughter I'll miss the most. Despite having been shuffled through a succession of foster homes, he was outgoing and curious. He was an intelligent young man and had he been given a chance, I know he would have been a great success in life. Pam has a song she'd like to sing for him, and then I'll invite anyone who'd care to, to share their memories of Nick."

Tears were now rolling down Catherine's cheeks as fast as she could wipe them away. She hadn't expected Pam to sing so beautifully, but the secretary had a lovely voice which made the wistful hymn she'd chosen even more poignant. It was a song to celebrate life rather than a sorrowful lament, but still, most of those listening were in tears.

So many of the kids wished to relate an incident they'd shared with Nick that the service lasted more than an hour. At the close, they all joined Pam in singing "Amazing Grace", but then no one seemed anxious to leave.

"We're scattering Nick's ashes at sea," Luke announced. "There's a bus to take anyone who'd like to go, and volunteers are most welcome to drive their own cars to the harbor."

Polly pressed close to Catherine. "Are you coming with us?" she asked. "I went once last year when another kid died. It's a nice boat, and everyone had a good time."

That Polly would describe scattering ashes at sea as though it were merely a nice outing was too much for Catherine, but fortunately, she had a handkerchief in her hand to cover her dismay. "No, I'd rather just say a prayer for Nick here, but thank you for wanting to include me."

"I'm staying here too," Tina said. "Charlie doesn't care much for sea cruises. Maybe we could work on the mural."

Luke hadn't looked her way once, and Catherine supposed he would ride the bus with the kids. That meant she wouldn't have to worry about running into him that afternoon.

"I have extra clothes in my car," she replied. "Give me a minute to change into them, and I'd like to do whatever we can."

Tina beamed. "Thanks, Mrs. Brooks, you're the best."

Catherine gave her a quick hug, but she couldn't respond, not when the man she loved hadn't even wished her a good day.

Chapter Eighteen

Ford Dolan had never had any respect for housework, and with Violet gone from their dingy apartment, dirty dishes had piled up in the sink and filthy clothes lay strewn across the floor. He cursed Violet every time he tripped over something he'd left in his own way, but as he saw it, it was her fault for running out on him.

"Ungrateful slut," he muttered. He tightened his hold on his empty beer can to crush it and tossed it onto the heap of fast-food wrappers littering the cab of his truck. He pulled into a parking place in front of his apartment building and carried the rest of the six-pack and box of fried chicken he'd bought for dinner up to the door.

The light was burned out in the hallway again, but he made his way to his unit without careening into the walls too many times. He'd just unlocked his door when he felt someone move up behind him. Expecting one of his nosy neighbors, he sneered as he looked over his shoulder.

The blonde smiled and took another step closer. "Something smells awfully good, honey. Why don't you invite me in for supper?"

Ford's mouth fell agape. The woman's red dress barely concealed what appeared to be a gorgeous figure, and while he wanted desperately to invite her in, he feared she might take one look at the mess and run right out again on her spiked heels.

"Sure," he mumbled. "Just give me a minute to tidy up a bit."

The blonde edged closer still. "Sorry, your time's run out."

"Huh?" Ford had left a light on, and he caught the bright gleam of her knife in the second before it entered his belly. He tried to scream as the blade tore through his flesh, but no sound came out of his parted lips. Warm blood poured down his pants, and he died thinking he would finally have to go to the Laundromat.

Saturday morning, Rafael stood out on the sidewalk studying the mural with Catherine, but he hung his head in disgust. "I can hardly stand to look at it now that Nick's dead."

Catherine understood his despair but refused to be trapped by it. "When Dave and I first discussed the possibility of a mural, I suggested including a panel where people could write the names of their own angels. Somehow I failed to mention it to you, but it's still a lovely thought. We'll have to ask Toby's permission, but what would you say to dedicating the mural to Nick's memory?"

Rafael had gotten an early start that morning to paint the angel he'd based on Nick. He'd created not only a perfect likeness of his slain friend, but in one of Nick's characteristic poses, the angel was looking back over his shoulder and laughing at some private joke.

"It's a nice idea, but it wouldn't stop the hurt," Rafael answered. "Even when good things happen, like this mural, they're always followed by something incredibly bad."

"That's no excuse to quit," Catherine argued.

"What's the use when there's no point in anything? I'm not going to get a scholarship from Art Center. You know I'm not."

Rafael had been so broken up by Nick's death that all trace of his former arrogance had vanished. He was as frightened as the rest of them, Catherine realized, and she would get him the scholarship he deserved even if she had to put up the money herself.

"Keep working on your portfolio. The scholarship will come through," she promised. "Now let's talk to Toby about adding a memorial panel."

Unable to focus on his work, Toby was sitting on the porch. He nodded as Catherine explained her idea for adding names. "Sure, I'll put some permanent markers out, but I'll anchor them on cords so that no one draws a mustache on one of the angels."

"Who would do such a thing?" Catherine cried.

"Plenty of people," Rafael offered with a rude snort. "For guys who'd shoot someone they don't even know, drawing a mustache would be nothing."

"I suppose you're right," Catherine conceded. She turned to find Detectives Salzman and Garcia approaching. They were both rather severely dressed in navy blue that day, and neither offered a friendly smile.

After a brief greeting, Garcia got right to their news. "We checked out the license number of the green convertible. It belongs to a retired sheriff's deputy. On Wednesday night, he had it on display over at a Bob's Big Boy restaurant for their classic car night. So he's in the clear. The slugs we dug out of the house don't match any we've gathered at any other crime scene, so for now, all we have is dead ends."

Disappointed not to have supplied a crucial lead, Catherine chewed her lower lip. "Whoever shot Nick, must have driven by here before that night, and he'll probably drive by again. Could we set up a camera to photograph traffic?"

Garcia turned to Salzman and rolled his eyes. "Sure, but drivers tend to use the same routes to work or to run errands and back. All we'd have is a lot of license plate numbers rather than viable suspects, and we sure as hell don't have the time to check hundreds of alibis."

Toby stood and stretched. "You know what kind of cars gangbangers drive. There'd be no reason to check up on little old ladies in Toyotas."

"Everyone's a detective," Salzman murmured under her breath. "You're here every day. Have you seen any cars, other than the green convertible, that seemed out of place?"

"No," Toby admitted, "but it's difficult to believe no one saw anything that night."

"It had just gotten dark," Garcia reminded him. "People were turning on their headlights and hurrying home. The patrons heading into the bar were already tasting their first drink. No one was on the lookout for a shooting."

"I am now," Toby responded. "I make sure all the kids leave at four, and after dark, I don't come back out here in front myself. I'd like to rig lighting for the mural, but not until you catch the guys who shot it up."

"That may be a long wait," Catherine murmured under her breath.

"Thank you, Mrs. Brooks, we're well aware of our conviction rate." Garcia took several steps away to study the mural up close. "You've got a masterpiece here. I hope you know it."

"It's a masterpiece, all right," Rafael complained bitterly, "but look what it got us."

"You ought to have a big jug out here for donations," Salzman suggested. "At least earn enough to buy yourselves hamburgers for lunch."

"Starving artists don't win much sympathy," Toby countered, "but thanks anyway."

"We strive to serve the community," Salzman replied, and she and Garcia walked back across the street where they'd left their car.

"Where's Luke this morning?" Toby asked. "Isn't he coming in again to help us?"

Catherine shrugged off his question. "I have no idea what his plans are, but we need to keep working."

Rafael headed for the porch to pick up paint. "I'm on it, Mrs. Brooks. Let's wrap this damn thing."

Toby swept Catherine with a perceptive glance and lowered his voice. "Something's wrong here. You and Luke have a lovers' quarrel?"

"Give it up, Toby, you're the very last person I'd confide in."

"Well, that's flattering." The artist laughed.

"I'm sorry, but I just don't need your prying today." Nor any other day, Catherine thoughtfully didn't add.

"There's no need to pry when I see from your expression that something's catastrophically wrong. Dave will be thrilled. He's madly in love with you, you know."

"Could we just paint the mural," she exclaimed. Since the shooting, she'd been unable to sit with her back to the street and now began pacing the yard. She was relieved when Toby went to his studio, but when they began to clean up for the day, he reappeared carrying a package.

"I made something for you. Go on, open it now so I can see how you like it."

Catherine tried to back away but bumped into a wall of kids eager to see what Toby held. "I can't accept presents from you," she insisted.

"Don't think of it as a present. It's just something to set out in your yard, and if your neighbors ask where you got it, you can send them to me."

"You expect me to display your work in my yard?" Catherine asked incredulously.

"Yeah, go on, open it up." Toby set it down on the ground and gestured invitingly.

Polly stood at her elbow. "Open it, Mrs. Brooks, we all want to see what it is."

Catherine hated to give in, but with a chorus of kids chanting to encourage her, she had no choice. She knelt to untie the twine and then peeled away the brown wrapping paper. To her immense delight, what she found was one of Toby's wonderful metal cats, but at only two feet in height, with three-inch nails for whiskers, it was just the right size for her yard.

She looked up at Toby and shook her head. "I love it, but this is much too valuable for you to give away."

"Hell, no. It's just leftover bits of wrought-iron, scrap metal and springs. Go on, take it, and you'll help me clean out my studio."

"Aren't you going to kiss him?" Tina yelled.

Toby's smile widened, but while Catherine rose to her feet, this time she refused to oblige. "I'll take it, but only to showcase your work."

"Fair enough. I'll carry it to your car. Come on kids, it's time to go."

Catherine and Toby waited until the last teenager had straggled across the street before they walked around the house to where she'd begun parking her Volvo. "Thank you, I really do love cats, and this one has such a charming personality."

Toby slid it into the back of her car, used the wrapping paper as a cushion, then straightened up. "I wish you thought that highly of me."

"You'd be surprised," she remarked wistfully. "But now that we have a minute, tell me something. Is there really a chance Art Center will offer Rafael a scholarship?"

Toby slammed the Volvo's rear door shut and stepped back up on the curb. "I think so. Nowadays, lots of kids are into computer animation and dreaming up wild, interactive games. To have Rafael walk in with such exquisite drawings just blew them away."

"Good. I'd like for him to have that opportunity. Could you check with Art Center? If for some reason they can't swing a scholarship for him, then one can be arranged through a private donor."

Toby stared at her as though she'd just sprouted a second head. "Are you talking about yourself? Have you really got that kind of money?"

"Let's just say I enjoy donating to a good cause. Thank you again for the cat. Now, it's been a rough week, and I need to get home."

Toby closed the slight distance between them. "Why not stay here with me? I can promise you a memorable night."

He was a damnably attractive man, but his seductive invitation didn't even tempt her. "Don't you ever give up?"

"Not when I see something I want, and I've wanted you from the day you and Luke wandered up on my porch. Why do you think I was so eager to have you paint the mural here?"

In Catherine's mind, it was a short leap from choosing his house for the mural and needlessly putting kids at risk for a drive-by shooting. Unwilling to go there, she just shook her head.

"I'm going home before I say something I'll regret." She already had her keys in her hand and hurriedly walked around to the driver's side of her car.

Toby remained on the curb and watched her drive away.

Without the sweet memories of Saturday night with Luke to soothe her longing, Sunday was impossibly lonely for Catherine. Too anxious to read or even iron in front of the television, she put her new metal cat out by her front porch and then worked in her yard until the flower beds were completely free of weeds.

Forced inside at sunset, she studied the duplicate sets of photographs she'd taken at Lost Angel and laid those of Luke aside. While there were a couple she planned to enlarge, she was in no danger of forgetting the man she adored. She'd never told him she loved him, but she wouldn't give up hope that one day soon, those would be the exact words he longed to hear.

She recalled seeing only one framed portrait at Luke's place, and rather than his beloved daughter, it had been the drawing Rafael had done of her. She hoped it still sat on his dresser as a constant reminder she hadn't been the one to walk away.

With Dave and Pam handling the holiday cards from the contest artwork, once the mural was finished, she would have no excuse to return to Lost Angel. It pained her to think after that day, her path would never cross with Luke's.

Next Saturday she would take the CBEST test and with any luck, she would pass and be able to teach, but now she was no longer eager for a job. Instead, she wanted to stay at home and concentrate on being a mother for a year or two. She couldn't plan any further, but knowing every child deserved a happy life, she hoped the future would bring her and her baby something good.

Luke had stayed home on Saturday night and gotten drunk. When he awoke Sunday morning with a wicked hangover, he poured himself another stiff drink to ease himself into the day. He was too smart not to recognize his behavior as self-destructive, but he simply didn't care.

Life had become so bleak that he no longer wished to live it. Then he would think of Catherine, as he did every few seconds, and he refused to torture her with the death of another lover. He'd been cold to the point of cruelty to break up with her, and yet she'd responded with a promise never to turn him away. The generosity of her undeserved offer haunted him.

He would have welcomed fierce anger, but that she still wanted him gouged a deep furrow in his soul. Awash in self-loathing, he poured out every bottle of liquor he had in his condo and forced himself to go out and run.

He felt sick clear through by the time he returned home and slept without waking until Monday morning. Then he had the challenge of cleaning himself up so he didn't resemble death warmed over, but he left home afraid he'd failed. He would push himself through the day, and the next, but he knew he'd lost the ability to lead and would soon have to resign from Lost Angel.

That same morning, Detective Salzman crossed the street to summon Catherine to the Lost Angel office. "We have some news you ought to hear. I'd like you to come with me."

Her authoritative tone convinced Catherine she had no choice, but she waved to Toby to let him know she was leaving, and that he'd be in charge. "Have you found out who killed Nick?" she asked.

"We're working on it," the taciturn detective replied.

Catherine was more eager to see Luke than hear about their investigation if they were no closer to arresting the killer than they had been on Saturday. She followed Salzman into the office where Pam, Luke, Dave and Detective Garcia were already gathered.

Catherine exchanged hellos with Pam and Dave, but she could only stare at Luke. He was noticeably thinner, which sharpened his handsome features, but it worried her to think he wasn't well. When he refused to glance her way, she smiled at Garcia.

"Now that you've joined us, Mrs. Brooks, I hope we'll have greater success at reaching the truth. A man named Ford Dolan was murdered near here Friday night."

"Murdered?" Catherine gasped.

"Good, I see you knew him too. It looks like the work of the Lady in Red, but this time no one saw her. She kicked Ford's body back into his apartment, so it wasn't discovered until Sunday afternoon when a neighbor reported a peculiar odor coming from the apartment."

Catherine shuddered. "How awful."

"Apparently Ford had just arrived home carrying what was left of a six-pack of beer and some fried chicken," Salzman added. "The receipt showed he'd paid for three pieces, but there were only two in the box. We think the Lady in Red had dinner on him."

Pam nearly shrieked. "Are you saying she sliced up Ford and then walked off chewing his chicken?"

Garcia nodded. "Real cold bitch, isn't she? But Ford's girlfriend, Violet Simms, hasn't been seen for several days, and we've learned she often came here. By some extraordinary coincidence, she fits the description of the Lady in Red."

Luke's response was a particularly inventive curse, but he quickly apologized. "Look, I took Violet to a battered women's shelter last Monday morning. I've called to check on her every day, and she's still there. She's not your killer."

"We'd still like to speak with her," Salzman insisted.

Luke shook his head. "Shelters don't advertise their location to protect their residents, and I'm not telling you where she is."

Garcia did a quick survey of the room. "We know where the shelters are, and we'll track Violet down eventually. Anyone care to point us in the right direction?"

Catherine shrugged helplessly. "I've no idea where she is."

"Neither do I," Pam added.

"I just mow the lawn here," Dave insisted.

"We'll find her," Salzman assured them. "But if Violet isn't the Lady in Red, then it's someone who knew her and knew Ford abused her. That leads us right back here to Lost Angel. One of you must know a whole lot more than you're telling. If you don't speak up soon, you stand the risk of being named an accessory to murder."

"Let's remember who we're talking about here," Luke advised. "Felix Mendoza, and Bobby Clyde Flowers, who pimped underage girls, and Ford Dolan, who got his kicks punching Violet Simms around. Most of the public would be honored to be named an accessory in those murders."

"Don't try the victims. We're not in court," Garcia cautioned. "We'll find Violet and have a nice little chat, but something tells me we'll be back here before the day is out."

"The office closes at five o'clock," Pam offered agreeably.

"Wait a minute," Catherine interjected. "Violet has an alibi, but it's possible Ford was lonely without her and hit on a prostitute. That she appears to have been the Lady in Red may be nothing more than a gruesome coincidence, rather than proof of a direct link to Lost Angel."

"That's really good," Dave enthused.

Garcia responded with a low chuckle. "That's precisely why I insisted you be here, Mrs. Brooks. I knew you'd come up with a theory no one else would."

"It's actually quite logical," Luke argued. "Ford couldn't speak without insulting anyone within earshot. If he approached a prostitute, then it's likely he did it with language several notches below crude."

"Nothing surprises the whores in this town," Salzman countered, "so I doubt that Ford could."

"But you didn't know him," Catherine insisted. "We did."

"That's not a point in your favor," Garcia warned, and after a nod to his partner, the detectives left.

"I refuse to believe it's one of the kids," Luke exclaimed.

"So do I," Dave agreed. "But it makes me real uneasy to think that it might be."

"The kids stick together," Pam reminded them. "If they wanted to kill someone, they'd hunt him down in a vicious pack."

Luke nodded. "You're right. Now, while you're all here, I need to tell you what Pam and I were discussing before the police arrived. Dave, you'll leave for a better job soon, and Mrs. Brooks plans to teach in a high school in September. I'm seriously considering an offer from an Ivy League university that's shown a flattering interest in me over the years. Pam won't remain here without me, which means in a few months, all of us will be gone.

"If the Lady in Red hasn't been caught, our intrepid detectives are sure to consider our mass exodus suspicious, so for the time being, let's not discuss our plans with them."

Catherine was too stunned to speak. There were tears in Pam's eyes, but Dave reacted with anger.

"What's going on here?" he cried. "A week ago you and Cathy were a couple, and now you're considering job offers back east without telling her? I don't believe you, man."

Dave slammed the door on his way out, and unable to remain in the same room with Luke, Catherine followed. Feeling unsteady, she sank down on the steps and tried to think what to do. It had never occurred to her Luke might leave Lost Angel, let alone the state.

Hearing the door close a second time, Dave turned around and came back. "That rotten son of a bitch," he yelled. "I'll bet anything you name that he knew he was leaving the whole time he was with you. You know that, don't you?"

Catherine shook her head. "No, I don't believe that at all. Luke has been a rock here, and if he shatters now, then he shatters. But that doesn't change the fine man he is."

"Love!" Dave fumed, and clearly exasperated that she would defend Luke, he walked away with a long, brisk stride.

Catherine wrapped her arms around her knees and rocked back and forth. She missed Luke terribly, ached for him, but the thought of him moving to the East Coast was so unexpected, she didn't know what to do.

Maybe what he needed was a complete change of scene, but what she needed was the man she knew him to be. Fearing his departure might be imminent, she could no longer justify waiting to tell him about the baby. She just hadn't expected to be forced to do it that day.

Pam would be gone before the end of Luke's afternoon session, and rather than go home at four, she would stay and wait for a private conversation with him. She doubted anything he could say would equal her fears, but just getting the dreaded confession over with would be a relief.

She tried to stand and still felt too shaken to walk. She sat to rest a moment longer and wished someone would bring her a strawberry shake.

Shortly before four o'clock, Pam Strobble crossed the street to Toby's house. After quickly admiring the stunning mural, she drew Catherine aside.

"The detectives just picked up Luke for questioning," she whispered.

"My God, have they arrested him?"

"No, but I don't like it. He told me to cancel his afternoon session, but I've always wanted to lead it myself, and with everything going to hell here, I might as well. Could you cover the office for me until five?"

"Sure, I'll be happy to. I wanted to speak with Luke anyway. What time do you suppose he'll be back?"

Pam just shook her head. "There's no way to tell, but my husband and I have tickets for a play we've waited a long time to see, so I can't stay and wait."

"I'll stay," Catherine promised.

As soon as the teenagers had cleaned up for the day, she moved her car into the Lost Angel lot and parked it next to Luke's. She then left a note under his windshield wiper asking him to stop by the office before he left for home.

With telephone calls to field, her first hour in the office went quickly, but once Pam had left for the day, it was unnaturally quiet. Occasionally she would hear the sound of a horn from the street, but otherwise the office was silent. She walked around, stretched and tried to compose a coherent sentence for an opening with Luke, but none of her efforts made much sense.

Another hour had passed before she went into Luke's office and sat in his chair. She wished she had Violet's telephone number so she could check up on the shy girl herself. Thinking Luke might keep it in his desk, she slowly slid open the middle drawer, but it contained only an assortment of pencils of varying sizes, pens, a few rubber bands, paper clips and a box of Band-Aids.

She understood why he might need his own personal stash of bandages, but it still made her laugh. There were three more drawers on the right, but the first two held only additional office supplies. About to give up, she yanked out the deep lower drawer.

At first she was merely startled to find a tangle of red satin, but a quick inspection proved it to be a cocktail dress. A long blond wig had been hidden beneath it, and a pair of dark panty hose, and red heels lay at the bottom of the drawer.

Horrified, Catherine shoved everything back into place and slammed the drawer shut with a force that shook the whole desk. The Lady in Red's disguise had been described to her often enough for her to recognize it at a glance, but that there could be only one explanation for Luke to have it made her ill.

She stood and would have run from the office, but Dave was blocking the door.

"I think you better sit down again," he urged softly. "We need to talk."

Unwilling to return to Luke's place, Catherine collapsed into her usual chair, but she couldn't stop shaking. Luke had always been so convincing, but dear God, was he truly a murderer?

She looked up at Dave, but his expression was far too serious to offer even a glimmer of hope.

Chapter Nineteen

Dave leaned against the doorjamb and folded his arms across his black Doors T-shirt. "I was running the vacuum cleaner in here last night and the cord caught on the corner of Luke's desk. I opened the bottom drawer to free it and discovered what I think you just did. Scary as hell, isn't it?"

Catherine shuddered. "I just want to get out of here."

"I don't blame you, but I don't know what to do, and I need your help. I'm furious with Luke for the way he treated you, but that doesn't mean I want to see him tried for murder."

"I can't believe Luke murdered anyone." Yet even as she spoke the words, she recalled his steely strength and the fire of his temper. But she refused to brand him a serial killer.

"I don't want to believe it, either, but those sure aren't Luke's running shoes in that drawer."

Catherine could think of no plausible explanation for Luke to have a copy of the Lady in Red's costume, so it seemed likely those were the murderer's actual clothes. That they were stashed in Luke's desk was damning evidence against him.

Dave shifted his position slightly. "Luke was lucky the detectives didn't arrive with a search warrant this afternoon. When he gets back, we've got to convince him to get rid of his disguise."

"How can you focus on the clothing?" Catherine cried.

"It's incriminating evidence. You want Luke to get caught?"

"No, of course not. I want him to get help."

"What kind of psychiatric help do you imagine he'd receive in prison?"

"Stop it!" Catherine begged.

Dave softened his tone. "It's Luke we need to stop. Stay here with me, and as soon as he gets back, let's confront him."

"Confront him with this horror? How?" Catherine wanted to scream and then run, but she was shaking so badly, her legs would never hold her.

"He's bound to have something to say about the detectives' interrogation. Let's let him talk first, and then tell him what we've found. Or, we have another choice. We could call the detectives right now and let them know they've got their man."

"No, I want to hear Luke's side of this."

"I think you heard it this morning when he dismissed Felix and Bobby Clyde as men who pimped underage girls and Ford as abusive. If he didn't actually cheer for the Lady in Red then, he came awfully close."

With a sudden eerie chill, Catherine recalled the day Ford had accosted her in the parking lot. Luke had sworn he could kill him that day. Could he have carried out his threat?

Felix had been killed around the time she'd met Luke. Dear God, had she fallen in love with a murderer? Luke definitely had a dark side; indeed, it was that stormy part of his nature that had overwhelmed him when Nick had died. But was he a cold-blooded killer who stalked his victims and then sauntered away eating their fried chicken?

She looked up at Dave. "The chicken bothers me."

Dave frowned in dismay. "What chicken?"

"The part of Ford's dinner that the Lady in Red supposedly helped herself to, or I guess, himself."

"I thought it rather bizarre myself. You'd think he'd just want to get the hell out of there, but if he was out stabbing people, his thinking couldn't have been all that rational. Obviously, an insanity defense makes perfect sense. Then again, Luke has already made plans to move back east, so maybe he fears the detectives are getting too close."

"Do you think he can just get out of town and leave behind a string of unsolved murders?"

"With the fine record the LAPD has going, he's got a fifty-fifty chance."

Those seemed like excellent odds to Catherine, but she hated to think of Luke as a murderer no matter how despicable his victims might have been. It was a horrible legacy to give a child, and that frightened her all the more.

It was after eight o'clock when Luke got a ride back to Lost Angel. He was surprised to find Catherine's Volvo still in the lot and hastily read the note left on his windshield. With the afternoon he'd had, he was in no mood to talk with her, but it appeared unavoidable.

He hadn't expected to find Dave sitting on his desk, however, and that changed everything. "I got your note," he told Catherine. "We'll have to talk another time. Go on home."

Catherine didn't budge. "First tell us how things went with Garcia and Salzman."

"Tomorrow will be soon enough. Go home."

His tone had become more emphatic, but Catherine still refused to leave. "Just tell us how much the police know," she asked.

"We're dying to hear," Dave added.

Clearly displeased, Luke drew in a deep breath. "All right, since you insist. The police didn't check out Ford's truck before it reached the impound lot. He was the victim, remember, and not suspected of any crime, but when they opened his toolbox to take an inventory, they found a gun.

"Ballistics tests prove it was the one used to kill Nick."

When Catherine found her voice, it was strained and hoarse. "You thought Ford would come after you, but instead he shot up the mural? Violet begged me not to let Rafael paint her. If I'd just convinced him not to, then none of this would have happened, and Nick would still be alive."

Luke took a step toward her. "It's not your fault. Once Violet entered a shelter, where she should have gone months ago, Ford turned his virulent hatred on us. He might have walked in and shot everyone in sight. It's a miracle only Nick died."

Seeing she was unconvinced, Luke addressed his next comment to Dave. "Garcia believes Ford's murder is directly linked to the mural shooting. While no one admitted seeing the shooter, he's certain someone must have and tipped off the Lady in Red."

"Give it up, Luke," Dave chided. "Catherine and I found your disguise."

Puzzled, Luke glanced toward Catherine, who was staring at him through tear-filled eyes. "What are you talking about? I don't own a disguise."

"I was looking through your desk for the shelter's number to call Violet," Catherine admitted hesitantly. "Your Lady in Red outfit is in the bottom drawer."

"Now I know it's time for you to go home," Luke replied. "Please leave."

Catherine shook her head. "I just want to know why."

"Why is some goofy disguise in my desk drawer? Someone must have planted it there. I've already given you my opinion of vigilantes. Even if I agreed with those who move outside the law, there are too damn many evil men who prey on kids for me to kill them all. So what would be the point?"

As usual, he sounded convincing, but Catherine was too frightened to judge clearly. "I'll never say a word to the police, but you've got to get rid of your disguise and promise you'll not kill anyone else."

"For the last time, I don't own a disguise, and I haven't killed anyone," Luke argued. "What's been going on here, Dave?"

Dave shrugged. "There's no need to play dumb with us. We're not afraid of being named accessories to your crimes. We just want the Lady in Red to disappear tonight."

Luke shot Catherine a dark look. "For the last time, get out of here."

He was truly angry now, and Catherine wondered if it was because he was innocent, or God forbid, guilty and infuriated at being caught. She and Dave had backed him into a corner, and she couldn't bear to listen to anymore lies. She rose, but rather than stand to move out of her way, Dave came off the desk to block her path.

"Catherine stays," he said.

Luke backed out into the outer office. "Come on out here where there's more room to talk."

"Not if you're just going to lie," Dave countered.

"I'm not the one lying here. Garcia is close, but he's too committed to the idea one of the Lost Angel kids is the killer to consider any alternatives. In his mind, Ford's murder merely proves his theory. I have another one."

Standing behind Dave, Catherine saw the clear outline of a knife tucked in his hip pocket. She didn't recall ever seeing him carry a pocketknife. While she might have missed it, that night it struck her as an ominous sign. He had easy access to Luke's office and could have planted the disguise in Luke's desk any time, even that afternoon while Pam had been away to summon her.

She'd thought the death of Luke's daughter might have compelled him to murder, but Dave had suffered tremendous losses of his own. He was always eager to be helpful, but had he struck out on his own to fight the dangers threatening Lost Angel's teenagers?

She backed away from him, but with him blocking the aisle, she was trapped between the chairs and file cabinets. "I'd like to hear your theory, Luke. Please tell us."

Luke came back to the doorway. "In some respects, I've been as shortsighted as Garcia. I was certain none of the Lost Angel kids was the Lady in Red, but I hadn't given any thought as to who it might be. Then Ford was killed, and it seemed much more likely the murderer was somehow linked to the center.

"This afternoon I asked Garcia why they'd pinned Ford's murder on the Lady in Red if no one had seen her, and he told me no one else slices up her victims in the same way. The coroner recognized the knife wound in Ford's belly instantly.

"Catherine, you asked Garcia once if it didn't take tremendous strength to stab someone the way the Lady in Red has, and he just shrugged it off. I asked myself who might have the necessary strength, and who might have recognized Ford Dolan's truck when he fired on the mural. Only one name came to mind."

"That's funny," Dave interjected. "We came up with yours."

"Leave Catherine out of this," Luke demanded angrily. "We've got all night. You and I can work something out on our own. Let's send her home."

There was an alarming edge to Luke's voice, and easily following his line of reasoning, Catherine knew she would be wise to get away now and call the police. "I think I will go. Excuse me, Dave, I need to get by."

"Sit," Dave ordered. "No one is going anywhere."

Catherine tried to ease by him. "You're scaring me, Dave. I want to go home."

With a sudden quick turn, Dave shoved her back into her chair with his left hand, and drew his knife with his right. With the tap of a button, he flicked open a razor-sharp blade.

"Catherine and I are leaving together," he told Luke. "You're going to pretend you didn't see us tonight. You call the police, and she'll be the one to suffer."

Without a second's hesitation, Luke came out of the doorway and with an explosive force, punched Dave in the face. He slammed him back into the desk, but Dave struck out with his knife and tore at Luke's left biceps.

Blood sprayed across Catherine's face, and she screamed as she scrambled out of her chair. The men were fighting for control of the knife, shouldering each other with brutal strength, and she was forced back against the window to avoid being hit as well.

Luke had hold of Dave's wrist, but Dave shoved him off-balance, broke free of his grip, and slammed the knife into his shoulder. Desperate to help Luke, Catherine kicked Dave in the knee, causing him an instant of inattention that allowed Luke to recover. Then Dave turned and slugged her.

Catherine careened into the file cabinet, and the philodendron bounced precariously toward the edge. It tottered in a blurry dance before her vision cleared. The flowerpot was the only weapon at hand, but as she reached up to grab it, the jostling men had turned so that Luke was now closest to her. She dared not risk hitting him and so hugged the plant close to her chest.

Luke's shirt was stained with blood, but he was still slamming his right fist into Dave as they wrestled for the knife. They fought with the fury of bare-knuckled champs. Blood streamed from Dave's nose, but he seemed as unaware of the injury as Luke was of his.

It made Catherine sick to watch them, but she couldn't turn away. When Dave caught Luke in the chest with the tip of his blade, the pair swung around again, putting Dave within striking distance. Awaiting a clear shot, Catherine swung the potted plant up against Dave's head.

The pot shattered, showering her with dirt, and for the briefest of instants, Dave froze, apparently uninjured. Then he swayed, and when Luke caught him on the chin with a fierce right, he went down.

Luke wrenched the bloody knife from Dave's hand and then collapsed beside him. "Call 911. Tell them we need an ambulance, and police, quick."

Catherine shook off the dirt covering her clothes and then had to step over both men to reach the telephone lying on the floor behind the desk. She immediately called for help, then bent to check Dave for a pulse.

"Have I killed him?" she asked fearfully.

"No, you just stunned him, but he damn near killed me, and I appreciate your help."

Still shaking, Catherine went into the outer office for the twine stored in the supply closet. She grabbed the scissors from the desk she often used, and swiftly tied Dave's hands behind his back before he had a chance to awaken and attack them again. Then she lashed his ankles together.

"I don't want you sitting next to him. Can you move into the outer office?" she asked.

"I could crawl, but that wouldn't be very manly."

"How can you joke at a time like this?" She knelt beside him and began to unbutton his bloody shirt. "I'm going to rip this up to cover the cuts. I'm afraid you'll bleed to death before the paramedics arrive."

Luke rested his head against his desk. "Sorry, but it wasn't a fair fight."

When he closed his eyes, Catherine shook him. "Don't you dare die on me! Stay with me, Luke."

He glanced toward her, but his eyes were dulled by pain. "I'm a long way from dead, but did you really think I was the Lady in Red?"

She was too ashamed to admit the idea had even crossed her mind. "I was so frightened, I didn't know what to think, but I definitely wanted to hear your side. It's a good thing I didn't leave the first time you asked me, or you'd have been on your own."

"I doubt Dave would have let you go even then." He watched her quickly bind the cut in his arm, but all she could do was apply pressure to the deeper cuts in his left shoulder and chest.

"I've been a complete idiot," he murmured.

"There was no way you could have known Dave was the killer." She pressed down hard, but blood was still oozing from his chest, and she feared the wound was even deeper than it appeared. She tried to smile as though she had everything under control, but her lips trembled and gave her away.

"No, I meant about you."

"Don't talk," she urged. She turned to make certain Dave was still out cold, and he hadn't moved.

Luke felt dizzy, and the sight of his own blood splattered across her cheek and shirt made him sick. "Fool that I am, I actually believed it would be better if we went our separate ways. Then I found you here with Dave, and all that mattered was protecting you. I would never have let him take you. You know that, don't you?"

The ambulance and squad car pulled into the parking lot before Catherine could respond. She shoved herself to her feet and ran to the door to meet the paramedics, a man and a woman, and two powerfully built male police officers. While the paramedics tended to Luke and Dave, she attempted to string together what had happened for the officers.

When Toby came running through the door, she was overjoyed to see him. "Dave tried to kill Luke," she rushed to explain.

"I heard the ambulance and was afraid someone else had been shot. My God, is that your blood all over you?"

Catherine glanced down at her once pale green T-shirt and jeans. "No, but it's a good thing I was dressed to paint, isn't it?"

The paramedics were able to rouse Dave, but as the police officers began to escort him out to their squad car, Catherine called out to them. "There are some clothes in the bottom drawer of the desk that you ought to take with you. They belong to the Lady in Red. DNA testing should prove Dave wore them."

Once the officers had Dave confined to the back seat of their patrol car, the younger of the two returned to retrieve the suspicious garments. He bagged them, then shook his head. "You telling me that guy out there is the Lady in Red?" he asked.

"Apparently so," Catherine replied.

Toby appeared to be equally astonished. "I've been hanging with the Lady in Red? You got to be kidding."

"Does Luke look as though this were a joke?" Catherine countered. "Now I doubt they'll let me ride in the ambulance, and I'm too upset to drive my own car. Will you give me a ride to the hospital?"

"Of course. I didn't mean I doubted you. It's just that, well, nobody expected the Lady to be a man in drag."

"I did," Catherine claimed proudly. "Now come on, let's get out of the paramedics' way."

Kids had begun to gather in the parking lot and crowded around the ambulance when Luke was carried out on a stretcher. "Is he gonna die?" Max called out.

"Hell, no," Luke shouted.

"A few stitches and he'll be fine," Catherine assured them. She crossed the street with Toby, and while he failed to drive with Luke's manic speed, they arrived at the County/USC Medical Center only a moment behind the ambulance.

"I don't like coming here again," she said.

"There're not that many trauma centers operating anymore, and Luke is a bloody mess."

"I could have done without that."

"Sorry, but I'm not happy to be here again either," Toby complained.

"Just drop me off. I want to stay with Luke."

Toby dug a business card out of his wallet. "Here's my number. Call me if you need anything, a midnight snack, donuts at dawn, a ride home in the morning, whatever."

"Thanks, Toby." Catherine leaned over to kiss his check. "Oh, there is one thing. In the morning, will you please tell Pam what happened? I'll need to buy a new pot for the plant, but I don't want it thrown out."

"You got it," Toby assured her.

Catherine left his truck to follow the paramedics inside. She caught up with Luke's stretcher and reached for his right hand.

"I'm not leaving you."

Luke tried to smile, but winced. He was close to blacking out, but squeezed her hand. "Good. I want you to stay."

She bent over to kiss him. "Hang in there, hero."

Luke didn't feel much like a hero, but he liked hearing it. His left arm felt as though it were on fire from his fingertips to his shoulder. The paramedics shifted him from the stretcher to a treatment table, and he couldn't help but wonder if he were in the same room where Nick had died.

He tried to sit up, but a whole crowd of medical personnel appeared to hold him down. The bright light hurt his eyes, and he shut them tightly. "Just sew me up. I want to go home."

They numbed Luke's pain, but Catherine couldn't bear to watch the doctor stitch up his flesh. She kept a firm grip on his hand but looked the other way. A nurse cleaned off her face and brought her an icepack for her cheek, but she cared little about being bruised from Dave's blow.

It was early morning before Luke was released, and they were both too tired to think clearly. "I can call Toby to give us a ride to Lost Angel to pick up my car," Catherine suggested, "or we could just take a taxi to my house and worry about our cars later."

"Call the cab," Luke urged. "I can do without Toby today."

Luke's left arm and shoulder were so heavily bandaged, he could hardly move, but he slept easily in Catherine's bed knowing she was cuddled by his side. They didn't get up until late afternoon, when hunger made further sleep impossible.

"Do you still have the steaks?" Luke asked.

"They're in the freezer. Do you feel well enough to sit out on the patio while I set up the grill?"

In truth, Luke felt sore all over from the fight, but unwilling to appear an invalid, he rolled to the side of the bed and sat up. "Sure, I don't feel nearly as bad as I look," he lied. But after Catherine had showered and dressed, he entered the bathroom and swore when he discovered another black eye.

He made it out to the patio under his own power, while Catherine was busy lighting the charcoal. "I hope you won't mind my coming to dinner without a shirt, but even if I had one, I don't think it would fit over the bandages."

Catherine kissed him rather than complain. "Even if you may look as though you were hit by a train, you still look awfully good to me. Besides, we're outdoors rather than in the dining room, so we needn't worry about maintaining the proper decorum."

"That's a relief." Luke felt right at home in her backyard, but after watching Smoky chase butterflies through the colorful flower beds for a moment, he pulled her note from his pocket. "The last time I was here, there was something you wanted to tell me. You wanted to talk last night too. We've got plenty of time now."

Satisfied the charcoal was burning nicely, Catherine sat beside him. "Maybe you ought to eat first."

"Is it that bad?"

Catherine had been too frightened in the last twenty-four hours to think of the baby, but now she was resigned to telling him the truth. "It's all in your point of view."

Luke nodded to concede the fact. "Well, I've already acknowledged being an idiot where you're concerned; but maybe you'll overlook it. You want to get married?"

Shocked, she sat back in her chair. "You've asked me some startling questions in the past, but that takes the prize. You're still running on adrenalin. You need to wait a few days and then decide if you really want to propose."

"You see what I mean about a dance? If I move forward, then you move back. You said you'd never turn me away."

That he recalled her promise made her smile. But when he'd given her such an off-hand proposal with no mention of love, she was reluctant to accept. She loved him dearly, but a one-sided marriage would never last.

Luke pushed his chair away from the table and patted his thighs. "You're too far away. Come here."

"I don't want to hurt you."

"You won't. Just come here and sit," he coaxed.

Willing to at least give it a try, she left her chair, carefully eased down into his lap and smoothed out her skirt. "Let me know if this gets uncomfortable."

Luke hugged her with his good arm. "No, it feels great. I've really missed you. I'm sorry for getting so lost in my own misery that I wasn't there for you. It won't happen again."

"Is that a promise?" she murmured wistfully.

"Absolutely. No matter what you need, I'm your man."

"Thank you." Catherine took a deep breath to force out the words. "I'm pregnant."

"What?" Luke would have leapt to his feet had her weight not held him down. "Are you sure?"

"Sure about being pregnant, or sure the baby's yours? Yes on both counts."

Stunned, Luke felt as though the breath had been knocked out of him. He braced himself, but the thought of having a child with her brought only a curious warmth rather than the expected agony. His lengthy silence prompted Catherine to leave his embrace, but he pulled her right back down again.

"No, stay with me. I was careful, so it's no wonder I'm surprised." In truth, he was completely overwhelmed by the prospect of fatherhood. "Give me a minute to get used to the idea; then tell me what you want to do."

Catherine combed his hair softly with her fingertips. "If you loved me, my first choice would be to marry you and raise a family. But if you can't—"

"Of course I love you," Luke cried. "I haven't been able to get you out of my mind from the first maddening day you walked into my office and gave me such a hard time. If I'd had any sense, I would have known you were the woman for me right then."

She rested her cheek against his silvered hair. "I love you too, but a man really ought to mention love when he proposes."

"Thanks for the tip."

"I hope you won't need it, but Luke, if our having a baby together is going to be too much for you, please say so now."

He could still feel how Marcy had felt in his arms when they'd brought her home from the hospital; refusing to allow her tragic death to spoil their future, he choked back the poignant memory.

"Because of Marcy, you mean?"

Sitting back, she saw the threat of tears in his eyes and gently kissed them away. "Yes. I wouldn't have done this to you, but it truly was an accident."

"I know, I was there, remember? But there's nothing accidental about us. We've made choices all the way, and except for the brief lapse into idiocy when I told you good-bye, I happen to believe they're the right ones."

He hugged her again tightly. "I admire the way you remember Sam. From now on, I'm going to focus on the happy memories too, rather than dwell on the pain."

It made her proud to think she'd taught him such a valuable lesson. "Thank you, but I do have one more confession. I'm about as impulsive as an abalone, but I just couldn't resist you."

He laughed and ignored the resulting pain in his chest. "I have the same problem with you." He hadn't been so wonderfully content in years, but then his stomach began to growl.

She eased off his lap. "I'm starved too. I'll get the steaks."

As she started toward the house, she caught sight of Joyce turning away from her side gate. "Joyce, wait, come on in. I want you to meet Luke."

"Are you sure?" Joyce entered and crossed the grass with tiny steps.

Luke grabbed hold of the table to haul himself to his feet. "How do you do? Please excuse my appearance. I got into a knife fight last night, but I intend to avoid them in the future."

Startled, Joyce stopped several feet from the deck. "I thought maybe you'd been in a car wreck. Who won the fight?"

"I did. The other guy's in jail," Luke replied with a ready grin.

"Oh, Catherine, even with a black eye he's cute."

Luke laughed at her compliment. "Thank you, but I hope to look a lot better by the wedding."

Joyce squealed and hurried to give Catherine a hug. Then she whispered, "I told you he might be thrilled."

While that hadn't been precisely Luke's reaction to news of a baby, Catherine's joy shone in her smile. "I want you to help me plan. I'll give you a call in a couple of days."

"I'll look forward to it." Joyce hugged her again, waved good-bye to Luke and nearly skipped out the gate.

Catherine went in the house to get the steaks. The coals glowed with the perfect heat, and she put the meat onto grill. "This seems so incredibly normal."

Luke walked over to her and slid his right arm around her waist. "Isn't that what you want?"

"Yes, especially after last night. What do you think will happen to Dave?"

"The Lady in Red was becoming a celebrity, so some hotshot attorney will take the case for the publicity. He'll liken

Dave to Zorro, who only killed those who deserved to die. Who knows, he might go free."

"Zorro is a fictional character, so that might not work," she chided. "You're also forgetting Dave tried to kill you. Won't a jury have to find him guilty of attempted murder?"

"Maybe not. I hit him first, and we were fighting over you. A clever attorney could spin our rivalry into quite a romantic tale. I was also his therapist and obviously totally ineffective. That'll also help Dave's defense."

"I can't tell if you're being cynical or optimistic."

"A little of both, I'm afraid." He nuzzled her neck and placed a teasing kiss in her ear.

She giggled. "Are we really moving back east?"

"No, I'll stay at Lost Angel. I was just trying to outrun myself again, something you once warned me against. California's home, and it's still a good place to raise kids. I keep thinking your Sam must have been a hell of a man. If we have a boy, would you like to name him Sam?"

Catherine burst into tears. "Oh, Luke, that's the sweetest thing I've ever heard. You're a hell of a man too."

He drank up her eager kisses and then whispered, "I'm sorry not to have offered a more romantic proposal, but at least I get some things right."

"Well, you sure got me," she whispered against his lips.

Her next kiss convinced him that, together, they would survive whatever tragedy came their way, and better yet, create all the joy they would ever need for a blissfully happy future.

About the Author

New York Times bestseller Phoebe Conn loves to read and began writing her own novel as a fun project for a summer vacation. By the time she returned to teaching in the fall, she had begun her own mythic journey into the land of romance. *Where Dreams Begin* is her thirty-fifth book. With more than seven million copies in print of her historical, contemporary and futuristic books written under her own name as well as her pseudonym, Cinnamon Burke, she is as enthusiastic as ever and still loves writing.

She loves to hear from fans. www.phoebeconn.com and phoebeconn@earthlink.net.

Loving him could be an adventure that gets her killed.

Defy the World Tomatoes
© *2010 Phoebe Conn*

Darcy MacLeod's Army brat childhood drives her to sink roots as deep as the plants with which she works. As part owner of a nursery/gift shop in Monarch Bay, she's well on her way to her dream. Though she's haunted by the lingering fear that her one chance for true love has come and gone.

When Griffin Moore asks her to landscape his sumptuous new estate, she's entranced by the internationally renowned pianist's air of mystery. Yet as she is inexorably drawn into his bed, her instincts tell her that secrets lurk behind his sophisticated mask.

With her carelessly styled hair, grubby overalls, and hands that see more dirt than an earthworm, Griffin finds Darcy a refreshing ray of light in his shadowy world. His globe-trotting concert schedule makes him the perfect Interpol informant—and makes a permanent relationship too dangerous to risk.

Their passion rivals the music of the great classical masters, but even as Darcy dips a toe into Griffin's extravagant world, darkness reaches out to strike a dangerous chord. And Darcy must fight to keep her second chance at love—and her lover—alive.

Warning: Contains meddling friends, high adventure, down and dirty sex, and a couple who make beautiful music together—in bed and out.

Available now in ebook and print from Samhain Publishing.

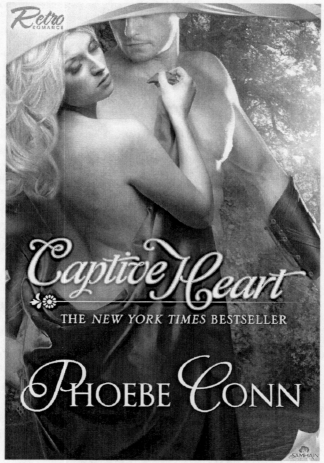

It's all about the story...

Romance

HORROR

www.samhainpublishing.com

CPSIA information can be obtained at www.ICGtesting.com
Printed in the USA
LVOW092201260612

287820LV00001B/106/P